To my family

For your endless support

The Tin Man's Journey

Dan White

Copyright © 2022 Dan White
All rights reserved.
ISBN-13: 9798835235407

Contents

How To Really Destroy A Man	7
The Inexplicable And Lamentable Birth Of Version 2	19
Silly Boy	37
And The Band Played On	53
The Making Of A Man	63
A Strategic Lapse Of Judgement	73
Solitary Confinement And Other Forms Of Torture	85
Let It Rain	97
And The Award For…	115
Highway To Hell	127
The End Is Nigh	145
Plan B	165
Dog Days	173
Bend Over. This Won't Hurt A Bit	187

Over The Rainbow	201
Easy Come, Easy Go	221
Not Quite Wales But Somewhere Like That	235
White vs. White	251
Booby Chains And Small Knickers	267
Bring It On If You Have To	279
Don't Let The Fat Lady Sing	293
Balls And Bags	311
Deck The Halls	327
The Lion, The Witch And The Wardrobe	345
More Than Any Man Should Have To Bear	357
Done	371
Poker Face	385
Everything Is Awesome	399
Closure	411
Thank You For Having Me	423
And The Bell Tolls	437

How To Really Destroy A Man

'You're pathetic, Daniel. An embarrassment. Look at you, for God's sake. It's like dealing with an imbecilic child. I need a *Man*, Daniel, I need a *Real Man* like your dad. Your dad's a *Real Man*. Christ, even your grandad would be better than you. He's a *Man* at least. A *Real Man* like I need. You on the other hand, you disgust me.'

I savour these words as I lie slumped in the hallway of my first floor flat in Dalston or as I prefer to call it, Stoke Newington (much nicer for those of you who don't know the area). It comes as something of a surprise, not in the least because until that very moment, my girlfriend had insisted she hated my father and grandfather as much as the rest of my poor unsuspecting family, but nonetheless, I don't comment. I've already learnt by this point to wait passively in quiet contemplation of the threadbare brown carpet and the underlay that is turning to dust.

I have time amid her observations to reflect on the fact that if I can hear my neighbour break wind in the dead of night through the gaps of these same floorboards, he must surely be privy to this unprovoked attack on my manliness, or lack thereof, and may well agree given the circumstances, but I digress.

'Nothing to say, you spineless arsehole?'

I'm only a matter of months into a relationship with the person I had proudly (and it would appear prematurely) announced as being The One and I'm getting a royal chastising, though I will never know quite why.

'You're ridiculous. I'd laugh if it wasn't so embarrassing.'

She's leaving I'm told and I'm okay with this. In fact, I actively want her gone. The initial attraction has quickly waned and to be perfectly honest, I'm beginning to suspect she might not be that nice. She keeps getting sacked and has an impressive, ever-expanding mental record of all the people who've unwittingly offended her in some way. It's a somewhat hefty list and one I seem to have made my own way onto by the sheer provocation of my presence. But I'm not alone there at least. My friends and colleagues joined me weeks ago and the names of every member of my family, my father and grandfather included, despite their recent elevation to the position of *Real Men*, are written in capitals and underlined in red.

'You're a loser. Do you hear me? A loser.'

For the record, she's not wrong about my dad and grandad, in this aspect at least. They are real men, who I like to think would've had the balls to turf her out and never look back, but that isn't me. Confrontation isn't my strongest suit, so I'm content to remain slouched and defeated until the tirade is over and I can raise myself stiffly and relieved at the sound of the door slamming behind her. Any minute now.

Did I mention I'm on the floor? I'm still there and being told quite implicitly, lest there be any doubt in my mind, that I am essentially a worthless and unlikeable turd, but again it's okay. I just want her to leave. Another few minutes and a couple more good old fashioned metaphorical kicks to the testes of my self-confidence and she'll be gone.

But there's a problem. We have, despite the inconceivably brief period since our initial meeting to our co-habitation, adopted Mavis, a tan and white Collie from the RSPCA. And I am in love with her. She is my first ever dog following a series of narcissistic childhood cats who would sooner empty their bowels in a shoe than trouble themselves with bringing it to me, trailing with drool and lovingly wrecked beyond recognition.

And Mavis, my one true love, is still there where she's been since I first sagged browbeaten onto the tattered remains of my carpet. Right next to me, loyal friend that she is. The finest animal ever born. Beautiful and graceful, devoted and kind. She is a gem and as I make the mistake of looking into those doleful, knowing eyes, I quiver and waver and realise all at once that I can't let her leave. Mavis that is – not my girlfriend – but sadly there is only one way this can happen. In years to come I will lament this decision and reflect, no less than constantly, on how I voluntarily buggered up my existence out of affection for a dog who, God bless her, would die less than three years later.

Regardless. The mistake had been made. I had revealed my weakness and proven I could be bent to my girlfriend's will. That if pushed, I could and would fold and crumble. I had unveiled my complete lack of backbone and presented her with a complicit victim. A compliant prisoner. Her perfect man.

And so to the events that set all this in motion back when there was no us, only me. The last night, as it turned out, that I would ever be carefree and oblivious. That I would sail along unsuspicious of life and untainted by fear.

Not the self-imposed artificial fear of standing in front of a room full of strangers hoping I could make them laugh, as I was about to do then. Not the mere culmination of adrenaline and nervousness that would fire my performance and lend me an onstage bravado to see me through the next fifteen minutes like an old friend, but real fear. The sort that would wake me in a cold sweat in the middle of the night, my muscles clenched in instinctive panic, my very breathing muzzled at the thought of inadvertently unsettling the silence and setting off a new chain of accusations which would render me useless the following day. The sort of fear that would force me to head intentionally down a road from which I could never turn back. A road that would age me and break me countless times. A road that spanned years and even crossed an ocean. Twice.

And that is the moment, standing backstage at the comedy club, feeling sick like I always did before I went on, that first moment I will always look back on and wonder how everything would have been different if I'd listened to my instincts and bolted that night. If my churning stomach and stretched nerves had only done what thousands of years of evolution had trained them to do and made me defecate myself right there on the spot.

But they didn't, so instead I let a beat pass and resisted the urge to raise my hand against the glare of the spotlight as I stepped onto the stage with a confidence I wouldn't feel until my fourth pint later that night.

'Ladies and gentlemen! How are we this evening?' I reached for the mic, nodding to Bob who'd introduced me and was backing away with a self-important swagger I hoped would trip him. A murmur of expectancy rumbled around the darkened room as a couple of dozen faces, illuminated by the soft glow of LED tea lights garnishing the tables turned towards me, smiles already half-formed, the atmosphere charged. I dispensed with the pleasantries.

'For those of you who don't know me, I'm recently single.' I held my hand up against the obligatory sympathetic groan. 'Don't feel bad for me. It's for the best. I don't think my ex was ever really that into me. I say my ex. She never formally broke up with me so you never know... I just came home to find all her stuff gone. And my stuff. I wasn't sure if I'd walked into the wrong house, you know what it's like when you suddenly find yourself in the kitchen when you were aiming for the loo?' I froze, my legs parted, my arms poised, a look of pure confusion on my face. 'No? Just me?'

They laughed. I don't even know what at. People always laughed whenever I started talking. I could ask them to pass the milk and they'd stare at me with inane grins like I was about to launch into some hilarious diatribe about udders or cow pats. I must have one of those voices, I guess. Or one of those faces. I'd learned to make the most of it.

'It's alright though. I got my own back. Bought the whole lot back off of her on eBay. Ha! I showed her, huh?' I surveyed the room, a self-satisfied smile playing on my lips, a casual strut across the stage. A ripple of reluctant laughter filled the pause. 'Don't mess with me.' I bounced my eyebrows smugly. The noise picked up a little. I let it build some more.

'So, my ex, she tells me once I've got tiny hands. I said what? What do you mean I've got tiny hands?' I twisted them in front of me with a sneer. 'She said *you have, you've got tiny hands. It was the first thing I noticed about you.* I said the first thing you noticed about me? The first thing I noticed about you was how beautiful you were and you were sat there thinking I had abnormally miniscule hands? She said *yeah. It's not like you're tall or anything but even so, they are small.*' I looked around the audience incredulously. They started to laugh. They wanted to laugh. People were like that. They needed to enjoy themselves. Feel better for a few hours. It didn't take much. I drew my hands up and down the length of my torso, my face suspended in a cloud of bewilderment.

'I said I'm over six foot. I mean, I'm not going to be joining a basketball team any time soon, but even so, I'm comfortably above average in the height stakes, in this country at least. She said *my ex-boyfriend was six foot four.*' I pulled a face, a horrified grimace. A slow snigger rolled out across the room. '*He had massive hands.* I thought Jesus, when do I get to meet this Herculean giant? I might take this sort of judgement from him. You're five foot three.

'Your hands are tiny, she says. And she wasn't being mean or anything. She was laughing. You know when it gets awkward, when someone's laughing at something so much but you can't join in and you just have to sit there and wait it out. Like with that lady at the back there.' I pointed to a woman in the audience and her whole table erupted with cackles as she coiled over, giggling and mortified in equal measures. I waited her out, an impatient roll of my eyes, a placating lift of my palm setting her off again, making the rest of the room strain around towards her.

'You alright?'

She nodded, hid her face behind a pint glass.

'I'm going to carry on.'

She nodded again, cheeks red from exertion, tears ruining her mascara. Her eyeliner was a mess. I sighed audibly one more time.

'So she says... *your hands are tiny.*' I stretched them out, my eyes darting back and forth between the audience and the comical claws I was swivelling sceptically in front of me.

'I said I've been called a lot of things in my time, but no one's ever, ever told me I have ridiculously disproportionate appendages and honestly, I'll be frank with you all, I can't tell you what that does to a man.

'It doesn't sound on the surface of things like it's that big a deal, but they're your hands. They're right here. You can't hide the bastards, even if they are tiny. You use them for everything, all the time and then suddenly you become aware that for years for all you know, everyone around you has been secretly judging this weird deformity of yours. Not that there's anything wrong with being deformed, you just didn't know you were, and in an instant every time you reach for a cup of coffee you start worrying it's going to slip through your tiny toddler-like fingers.' I pretended to struggle with the mic. 'You start comparing yourself with everyone you know, sidling up to them and letting your hand edge across to theirs when they're not looking. I'd be sat on the tube...'

I imitated myself casually creeping my arm across to some fictitious stranger and glancing down, measuring my hand against theirs and pulling away with a frantic innocent twist of my head as they turned towards me.

'I thought I was going mad. Got to the point where I was disguising them.'

I tucked my hands across my chest and pretended to pick things up with my elbows. Lift a glass with the jut of my chin and an exaggerated overbite. The audience were roaring now. The woman at the back was wiping her face again. Her friend was staring at me, her head lowered, shiny dark hair falling across her eyes. I knew that look.

'I said to my mate, Johnny, you'd tell me wouldn't you, if I had horribly small hands? And he said *mate, I've known you all my life – you're like a brother to me. You look like a ninety year-old alcoholic, your legs are too skinny, your neck's too fat, that tattoo looks like it's been drawn on with board pens and your breath stinks, but no, I've never thought of you as having particularly small hands.* But then you look at them, right.' I held my hands out in front of me, studying them, contorting them. 'And the more you look at them, the smaller they get. Look at them! Yours, not mine! Jesus! Mine have had enough scrutiny.'

One by one, the audience began to unfurl their crooked fingers like a lawn full of daisies opening towards the sun. Started examining their own hands and laughing without even knowing why, comparing theirs to each other's as intense observation made them fluctuate disproportionately. The laughter rose as it fed on the contagious wonder sweeping the room. The brunette lifted her eyes from her own outstretched arms, her shoulder leaning against the dishevelled friend, a knowing smile on her lips, her stare intense.

'So my advice –' I stared straight back at her. '– is if you really want to hurt a man, if you really want to screw him over, don't sleep with his best mate – that's just bad manners, he'll get over it. And don't walk out without telling him – he probably won't even realise for a few weeks. He'll just think you're being a bit quiet. Don't even, and I mean this, put all of his worldly possessions on eBay. There's a shed load of hidden charges and don't even get me started on PayPal.

'No, if you really want to damage a man, if you want to ruin the rest of his life, all you've got to do is tell him he has tiny hands.' And I finished with a self-conscious scramble at replacing the mic as the audience, now incandescent with crazed euphoria erupted with glee.

At least that's how I like to remember it. There were definitely a few chuckles anyway, which may or may not have been me laughing at my own jokes.

Not that it was a joke. It was a true story. I still worry about it to this very day. The fact I've been walking about in full view of everyone with mitts the size of a five-year-olds hanging off my arms, but when I think of that night, I feel nothing but sorry for that poor sap who stood there on stage in all his blissful ignorance thinking the worst thing that could ever happen to him was someone saying he had tiny hands.

Him, I pity. The late Version 1 of myself as I like to think of him now. Version 2, the one convincing himself that overreactions and temper tantrums were par for the course in a relationship – him, not so much.

I would smash Version 2's head against those floorboards until his brain spilled from his ears. I would stamp on him until he lost consciousness and was incapable of falling into the sorrowful depths of that adorable dog's eyes, until he was oblivious to her desperate pleas as she was dragged for the last time out of his flat and out of his life. But I didn't have the luxury of foresight back then and I'm not sure I'd have had the strength in that moment to walk away even if I did. I was twenty-seven years old and my life, as I knew it, was over.

The Inexplicable And Lamentable Birth Of Version 2

And so back to that fateful night. My slot was over and I was drenched with relief, giddy with the cocky self-assurance that always accompanied making an audience of perfect strangers laugh. I was high on the thrill of admiration, swaggering confidently as I headed straight towards the bar where I knew if I waited long enough the brunette would find occasion to sidle over and feign ignorance until I ordered her a drink. Which is exactly what happened, as it had a dozen times before in similar circumstances only this time I was the one caught unawares, thrown off guard by her penetrating stare, her perfect symmetry, the posh accent I would only discover in time was put on to complete the façade she portrayed.

Her friend was with her, as flustered with awe and embarrassment as the brunette was composed and I apologised for singling her out, but she just giggled as I knew that she would. Hung around for a few minutes more. I was well versed at making people comfortable, but the banter was going nowhere and the brunette, sensing my attentions would be better directed at her alone, sent her sidekick back off to the table while she waited for the drinks. If they ever came. We had yet to order and I was in no hurry to disturb the undercurrent of attraction simmering between us when we did.

I wasn't to know it but that was the last time I'd ever see that particular friend as they were shortly to fall out and she'd find herself joining the rest of the condemned on the aforementioned List. But all that was irrelevant at the time. I had no idea such Lists even existed, indeed that people who kept Lists existed in real life. Let alone in my life.

'The name's Philippa,' she purred. Naturally, for what other name would be befitting of such beauty?

'Dan. But you know that. From the show. Or maybe you don't. I was just – Dan.' Her laugh tinkled, the charge of electricity flickering between us virtually visible. I was unnerved, losing my touch. She was dazzling me when it should have been the other way around and I fell for her fast, right there at the bar as we ignored the staff's impatient interruptions, creating a scene with our very indifference to the rest of the world.

'Come here often?' Her voice was playful and sensual, a seductive murmur and I hung on to every word like a teenager enthralled by a crush.

We shared our first kiss in the back of the cab that was to take us to her new flat – my flat at the time actually, though I didn't know then that it wouldn't be mine for much longer.

She stayed overnight and by the time she left, I already wanted to see her again.

I hate myself for that now, for that weakness, that naïve desperation, but back then it was the summer of 2006 and the biggest worry I had was En-ger-land being about to underperform once again in the World Cup.

She met my flatmate, Jake, in an awkward underdressed dash to the toilet that morning and they seemed to hit it off, which made it easier when that first momentous meeting rolled on and on like a tumbleweed in the otherwise barren landscape of my love life.

I introduced her to my parents – separately since they were divorced – but they were impressed both by the classy accent and the apparent worldly-knowledge she held about everything that had ever happened anywhere. She met my sister, who said all the right things afterwards. She had no reason not to. Philippa was charming, attractive, educated and intriguing. And if they did voice any concerns, I can categorically state I was not prepared to hear them. Quite the opposite, in fact. I was ready for a relationship.

I'd been living in London for four years by that point and I loved it. The dark seedy corners in the edgy backstreets as much as the glorious, statuesque grace of the landmarks flanking the skyline.

I divided my time between the job I wanted – doing stand up in gloomy bars and comedy clubs which would do me until I got my big break – and the work that actually paid for my disproportionately costly lifestyle living on kebabs in a two bedroomed flat my parents could've bought with their pocket change when they were teenagers (if they'd only had the forethought). But they didn't so it now swallowed up over half my wages every month. Wages I earned as a Metropolitan Police Officer, a respectable position I was careful not to refer to in front of an audience of potential hecklers at any time. I wasn't a fool after all but the truth was, I was good at what I did. I was the youngest detective in my team and I was flying up the ranks without the slightest desire or particular interest because I knew what I really wanted to do and that was make people laugh. But that, as of yet, didn't pay the bills.

Nevertheless, I was happy. I had a rosy future in the Met if I wanted it and a small but significant following on the comedy circuit that I definitely did want. And I had friends. Lots of friends, but it wasn't enough, not for the greedy, grasping bastard I was back then. I was lonely at night and deep down, despite being the owner of a pair of testicles, I'd been broody since the age of seventeen. I knew enough not to admit this to my satirical mates but while I should've been running around trying to knob anything that moved and masturbating seven times a day, I found myself distracted – primarily by the masturbation which took up an unreasonably large proportion of my time – but also by the ache in my movaries.

By the time I met Philippa, I was ripe and fully primed for commitment, fatherhood and everything that went with it (though in hindsight, had I known what that was, I'd have stuck to my five-knuckle-shuffle-workouts instead).

However, it wasn't to be and Our Relationship, as I was proud to call it, continued to flourish over the following months. I took her to Italy where we spent our days drinking Aperol Spritzers by the pool and every evening strolling hand-in-hand through the cobbled streets of Sorrento until we found a restaurant where we could watch the sun set on a terrace overlooking the sea. She said *I love you* there and I said it back for the first time, though I'd known it since the night we'd met.

She was captivating, sharp and witty and she thought I was amazing. It was almost embarrassing. There was no one in the world better than me it turned out. No one who could make Spaghetti Carbonara out of a jar quite like yours truly, no one who could sink a tea bag into a cup and let it stew for the exact time it took to infuse perfectly, no one who could handle the speed bumps along Stoke Newington High Street like I could and her face when I parallel parked for the first time could have resurrected Christ himself.

I'd never felt so accomplished and adored and so when it turned out the job she had was only a temporary one, I didn't think anything of it. And when she jacked it in because she didn't like her boss, I was sympathetic and generous to a fault. And she got another job soon enough, although she didn't like that boss either but she was working (on and off) in Central London and even part-time jobs paid well there so what did it matter if she took a few months off? I wasn't after her money anyway.

And when it turned out the Mercedes key on her fob wasn't really hers – *it's just a spare to my Mum's* – I didn't flinch. When she revealed – *I'm actually 31, not 28* – I couldn't have cared less. Big difference. When it transpired her name wasn't Philippa, but *Lisa*, I could sort of understand why she'd changed it. When it came about that her flat actually belonged to her mum – *it'll be mine when she's dead* – I was surprised but I got over it quickly. When it emerged her mobile phone was in her mum's name too – *what? It's not that weird!* – I should have probably considered the fact she'd reached the grand age of 31 (not 28) without the necessary credit history to get a cheap as chips Nokia as a bit of a red flag, but I didn't because I wasn't after her money and I was happy, right? She'd told me I was – *you're so happy* – and I have to admit, she wasn't wrong.

My free time became our free time and there wasn't a moment of it that wasn't filled with some new experience or activity. Some exhilarating adventure or eye-opening event. A weekend didn't pass by without trying a new bar or restaurant or actually going into one of the museums or galleries I'd walked past so many times before. She opened up a whole world to me I'd always known existed but had never bothered to explore. She sailed through life with such enthusiasm and vitality, it was contagious and addictive and the more time we spent together, the more I wanted to.

And so after that first few heady months it was decided that her (mum's) flat would be sold and we should move in (to my flat) together. She (her mum) had spent some money on the place in the year she (her mum) had owned it and with the insane property market being what it was, it sold quickly and before I knew it we were co-habiting.

Fortunately, by this time Jake had moved out, uncharacteristically and without much warning but I had to admit I was too relieved to question his motives. It'd been difficult towards the end trying to have a relationship with him still there. I couldn't quite place my finger on it at the time but although we'd been as tight as brothers since we'd met at primary school, things had become strained in the flat and an atmosphere had crept into the living room where once there'd only been beer cans and endless sessions of Call of Duty.

So now we lived together, pretty much to the surprise of everyone I knew and to make matters better or worst, depending on how you look at it, we staked our futures to each other by adopting Mavis from the RSPCA where Philippa had once worked. It would come to pass that she'd only been there for about a year before falling out with the management. It would also turn out this was one of the jobs she'd held down for longest but nonetheless, I was by now au fait with her chequered employment history and while not entirely swayed by it, nine years as I was into a career I'd thrown myself into fresh out of school, I was still unsuspicious enough to be persuaded it was of little or no consequence.

In my capacity as an indifferent member of The Filth, I'd observed the putrid gases of a bloated four-day old corpse explode when undertakers tried to lift it into a body bag, I'd looked on appalled as maggots crawled out of the eyes of somebody's decaying, neglected nan, I'd testified against gang leaders who would sooner slit my throat than look at me, but nothing, and I mean nothing, could've prepared me for what was to come.

It started uneventfully enough. That is to say that soon after moving in my girlfriend – my partner – suggested we *open a bank account together!* (Note - never do this.) *If we both put in a few hundred pounds every month, we'll be able to save up in no time. And pay bills directly. It makes more sense that way.*

What I'm certain she didn't say, no matter how many times I've gone over it is *then you can put all your money in it and I'll open a separate one in my own name. But we'll only spend whatever's in the joint account. As long as you run it by me first.*

May I point out at this time, I still hadn't seen anything untoward coming... Dry applause please.

It was also around this period that she embarked on an Open University degree, which I paid for in the old fashioned sense that I was the only one earning money on a regular basis, if at all, but I was happy to help. We were, after all, launching ourselves fully into a promising future together. I can't remember exactly what the degree was in because the subject matter changed every other week and besides which before she could start the foundation course, she had to retake a load of GCSEs. Just the silly ones like Science, Maths and English because she hadn't got around to doing them – any of them – in school.

There was a reason for this. She didn't take kindly to being told what to do and so the irrefutable laws of nature, physics and numerical certainties were a constant and vexing source of trouble even she was hard pressed to dominate and control. And so this simple act of self-improvement through education would prove to be her undoing and the first indication that anything was wrong. Or the one hundred and ninety-third to those of a more sensitive disposition to me.

It began with a disastrous lunch at our (my) flat when I still had permission to see my own family, albeit somewhat infrequently and not without the occasional unforeseen consequence. Her mum, Linda, who was present as well and revered me with a misplaced level of admiration I found both flattering and slightly disconcerting, would tell my mother that very night she couldn't believe Philippa had managed to bag someone as nice as her son, which at the time, even my own mum thought was excessive, but that was early in the afternoon and a great deal was yet to happen.

Perhaps it was the wine or the E numbers in the Pringles, but Philippa was feeling a little over-confident and knowledgeable in her current role as an Intellect which resulted in a disagreement between her and my brother-in-law concerning the legality of the recent invasion of Iraq. History – which she would also briefly flirt with – would eventually prove there were no weapons of mass destruction, but at the time she'd just read an *Article Online* which countered all of Andy's arguments and fully supported the legitimacy of the American government's dubious claims.

'Haven't you read the bloody news?' Philippa was on her feet, her nostrils aflare.

'Not the Daily Mail, no.'

'There are articles about it everywhere online! What are you, an idiot?' Something about her tone [the volume, shrillness and mild threat] made me shoot across the room armed with only a manic grin and a bowl of snacks. 'Of course they've got nuclear weapons. They've had them for years.'

'Cheese ball anyone?'

Andy shook his head, either at me or with incredulity. 'That's what the West wants us to believe but they're just protecting their own oil interests.'

'Are you seriously defending Saddam Hussein? You know he's a war criminal, right? He's killed thousands of people.'

'Cheese ball?'

'I know. It's terrible. So why didn't anyone do anything about it at the time?'

She threw her arms up triumphantly. 'Well, did you?'

What began as a mild-mannered difference of opinion, ended with her shouting ferociously at Andy at length and screaming *what about Rousseau?* in case anyone forgot she'd studied a unit of pre-grad philosophy. Unfortunately everyone else had finished school several years before and couldn't remember a thing about Rousseau so all that followed was a silence that slammed through the room like a sledgehammer.

It was shocking. My family didn't do confrontation like that and neither did I. The whole row was unnecessary and came out of nowhere. Even I, in my dim-witted capacity as a gullible fool was taken aback that she could be bold enough to shout at a close family member of mine despite hardly knowing him, but I was yet to discover this was more of a speciality rather than an exception.

It would also become apparent fairly soon that Andy had just made The List and by virtue of her lousy taste in men, so had my sister, Julia.

And that was the point where I have to start taking some responsibility for the hellhole I was allowing myself to fall steadfastly into. It was a warning sign and one I heard loud and clear, but still I kept digging deeper underground.

'Why didn't you back me up just then?' Her back slammed against the door as it reverberated behind my mildly traumatised family and all I could say was *I*... 'That's the way it's going to be, is it? You all ganging up on me?'

'That's not –'

'Don't you dare!'

'Philippa, darling –' Linda slid out of the shadows.

'Oh, piss off, Mother. I don't even know why you're still here.'

'I was just…'

'Get out!'

'Sorry, darling. I'll be off then.' She faltered, on the brink of intervening, thought the better of it and scuttled away. A sensible move all in all. Philippa rounded on me, her eyes narrowing, her lips white and thin.

'And why are you sitting down? You haven't cleared this lot up yet.' I was back on my feet and it made sense in that moment to apologise just to make it all go away. It didn't. 'Don't leave the dishes in the sink'.

'I was going to rinse them.' A plate sagged uncertainly in my hand.

'Ha! That'll be a first. What are you doing?! Scrape it in the bin first. And make sure you stack the dishwasher properly. I'm sick of having to take it all out and do it again. Jesus Christ. Look how much wine they've wasted. Not the crappy stuff they bought, you notice. They drank ours and left the shit stuff for us, tight bastards. Don't put it away. Chuck it. I said, chuck it! Oh, for God's sake, pour it away first. No wait! They can have it back the next time we have to go over to theirs. I can't wait to see their faces.' It was the happiest I'd seen her all day. It didn't last.

'What are you doing with those crisps? I might want them later. I barely had a chance to eat all afternoon I was so busy running around after everyone. And thanks for leaving me to it. It's no wonder Andy thinks it's alright to talk to me that way, the chauvinistic pig. He takes his cue from you ordering me around, demanding food and drinks for everyone like I'm some downtrodden maid. Is that it? You think I'm just here to serve you and suck you off whenever you want?'

'No, of course not!'

'Because that's what it feels like. It feels like you've forced me to give up my flat, my independence, my life and tied me down here and you're not even grateful.'

I dropped the pretence of washing up. 'I am. Look, can't we just –'

'What? Can't we just what?'

'I'm sorry.'

'Are you? It seems like sometimes you don't want me here.' I turned my head stiffly towards her, softening at the slump in her shoulders and dejection on her face.

'Of course I do.'

'Really?'

'Really. You know I love you. I didn't mean to make you...'

'But your family, Dan–'

'I know. Let's not talk about them anymore. Why don't you sit down and put your feet up. You must be exhausted.'

She pulled me towards her, her head resting on my chest, her fingers trailing my waist and then she kissed me.

'Thank you, babe. I just don't know how you put up with them. It's always so much nicer when it's just you and me.'

And in a sense she was right.

A couple of days later we received a card from her mum. It said *thanks for a great afternoon and such a wonderful discussion.* This was warning sign number two. That had been no discussion. It was an attack, it was humiliating and it was being applauded.

I would later identify this pattern of appeasement in the psychology books I'd come to read as I tried to understand the new, terrifying world Philippa was constructing around me. In fairness to her, I'd also note the destructive effect of her turbulent childhood which included moving house about thirty times and changing schools just as many until at fifteen she was packed off (with more than one kind of baggage) to live with her grandparents in England. She wasn't to know it but it would be several years before her mother re-joined her from Canada – minus her father who she never set eyes on again.

Did I mention she's Canadian? Her dad is too, though her mother's British but Philippa had been born there and was fully devoted to the True North, which was, as far as I could glean through her endless glowing examples, better than the UK on every single level (except apparently for the accent which she'd dropped like a warm turd the second she mastered the inflection of a minor royal). In fact, she'd already lived there and left twice by the time I met her, having been inspired to return for five years in her early twenties after watching *Good Will Hunting* at a cinema in East Grinstead. But she was back now and comfortably lodged in my home, though anyone would be forgiven for thinking she was not happy about this arrangement.

'Jesus Christ, why are English flats so tiny? I had dog kennels bigger than this in Toronto.'

Over the course of a few weeks, the energy she'd previously poured into impromptu sightseeing tours or trying out rooftop restaurants and little known back street bars was redirected towards me and she had no problem leaving a scathing review.

'Do you have to breathe on me? You smell like cat food. Jesus Christ. Suck a mint or something, can't you? It's like your mother's crawled inside your mouth and died.'

I wasn't used to this sort of exchange, which is perhaps why exchange is the wrong choice of word. I didn't usually know exactly what I was supposed to have done but it was clearly too awful to confront me about so instead she would tear strips off me for some other offence. At any rate, this was the only explanation I could come up with for the vehemence of her reactions to me fast-forwarding a programme too far or answering a text before she'd finished her dinner.

'How many times do I have to tell you not to do that?'

At first I simply apologised for overdoing the pasta or walking too quickly or making a noise when I chewed, but that wasn't enough. I was expected to listen in silence as she listed in detail my failings and I learned that if I tried to defend myself, the list grew. I did what I could to make it up to her, to get us back to the place we'd been so happy in before I'd inadvertently screwed it up somehow but without knowing exactly what it was she was so angry about, I never seemed to get it right.

'I swear you're only pretending to be completely incompetent to get out of doing anything round here.'

And so maybe this was the point in the story when I should have walked away, or simply stayed where I was since at that time I was still the sole owner of a fairly pricy two-bedroomed property on the borders of an affluent, up-and-coming borough in one of the most exciting, extraordinary and expensive cities in the world.

This was the point rather, that I should have reclaimed my existence, my finances and my sanity and thrown Philippa out of my life like a baseball (which incidentally, is infinitely superior to a rounders ball), but I didn't. I was still a few months away from learning that I was not a *Real Man* but since this was not to be an isolated incident, by the time it occurred, I would be under no illusion that I was.

So maybe that was the point when I should have kicked her to the curb, but let's not forget Mavis in all of this who as I mentioned before was by then my main source of comfort and joy. Not to mention social life, confidante and emotional crutch.

So instead of making a clean break of it and continuing my life all the better for my narrow escape from a mentally unstable, intimidating and verbally aggressive megalomaniac, I allowed her to contribute the ten grand she'd made on the sale of her (mum's) place to the renovation of my (or I should say from that moment on both legally and unequivocally, *our*) flat. The trap had been laid and I had skipped in, sealed the door and bolted myself in behind it.

A few weeks after the building work was completed, she booked a one-day yoga course at a Swiss retreat (where else!) and I was told that when she returned I was expected to propose. And so in an act of utter lunacy driven by the vain hope that it would make everything better once and for all, that's what I did. Silly boy.

Silly Boy

My chair leg screeches against the dented, exposed floorboards lining the private rooms upstairs in the Blacksmiths Arms. Teeth on edge, I push the seat back to the wall and rise to my feet. I clear my throat as all eyes turn to me and survey the eighty or so glittering, slightly bemused faces of my dearest friends and family.

All the bride's guests are sitting at the head table with us. There's only a handful of them and apart from her mother, they're strangers to me. My own mum and dad have been placed together for the first time since he left her two decades ago for the woman staring wide-eyed and anxiously at him from the back of the room. They're all as uncomfortable with the situation as each other, but none more so than me.

My closest mate of twenty years and my best man, Jake sits wretchedly thumbing his napkin next to Philippa's maid of honour whose name I don't know as she's a hasty replacement for Bethany, a *BITCH* who was recently assigned to The List. Bethany's dress billows unflattering around this substitute best friend like a yurt. But no matter. She will not be around for much longer either.

The lighting in the pub is fairly dim which I hope disguises the dark shadows that have appeared around my eyes in recent weeks and lends an element of depth to the stiff grin I'm wearing like a shield. I brush down my tuxedo and glance at the notes in my hands as I soak in the sobering reality that I've just signed my life away on a piece of paper which would have served me better had I wiped my arse with it and swallowed it whole.

I am now the legal property of someone I'm almost certain I don't love or even like. And I have a speech to give in which I must sound as though my balls haven't been split open like an avocado and scooped out with a spoon.

I can't explain how I've arrived at this particular crossroads in my life but I'm comforted throughout my wedding day by the knowledge I can always get divorced. I don't mention this in my speech of course. Nor do I allude to the joyous occasion of Philippa's homecoming from Switzerland or try to justify why, with all spontaneity and excitement removed from the process, I did what I was told that day and proposed in the overgrown back garden of my (by that point, our) Victorian conversion.

It was the least romantic proposal of all time. A complete lack of effort and zero surprise. Her bloody mother was already at the flat to celebrate before I even popped the question.

'Wonderful news!'

'Back in your box, Mother. He hasn't even asked me yet.'

I'd flung a new set of garden lights over a dead shrub, chilled a bottle of her favourite champagne and wiped down the engagement ring she'd supplied me with before she went away. It was her grandmother's, a woman I'd never met and who was often described as *not being very nice to people* by someone who could have ended the troubles in the Middle East with one penetrating stare.

Laughably, I was pleased at the time because it meant I wouldn't have to splash out on a ring! All I needed was forty quid to have it reduced in size to fit snugly upon her beckoning finger. What savings! Particularly at such short notice! Never mind the fact no one should have a ready-to-go engagement ring and be prepared to use it less than a year into a relationship. And not a great one, I've got to say. No further proof of insanity is required. But to me, poor dumb weak stupid me, it represented a nice little saving so I took it in my greedy hands and to the jewellers I went.

Initially merely hooked, I'd now well and truly landed myself. Had I been a fish, I would have not only jumped out of the water into the boat, but I'd have promptly grabbed the nearest knife and gutted myself.

In times to come people will ask me how I let it go so far and I wish I had a nice tidy explanation I could engrave on a mug, but I don't. All I can say is there's an almost imperceptible line between banter and abuse, between flattery and manipulation. Before persuasion turns into control. It doesn't take long and it doesn't take much to become incapable of distinguishing between unexceptional and unacceptable behaviour in an altered reality where your judgement is consistently undermined.

And in addition, of course, please let me state for the record, things were not always mind-blowingly bad between us. Between the turbulent periods of darkness, there were actually weeks of exhilarating highs and affection amid which I would regain my hero-like status. At these times I'd revel in the adoration bestowed on me. The hair-raising passion and spine-tingling love. And during these periods the sex was intense and relentless.

'I swear, you've had lessons in this.'

Following the proposal, things returned to the heart racing heights of excitement and mutual attraction of the months following our initial meeting. My poor battered todger had an easier time of it when I was a teenager perusing certain dog-eared pages of the Littlewoods catalogue but I wasn't complaining. I was happy. I was relieved. I wished she'd made me ask her to marry me months before and to my absolute delight, in this delirious happy short-lived phase, my Supersperm (for there was no better) fulfilled its potential and impregnated my soon to be wife.

Life couldn't have been better but nonetheless a dark shadow crept back over our relationship much like a black cloud on a summer's day when it's too late to nip back to the house for a jacket. The comments began, but she was pregnant after all so I put it down to hormones. She stopped lifting a finger in the flat but her ankles were apparently swollen so, of course, I insisted she rest. She was unable to cook due to the sickening smells emanating from the kitchen although eating was never a problem despite the disappointing quality of the food.

'What's that smell?'

'Thai green curry. You're fav-'

'Curry! Are you trying to kill me? Curry? Jesus Christ! That's what you eat to induce labour, you ignorant prick. Do you want me to have this baby right now?'

'God, I'm sorry. I just thought – '

'No, you didn't think, Dan. That's your problem. You never do! Get me something bland to eat. Something I can keep down, you inconsiderate bastard. Bland food is never usually a problem for you. Or do I have to get up and do it myself along with everything else?'

As the weight piled on, she became increasingly self-conscious and ever more short tempered but I understood. This magical feat of nature did not come without its drawbacks and so I rubbed those swollen ankles and made a special effort to cook the sort of food her hapless stomach could tolerate. I let her petty criticisms sail over my head and didn't dwell on the sharp tone that had entered her voice whenever she spoke to me.

'Can't you at least do something about that disgusting smell? Christ, I think I'm going to vomit. Open a window or something. You really are the most self-centred idiot I've ever met. To think you're going to be a father in a few months. I swear to God, if you don't sort yourself out, I'm not letting you anywhere near this baby.'

A few weeks on and with the wedding plans still underway she began to refer to the affair I was harbouring with the typist at work. I'd described her in a throwaway conversation once as a really lovely lady and shortly afterwards a colleague – who was immediately struck off the guest list – sent me a photo of us standing together, my arm around her shoulder. It was an unremarkable gesture performed for a few moments only with a woman who was visibly old enough to be my mum, but it cost me a week's worth of sleep, several kilos in weight and the loss of control over my credit card.

'Should have kept it in your pants then, shouldn't you?'

The honeymoon period was over before the marriage had even begun and so I could have been forgiven by many for quietly slipping away but if I thought my love for Mavis was good enough reason to nail my balls onto the cross I was already dragging around, the unsurpassed bubbling euphoria I felt at the impending birth of my first child would have seen me walk through flaming rings of fire to get to the registry office. The love and hope I had for this little person I had yet to even meet defied reason and spanned space and time. I would have swallowed a pineapple whole for this baby and leaving, no matter how bad things had got was not an option.

And so it was. The wedding was set for a few months away. No sense in wasting any time after all. She was pregnant and our (my, *MY*) two-bedroomed first-floor flat was deemed inappropriate for a child, which I couldn't disagree with. Foolishly, I was too grateful she picked up another job so as to ramp up our mortgage application to really question what would happen if she decided never to work again, ever.

So onto Rightmove the bachelor pad went and with the property market still being insane, it sold almost immediately and at a ridiculous profit. Happily for the people we were buying our three-bedroomed cottage-style semi-detached in Epsom from, theirs had also benefitted from a massive mark up in price too, which was proportionally higher.

There were too many things happening all at once in my life and too many things to control. There seemed to be no means of stemming the incoming tide of events and no way to turn back. In the three months that followed our whirlwind and coerced engagement things went as so. I;

Enjoyed a brief, but fateful resurgence of happiness and normality which was to end more or less the moment I;

Impregnated Philippa, which provided me with almost as much joy as England beating Australia at the Rugby World Cup in 2003 but meant we then;

Had to upscale our lifestyle and exchange a ludicrously expensive but just about affordable flat for a house in the suburbs of Surrey which was close enough to commute to Central London from but still posh enough for Philippa to revive the fantasy that we were rich, all of which;

Was a huge stretch financially and here's the crucial bit, was based on two incomes, which would over time feel like such a weight around my neck, had I ventured into water I'd have sunk.

In addition to all this, Philippa was arranging every aspect of our wedding with the gung-ho exuberance of a child who'd been locked in a sweetshop afterhours.

'This is going to be so much better than your sister's!'

She chose Chelsea Town Hall as the venue, following the footsteps of Patsy Kensit and Pierce Brosnan (of course!). She chose the pub for the reception after reading an *Article* about it *Online*. She chose the tuxedo my father, my best man and I were to wear without troubling us all with opinions. She chose her dress (seemingly from the wardrobe department of an amateur panto production of Cinderella) which had to be taken out several times during the lead up to the big day and brought a tear to my eye when I saw it – though not for the right reasons.

I was allowed a stag do in custom with tradition. It was a twenty-two-man trip to Warsaw where I spent three days being beaten and stripped and awoke daily to a bagful of human excrement warming my bare chest. I can honestly say it was a lot less enjoyable than I hoped it was going to be. She didn't have a hen do because she didn't have any friends to have it with. But still with alarm bells ringing I walked on. I had been told after all.

The night before the wedding I stayed with Jake in his new place. We had some drinks at his local and I couldn't possibly have felt less excited. It was strange because I'd always wanted to get married. My own parents were divorced and it'd always been my big thing not to do that. I wanted my life to be defined by my marriage and kids. To provide that stable perfect family for my children. I wasn't to know at that point quite how spectacularly I would fail at this but even then I knew I was making a mistake.

I remember going to bed, totally sober and with the most surreal feeling imaginable, knowing that when I woke up, I'd be getting the tube downtown to marry someone I didn't really love but somehow didn't seem able to walk away from.

The more I'd learned about her in recent months, the more I was concerned. She really didn't have friends to speak of and those she did never hung around for long. She couldn't keep a job. She didn't seem to like my friends or family and was beginning to feel comfortable with actually telling me so. Not with the level of sheer unshakable hatred that would follow, but it was already enough. Yet there didn't seem anywhere else to go but ahead.

I woke up bright and early, puked my guts up in the bog and staggered to the mirror where I stared at myself, complete with white sweat and bloodshot eyes, and knew for absolute certain that I didn't want to get married. Not that day and honestly not to her. But people were waiting so I composed myself, showered, dressed and tubed it down to King's Road. We were husband and wife by midday.

And now, too late to do anything but march with the band in the small celebratory reception above a pub I'll never frequent again, I lift a clenched fist to my dry mouth and cough, smile self-consciously and address the dozens of people I'm silently hoping will tell me it's not too late and I don't have to do this.

'Thank you for coming, everyone,' I say instead. 'Especially those of you who've travelled from the other side of the world in order to share this special day with us.'

I raise my glass towards the huge Canadian who's flown over especially in what must have surely been a whole row of seats. Mitch (naturally) loosely represents a father figure in Philippa's tempestuous life and is rewarded a surprising degree of respect. Or not so surprising given his bank balance and the fact he's besotted by Philippa's mother, who keeps him dangling at the end of a very long leash and will continue to do so – despite his obvious downside – as long as he keeps paying for exotic holidays and the odd piece of high-end jewellery. This is not a family of fools.

'Some of you are probably wondering what took us so long to tie the knot, so thanks for your patience.'

There's a titter, a slight adjusting of seats. I pick up my glass of champagne. Take a swig from it.

'As most of you already know, I met Philippa at one of my gigs, just over a year ago now. I knew I'd fallen in love with her within the first few dates. She told me so. Best not to argue.' There's a thin line of tension in the smile she bares to blend in with the laughter. 'And she was right of course!'

I lift my glass beaming at her, at all around us. A small applause ripples through the room. A couple of enthusiastic whoops authenticate the charade.

'I was first attracted to her mind of course, and so now she's pregnant, I'm delighted to note that her boobs are both as big as her head.'

She likes that one. Any reference to her big boobs always went down well. My mum is less impressed. I look down at my notes. Wish I'd written more than *Thank you, Baby, Happy, Thank you again*.

'We're still trying to figure out how it could have happened out of wedlock. Linda, I swear I was just looking for the remote...'

Mitch's sweaty palm presses against Linda's coiled fingers as though protecting her from a barrage of famous British dry wit. This is going badly. I'm used to winging it on stage but this is different. I haven't quite taken into account the conflicting sentiments of a roomful of drunken

47

policemen, all-knowing childhood friends, a psychotic bride and my mother. I throw back the last of my drink and indicate to the waiter for another.

'And thank you as well to all the fine gentlemen who joined me for a cultural sightseeing tour of Warsaw on what I'm told will be the last holiday I ever have outside a Eurocamp. Highlights included a seven hour wait in the A&E department with the fiery remains of a hot chilli pepper seared between my raw enflamed buttocks.'

'You loved it!' my old Superintendent, Jim Nichols, roars from the back of the room to an onslaught of indistinguishable heckles.

My sister's grimacing at me. I don't dare look to my left. This is all going horribly wrong and I have no way to stop it, which seems appropriate.

'Still it was pleasantly surprising to discover the hospital food was no worse than anywhere else in Poland. It was all pretty awful and every meal was brown. Not that I'm the most accomplished chef in the world, though goodness knows, I'm getting plenty of practice now, my sweet,' I turn to Philippa with a disarming grin. Wait for the rumble of laughter to fade along with her feigned eye roll and shake of the head.

'But my God! Even the ketchup was boiled. Still, can you blame them? These people survived the horrors of the Nazis, endured years of a repressive regime, overcame communism and have produced some of the hardest working builders known to man, but my God, they draw the line at using an Oxo cube.

'And I can sympathise! Have you ever tried to open one of those bastards?' I said bastards in my own wedding speech. Is that okay? I think it's probably not okay.

'Their entire design is centred on the premise that it's easy to stack into the shape of a brick. A brick! You've got to admire the engineering, but it takes special safety equipment to get the damn stuff out of those little silvery packets. And you never know whether it's going to come out in a single solid lump that you'll discover in one staggeringly concentrated mouthful –' I blew my cheeks around my pursed lips, my eyes wide and crossed. '– or if it'll explode all over the kitchen as you rip one tiny corner of it open. And that stuff gets everywhere.

'I'm telling you, I was making Spaghetti Bolognese the other day and I had to use five of them just to get enough in the pot. Philippa came in to find out what was keeping me and I told her I'd been grouting the kitchen.' Something about the look on my bride's face tells me I'm going off course again.

'But Oxo cubes…' For the life of me I cannot think why I am talking about Oxo cubes at my wedding. 'Philippa, my lovely Philippa –' *Whoop!* I stretch my palm out and all eyes turn towards her. She sizzles playfully in the spotlight, the effervescence bouncing off the sequins on her dress like a disco ball. '– is a bit like an Oxo cube.' Even I'm not sure where I am going with this, but I have to pull it off.

'She takes something ordinary – like my life, for example and she turns it into something totally different, something bursting with new sensations and experiences. She turns the bland into the exciting, the mundane into the unimaginable and so the person I would like to thank most of all in this room is my wife, the mother of my unborn child. Philippa, it is an honour to spend the rest of my life with you and I look forward to you spicing it up for me… Like a… Stock. Cube.' Shit.

The rest of the evening passes in a blur. Mitch rises arduously to his feet and lists at length Philippa's impressive array of talents and accomplishments, none of which sounds familiar or even feasible, except for her latest feat of triumph, which is apparently snaring me. My dad has also prepared a speech but when the time comes he's not allowed to give it and I'm ushered instead to the swiftly cleared floor space where I must participate in a grotesquely defective performance of *I've Had The Time Of My Life*.

We don't have a honeymoon because we've spent all our money on the new too expensive house. There's no carrying over the threshold and no wedding night sex (which I'm quite happy about). Rather, we return home at about 11pm and are met with, first the smell and then the sight of Mavis's uncannily astute diarrhoea, which she's gone to great lengths to spread liberally across the kitchen floor and roll around in.

'Oh, for God's sake. You can clear that up.'

By the time I get to bed an hour and several stiff whiskies later, my wife's asleep and I lie in the dark weighing up the soul crushing stupidity of what I've done against the awe-inspiring, life-affirming reason I did it. The innocent, unsullied being growing inside of her. That perfect person I can already imagine holding in my arms and keeping safe. Loving unconditionally no matter what hardships I have to endure to protect them.

It's worth it. Whatever mistakes I've made, I've redeemed myself. Whatever misery awaits me, I can tolerate, so long as I'm a father. So long as I have that one light in the darkness that has inexplicably taken over my life. Only the thought of which is keeping me sane.

Two days later, we lost the baby.

And The Band Played On

It's not the inevitable result of eating blue cheese and oysters. It's not simply because of a bad fall or an addiction to crack. Miscarriages happen more often than you think and most of the time, no one will ever know why. Sometimes nature just knows better. It's a miracle so many pregnancies work out so well, go full term and produce perfect, flawless creatures we can mould with our own hands and screw up ourselves. It's nobody's fault when it doesn't work out, but that doesn't change the fact it's devastating and bewildering to lose what was never meant to be.

From the moment you stare down in wonder at the pink line on a white plastic tube soaked in fresh, potent urine, a child is born in your mind who'll cuddle up next to you on the sofa, who'll look up at you with big eyes as you reach down and take their small plump hands in yours, who'll giggle contagiously as you swing them around you in the garden of your cripplingly expensive semi-detached in the suburbs. A vague outline of loose, crumpled hair above a bleary, all-trusting expression will appear in your head at the least expected moment – in a meeting, on the bus. The blurry vision of a tiny, fleshy being that's more of a feeling than an image will tighten your heart and spread warmly from your fingers to your toes like a spilt cup of tea on a tablecloth. And when that tangible fantasy is torn away violently, it's natural to feel grief, even though you may not feel entitled.

I'm crushed but stoic. I understand how in addition to the devastation I'm experiencing, Philippa's own body is raging against her. I know her hormones are unsubtle and cruel, deflating her swollen breasts almost overnight and leaving her bloated with the weight she'd stored in preparation for nourishing that new life inside her. I know she has no control over her feelings and it's normal that she should react to this overwhelming turn of events and so, while dealing with my own remorse quietly, I absorb the animosity and anger that rains down upon me, the vilified outbursts.

She's no longer pregnant and hormonal. She's in mourning and hormonal and a small window has opened through which I could climb out, but I'm not the sort of person who could do that, though in times to come I'll wish I were. She's overbearing and surly but she's suffered a loss and I hope it'll pass.

'Leave me alone. Just leave me alone.'

The doctors tell us not to try for at least a month. That if we were to get pregnant again, the risk of a second miscarriage is higher, but Philippa's urge to fill the empty void in our lives and inside of her is more powerful than her fears and for once I'm glad she refuses to listen. She's pregnant again within her next cycle and this time it's to last. The initial relief and excitement upon hearing the wonderful news however, is not.

'Oh, fuck off.'

Perhaps it's the trauma of our previous loss or the dread of another, but with this pregnancy comes a new level of angry, aggressive behaviour, far worse than the frequent but fleeting glimpses I have seen before. I become afraid of her for the first time.

'I said FUCK OFF!!'

She wants to quit work immediately even though it'll disqualify her from maternity pay. It's worth ten thousand pounds and we're the proud recipients of the world's heftiest mortgage, don't you know? I'm terrified that she'll throw that away when all she has to do is stick it out for two more weeks until she can leave her job and still be able claim nine month's worth of most of her salary. She asks Linda for her opinion and continuing the sound motherly advice she has provided since childhood, she tells her to walk away from it.

'You don't need that sort of stress, darling. You're doing enough.'

Fearing, genuinely, for our survival, I'm somehow able to convince her otherwise, thank the sweet Lord Jesus and she manages to drag herself to work where she apparently does nothing but dislike people for two more weeks, but she's not happy about it. I'm not to know it but that will turn out to be the last day of actual honest paid work she'll do for the remainder of our marriage. Financial reckoning is on the horizon, not to mention the arse is about to fall out of the economy anyway.

The next six months are to be a good precursor for what the years to come will be. I find I live with someone who's furious at me. Someone whose sole contribution to the house is existing within it. Our outgoings far exceed our incomings and yet a delivery from eBay, John Lewis or The White Company appears on the doorstep virtually every day. A collection of items perhaps most easily described as needless shit. At the point at which we're down to one wage, she's decided to do her bit by attempting to buy everything on the Internet.

'But why don't we have any money? And I hate your sister by the way.'

She buys an old lady's tea set in the charity shop and tells everyone it belonged to her grandmother. She buys a violin because she wants to be seen as the sort of person who plays. She buys a piano for the same reason which is larger and more of an encumbrance. She can't produce more than a tone-deaf estimation of a melody because she can't read the notes and absorbing this skill as though by osmosis evades even her stubborn determination. So the violin is delegated to its display stand and the piano becomes the world's most opulent sideboard for piles of crap that appear on top of it, unloved, the lid unopened, the middle C inexplicably chipped and forever silenced.

Her affection for Mavis is withdrawn. She's grown to be a nuisance, an inconvenience and I don't argue when Philippa refuses to take her for her daily walks anymore. It becomes our private time together, just me and the dog, out of the house, away from the noise and the judgement, afar from resentment. And as I seek out quiet lanes in which to hide, tears flow freely down my face and I have no way to stop them. Instead I howl in pain and utter helplessness. In disbelief at the unending misery I've allowed to take over my life and then I pull myself together for there is nothing I can do to change any of it and at least I have these few moments alone with my faithful hound. Except on Sundays when a stroll to our local pub for a lunch we can ill afford invites the attention of strangers who encourage my loving wife to revel in her role of Expectant Nurturer and All Round Benevolent Care Giver.

I put all this down to the pregnancy. I need it to be because of the pregnancy. I understand it must be a shocking experience for any woman, particularly for those whom it seems to affect the hardest and if it is the price I have to pay for having a child, so be it. Philippa's snappy, but weepy, she's hot headed and petty, insensitive and agitated but she's subject to physical demands I will never be able to comprehend. It isn't ideal but it is temporary. There's an explanation for it all and anyway, I'm sure this new level of resentment will clear up after the birth. It's inconceivable that it won't.

Katie is born at home on a perfect spring day in May 2008. We were in agreement about not confirming the sex of the baby but the rest of the decisions as to home birth or hospital, natural or caesarean, I leave entirely to her. I'm firmly of the opinion that since she has to squeeze the equivalent of a watermelon out of an opening the size of grape while I merely look on in horror, she has the right to choose how and where she will do it.

She decides on a water birth in the maternity suite of Epsom hospital's newly refurbished birthing centre. She choses soothing music to accompany the serene rhythmic breaths that will gently encourage our child on its journey down the birth canal. She choses eye-wateringly expensive lingerie for the photos she'll post of herself on Facebook afterwards, babe in arms, her hair tousled flatteringly around her lightly powdered, flushed face. The baby and I are given very specific instructions regarding the labour and I am happy to support her and let her take the lead.

That changes the day I find her in the upstairs bathroom moaning in agony with two hands on the radiator trying to wrench it clean off the wall. I spend the next ten minutes trying to prise her clenched fingers off it and heave her into the bedroom without ruining the carpet. Ambulances are dispatched, midwives called, it's too late to go anywhere and in absolute credit to her she goes through the whole thing without drugs or gas. It is my honour to be present for it all.

The midwife hands me Katie the second she's out and I'll remember, for the rest of my life, watching that beautiful tiny being suck in her very first breath. She's a girl. She's my girl and she's perfect.

I've always known that being a Father would change everything and I'm not wrong. It becomes brutally apparent quite how selfish a life I've been able to lead up to that point. It isn't the hard work in those first few weeks that really hammers the point in. It isn't the sleeplessness, the worry, the sleeplessness, the weird black poo, the wonderful harrowing first night anxiety of being a parent, the sleeplessness or the sleeplessness, it's the fact that this is it. That it isn't about to change or get easier. It isn't a busy period at work or an unnerving holiday at Butlins. This is now my entire life. I've been given a miraculous, fragile gift that I'm never going to stop worrying about. That I'm going to have to lead through this world, through the good times and the bad. Through school, through boyfriends – or girlfriends – through the pain of being an England fan. The responsibility is mine, the almighty honour that it is. This is forever. I wouldn't have it any other way but I know I'm going to be knackered and worried until, well, death.

I'm not one to blow my own trumpet (we don't have one of those, believe it or not) as I'm not good at much. But paaaarp... the parenting stuff makes sense to me. There's nowhere on earth I'd rather be than by Katie's side. She's a revelation to me. She's so much more than I could ever have hoped for, the perfection to my fallibility. The beauty to my beast. She's everything that's right with the world and I'm determined to be all she ever needs in a father. That's my mission. That's my goal. Life is crap, but while there's still breath in my tired, splintering body, I will not let it crap on her.

But I've always known that was how it would be. I'd envied too many fathers over the years not to know how I'd feel when I had a child of my very own. What surprises me on the other hand, what I am totally unprepared for, is Philippa's reaction to Katie's arrival.

The occasional concerning eruptions aimed firmly towards me become more intense and a smattering of distain underlines our every exchange. This effect is as immediate after the birth as a fart following a curry, but with tiredness comes irritation so it's almost inevitable. What worries me however, is that she doesn't seem to connect with Katie at all. She is lost and angry and unable to relate to the needs of the tiny helpless life we've made.

I carry Katie close to my chest whenever I can, breathing in her new baby scent, feeling her heart beat against mine. I take the lead in changing nappies. I cleanse her mottled skin with a warm cloth until the ugly purple remnants of the umbilical cord dry and heal and then I bathe her, her delicate head cradled in one hand, her wrinkled plucked bird-like body nestled in the crook of my arm. Meanwhile, Philippa channel surfs and devours the web as though we only have it on a free one-month trial.

For days she's unable to breastfeed Katie. We take advice from the nurses who come to visit the house but nothing seems to make a difference. It isn't a big deal to me and it's certainly never a question of failing on her part, which I emphasise as often as I can. A lot of women struggle to produce milk. It happens. That's what formula is for, but when I suggest we buy some, I'm met with a volley of rage and resentment unlike anything she's conjured before. Her face contorts and twists and even her eyes seem to change shape. To state the obvious, I drop the subject.

For days Philippa sways back and forth in the rocking chair she bought especially and cries with frustration and pain through Katie's blood-curdling wails as she suckles desperately at a nipple, which through nobody's fault, is unable to provide what she needs. Katie loses a little weight as a new-born baby always will. Then she keeps losing weight. And she keeps crying.

One night, at least a week after she was born, I'm changing her nappy. She's lying on her back, still screaming, her tiny arms spread wide up toward the ceiling, reaching out to me. I know exactly what she wants and as I look down at her, for the first time I see her ribs showing clearly through her tight little skin. It's enough. No, it's too much. I know

I'm not wrong and I know whatever her mother's dealing with doesn't justify starving this beautiful creature.

I finish changing the nappy and drive to the local petrol station, where I buy what will turn out to be the first of hundreds of bloody powdered milk cans. I drive straight home and make it up following the instructions I will later be able to recite in my sleep. My wife is livid at my arrogance, at the audacity of me daring to interfere.

'I am her Mother and I know best.'

But I don't care, I've had enough and I'm going to feed my daughter.

We don't own a microwave because Philippa doesn't like them (always handy) so I make the bottle up with hot water, which I then cool. I put it to Katie's mouth and I'll always remember how amazed I am at the aggression with which she latches onto that thing. I swear she jumps a couple of inches out my arms and attacks it like a piranha stripping flesh off a horse. She drinks the entire lot in one sitting without pausing for breath and for the first time in what will be thousands of times, she pukes up all over me.

I make another bottle and on this attempt I'm more careful to give her a little at a time. It stays down. She stops crying and she sleeps. From that day forth she has nothing but formula milk. From that day forth I genuinely believe my wife hates me.

The Making Of A Man

I am a father, I am complete and my life's changed unrecognisably, though no one could ever have prepared me for how much. It's five o'clock in the morning and she's been screaming her head off since three. I've tried everything I can think of to quieten her down. Pacifying her, pacing, ignoring her, lying stock still and barely breathing, murmuring gently but nothing works and I have to get up to walk the dog before I go to work in half an hour.

Miraculously the baby's slept through all of this, although Mavis has not and can be heard scratching at the knob on the kitchen door behind which she's locked every night now. My eyes droop closed involuntarily and I'm immediately awoken again with a blistering tirade centring as it has for the last two hours, on the fact that I don't do anything around the house or help with Katie. At all.

'I have to do everything around here!'

I resist the urge to point out that when I return from taking Mavis for her early morning dump so Philippa doesn't have to during the ten hours I am at or on the way to work, I will change Katie's nappy as I do every morning while I wait for her bottle to cool and when she's dressed and fed I'll bring her upstairs to my wife who'll be fuming as always since I will have to wake her in order to leave.

She'll be understandably exhausted having been up all night shouting at me and so when I return I'll be expected to feed, bathe and put Katie to bed (which I'll have looked forward to all day), pour out a couple of glasses of crisp white wine (for her), prepare an evening meal for us both and while it's simmering on the stove or baking in the oven (an Aga, of course), I'll take Mavis for her evening walk and return in time to serve. And pour Philippa another glass of wine. I'll then sink into an armchair at nine o'clock and watch one programme before I crawl to bed, where I'll sleep for a couple of hours before I'm woken by a shrill assault on my eardrums.

I resist saying this because Philippa is screaming only inches from my face and without pause. Flecks of spittle fly like poison darts onto my cheeks but I steel myself against the instinct to flinch. If I'm lucky, she'll wear herself out and collapse fuming with anger and frustration onto her side. My internal clock's already counting down the minutes until the alarm will ring and any hope I may be harbouring of a few moments' sleep will vaporise, much like my love for this woman.

'You think you're so hard done by, don't you, poor baby? Off all day boozing it up and shagging whoever you like while I'm stuck in the house like a good little wife.'

If I'm *really* lucky she will wake up in an inexplicably good mood and spend money we don't have on tat we don't need that she will later sell on eBay at a massive loss, allowing her to claim she is still contributing to our eye-wateringly stretched finances, which will in turn enable her to spend the afternoon emptying the boutiques of Epsom of their high-end merchandise and baby clothes which cost more than my entire wardrobe. This will stretch our finances further but will mean that she's too busy to phone up my boss, the superintendent at Lambeth nick and berate him for not allowing me to leave earlier to help out with the baby.

'There must be someone else who can do it. I need him back here.'

Or me, who she will continue our current conversation with at a volume that will resound around the office as though on speakerphone. This will be witnessed by all my piss-taking colleagues, who despite usually revelling in one another's misfortunes (tiny hands in particular) – no longer ridicule me after these calls in much the same way as they draw the line at mocking the disabled or infirm. It won't matter what I'm in the middle of dealing with, be it interviewing a drug dealer, arresting a paedophile, or applying for a warrant from a judge. I will answer my phone or face the consequences. Or rather Katie will face the consequences.

'Stop crying. Shut up. Shut UPPP!'

She's four months old and the sweetest, most docile loving thing I've ever known. Her very presence in this world has made it a better place but I'm afraid for her. Not so afraid that I could possibly get away with packing a bag for us both and running so far away Philippa will never find us. She'd never allow it. Katie's too important a prop in her current role as an Excellent Mother, which she performs with a glittering star-like quality from the moment she leaves the house until she returns.

Once inside however, she appears to be incapable of remembering where she's left the baby and despite never seeming to move from the sofa all day, she manages to trash the house so completely I'm always surprised not to have caught the tornado warnings over the radio at work.

I'm finding myself increasingly grateful to my mother-in-law who's become an almost permanent feature in our lives during daylight hours and who confides in me her fears about Philippa's mental health. We agree it's most likely postnatal depression and it'll pass. I'm sympathetic to such things. My sister, Julia, had a little boy only last year and tells me she had a touch of the baby blues too. By this she means she was tired and a little bit teary after three hours' sleep every night for about six months.

'I'm not sure it's the same,' I say.

'Well... Don't worry too much. She's bound to get over it soon.'

My own mother's been banned from showing her face other than for a few hours one Saturday a month when Philippa will refuse to come out of our room feigning exhaustion and will keep me up for hours after she's gone, describing in detail quite how much she hates her. So far she's only phoned my mum up to tell her this personally twice.

My father, for some reason, is still welcome and is praised for his prowess around an electrical circuit. His wife, Elizabeth is a *BITCH* however, who must burn in hell, which is a little harsh since she apologised profusely for giving Katie a pink blanket only days after Philippa had read an *Article Online* about the dangers of gender stereotyping from an early age.

The cracks in our relationship are beginning to resemble subsidence but she's the *Mother* of my child (as she likes to shout at me five times a day), the shared owner of a house I won't see a penny of if I leave and the co-guardian of a dog I'm almost certain she'd put down if I gave her one ounce of incentive.

She routinely throws her wedding ring at me demanding a divorce now and as much as I'd like to take her up on the offer (albeit empty) I work full-time supporting us all and I know enough about family law to recognise no court in the world would award me custody in these circumstances. Not simply because of a hunch I have that something isn't quite right. Not because the woman I married turned out to be as unpleasant a wife and a mother as she was a girlfriend.

I could move out and be prepared to fight for weekend visitation rights and hand over what remains of my salary to lawyers once the cost of maintaining two houses has already been deducted (well, one house and a hole for me). It's been done before many times by men with even more to lose than me, but the thought of seeing Katie any less than I already do leaves me cold. I may love my daughter more than life itself, but sadly, I'm also lacking a pair of boobs which society deems an obstacle to good parenting. This is not a fight that I want. Philippa is her *Mother* after all.

'It's thanks to me you've even got her.'

And so I stay, snatching a few hours of sleep where I can between my wife's furious outbursts and her unfounded accusations because in fairness, she's depressed and she'll get over it, right? But not today. It is seven minutes past five and there's a small chance I can still grab twenty-three minutes of sleep if Philippa runs out of steam. Twenty-two minutes. Twenty-one.

'I can't believe you told your mum it was okay to come up again so soon. She only came up a few weekends ago and you know I'm trying to get Katie into a routine. Not that I'd expect *her* to have any consideration. I thought my own mother was bad until I met yours and she's a fucking idiot!

'Take that cheap plastic teether she brought with her last time for one. It's probably toxic and Katie hasn't even got teeth yet. It's just more junk I have to tidy up. And it's not like she'd ever lift a finger to help out, is it? The old wizened bitch.

'It's no wonder your dad left her. Who can blame him? It's just a shame he ended up with that other stupid cow. You'd think he'd have learnt his lesson the first time around, but nooo. He swapped a tight-fisted cheapskate for a money grabbing, blood-sucking, home-wrecking whore and I have to put up with them both! I honestly don't know who's worse.

'Between them and your twat-faced sister... Looking down her nose at me just because she managed to shoot Golem out a few months before I had Katie. Bloody had him exorcised out of her more like. Makes my skin crawl just looking at him. You should put him in one of your acts. He'd get more laughs than you ever could.

'When was the last time you said anything remotely funny? Oh, don't tell me. It was the Oxo cubes. Fucking Oxo cubes?? I should have walked out right then, but I wasn't even surprised, that was the trouble. I knew you were a fucking idiot when I married you, I just didn't realise how deeply shit you were at everything else too. Kept that quiet, didn't you? Didn't bloody mention you were going to do sod all for the rest of your life, did you? I'd be better off alone, I swear, for all the bloody use you are around here.

'And I wouldn't have to put up with your snide comments about how fucking poor we are every time I blow the dust off your wallet. Well, it's my sodding money too, you know? It's all half mine. I don't have to justify or explain why I'm spending my own sodding money.

'It's not the effing dark ages, you wanker. Why don't you sort your fucking life out and get a promotion if you're so worried about living on a cock sucking shoestring? Pull your finger out and do a bit of overtime once in a while instead of moaning to me about money.

'What do you think I'm going to bloody feed you? Air? Jesus wept. I should kick you out on that sorry, pathetic arse of yours right now. I'd get the house to myself for a start, not to mention maintenance, instead of having to beg you for every penny I spend.

'And as for Katie, you can forget about seeing her again. There isn't a court in the land that wouldn't award her to me. There are some stories I could tell about you, don't think I wouldn't. You'd be lucky if they let you see her before she's twenty, you sad old alcoholic womaniser. Not that you'd give a shit. You'd be off screwing every other piece of arse out there, if you're not already. You'd give a shit about the money though, wouldn't you?

'Oh great, now your fucking dog's woken up the baby. Don't think I'm going to deal with it. Go and sort out your own damn mess before you piss off and leave me to it all day. I'm going to be fucking knackered now as well. For fuck's sake. Well, fucking GO THEN!!! Arsehole.'

And so I lift the new Version 3 of myself out of bed and drag him, half delirious with glee at his dismissal and nourishing the faint hope he can nod off quietly for five minutes on the sofa as Katie feeds peacefully in his arms. Version 3 is a changed man. He's a father, a protector. It's not enough to curl up into a ball and hope he loses consciousness so he doesn't have to deal with the crap he's inflicted on himself. Now he must stand up and be counted, by which, do not imagine I mean he must actually stand up for himself, which would be infinitely worse than simply not popping home and doing the dishes during a night shift or asking if it would be okay to attend a friend's birthday drinks in about two months time. I simply mean, not rocking the boat, in so far as he can given that he has no idea what makes the boat rock in the first place.

Version 3 of myself is just as worthless in my eyes and probably those of the rest of the world, as Version 2, but Version 3 must survive and preserve. He has a job to do and he must do it well. There's nothing clearer to me than the knowledge that no matter what, no matter how bad it gets, Version 3 cannot leave.

In fact, it dawns on me as I lift my gurgling child out of the cot and into my arms, as she rests her little head on my shoulder and I walk tentatively down the stairs to the kitchen where Mavis jumps on her hind legs and scrapes her paws down my thighs, tongue lolling through a magnificent smile, that Version 3 cannot even die. Ever. Version 3, as you may have already realised, is well and truly fucked.

A Strategic Lapse Of Judgement

My sister, Julia is pregnant again which is wonderful news but my heart sinks like a stone. Within hours my ailing knackers are in demand again and although I'm certain on a number of levels that bringing another child into our already dysfunctional dynamic is not a good idea, I'm also aware that I won't hear the end of it until we have.

I feel no attraction to my wife whatsoever and have absolutely no desire to spend any more time in her orbit than I already do, let alone grind any part of myself against her but there's no way Julia's going to get away with breeding more efficiently than Philippa. The spotlight's beginning to fade as it is and I sense Katie's been a disappointment so there's nothing to do but replace her.

'Let's see if you can even remember how.'

To be fair, I actually like the idea of having a second child and I reason that maybe if we have the two of them close together, it may make things easier (I know, I know). I always saw myself with two kids, though I guess when I pictured that particular idyllic scene, I wasn't sharing it with someone who hated me. Still, there's a chance a new baby might finally sort Philippa out and provide Katie with some much needed support and company growing up. Quite honestly at this stage I'll try anything.

I also need to put an end to the obsessive focus my wife has suddenly developed towards my man eggs and so I summon the willpower of a flame-grilled Tibetan monk (ironically) in order to satisfy these latest demands. At the very least she stops talking for a few minutes while in nothing short of a miracle – given the state of my libido – I do it again. Philippa is pregnant and even more irritable and exhausted than before.

My mother tells me I'm an idiot and she's right but as much as I'm dreading the next few months, not to mention the arrival of another mouth to feed and vex my already emotionally-strained wife, I'm also delighted it's happened so quickly. I've been released from my duties but more importantly I've already calculated how long I must stay before both kids are old enough to legally choose to live with me and this will only put me back fourteen months.

Not that I can imagine ever loving anyone as much as I do this bundle of glorious wonder I gaze at in my arms. But as I opened my heart to Katie despite my love for Mavis knowing no bounds, I know I'll feel the same unquestioning, unconditional love for this new little pawn I've introduced to the game. In the meantime however, Philippa's struggling with morning sickness, swollen ankles, prenatal depression, postpartum depression and a horrible personality.

Her mother is the current object of her animosity and contempt following her second platonic minibreak away with Mitch on the back of a ten-day Artic cruise around the Norwegian Fjords at a time when Philippa feels she should be on hand to help out with whatever cup might need washing in the sink or to look after Katie while she surfs the web. The result of this (apart from being woken at three o'clock in the morning to talk about the neglectful *BITCH*) is that my mum's now heavily in demand from the minute I go to work until I return and am able to resume my responsibilities in the house. Namely everything.

As well as being afforded a brief respite from being the worst grandmother in the world, my mum's actively enjoying being amazing at everything. There's no one on earth who can make coffee the way she does or melt cheese on toast quite as oozingly perfectly without burning the edges. She's *excellent at patting and burping and pacing with* our child and in the hour long attempts to squeeze pureed vegetables through Katie's pursed, stubborn lips, she's a *dab hand* and *extraordinarily patient*.

My mum is giddy with gratitude and relief at the turn of events and the sharp tone in her voice when she refers to my wife has softened. She has explanations now for past grievances and the injustices inflicted upon her in previous years.

Philippa is a victim of circumstance and who can blame her for not always being happy after the life she's had? It's Linda's fault really and I agree she certainly didn't help, firstly by destabilising Philippa and then encouraging her instability either through stupidity, bad parenting or fear.

I warn my mum it may not last and she's understanding because it's difficult for Philippa to control her emotions now that she's pregnant again and still dealing with the demands of looking after a small child.

Fortunately Linda remains on The List throughout the course of the pregnancy, despite still being required to look after Katie and clean the house on the days my own mum's unable to. This is accompanied by slanging matches the likes of which the mannerly residents of Epsom would have only previously witnessed on an episode of Eastenders. Yet mother and daughter are drawn together irrepressibly like magnets, crashing into one another time and time again. They are caught up in the drama of the strange, fabricated world in which they star and as much as they hate each other, they're inextricably bound together in a quagmire of condemnation and blame.

All of which serves to terrorise my own daughter who is not yet anaesthetised to the ten thousand decibel discussions about whom is the most useless waste of space between the two of them. I, for one, am elated that Linda's absorbing the bulk of Philippa's hormone-infused anger, but Katie needs tranquillity and calm so I encourage my mum to visit as often as she can and surprisingly she's welcomed with open arms every time (as long as she makes herself useful, of course).

This ends the day Julia gives birth to another beautiful, bouncing baby – a girl this time and my mum makes the mistake of telling everyone how sweet she is. A switch has been flicked in Philippa's head, but the doting grandmother is oblivious in her gushing chatter and ill-advised joy.

She has become, in the blink of an eye, a necessity that must be endured but not enjoyed and only I can see the tightness cross Philippa's face as she navigates the thin line between tolerating my mother for as long as she continues to babysit or hoover, and wishing she'd die.

By the time she's nine months pregnant, my mum's staying with us four or five nights a week, partly to ensure that she's present when Philippa goes into imminent labour so she can look after Katie, but also to keep her away from my sister and her family as much as possible. My mum's not entirely comfortable with this arrangement, but she's needed and must rise to the occasion.

In addition, amateur psychologist that I've become, I realise she's tasted the vindication of complete adoration and while not implicitly certain it's been withdrawn, she's chasing the opportunity to levitate back to the dizzy heights of veneration she experienced before she blew it by loving Julia's new baby too.

At last the big day arrives, two weeks late and not entirely without apprehension, but once again Philippa performs like a pro and I'm proud of her. There are moments of real connection between us and it is not like in films where the woman insults her husband throughout and screams at the top of her lungs that she hates him (which makes for a nice change). Her attentions are focused on the unfortunate midwives instead and so it's almost relaxing for me.

By the time the blood-coated cap of my baby's head peeks out from between Philippa's legs, I'm thoroughly enjoying myself. I have another daughter, another beautiful perfect little girl and as I hold her in my arms, I see her for the first time as a person in her own right and not purely a playmate for Katie or a tool to distract my wife until such a time as I'm able to leave her.

Philippa's reaction is very different this time and I'm relieved that she immediately bonds with the baby who we decide, almost mutually, to call Lauren. She's joined several forums online berating the pressure men and society in general put on mothers to breastfeed or face unfair judgement so she is fully committed to using formula and championing the cause. The chastised midwives are wise not to contradict her on this.

When my mum brings Katie to the hospital to meet her new little sister, Philippa is doting and sweet to them all, but then of course, we are in public. By the time we return home, we've more or less fallen into a routine in which Philippa is unaccountably occupied by the baby and Katie and I are able to enjoy each other's company in peace. Linda (Mitch) spends a fortune on baby clothes, a double buggy and a new moses basket to replace the one Philippa sold recently on eBay. She's back in the good books and though my own mum doesn't know it yet, she is not.

It begins subtly enough with a few comments – the meaning of which my mum is not sure she's quite caught – and deteriorates rapidly into sharp observations about the state of the house (our house) and the fact Katie hasn't been fed yet. To top it off she remains obliviously cheery about Julia's kids and never short of a story or two insists on telling me, within Philippa's earshot, agonisingly explicit step-by-step accounts of all their latest adventures. This does not go down well.

Whereas the first time Philippa could hardly bear to be around Katie, with Lauren, she's loath to put her down. Even Katie's less of an irritation now she's learnt to sit still in front of the television for long periods of time. But along with this newfound ability to give selflessly to others, she's also begun to throw herself (occasionally at least) into her current role as a Martyr. This entails insisting she can do everything herself – possibly in competition with Julia, who can.

Unfortunately, it's not a role to which she's suited and in fairness, it shouldn't be a priority for any woman who's recently given birth. There are no expectations put upon her other than those she lays down for herself, but my sister's set the bar unattainably high by managing to both get dressed in the mornings as well as feed her own kids. All without seemingly screaming at them, so poor Philippa's set herself up for a fall and as we all know by now, or at least we should, she will not fall alone.

'You have never liked my children!' she screeches down the phone at my dumbfounded mother, who has unwittingly picked up the receiver with nothing but the vague hope it isn't someone who's heard she's been in an accident that wasn't her fault. Moments later she would happily crash into the back of a minibus so as to hear the familiar tone of background noise echoing around a northern call centre instead. 'All you talk about is Julia's bloody kids. When was the last time you asked about mine? It's not like they're even that amazing. Mine are much better looking but all you do is go on about hers.'

'Philippa. That's not –'

'Don't you dare try and deny it. You have photos of them all over your house.' She has hundreds of the girls too, but admittedly Julia is very good at printing pictures of her family out and presenting them to people at birthdays. It's annoying actually.

'And I'm sorry,' She isn't sorry at all. 'But what is the point of you coming to *help out* when all you do is sit around drinking coffee and reading the paper?'

I know what's coming. I heard about it the day it happened a week ago but it's festered and raged inside Philippa's disgruntled mind since then.

My mum, withering in status but a necessity around the house nonetheless, had been staying for a few days and I'd been at work. Philippa had taken the washing out into the garden to hang on the line (the only part of the story that would have seemed implausible only a few weeks before) so my mum had offered to hold Lauren for her, while she continued to play with Katie in the lounge.

Error number one was not recognising that Philippa had a cross to bear and so she insisted on taking both the girls outside with her to further complicate the task in hand and spoil a perfectly nice game of Doodlebugs to boot. In retrospect, my mum realised she was supposed to have taken over the laundry duties, but instead she took my wife at her word.

Error number two. Philippa took her sweet time so my mum picked up the paper and read it while she waited for them to come back inside and when they eventually did Philippa was still bustling around the kids so (error number three) she finished the article. Not the paper. Not the crossword. Just the article, which for a free local rag that had been pushed through the door, probably comprised of three paragraphs. But it was long enough to hammer the last nail into my mum's coffin. She had not only completed her fall from the world's highest pedestal but she'd burned to ash on the way down.

'You're a disgrace,' Philippa continues while my mum, heart thumping in her shocked chest, mouth agape, clings to the bannister for balance. 'You have no fucking shame. They're your grandchildren and you can't even be bothered to spend any time with them. How do you think it makes them feel? They were in tears when you left last time. They know you can't stand them and don't think I'm going to lie to them for your sake. If you can't be bothered to make an effort for them, I'm not going to pretend that you give a shit.

They don't need you. Any of you. They've got me and *my* mother who actually helps out when she comes over instead of expecting meals to be made for her. When was the last time you bought any presents for the girls? Or did anything around the house?'

She'd turned up with three bottles of wine, a load of coffee and the spare shampoo she'd got in a two-for-one deal. She'd brought her own towels and bedding to save on the washing. She'd made two of the three lunches she'd eaten and tidied up afterwards. She'd emptied the dishwasher twice, loaded it three times and wiped all the surfaces in between doing jigsaws and Play-Doh and reading stories to Katie from six o'clock in the morning all the way through to bed time. The only thing my mum didn't do was make our dinner, though she did do the girls' tea but all she can say is *I...* before Philippa interrupts to tell her she is utterly despicable and shouldn't be allowed around children.

She is spitting into the phone in a voice that sounds like glass smashing into jagged splinters. Like empty bottles transformed instantly into instruments of death. My mother's petrified throughout the ordeal. Defenceless, vulnerable and taken wholly unawares, but when she tells me what happened later, all I can do is laugh. Hysterical nervous hiccups of laughter that accompany the cold sweat beading on my forehead as I pace the kitchen, phone in hand and my heart in my throat.

It is one thing to be continuously spoken to like an unruly child who's disembowelled the family cat but to hear the fear and bewilderment in my own mother's voice and be helpless to prevent it from happening again is a whole other level of awfulness. To know this is not the last time she'll be on the receiving end of such a venomous lashing without any warning or the experience to ride it out but I'm delirious in that moment and the only advice I have is that she should hunch down and accept it. Just continue to back me up in this charade and make that extra effort, even if it's a pretence, because if she or any of my dwindling group of supporters don't, if they pick up the paper and read it, even though they've offered to help and been turned down, one of us will pay the price and if it isn't the perpetrator of the offence, it will be me or my children. And so I laugh because if not I'll cry and I don't have the words to tell her that all hope is lost.

It's not enough to do everything you can. It's not enough to sacrifice your family and everything else you love. You must be alert at all times. Vigilant, guarded and most importantly, you must never, ever fall for the charm. It's short-lived and it will slice through you like a knife when it's taken away.

And when it is, you will not know what hit you.

Solitary Confinement And Other Forms Of Torture

Over the course of the next year and a half I become increasingly alienated from my family and friends. There's no one specific event that causes this but rather a series of small incidences which in the end make not seeing them so often, the easier option.

My sister was banned about six months ago after she refused Katie a breadstick (very sweetly and in the same tone you'd use on a puppy) because lunch was a few minutes away and she'd spoil her appetite. Katie was as chirpy at the prospect of having her aunty's special invisible pasta (tons of blended vegetables camouflaged in a tomato sauce) as Philippa was affronted by;

Firstly, Julia's attempt to offer anything other than beige carbohydrates to the children;

Secondly, by the cheek she had at turning down a request for any such beige carbohydrate regardless of timing;

Thirdly, at the suggestion that beige carbohydrates were therefore less nutritious by comparison to *that fucking pasta sauce she does every time we see them* and;

Fourthly, by the fact *that fucking pasta sauce* was Katie's favourite meal on earth.

Oh and also, Julia was a *BITCH*.

The afternoon ended in tears, as I knew it would, with Philippa deciding abruptly that all beige carbohydrates were now off limits and it had, by rights, been her decision to stop Katie eating them (at some inconvenience since until then 90% of the kids' diet consisted of breadsticks and rice cakes). And so into the bin went the wholemeal fusilli complete with invisible pasta sauce, broccoli and cheese, which was *not fit for pigs*.

Even I was shocked. She normally managed to hold it together in company or at least restricted herself to the odd snide remark but in my wife's defence, Julia had been on particularly good form that day and Andy hadn't helped by building a *pretentious and fucking lethal* tree house in the garden. Even the weather was better there. We'd left in drizzle and arrived at the bottom of a glorious rainbow. Philippa could hardly be blamed for being a little on edge and never wanting to see *that pair of bastards* again.

I stay in touch over email (a new account only a few people know about) and occasionally on the phone, but I have no desire to put my wife and my sister in a room together ever again and so as much as I love her, I push Julia away. My loyalty is to my girls and my job is keeping their mother stable or as stable as can be given she's nuts.

From that day on and for pretty much the next three or four months, she only gives Katie and Lauren peas, broccoli and sweet corn, which they eat from a bowl wherever they happen to be. I'm chastised if I attempt to feed them anything more substantial so I have to sneak sandwiches and pasta to them in secret until, thankfully, Philippa reads an *Article Online* about the dangers of eating too few carbohydrates, which apparently vindicates her and puts my sister to shame. *Ha!*

The house is a mess all the time. When I get home from work, I tidy up all the toys that have been spread across the floor of every room throughout the course of the day. Philippa is exhausted by then because she has apparently been playing with the children and said toys without a break, so it's my turn to take over cooking and cleaning and looking after them before I head out again with the dog. I don't mind this. Being with them and Mavis is the best part of my day and I'm glad they've been playing so much although I don't believe for a minute they've been anything but alone. This is fine too and had been after all, a huge part of the reason I agreed to having two kids in the first place.

I do wish however, that they weren't encouraged to spend the bulk of the day smearing peas into the carpet, planting stickers all over the furniture, scattering thin curling shreds of ripped wallpaper on the floor and scribbling on the walls with permanent ink.

It shames me to admit they're a little bit feral and when they pounce on me as I walk through the door every night, it's as much out of the excitement of seeing another human being as it is because they love me. And they do love me. We're a team and when I'm not there, they team up together. They're as close as any two people can be and it's a delight to listen to their little conversations, their cute childish voices making every sound that comes out of their mouths completely adorable. It's a shame Philippa more often than not has a headache and must scream at the top of her lungs until they are quiet so she can have two minutes of peace without having to listen to *their crap*. I, on the other hand, could listen to them all day.

'Daddy. If my body falls off, will you take me to the hospital?' This in the middle of breakfast.

'Yes, darling. I should think so.'

Katie chews for a moment and swallows her mouthful. 'And if my eyes fall down?'

'Yes, I'll take you to the hospital.' A dribble of milk slides down her chin and I wipe it away with my thumb.

'But what if your body falls off? And your arms and your legs and your head?' She sticks her spoon against my throat for emphasis. It still has a honey nut cornflake on it.

'Well, we'll have to see in that case.' I have more pressing things on my mind like the soggy mark on my T-shirt that'll probably dry like a jizz stain. 'I can't make any promises.'

'Will Mummy will take us to the hospital?'

I dab at my top with a damp napkin, my eyes firmly focused downwards. And then I breathe in and force a smile on my face. 'I really don't know, love. You'd have to ask her.'

Paradoxically, whenever anybody else is around Philippa's suddenly consumed by the desire to take them wherever she goes, be it upstairs or to the garden or the toilet. She's careful to make sure they know they have nothing to worry about if she does leave the room by pointing out multiple times they have nothing to worry about if she does leave the room. She'll repeat this emphatically so many times it will leave the girls in no doubt that there is absolutely something to worry about if she does leave the room and so when she does eventually leave the room they will follow her, leaving whoever has attempted to visit alone and worrying that there really is something to worry about.

We don't have many visitors these days. The girls are easier to look after now and sleep better so we're not permanently frazzled, unless Philippa has something on her mind which she feels she must share in the middle of the night. Her mother's still the main source of childcare when needed, but when they fall out, which is often, my own mum is called upon to help again.

She's wary now and timid around Philippa and the girls, fearful that any display of affection from them towards her will set off another perverse outburst and yet equally conscious of having to gush over their every move or face accusations of not caring enough.

It's fortunate that both my daughters are breathtakingly gorgeous and I don't mean this in an indulgent rose-coloured glasses sort of way that makes parents with children who look like potatoes continue to put photos of them all over the house. My girls are stunning individually but together they make trips to the supermarket a royal pain unless I'm in the mood for chatting to every old lady and shop assistant within a three-mile radius as they insist on telling me how beautiful the two of them are.

And I understand they don't need to be good looking in order to succeed in life, I appreciate this doesn't validate them but I've got to say it helps.

It's impossible to look at them and not fall in love no matter how many pictures they've drawn on the newly repainted walls and for my mother, their appearance is a fountain of compliments she has come to rely on when she can't bring herself to congratulate them on redecorating the hallway with toilet roll or for bouncing up and down on the trampoline with their lunch.

At the other end of the spectrum, my dad is cheerfully incompetent around the girls but this is forgiven because what he lacks in babysitting skills he makes up for in Manliness, which, much as I love him, seems to involve falling asleep in an armchair and worrying about the news. His only flaw, it would seem is his appalling taste in women and it's galling to my wife that he never goes anywhere without Elizabeth, who Philippa tells the children to be careful around *because she cannot be trusted.*

There are a few friends I'm still allowed to see although they're less inclined to visit, so reunions have been reduced to special occasions such as the kids' birthday parties which are grandiose affairs with entertainers, bouncy castles, petting zoos and not nearly enough alcohol to make paying for it all tolerable. Oh and attendance is mandatory regardless of how offensive your pasta sauce may be or whether your husband has recently passed which was the case with my gran when Lauren turned two.

I'd always been close to my grandparents. My father, having walked out on the family he hadn't honestly really noticed until then, had suddenly found himself the proud recipient of two suspicious, stroppy children every Sunday. There were only so many times he could take us bowling and so off up the M27 we would go twice a month where my gran would knock at least fifteen minutes off our lives with every roast potato she served up in a sizzling puddle of oil and salt. It was heaven. Not only was lunch an invitation for open-heart surgery, but spending time with my grandparents was actually entertaining.

Their drawers were literally bursting with every broken comb and piece of string they'd ever owned. We'd spend hours trawling through them for treasure and occasionally we'd find some, which when you're eight usually takes the form of a half-mangled toy soldier with chipped toxic paint.

At the end of every visit, my grandad would press a hot shiny pound coin into the palm of our hands and say *'ere, put this somewhere safe* in a gruff Irish accent and we'd stuff it in our pockets with a grateful hug, looking forward, before we'd even left, to seeing them again.

My grandad was the toughest man I'd ever met. He didn't try to be, that's just the way they were in that generation. You'd only know he'd injured himself when he turned up clad in Sellotape. Not for him hours wasted in A&E with a half-sawn off thumb if he still had the strength to sort it out himself. Even breaking all ten fingers in a motorcycle accident didn't stop him reaching for the sticky tape. If you'd opened my grandad's first aid kit all you'd have found was one big old roll of the stuff. And I'll be buggered if it wasn't all he ever needed.

The first time that man ever went willingly to hospital, he was nearly ninety-three years old. He walked in unassisted and proud and there he stayed, dying one week later. It was in the middle of the night and I had the almighty privilege of being the only person with him. I closed his eyes, combed his hair and kissed his head before calling my gran and my aunt. I didn't tell them he'd died because I didn't want them to crash on the way to the hospital and besides, I wasn't ready to say it out loud.

When my gran had found Grandad lying in bed and barely able to breath, he'd said to her *I've always loved you.* He knew it was the start of the end and in the darkness of that moment that was his most enduring thought. They'd been together since the war, through the good times and bad and those were the words he chose.

That was the sort of marriage I had always wanted, that I'd aspired to, but it wasn't the sort of marriage I'd got and we'd enjoyed all those Sundays growing up so I wasn't completely opposed to divorce once the girls were old enough to choose to live with me. It hadn't been on my list of things I hoped to accomplish, but I knew from experience it could have an upside if it was handled with dignity and class. It could change the dynamic in a family in a positive way, strengthen relationships and introduce new experiences people would otherwise never have had. I'm not exaggerating when I say we could have sailed through our childhood without ever tasting a McDonald's were it not for my parents parting of ways, which though traumatic and unsettling for us all (not least for my mother who did not get taken out for fast food), it did force us to spend actual quality time with our dad who until then had spent most of our existence behind a newspaper or playing the trumpet in the downstairs loo.

And it also meant more time with our grandparents, who as I said, I became increasingly close to, so I'm gutted when my grandad dies. It isn't a tragedy but it affects me deeply and then two weeks later, Mavis, my best friend in the world who has seen me through the very worst of times with no expectation other than to be loved in return, becomes weak and lethargic.

Three days later, with no improvement, I take her to the vet's and discover she has kidney failure and the kindest thing would be to let her go. I return to the house with her so the girls can say their goodbyes and then I cry all the way back to the surgery. It's a Wednesday, the sun is shining and she dies in my arms.

I can honestly say I have never felt so broken in my life as I do then. I'm married to a woman I hate and fear, I have two beautiful daughters I feel guilty about every moment of every day, I'm estranged from the majority of my family and friends, I've passed my Inspector's exam but since police budgets have been slashed, there's no chance of an actual promotion or pay rise for the foreseeable future, I haven't done any stand up for months and I've lost two of the most important relationships I've ever known in quick succession.

And so when Philippa's occasional unflattering comparisons between England and Canada become more frequent and more vicious, I start to wonder if maybe she's onto something. The cost of living there is much lower while wages are the same. I love my too-expensive semi in the suburbs but we can swap it for a mansion over there and still have change to go skiing every weekend and shoot moose.

Canadians need policemen too obviously although they have a much lower crime rate and the education system's rated one of the best in the world. Even on one wage we can live the sort of life Philippa aspires to. The sort of life she might not criticise and complain about all the time. She could drive a nice big car – a new one – live in a nice big house, buy as much crap as she wants from nice big stores and in my desperation to find an escape from the life I feel trapped in, I think she might even be nice about it. That if she has everything she wants, she might finally be happy.

I should have known but that was my problem. I always expected too much.

Let It Rain

My dad thinks emigrating is a brilliant idea. He's always wanted to go to Canada and this will make it much easier. He approves of big houses and big cars and having somewhere nice to stay when he visits. Julia tells me it is a bad idea and cries. My mum says Philippa will be bored within five years and demand to come home. I tell her I know but ask her what I can do. She can't come up with anything and so from that moment on facilitates as I deconstruct what little still remains of my life.

Philippa is happy. She's excited and busy making plans. For her, this entails trawling the Internet for big houses and big cars. For me, given that I still have a job, a tenuous involvement with the comedy circuit, an enormous debt, an even more enormous mortgage, a too-expensive semi in the suburbs we will no longer need as well as a smattering of friends and family around me, matters are slightly more complicated.

I begin by contacting the various Canadian police departments to find out how to apply for a transfer. I won't bore you with the inexplicably ball breaking process which finally leads me to the knowledge that although I've been a policeman for over a decade and have passed my Sergeant, Detective and Inspector's exams, although I was handpicked for an elite team in the Homicide and Major Crime Command and have worked in the busiest and most dangerous of London boroughs running my own team of detectives, I will have to enter the Canadian police force at the same level as every one else. The bottom. There's to be no sliding seamlessly into a lateral position, no sharing my wealth of skills and expertise with our North American counterparts.

Rather I'll have to retrain with all the eighteen-year-old Chucks and Chads fresh out of high school and braces. And not for a moment will the salary reflect the thirteen years of experience I'll bring to the role.

This is not ideal, obviously, but I am reminded that I worked my way up pretty quickly the first time so I can *suck it up*. While also doing some stand up on the side to prop up the family coffers. I'm not overwhelmed with joy, but no decision has been made and we'll decide what to do on balance when we have all the information to hand. Philippa's certain life will be perfect out there and while I'd rather not go, I can't take being shouted at anymore.

We put the house on the market because it's easy enough to do and we can always take it off again if our plans change. We're on a fact-finding mission after all. No firm decisions have been made. Fortunately the girls are still too young to go to school over there and we don't cancel the place Katie was lucky to be offered at the pre-school up the road because we're a long way from committing ourselves to actually leaving.

We book a two-week holiday to Toronto. This is merely to see if I even like the place. My expectations are fairly high having heard so much about it over the last few years, but even so it is hard to imagine the streets really are bejewelled and dripping with gold. I've been informed many times that every single aspect from the people to the standard of living, the shops, education, healthcare and every other service or policy are better than in the UK and this is not so hard to imagine.

However, I still have an open mind and in so far as I can, I refuse to commit myself entirely to the prospect of emigrating until I've at least been to this utopian paradise and weighed up the pros and cons. Obviously at the top of the pros is the possibility that Philippa may finally be happy and our relationship can return to the joyful days when I scaled the peaks of my godlike status with a finesse and gravitas unlike any man on earth. Top of the cons, obviously is that nothing will change and we will be all that we are here or worse, and the only sane people I know will be three and a half thousand miles away.

No matter. I reserve the right to judge for myself. We arrive on a blistering hot summer's day. The light glints off the skyscrapers and bathes the gleaming wide streets in a blanket of glistening gold (she was right!). The whole place has the look of a shiny, new film set and I feel strangely nostalgic at the sight of the green road signs, the yellow traffic lights, double-fronted stores selling nothing but doughnuts and burger joints serving milk shakes in buckets and heart attacks on bread.

I have to admit, I'm impressed and the mood has lightened considerably. The flight on the way over had almost crushed my final reserves of strength the way only a long haul transfer across the Atlantic with two small children and a cantankerous, belligerent wife ever could.

By the time we landed, I'd walked up and down the tight aisle of that no frills, economy flying tin can no less than ten million times, I'd jiggled both girls until my arms hung down to the floor like spaghetti (which admittedly helped with the endless stooped shuffle along the gangway), I'd sung fifty thousand renditions of Incy Wincy Spider and endured the consequential verbal battering I received for tickling the kids in a confined area.

As the plane lowered it's wheels onto the baking hot tarmac at Toronto Pearson International airport, the other passengers in the vicinity put their hands together for a thunderous round of applause for me, probably less in response to my singing abilities than at my efforts to prevent Katie and Lauren screaming the whole way through the eight-hour flight, but it was gratifying nonetheless. Philippa was less complimentary ('They'd have never have done that if you were a woman') but having battled our way through the ubiquitous arse of Passport and Customs Control and out into the glorious sunshine, she finally thawed and I allowed myself the luxury of believing we were on the right track after all.

The houses are big over there. Not quite as big as I'd dared to hope but certainly big enough to afford to live comfortably in a four-bedroom detached with a huge front and back yard with a basement in a nice part of town (or just out of town. Alright, you've got me. In the suburbs). The schools in the area are all excellent, the shops are a car ride away, but so is everything because it's all massive. Burlington, where we are looking, is clean and pleasant. There are parks everywhere with well-maintained playgrounds and not a used condom in sight.

We view a few houses, just to get a better idea about what to expect. They're the typical wooden cladded North American style I've always seen on telly and they're nearly twice the size of our cute over-priced cottage-esque semi in Surrey. One in particular catches our eye, which is futile because we're months, if not a year away from even contemplating physically moving.

We allow ourselves to fantasise about living there. The girls are allocated bedrooms, the basement is mentally refurbished, a pretentious and fucking lethal tree house is imagined in the back yard along with a huge trampoline and basketball hoop. There is even, wait for it… a swimming pool and we bask in delusions of grandeur.

It's irrelevant but it draws us a little closer together and for once we're not arguing. Or rather Philippa's not arguing while I silently contemplate the number of ways she could die, painfully but without repercussions. The children are noticeably less uptight and anxious in the warmth of their mother's approval and self-satisfaction. It is fair to say, we're having a nice time.

I go for an interview with a recruiter at Walton Police Service, which is a small force outside of Toronto and I'm assured that after the agonising twelve weeks of training, I should be fast tracked back up to my previous rank. He's already spoken to the head of my department in London and he is looking forward to welcoming me to the team in the event that we do, eventually, decide to relocate our whole lives at gargantuan expense and inconvenience, to the other side of the pond.

There are definitely a few more points to consider on the pro side of our objectives, but I'm still not remotely comfortable with starting right back at the arse end of my career, even if it will take me less time to claw my way back. It'll still be a good couple of years at least and apart from the soul-destroying, mind numbing monotony of only dealing with the more mundane cases, sitting on traffic duty and walking the beat like a teenager again, the money will be shit.

There's a lot to think about. A lot to weigh up – financially as well as emotionally. We have a couple of days left to enjoy ourselves, but it's all gone pretty well, I have to say. I'm feeling optimistic and as though Philippa and I are finally on the same team. In the same family even. And then she tells me she's accepted an offer on our house (a low one) and won't be returning to England with me.

She has to say it again before I really understand. Before the words that have hit me like a punch to my gut finally sink in. Before my whole world stops turning in slow motion. She and the children will be staying at the hotel for as long as it takes me to work through my notice, pack our stuff together and ship it across to the new house she has just put an offer on. Which has been accepted.

She will not budge. No matter how much I plead with her, I am a monster for suggesting the girls should be put through another flight back to the UK as it is known now instead of home. And there's nothing I can do. Not without getting social services and the police involved which will take years to resolve. She is their *Mother*, she is Canadian and we are in Canada.

I can't believe my naivety. My staggering stupidity or my foolhardy assumption that I'm dealing with a normal human being. I can't comprehend how I've put myself in a position where my wife has to drive me to an airport in a car we're renting so I can abandon the two children I love, children I'm genuinely afraid of leaving alone in the company of a sociopath. But I have no choice and the quickest way to get back to them is to go along with it all, heart in my throat and my balls in the overhead locker.

When we arrive at the drop off point both Katie and Lauren are asleep and I choose not to wake them, a decision which will haunt me for the rest of my life, even after my sister tries to convince me years later when I cry at the memory of that day, that only an arsehole would wake their sleeping children so as to upset them. I say goodbye to my smug, content wife and I head to the check in desk to explain that I am the only one of my party who will be boarding that flight.

I've never felt so numb in my life. I have no idea if I'll ever see my daughters again but I have a perfectly lovely too-expensive houseful of crap to pack up, a successful career to piss up the wall, a small circle of family and friends to cut ties with, a car to sell at a crippling loss and a hundred million other things to organise and apply for, all on my own and without my whole reason for living by my side.

Suffice to say, if the flight out there had dragged, the journey back gives me nightmares to this day and I spend most of the time picturing my daughters waking up in the back of the car with no idea where I've gone or the real reason I've left them. Not to mention doubting they'll be told that I'm coming back.

When I eventually arrive home and share news of the latest events with my family, there's a collective panic, incredulous protests and shocked silences, all of which reflect my own anxiety and none of which help at all. I find it hard to stop crying but there's too much to sort out to allow myself to break down completely.

To my relief, Philippa still answers the phone and allows me to speak to the girls, if they're not sleeping or engaged in some other activity like playing or breathing, which seems to coincide with the occasions my daily updates fall short of her expectations. When I do get to talk to them, they ask me repeatedly why I'm not there and all I can do is choke back the tears and reassure them I'll come back as soon as I can.

But this is a long way off. I have a four-week notice period to get through at work, but the sale of the house will take much longer than that. I have to receive a formal job offer from Walton before I can walk away from the aforementioned much better job in London which I can't leave until I have been approved for a new mortgage on a house which is overseas and therefore a hundred times more complicated to organise and dependent on my acceptance into the police force over there.

Not only that but according to the Canadian real estate system, I must accomplish all this by mid-July, when I have to produce the deposit for my soon-to-be four-bedroomed shed in the New World and any failure to do so will result in losing the house but still owing 10% of the sale price. Which I won't be able to pay either, but I must or I risk bankruptcy.

Or worse case scenario, my realtor casually mentions, there's a chance I could be sent to jail.

Not for the Canadians, gazumping and chains that fall through at the last minute. Those savvy Canucks protect themselves from the catastrophic dilly-dallying of estate agents, lazy solicitors and reckless homebuyers by ensuring that once committed to buying a property, the repercussions are fierce following any attempt to pull out. Which is admirable, I think. Which makes a lot of sense and should really be replicated all over the world, particularly in England where no such laws exist and which mean that when the buyers of my too-expensive semi-detached in Epsom change their mind, I have three weeks to come up with £100,000.

I have to come up with it. Not my wife of course, which would be the perfect end to this story, but me, the dim-witted, obedient fool who signed the papers to make the noise stop. But all is not lost. My kindly mortgage broker offers me a bridging loan with an interest rate that puts my meagre worries about the minibar bill Philippa is racking up in a four-star suite the other side of the world into perspective. I'll be paying back both until the day I die but in case I wasn't clear enough earlier, I either come up with the deposit or I could go to jail.

Jail.

And then a week later, I hear at the conclusion of twenty conversations with forty-two different people – all of whom have no idea what I'm talking about or need a little more information – that we do, in fact, not qualify for a short-term loan, even at the ridiculous rates I'll gladly pay by this point for the rest of my pitiful life, because essentially Philippa's lacking the necessary credit history to get even a damn Nokia.

Jail time is beckoning with a red, throbbing head and a penchant for pretty policemen. There's a chance I'll get lucky and only be slapped with a debilitating fine and a criminal record, which will prevent me from working for the police ever again but may be less painful to swallow, so to speak. Either scenario is more attractive than having to tell Philippa what's happened. The only thing that assures me I will see her again is the fact I know where to find her, but if we lose the house I have no guarantee she won't simply disappear.

There's a light in the tunnel, however and as mercenary as I feel even thinking about it, there's no other option. My grandfather's death had knocked me sideways, but now as I lie in a pool of cold sweat, gripped with terror for the third night in a row following Josh from Epsom Estates breezy announcement about the sale falling through, I realise there is a way out of this nightmare.

My gran had packed up most of her possessions a week after the funeral and moved into a newly converted bedroom on the ground floor of the home my dad shares with Elizabeth. Her house sold quickly and painlessly and she currently has the best part of £195,000 sitting in a bank account where it will stay until she dies, unless she dies at five hundred. All I need is a loan to pay the fees due on the new Burlington property until I manage to sell the Surrey house. Which I will at some point, even if it takes a few months and in the meantime the money will be tied up so there is no risk to anyone involved.

I'm so relieved at the realisation it will all be okay that I actually sleep for twenty minutes before I have to get up and go to a job I would rather gnaw my testicles off than have to deal with right then.

I call my dad as soon as it's light. He's not sleeping well either as he's certain Philippa's going to kidnap the children, but when I tell him I've found a solution to what until then he hadn't even realised was an issue, he's less positive than I'd hoped. As far as he's concerned if it were his money, I'd be welcome to it, but it's not his money and so he must check with my gran who adores me and my aunt who shares control of the finances and who would also do anything for me. Except this, it would seem.

For a week and a half I beg, literally on bended knees as I've lost the ability to stand and as far as they're concerned, they really would do anything for me, but this is not for me alone. This is for Philippa and they feel (with good reason perhaps) that if they transfer £100,000 into her Canadian bank account none of us will ever see her or the money again.

I remind them I'll be sued for £40,000 if I don't hand over the cash within ten days and I may lose a lot more than that, but they still worry. I tell them I'll sign anything they like, but this won't stop her running away. I remind them I still own a too expensive semi-detached in the suburbs which is worth over half a million pounds, but they fear the market has slowed and the money could be tied up for years. I mention I won't need a house if I'm in jail so they can rent the damn thing out but they're still afraid Philippa will find a way to get it. She is after all a master manipulator and frankly terrifying, although somehow less terrifying than my own family have become at that particular time.

My mum tells my dad to stop fannying around and do the right thing for once in his life, which I think is a little harsh but in any event, I appreciate her enthusiasm. She tries a gentler approach with my aunt and gran and is reasonably confident after an hour-long tearful conversation, that she's persuaded them that even if it takes me the rest of my life, I'll pay back the loan, which I'm not in any way entitled to ask for, but will destroy my whole family if I don't produce.

And then Philippa gets involved with a phone call to my aunt – which I pay through the teeth for – in which things are said in a less enigmatic and grateful tone than I'd have perhaps opted for myself and suddenly any potential wavering on the side of the opposition is firmly resolved. And not in my favour, if that wasn't clarified. It is not in my favour and yet I must keep breathing.

My sister's moved house and for once has some money put aside for the refurbishment which she offers me, but that, alongside a couple of ISAs my mum can pull out and some of my dad's investments, still leaves me a mere thirty grand short. But I still have three days in which to either sell at least one of my kidneys or my soul, though sadly neither is worth enough.

I beg again and am told that nobody has slept all week for worrying about it and they love me and the girls obviously, but Philippa is as untrustworthy as she is ghastly which I can't disagree with, although I am beginning to side more with her.

Julia tells my dad she will happily forfeit her share of any inheritance, as will I obviously, in the event it goes tits up and besides if all it takes to make Philippa disappear is £100,000, it's money well spent.

However, this doesn't account for the fact she's currently in possession of my children whom she now likes to turn the camera on during our Skype calls in the midst of her angry, puce rages so I can fully appreciate, as she leans her twisted, incandescent face only inches from their now almost blank expressions and screeches relentlessly at them, that they're *impossible to deal with.* It doesn't help, of course, that all I'm doing is *pissing around packing up a few pots and pans* and probably *screwing someone else.*

'How hard can it be, Daniel? Why do you have to make everything so fucking complicated? I gave you one little job to do and you can't even get that right. You're a useless waste of space. Whoever it is you've got shacked up in my house is welcome to you, you cocking knob. Just be sure to let her know I'll be coming after everything you've got, including the kids. You'll be lucky if I let you see them more than one weekend a year. You've got no rights in this country, don't forget that, you loser, so I suggest you think twice about whatever it is you're up to.

'I've had it up to here with you pissing around dragging all this out and expecting me to do everything. Do you know how exhausting it is looking after two young girls? Of course you don't, you chauvinistic prick. They're out of control. It's a nightmare and Katie's getting more insolent every day. In fact, the pair of them are driving me mad. I've had it with them both, did you hear that, you spoiled brats?

'And *you*? You've got us holed up in this room while you laze around that whole fucking house pretending you're single, no doubt. What have you done? Hidden all the photographs of me and the kids? Don't bother. No one would ever believe you have children, you show such little interest in them. At least I'm here for them. It's not like they even need you. You never do anything anyway.

'I swear to God, Dan, if you don't get this all sorted by the next time I call, you'd better start making plans that don't include us.'

I don't know how to speed up this process to stop the shouting and regardless of where I find the deposit, I will have to send it to her anyway and take the chance her urge to buy another too-expensive house in the suburbs and bleed me dry for the rest of my humble existence, is stronger and more financially viable than any desire she has to fleece me of a paltry one hundred grand.

I've lost a stone in weight where there was not a stone to lose. I've handwritten promises on notes no one thinks will stand up in court, I've contacted solicitors to draw up contracts in the event I actually need them. I've pictured myself diving off every skyrise I see, swayed towards every train that's sped towards me, counted the number of pills I have dotted around my empty shell of a house and drunk myself into oblivion so many times I can hardly remember what reality feels like any more, but I remember enough not to spend too much time there.

The only thing preventing me from taking the easy way out is the knowledge my girls wouldn't survive it, not in any recognisable state anyway. As hard as it is, I can't leave them alone in this world with their mother and so I get up every day, even though I have yet to go to bed.

The day before the deadline and despite all of their misgivings and worries, my gran and aunt drag themselves to the bank and stand arm-in-arm in the queue as though they might keel over any minute. But they do it. They transfer the full £100,000 into the bank account of a woman we all hate, but is from that moment on, the only thing standing between me and quite possibly a large tattooed convict with a broom handle and a point to prove.

It's a full twenty-four hours before any of us breathe again and there are no words to describe the relief I feel for the first time upon hearing that Philippa has decided to stick by my side and see how much more she can wring out of me. She may be violently hideous and cruel but I have to give it to her. She is as ever, meticulous in her planning.

And The Award For...

I down the dregs of my lager and as I slam it on top of an amp off stage, I somehow knock into a half-empty glass which careers in slow motion around the surface, teeters for a moment on the edge and then falls. It smashes onto the unnaturally brown sticky floor and I marvel at the shards of light glinting off the curved fragments now shattered around my feet. One half of the glass remains perfectly intact, while the other lies in pieces but if you were to lift it at a certain angle, it would look exactly the same. Completely normal.

I usually limit myself to the one pint before I go on, but I had my first drink at midday today and the second, third, fourth and fifth all unwittingly followed. It's my last night in England and there's nowhere in the world I'd rather not be right now than here.

I've already said goodbye to what little remains of my circle of friends and family. There were tears, though not as many as you might expect and I could sense my parents' covert relief that the curtains were finally closing on the last five years of drama.

They are not to know of course, that this is merely an interval and act two will begin shortly, overshadowing everything that has gone before. And what none of us foresees is one of them will take a starring role. But more of that later. For now I'm simply plagued by exhaustion and an unfulfilled burning need to teleport myself nearly four housand miles around the world.

Against all odds, there's nothing left to do here in London, aside from this gig. My leaving drinks were an offensive and wholly abusive affair of which I have no memory after the tenth pint but I'm told I enjoyed. Certainly something preceded me waking up alone in an abandoned shopping trolley in Sainsbury's car park, but since I no longer work for the Met, I have no authority to request the CCTV footage.

I suspect it's probably for the best that I'm leaving the country and joining all my worldly belongings, which are currently sailing across the Atlantic on a six-week cruise that costs more than the sum value of anything on it.

The sale of the house has eventually gone through and I'm warmed by the knowledge I've sold my beautiful home to a lovely couple who, after putting in a cash offer just under the asking price, then proceeded to fart around and delay proceedings for three agonising months until the day of completion when they suddenly reduced their more fair than generous offer by twenty grand.

Not for the English, the sort of laws that would prevent them from turning the life of another human being into yak's curd. And there was, as they knew, nothing I could do other than agree and smear a fruit-infused fox turd over the doorknob on my way out.

I've been staying with Julia in West Dulwich for a month now as I still had to see out my notice period and apart from the mild inconvenience of her building works leaving a light pattern of dust over every last one of my meagre possessions, it physically hurts me to be around her children, lovely as they are. It's not their fault but I would settle for a screwdriver through the scrotum than have to deal with the pain of not being with mine for one second longer.

They moved into the new empty Burlington house weeks ago and I can see from the credit card bills that Philippa has lost no time in replacing the very furniture that is winding its way across the ocean to her now.

I've only seen the girls once in the four months since we first went to Canada for a quick recce and that was when I went back for a formal interview with Walton Regional Police. They were running up and down the hotel corridor naked and as soon as I got there Philippa washed her hands of them, and also of me, disgusted as she was by my lacklustre attitude to the move, which suited me fine.

'See how you like being stuck on your own with them now!'

I loved it but it took days to get them to stop spinning around like cornered animals in a cage. To even listen to what I said without growling in response to any contact or communication. By the end of the week, they finally felt like my daughters again and when they clung to my neck and begged me not to leave, it was all I could do not to open the balcony doors and throw the three of us six floors down onto King Street East. But there were people walking below and besides, at that time, I still hadn't paid back the loan to my gran so if I died, it would all go to Philippa.

Leaving was harder that time because I knew how heartbreaking being apart was for us all, but nonetheless I had to return to complete the sale of the house and oversee the packing and transportation of everything we own (although we will get to own two of everything anyway).

I received the news I'd been accepted on the training course within a few days of the interview but I had to wait until I'd been shafted up the kaiser by my lovely buyers before I could hand in my notice at work – there being, inconceivably, a worse scenario in which the arseholes didn't simply blackmail me into reducing the price but pulled out altogether.

I was finally able to pay back the money I owed and for which I will always be grateful, but it was mentioned repeatedly throughout the three-month ordeal, that it had taken its toll on my poor gran. It will be years before things ever really feel the same again between us all. I know it's my fault for creating the whole disastrous situation, but the truth is, that unshakeable faith I had in my family to be there for me unconditionally has been broken. The love they have for me does have conditions and the lengths they will go to save me has limits and leaves a bad taste in my mouth.

And so I've said my goodbyes to everyone but Julia and her lot as she'll drive me to the airport tomorrow where she'll make a scene, which will make me cry, but inside I cannot wait to get back to that screeching cauldron of hatred I call a wife so that I can absorb the full brunt of her rage and brutal outbursts and remind my children what it feels like, instead, to be loved every single day. Every moment of every single day, not only in public when the world is observing and thinks we all look adorable.

But right then I have one more gig to get through. It pays peanuts, but that is what I dance for these days. One of the waiters gives me a dirty look and knocks my foot with the dustpan and brush as he sweeps up the broken glass I have absentmindedly scattered across the floor.

'You're on,' he says and with that I hear my name being announced in a tone that suggests it is not for the first time. I stumble over him and jog, by way of recovery, onto the stage.

'Bob!' I cry to the compère. The mic in Bob's hand is reluctantly drooping but I reach for it anyway. He backs away hesitantly. 'On your way, Bob, I've got it from here.'

He shakes his head almost imperceptibly and only I catch it, but then I am known for my sharp wits and ability to read people.

'Bob, ladies and gentlemen,' I say again inviting a round of applause to accompany his slow exit backwards.

'I see we've got a pretty big crowd in tonight.' They cheer again. Well, someone does. 'All here to celebrate the last leg of the tour with me, hey? My last night in London. Who knows if I'll ever return... If they find an unidentified male corpse cut up in pieces and eaten by grizzly bears, assume the experiment failed.'

I jam the mic back into the stand and just manage to reach out as it topples over with an ear-splitting screech. I wrench it back out again. Jiggle it up and down instead. Stroll lazily towards the tables.

'Some of you might have heard...I think I told you last time... Canada...? I'm off to Canada. Everything's big in Canada. Have you been there?' A solitary shout came from the back of the room. 'Get shafted too, did you mate?' He doesn't reply.

'The other half's there at the moment. With the kids. We went on holiday. She decided she liked it – declined to come back.' Three dozen faces are staring at me, dumb grins half-formed already in anticipation of the punch line. 'I should count myself lucky it wasn't Chernobyl or somewhere, I suppose. Fucking Iraq. Now there's some perspective.

'Canada's alright actually. Canada's alright. It's the Canadians you've got to watch out for... Or one in particular. My wife.

'She said Dan, I've bought a house. Here. In Canada. I just need you to pay for it. Minor detail. S'alright though. We had a house already so no big deal. Just had to pop that on the market. Easy peezy. Fuck me.' I let it hang in the air. Let the curl of my lip do all the talking.

'Have you ever tried to sell a house in this country?' Somebody jeers. 'Would have been easier selling cocaine to the Colombians. Probably less fucking terrifying too. Quickest way to lose three stone and all that excess hair nobody wants on top of their head.' I rub my scalp. 'Saved myself a lifetime of barber's bills at least. Should break even by the time I'm six hundred. Like you, mate.' I hone in on some unsuspecting coot in the audience. Let my finger linger on the lights bouncing off his iridescent forehead as his good-natured grin turns to shame. 'He knows what I mean. He knows what I mean.

'And somebody tell me, what is the point of an estate agent? I swear they're actually Moss Boss models sent out to advertise tight-fitting suits and pointy shoes. Like a secret shopper, only the other way around. A secret seller. There's probably some database somewhere linking Rightmove and Moss Bros HQ. Every time a listing gets taken off the market, you know they've sold another nice suit. Because otherwise, what are they there for? They don't do anything do they?' I walk limply around the stage.

'This is the downstairs,' I flop my hand out, palm raised nonchalantly. 'And up the stairs… that's *up*stairs.' I hunch my shoulders in mock incredulity. 'I had the good fortune to be around when *Josh*, coz they're all called Josh these Millennials, aren't they? *Josh* brought someone over. Fucker didn't even point out where the windows were…'

There was a rumble of laughter. That sort of chuckle that always comes with a rolled eye and a reluctant headshake.

'I said to him, I could do this. How do you justify earning your commission? He said *what do you mean? I've sold three suits, a tie and some cufflinks this morning alone. I'm sorted.* He was sorted.'

Everyone laughs despite themselves. Everyone who's ever sold a house anyway. I survey the room. The lights in my face are too bright. I hold up my hand. Squint into the audience. 'Any estate agents here tonight?' No one replies. 'Yeah… you'd better hide.' I swagger confidently along the front row, my finger pointing warningly, head nodding.

'I'd say it's been nice and quiet without the wife, but she likes to phone up at three o'clock in the morning to get an update. Last time I said here's an update. It's an app you can download that tells you what time it is in other countries. It's amazing. Works all over the world.

'She wasn't happy. She said you're with another woman, that's why you don't want me to call you. I was like fuck me!' I lurch across the stage clutching my chest, swing an appalled grimace at the crowd. '*Another* woman! It's all I can do to cope with one.'

A couple of empathetic cheers feed my rant. I stare out beyond the lights into the darkness again, picture Philippa in the middle of the room. There with her friend that night, staring straight back at me. Drawing me in. I shake her ugly, twisted image from my head. Drag the corners of my mouth down with a swipe of my fingers. It's too hot in here.

'Jesus Christ… Don't get me wrong. I know some wonderful women a hundred times better than me, and men – men would be just as bad if they had the bare skills and intelligence to do it, but my God, you ladies like to hold back a few surprises, don't you?

'I've never seen a dating profile that says good-looking, fun-loving single girl, interested in cross-motorcycling and butterflies seeks innocent gullible twat to completely screw over. You never see that do you?' Someone at the front is guffawing. The rest of the table throws their heads back and laugh at the poor sod.

'There's one.' I say pointing to him. 'He's been stung before.' He gets a sympathetic punch in the arm from one of his mates at that. 'Still laughing though. Bless him. Probably lost his mind. Might as well. You'll lose everything else in the long run, mate.'

I stagger back across to the amp off the side of the stage to see if I have any beer left, but the glass has been taken away. I shrug and turn back. 'Watch out when they hand you a ring and demand you propose, that's never a good sign.

Especially not if you're so terrified of the mad cow you actually do it.

'Who even has their own ring?! I thought I was quids in. Didn't realise she was just making it easier for me to sign over the rest of my pathetic existence to her along with every penny I'll ever make.' There's barely a murmur. Maybe a couple of snorts. It's a slow crowd tonight.

'Still, they say married men live longer. Have you heard that? Married men supposedly live longer than single men? I think it's just that they're not allowed to die. They've been banned. They've been told categorically to keep working to pay for those luxury Saga cruises and Werther's Originals. Married men daren't die. That's all it is. Their wives would kill them. That's why so many only keel over when they retire. They aren't worth so much.'

They laugh at that. Finally. A couple of women are nudging their boyfriends and giggling like we're all in on the same joke.

'You wait,' I said, nodding at their boyfriends. 'You might think these two here are normal, but odds are, fellas, they're a pair of psychos. Pinned you down yet, have they? They will and fucking run when they do, boys.' The smiles start to freeze a little. 'No offence. They're probably alright. I'm sure you're both alright. Who can tell though? They like you, that's the main thing. You'd think anyway.'

The one with the drooping chest has drawn my attention. The sequins are glittering on her top like a disco ball. Like

Cineralla's pig ugly wedding gown. I can feel the bile rising up my throat.

'You could probably do better though. Never trust a fully-grown woman who dresses up like a child's play thing. Some crappy doll from China. Still, what does it matter once she's got her claws into you? You think you're screwing her, mate, wait till you knock her up. Then, you'll know who's been screwed.

'But don't ask me. I should be an expert on the subject. Should be able to recognise a vindictive gold digger when I see one, but I'm afraid to say, I… *cant.*' I pronounce can't with a short vowel and throw it away with a point of my index finger. Then I stare straight at Cinderella deadpan waiting for the penny to drop. For the roar of hilarity to break the moment of silence that always precedes the loudest laughs.

Bob is hovering at the side of the stage. The woman's bottom lip is hanging open but she just needs a second to register that it's funny. I catch an uncomfortable shuffle of backsides in seats out the corner of my eye. The hum of whispers hissed sideways into shoulders. One of the blokes is starting to stand and no one is holding him back. Bob flies across the stage and wrenches the mic out of my withering grip.

'Ladies and gentlemen,' he cries. 'Please give it up for Dan the Man, Dickhead Extraordinaire. Soon to be leaving our sunny shores. Thank fuck.'

He pushes me back towards stage left as I finally take in the disgusted expressions on every face in the room and I mouth *I'm sorry* over and over to the poor woman I've just vilified. The unfortunate bystander upon whom I've publicly unleashed all the anger and resentment I have never had the balls to convey. Not to the person who deserves it. Not to someone who has made it their life's work to break me.

I can't even look that person in the eyes, let alone give back as good as I get because Philippa's good will always be better than mine and her best is so much worse. Instead it takes all my strength not to shake in her presence and to hold back my anguish until I am alone. Until now. Until tonight.

Bob jostles me backstage and with that I am done. My residing memory of this country, of my flagging dreams and all the innocent hopes and expectations I had for myself have been shattered and for once I've got no one to blame but myself.

Highway To Hell

There had been, over the course of the last few weeks, a sight thawing of tensions between Philippa and I. Once the house sale had gone through and I had nothing to do but blow the building debris from Julia's new extension off the suitcase I was living out of and make the occasional half-hearted appearance at work, I was no longer terrorised by emails and phone calls demanding I chase up the same things I'd been chasing up for days. As though mere desperation had the power to blow fire up the arses of distracted solicitors and mortgage brokers whose sole purpose was to frustrate any attempt to get a mortgage. In fact, now it was over, we'd unexpectedly joined forces against the common enemies that had stood in our way. They were all bastards and for once, I was not.

Overnight, the emails that continued to fill up my inbox like spam from a website I'd once saved 10% on, were now loving and gushing. She couldn't wait to see me, she missed me so much. The girls were madly excited that I'd be with them soon. So was she. Only the other day she'd gazed out at the full moon that lit up the garden and as she pictured our new life together there, she'd laughed with delight.

In retrospect, the image of a crazed beast howling in the moonlight is somewhat telling, but at that time I was too relieved to make much of it. That's not to say that I was reassured enough to think all this would last, but I couldn't help but feel that despite everything, despite the way she'd done it, despite the ransom of my children, despite leaving me to sort out a momentous and heinously stressful move across the world by myself, that it really had been the right decision after all.

'It's going to be wonderful, you'll see.'

I'd burned bridges I wasn't sure I could rebuild, I'd missed out on months of my children's lives I could never make up for, I'd lost more money in one day than I'd ever lost before (spare a thought for my blessed soul at that time for thinking a mere twenty grand was a nut squeeze), and I'd probably shaved a couple of decades off my lifespan, which combined with the previous five years of hell, didn't leave me with long left.

However, it'd been just short of a month since I'd last had my ear blasted off in a phone call that would replay in my head repeatedly until the next one. In fact, the most annoying her emails ever got was the string of requests to bring over tins of formula and the like, as though the global giants that were Walmart and Shop n' Save were yet to think of it.

The night I arrived we had sex for the first time in probably years on a bed she would later give away because for some reason we had four of them. It was a good start. I was back with my family and we had a clean slate polished and ready to fill with memories.

That was the first one. The next was discovering Philippa had promised the girls we were going to Disney World, which as you probably know is in a whole other country to the one I'd just spent four months trying to get into. But as I watched the corners of my wife's mouth take on the guise of a tight puckered anus, I realised the decision had already been made - which is how I found myself, less than a few weeks later, at the wheel of a forth hand V6 Dodge Grand Caravan.

Just to be clear, this was not a caravan in any actual sense where the name would be an accurate description. Rather it was a people carrier, which was called a caravan for fun while actual caravans are known as 'travel trailers' because, well, God knows. Five per cent of the language was just one of many new and exciting things I was going to have to relearn over the course of the next few months. Another was driving in close proximity to a time bomb on a three-week road trip up and down the entire east coast of America.

But it wasn't all in vain. We took the opportunity to toilet train Katie and left behind a trail of sodden mattresses stretching the length of the Gold Coast, despite having any number of beds we could have ruined at home. We developed the girls' palates with two hundred hamburgers in two hundred diners, which was generally the most refined thing on the menu (not accounting for the one place where they actually put crisps in them). And we instilled a sense of wonder as we observed, open mouthed, Americans so gloriously huge they could barely move, inhale more food than all of us put together only to top it off with pie.

As for Philippa, the novelty of a new town every day gave her ample occasions to relish in her latest role of Interesting Guest from Overseas and the locals couldn't get enough of her posh British accent and our beautiful blonde-haired, blue-eyed angels. They also thought nothing of gobbing up a great honk of chewing tobacco mid-conversation so the threshold of expectations was fairly low. Even so, Philippa lapped up the attention like a needy Labrador and I for one, enjoyed the respite.

When we finally got to Disney World, we were greeted by masses of overgrown adults whizzing around in electric wheelchairs they'd rented to get around the attractions and collect autographs from college kids dressed up as Elsa and the Lion King. Without a child in sight, I might add, even on the Dumbo ride. The whole place was hideous. Garish, crass and expensive. And after spending thousands of dollars that we didn't have and travelling for sixteen days solid to get to that God awful place, Philippa's first words were *now that I'm here, I realise I'd rather be volunteering in an African orphanage.* Needless to say, she has yet to do this.

But it wasn't all bad and if I got nothing else out of the trip, by the end of it I at least had an airing cupboard bursting with Hilton-embossed towels and flannels that would come in handy if we were ever to divide up our assets. Philippa wasn't the only one who could think ahead.

And I defy anyone to spend twenty-one days cooped up with two kids and their partner and not incur the occasional fall out. There were times it was horrendous and soul-destroying, but there were other moments, minutes, sometimes even stretches of hours at a time when it was really good fun. Cold waves of dread would occasionally surface at the sound of the girls squabbling or if I raised an objection to a ten thousand-mile diversion to see the world's largest ball of string but more often than not, Philippa managed to keep her demons under wraps and her game face on. Comparatively anyway.

The problems really only began, or resurfaced I should say, when we got back to Canada. She'd been in Burlington for a few months by then and it was already beginning to lose its appeal. For days on the return journey home, she talked of nothing but moving to Washington DC and only the physical restraints of not having a visa or working permit (me obviously) held her back from charging into the nearest realtor and slapping down an offer on something, anything, right there and then.

She'd somehow made friends while I'd been away and their houses were bigger and better and in far nicer areas (two streets away). Ours was a tip, but that would always be the case no matter where we lived. She was still in the habit of giving the girls flour to play with which was caked like glue onto the kitchen floor by the time I arrived. I left it for a week to see if she'd clean it but it remained, turning grey and then hairy as the rest of the dust and crumbs floating in the hemisphere found a home there.

Long story short, she didn't touch it and I eventually took to it with a chisel that left sharp, elongated dents in the floor, which I'd never hear the end of. Three days later the bowl of flour was out again, this time with macaroni and some lovely green lentils that would wedge themselves into every crack and crevice in the house until, to everyone's delight, they eventually sprouted.

The swimming pool, which had set the whole ill-considered emigration in motion, was suddenly deemed far too dangerous to use and while I was still allowed to swim with Lauren and Katie, inflated up to the ears in armbands, Philippa never got in it the entire time we lived there. Instead I spent thousands of dollars and five hours installing a fence across the back of the garden because she became convinced the girls would fall in and die. A noble sentiment if it weren't for the fact the dream of outdoor living was our whole reason for being there.

I wasn't allowed to buy a hot tub after months of selecting one for the same reason, yet she was happy to let the girls play in the front yard a few feet from traffic while she ordered her weekly fix of squeezy fruit pouches and Percy Pig sugar-free sweets from Marks and Spencer. Marks and Spencer. In England. Which then cost forty quid to ship across but what could she do? The stores in Canada weren't as good as the shops in the UK.

It wasn't long before I realised the idea she could ever be happy was a laughable fantasy I'd staked my life on and lost. There was no reasoning with her and no understanding her condition. And it was a condition, which meant I should really have sympathised because the crazy inside her wasn't under her control, but I couldn't forgive her and I couldn't empathise. I'd been broken too many times to care why anymore. Philippa was simply not capable of change or contentment. For all my futile hopes of satisfying her need to live an enviable life, we had not crossed the Atlantic alone. The extra passenger on that plane was her mental illness and it continued to follow us all around like a parasite feeding off our anxiety and despair. It didn't need a passport to travel or a visa to stay. It was inside her but it infected every one of us.

This is not to say that she was constantly angry. The pendulum swung without warning between overindulgence and crazed adoration of the kids who were *wonderful* and *precious* and told mummy loved them *to the moon and back and back and back again* to screaming matches our new wary neighbours would hesitantly allude to over the coming months when Philippa was not around. I say screaming matches but Katie and Lauren never replied. Instead they withdrew into themselves, their eyes glazed and unseeing which only wound Philippa up all the more. Katie bore the brunt of her wrath having never really been forgiven for rejecting her futile attempts to breastfeed, but worse than that, Philippa would actively create test situations, which the girls would inevitably fail.

Once, as we stood in the Royal Ontario Museum having a seemingly ordinary conversation about one of the exhibits, I marvelled out of the corner of my eye as she staged one of her experiments with the calculated genesis of a psychopathic twat.

Lauren was still young enough to be on a weaning cup and Katie was not, but she would still try her luck as a three-year-old will. As we talked, Philippa reached down and pushed the cup along the tray of Lauren's pushchair towards Katie who was patiently standing beside her. Katie looked at it but didn't react, so Philippa pushed it a little closer, all the while never taking her eyes off me. This continued until the milk was staring Katie right in the face and as anticipated, she stretched out to take it. Philippa's reaction was immediate and ruthless, even in front of a crowd of shocked observers, but this was no time for niceties. Katie was not to drink from Lauren's baby cup. She was too old for it and she'd been told. Many times, many times!

She'd have been less concerned if her firstborn child had swigged down half a bottle of lighter fluid. Of course, since there was every chance the whole scene might have been met with squeals of glee as applauding onlookers gazed admiringly at the adorable display, there is no real way to predict or prevent this sort of scenario. The only certainty is that it will be dramatic and over as suddenly as it begins, which nevertheless fails to comfort me.

It's only a few weeks later that my training starts and I am finally allowed to buy the Ford Mustang I've had my eye on for weeks since we need two cars to get around and this beauty is vintage enough to be cool but also knackered enough to be cheap. As I pick up my uniform from Walton Police Station, I can already feel the tightness in my ball sack at the thought of what awaits me, both in terms of the excruciating agony of having to relearn everything I've already spent thirteen years doing and at the thought of leaving the girls alone with Philippa again.

The academy is in the arsehole of Amish county in the middle of nowhere. There's literally nothing but miles and miles of fields and roads surrounding it and little to see but the occasional horse and cart, which I'm initially entranced by but soon come to ignore. I'm to stay there for three months from Monday to Friday and only return home at the weekends and Philippa is not happy at the thought of having to take over responsibility for feeding and clothing both children as well as possibly spending time with them when no one's looking.

But I needn't worry. It turns out it's not impossible to drive for two and a half hours door to door from Alymer to Burlington and back again every other day when it transpires that Philippa cannot (*and shouldn't be fucking expected to*) cope with putting the girls to bed at night.

And I'll admit they are a handful. With her. And little angels with me so it's only reasonable that despite having to be present for parades at seven o'clock in the morning and sit through hour after hour of scrotum-twisting bollocks until five o'clock every evening, I should then leave promptly in time to get the girls changed into their pyjamas, read at least three stories and tuck them in by eight o'clock only to turn around immediately to make it back to the academy before half past ten. All in the middle of winter battling through storms from hell.

Another complication is that while I'm away, the building contractor we've employed to rip out the walls in our basement and refurbish it into a state-of-the-art media room slash playroom slash guestroom with en suite and utility, has the temerity to mention to Philippa (when she leaves the children asleep in the car in the shade of the garage awning) that she should be careful no one reports her to Child Protection Services as it's the sort of thing they get quite funny about.

Whether it's meant as good-natured advice or in the outrageous critical vein my wife takes it in, I'll never know as the hapless builder is treated to a vicious verbal flaying and thrown out, never to return. But then why would he since we've paid him almost fully upfront in order to ensure he has the whole project completed in time for Linda's visit at Christmas? Our basement is completely gutted and we have no financial means whatsoever to employ anyone else to clear up the mess.

But we don't need to, for by no lack of wishful thinking, I am not dead so as well as driving home three times a week to kiss the girls good night, I now also get to enjoy spending the weekends sawing up pillars and frames, cramming insulation into them, hammering plasterboard onto plywood, hacking up floorboards and laying them, sanding walls and painting them, all with Katie hanging off one leg and Lauren on the other because God forbid, Philippa could keep them out of the way. And there's a deadline, which my wife feels she can spur me along towards with observations about the substandard state of the workmanship and the fact I am a useless, pathetic excuse for a man.

'This is genuinely terrible, Dan. Even for you, it's outstanding. To the point of embarrassing. The kids could've done a better job. How are we supposed to put anyone up in this? They'll think we're trying to kill them. Look at those nails sticking out. And the splinters on that corner. I could literally push this whole thing over with my little finger. It's a piece of absolute shit. You've probably devalued the house by twenty per cent.

'We're going to have to get someone else in to fix this mess and don't you dare tell me after all of this that we can't afford it. You should've thought of that before you started making this shithole.

'Christ. If anyone ever sees it... It's fucking humiliating. How am I supposed to let the girls play down here? Or don't tell me. That was the plan all along. You thought you'd take your sweet time and make me deal with them both, like I don't have to put up with them enough all week while you're titting about on that so-called course.

'And don't think I haven't looked up that bitch instructor you keep pretending not to fancy. I know exactly why you can't be bothered to come home every night and take over your share of the responsibilities here. Well, just try to leave us. I could take you to the cleaners, remember that. If this place is even worth anything anymore now you've ripped the crap out of it. I could have done a better job with Lego. You are categorically fucking useless.'

For the first time in our relationship, in my life in fact, I lash out in frustration and smash a hole in the wall with my fist, which is so badly damaged I'm in agony for days and can barely use it, although I must. Philippa who's standing on the other side of the room smiles as though she's finally got what she wanted all along and as she spins around victoriously and bounds up the stairs, she trills *you'd better have this mess cleared up by the time I come back down.* And obedient boy that I am, I do.

It's almost a relief to actually go back to the academy and sit in a room full of cocky, gun-toting teenagers with their chests puffed out, who are too arrogant to ask any questions or trouble themselves with the answers.

To hear Mike Chan's daily announcement upon leaving the sole lavatory every morning that he has *a little diarrhoea*.

To run like an eager six-year-old when Ched O'Malley cries *Look! A seal!* only to find him pointing excitedly at a grey squirrel twitching its tail only metres away (in an area where there are no seals for thousands of miles).

To run slightly less eagerly when the same Ched O'Malley cries *Look! A fox!* only to watch him wander obliviously towards a huge, snarling coyote. And not to stop him.

To be taught how to shine my shoes.

To be pepper sprayed in the eyes in order to know what it feels like to be pepper sprayed in the eyes.

To be tasered for the same reason.

To sit through a two day tutorial about speed cameras.

To learn how to shoot a man in the head when I've never wanted to touch a gun in my life.

To be shown how to dismantle it into ten pieces and put it back together again without blowing a finger off.

To sit through a full day's seminar about issuing traffic violations, which I've also never wanted to do. All of this is a treat compared to what awaits me at the end of that two and a half hour journey every Friday.

But at last, after twelve long arse-numbing weeks it is over and at the passing out parade I hope never to see any of my thick, bragging, small-minded, bigoted classmates again. But more of that later.

I have a week in which to finish the basement before Linda arrives. There's not enough time but Philippa's sweet enough to follow me around in the early hours of the morning reminding me that I am a *cock* at the top of her voice, lest I start to feel sleepy and finally it's done.

Hours before Linda's plane is due to land at the airport, I sink into an armchair with one child under each arm, admire my substandard handiwork and enjoy the sound of gas escaping through the freshly popped lid of a well-deserved beer. The frothy hiss is replaced moments later by the thud of Philippa's feet thundering down the newly sanded, wood-treated stairs as she snarls through gnashing teeth, *I just had to see if you'd actually opened that.*

I'd like to state at this point, that I stand my ground and drink it, but from this moment on I am *a raging alcoholic* and Philippa starts sending concerned emails about me to my friends and family as well as messaging them on Facebook.

She has also concluded that I'm gay because we haven't had sex since the night I arrived in Toronto and am not exhibiting any inclination towards wanting to repeat the performance. They write vague supportive replies back and then heckle me ruthlessly on my secret account but it's galling to be put in this position. Notwithstanding, I appreciate their continued commitment to the role-play and the rules of this game.

I'm not sure what the purpose of these insinuations is, if there's a long game or if this is another manifestation of her madness but at the time I'm drinking no more than about one bottle of wine and five beers a week because that's all I have time for and while I'd happily roger any man on earth rather than sleep with my wife, I'm not actually homosexual. Let alone an alcoholic homosexual, though I don't suppose anyone would blame me for giving either a go under the circumstances, but again who has time?

But all this is yet to come (the emails, not the alcohol-infused rogering). Right now I am getting off my tits on one beer and congratulating myself on achieving something I'd have never attempted had Philippa not pushed me into it and so for that I must thank her, but I don't. Instead I drive (drunk out my mind) to the airport with my happy family to pick up her mother who'll be staying in my state-of-the-art media room slash playroom slash guestroom with en suite and utility for a month.

I give it a day before the two of them are at each other's throats, but I'm wrong. It's an hour and seems to hinge on the fact Linda's plane is forty-five minutes late and we overstay the time limit in the short-term car park.

She has shiny expensive wrapped presents with crumpled decorative bows for everyone which we won't open until Christmas Day, but she's bought the wrong teabags (Earl

Grey but not Twinings) and in an act of pure stupidity she declared ten sticks of Peperami on her landing card which have now been confiscated. Dinner is ruined but I sense I may at last have an ally.

We agree that Philippa's out of control and we will no longer bend to her twisted warped view of reality, for her sake as much as our own.

For a few days we stand strong and Philippa becomes visibly confused and upset by our stance. She doesn't understand when we politely disagree with her outrageous opinions or when we calmly point out all the flaws in her delusions. We're actually making a breakthrough, I can feel it. Philippa even turns to me one day as it finally dawns on her that she cannot control the world with anger anymore and says in a quiet, quavering voice *am I going mad*? And for the first time in five years, I feel sorry for her, for she's finally starting to see herself for what she really is – the way the rest of us see her.

But it's too much to hope that Linda can stick to the plan and on Christmas Day when my wife rocks on the floor surrounded by presents with her nightdress bunched around her hips, her knees bent to her chest and her genitalia staring us both in the face in some primitive apelike power display, Linda says nothing but it's the beginning of the end and by the time the girls have finished excitedly showing us the contents of their stockings, she's crumbled and is backing up her daughter in whatever fleeting lunacy she latches onto. In this case, insisting the girls, who've been bouncing around the Christmas tree for weeks desperate to open their presents, must wait until after lunch for absolutely no reason at all.

Linda agrees that this is character building but suggests, as they burst into tears, that maybe they could just open one. She quickly retracts any such motion when Philippa literally growls and spreads her ankles even further apart.

The girls are sobbing but this only serves to fuel her righteous determination further. I attempt to stare her down while maintaining an agreeable tone in my voice as the kids plead with me, through hiccupping wails, to make her change her mind but Linda interrupts gaily and takes them off to their bedroom to get them changed into the glittering dresses she's bought from Monsoon and I'm left in a Mexican standoff with Philippa's vagina. Neither of us know it but this will be the last Christmas I spend with her and with my accomplice firmly back in fool's paradise, the vulva wins hands down.

The End Is Nigh

Philippa's primary error when she strategically isolated me from my entire support network and almost everything I knew and loved, was to fail to realise my friends and family would follow me anyway. It wasn't in their nature to pass up the opportunity of a semi-free holiday and besides, for some reason, they missed me and my daughters. Philippa's presence was just a major drawback like delayed flights or a tsunami, but they were all well enough versed in the pretence to understand that if they came there were conditions they were expected to meet, namely shutting up and putting up.

However, as long as that was understood they were welcome and suddenly my wife found that instead of having to tolerate them all for an afternoon every few months, they'd be staying with us for weeks at a time. She was torn between hating the imposition with a venom that would have made ISIS retreat and taking advantage of the inevitable free childcare that came with any visit.

Her mother's stay had resulted in the house being clean for the first time since we'd moved there and in her desperation to get away from the children, Philippa had actually completed another module of the Open University degree she was still pursuing after five years. This entailed having to pretend she still lived in England so she'd listed her permanent address as my father's house in Bournemouth. This gave him countless sleepless nights as he was convinced they'd be caught and imprisoned for fraud, but also meant she didn't mind when he and Elizabeth were the first to book flights out to see us as it coincided with the delivery of the next six hundred books she needed to continue her studies.

I'd been working a four-day shift pattern since I'd started back in uniform in January. It ran from 7am to 7pm for two days and followed with 7pm to 7am for the remainder. After that I was rewarded with a couple of hours of shuteye prior to Philippa shouting *don't go in there! Daddy's trying to sleep!* right outside my bedroom door until such a time as I surrendered, half-hallucinating with exhaustion and took my cue to get up. Even if I hid myself away in the spare room I would hear her tell the girls I was in there so many times they would inevitably join me and she'd relish the opportunity to scold them, the little darlings. And then make a hasty escape.

I was so sleep deprived I looked about ninety-six and there wasn't enough caffeine in the world to keep me focused. My working day consisted of sitting alone on traffic duty for the first time in my life and I'd never been so unfulfilled. Katie's jigsaws were more challenging.

The downside of a low crime rate is that there's bugger all to do if you're supposed to be out there fighting it or at least cleaning up the mess afterwards. It's so safe shop owners leave thousands of dollars worth of merchandise out on the street overnight. I even called it the first time I came across it because I thought something terrible must have happened inside when all the while there was simply a shortage of lawbreakers. We would sit around at the start of every shift waiting to be assigned duties, killing time by watching YouTube and catching up with our emails.

Any hopes I had of never crossing paths with my classmates from the academy were dashed the first morning I walked into Walton Regional station and found everyone but Mike Chan and his *little diarrhoea* staring at me with the same self-assured dick-like arrogance as before only now they had a license to shoot people.

Every last one of them came across as an uncultured idiot and I don't mean they didn't stick their little finger out when they drank a cup of tea. They simply knew nothing about anything except national sports. Discussing politics and current events would have been as obscure as bringing up the latest paradigm shifts in quantum theory and the natural world was as alien to them as the far reaches of the galaxy. A bird the size of a pterodactyl could fly over our heads and when I'd ask in excitement and awe what it was, they'd have no idea of either its name or its existence.

They couldn't identify a mountain lion if they hit it with a sign saying *Beware Mountain Lions* and I have yet to meet a single person who doesn't think I'm Australian despite never coming across an actual Aussie the length and breadth of the country the entire time I live here.

The most exciting thing that happened in four months of being there was Ched O'Malley (he who mistook a squirrel for a seal) getting arrested and kicked out the force for stealing a pre-paid credit card from the scene of a burglary and buying a bread-maker with it. He'd have got away with it if only he hadn't used Amazon and had it delivered to his home address. *His home address.* That's the level of intelligence I was dealing with and I mean dealing with, instead of working alongside.

And there were much better cops in much better departments, I knew that. But I was some stretch away from being able to join them and in the meantime I was stuck with a bunch of machismo cocks in their aviators strutting around with their chests pushed out, guns on hips calling me Rookie. I could feel my soul wilting with every traffic violation I issued and every dim-witted, narrow-minded anecdote and observation I couldn't help but overhear.

So, I'm pleased when my dad says he's coming. I haven't seen any of my family for nearly a year and my memories of them all are becoming nostalgic and perhaps a little rose-tinted the longer I spend in the company of fools.

I give him a list of all the things I need brought over because they genuinely don't sell them in Canada or if they do, they just don't do them justice. This includes KP Dry Roasted Peanuts (because no matter what my dad says when he discovers an inferior brand in Walmart, they don't even come close to the real thing), self-raising flour (because all-purpose flour is nothing of the sort and I have a hankering for Yorkshire puddings that cannot be curbed), Peperami (because Linda's still in the dog house for not getting them through last time), Marmite (there was obviously going to be some Marmite on the list) and shower gel (because it's bloody expensive over here and he can get it from The Pound Shop in Bournemouth Shopping Arcade).

I provide him with strict instructions not to declare any of it which results him not sleeping for the month before he gets here and promptly declaring it all at customs control even though no one's noticed the white beads of sweat hovering on his top lip like a petrified teenage mule smuggling heroin up his arsehole. In fact he actually has to interrupt the officers' conversation to announce that he's moments away from leaving totally unchallenged with a suitcase full of contraband goods. Unsurprisingly he's given a warning and the whole lot is swiftly whisked away to the nearest incinerator. All except the shower gel, which is called English Rose and smells like an old lady who's had a little accident.

It's not an altogether auspicious start but thankfully they've managed not to have all of Philippa's reading material burned to ash on the way over too and they've brought enough cheap plastic tat across for the girls to keep them busy for at least half an hour so almost everyone's happy. Not least my dad and Elizabeth who can finally relax now they're no longer in danger of being subjected to an intimate search of their body parts and immediate deportation.

I have a few days before my rotation at work begins again but I have been strictly prohibited from taking any more leave as I'll need it for whatever madcap adventure Philippa has in mind for the summer. But it's fine. As long as I don't sleep, I can still take Dad and Elizabeth out and about with the girls while Philippa cracks on with her studies and Internet purchases. It's manageable and even enjoyable once I remember my mum's coming out soon and I can get her to bring over all the stuff my dad had blasted into the atmosphere.

For the first few days we cram in an island cruise on Lake Ontario, take in the spectacular views from the CN tower, visit the Ontario Science Centre, avoid the Royal Ontario Museum (which I haven't been back to since Katie embarrassed us all by drinking out of Lauren's sippee cup) and have lunch in Kensington Market because it reminds me of England, which is perhaps more impressive if you haven't come directly from there.

But after three days it becomes apparent that actually Dad and Elizabeth are quite happy to mooch about a bit, helping out with the children and feigning surprise every time they fall asleep in an armchair. So I go back to work confident nothing can go wrong and return to find the girls have painted the entire dining room table green. It isn't even a nice green but Philippa's delighted by their creativity and the only edge I note in her voice is aimed squarely at Elizabeth who's made the mistake of telling Katie and Lauren they shouldn't really paint on the furniture.

I heat up some pizza for the girls because my father and stepmother have been unable to work out how to turn the oven on and Philippa's all hands off deck now they're here. Then I cook us a meal as I do every night after my twelve-hour shift and because every other grown adult in the house is essentially useless when it comes to doing anything with the kids, I put them to bed.

'Da-da', Lauren gazes at me sincerely as I'm tucking her in. 'If the window falls on us, will you take us to the hospital?'

'Yes, darling.' For once I don't think I'm over-promising.

'But if the window falls on you, who will take us to the hospital? You'll be cutted in half and we'll be deaded under the glass.'

'Why are you thinking about things like that?'

'Everyone will see us and we'll be like that.' She sticks her tongue out and collapses on the pillow, eyes crossed, her arms spread open wide.

'Mummy can take us,' Katie interjects somewhat confidently.

'Will she, Da-da?' And for the life of me, I don't know, but I ruffle Lauren's hair and kiss them both on the forehead.

By the time I come down, one wine bottle's empty, another's open and the conversation's shifted to Iraq. I experience a cold chill that instantly shrivels my scrotum to the size of sultanas. We're having the same lively debate Philippa and Andy had all those years ago in my two-bedroomed flat on the Stoke Newington borders back when it really was my flat.

This time, however, it's Dad and Elizabeth who are clinging to the now proven misinformation about hidden weapons because they can't believe the American government would be able to get away with lying to the rest of the world (because this has never happened) and it's Philippa who's repeating all the points she lambasted Andy for in the same zealous tone as she's now using to persuade a couple of geriatric worry warts that they're morons.

'That's exactly what they want you to believe! Anyone with a grain of intelligence can see they're only interested in the oil!'

My dad's slipped into stealth mode but I fear his wife can give as good as she gets, especially with the flush of a few glasses of Merlot warming her cheeks. Thankfully, I arrive in time to diffuse the situation and although I can tell my dad and Elizabeth are on edge for the next few hours, the whole confrontation has slipped from my wife's chaotic mind as though they were simply discussing the weather.

The evening ends early and as we retire, Elizabeth, creamed up to the eyeballs, re-opens the spare bedroom door to allow the air to circulate. It's straight across the hall from our own room, so I bid her good night and close our door but as Philippa comes in, she deliberately leaves it ajar and for the first time in almost a year, tries to initiate sex.

Apart from the fact I have the libido of a cadaver, I'm less attracted to my wife than I am a tangerine and I'm gay, I can actually see the outline of my dad and stepmother's bed from my own and they're in it. As I pull away aghast and hiss, 'what are you doing?' Philippa replies, pulling her nighty off and straddling me, *I'm pretty sure they know we have sex, Dan.*

Let me put it right out there emphatically that we don't, either then or apart from that once, at any other time in recent memory, but the whole creepy messed up display of overt sexual prowess is yet another symptom of her cracked-brain psychosis. From my decade odd experience in the police before I was reduced to watching traffic dry, half my encounters with mentally ill people involved references to, touching or actual flashes of their private parts and this was no different. It's gross and I really don't appreciate her doing it right in front of my dad. I mean, my dad. With the door open. Do I have to say anymore? (In case that's a yes, I do not fall for her charms then or any other time again.)

I leave for work before anyone else wakes up in the morning so I have no idea quite how awkward things are and console myself with the fact that Dad and Elizabeth are jetlagged and were probably asleep as soon as their heads hit the pillows. Plus, they are reasonably deaf.

By the time I get back, there's more wine on the table and I grit my teeth and hope I can get the kids fed and up into bed before anyone brings up Syria or cheap shower gel.

I make the mistake of asking the olds about their day and since Philippa's down in the media room slash playroom, (it's been downgraded from being a slash guestroom so as not to encourage guests) I get the full unabridged version which seems to centre on the fact that the 'salad' we had the night before disagreed with Elizabeth so she was up half the night and felt somewhat fragile in the morning.

Naturally they weren't offered breakfast and so after a few hours of playing ineffectively with Katie and Lauren, their stomach's rumbling and Elizabeth's head still suffering from the lettuce, they devised an escape plan under the guise of walking to the supermarket, some twenty minutes away. Twenty minutes if you're a normal person that is, walking at normal speed. Slightly longer if you're sixty something and not used to the pounding Canadian sun and about an hour if you are told just as you're leaving to take a three and four year-old with you.

'Pick up whatever you're having for dinner while you're there. And some milk. Organic. The biggest one they've got.'

To say they're feeling a touch frazzled would be like saying Philippa can be a bit of a cross-patch sometimes, but so far they appear to be holding it together, despite the crackling red veneer still sizzling on their faces.

Which is another thing, they whisper conspiratorially. They were told off for not putting sunscreen on the girls, who were admittedly looking a little pink. Nonetheless, they apologised for not having a clue how to look after children in the vague hope they wouldn't be called upon to look after them again. But they underestimated their only positive contribution to being in the house and despite a number of protests given the state of their already crisp, shell-like membranes, were immediately relocated to the swimming pool so the girls could cool down.

All in all, it's gone better than I hoped and I'm careful to thank them not only for taking care of the kids all day, but for holding their nerve around Philippa.

I'm onto my nightshifts at this point so I don't have to go back to work until the next evening, which means they can all have a break from each other, but there's a carnival in the centre of Toronto tomorrow and Philippa will not be dissuaded from coming with us.

There really is one thing Canadians do better than the Brits and that's a parade. The atmosphere's already charged when we get there and the kids yank me by the fingers to the front with a contagious innocent elation that crushes my instinct to pooh-pooh it all.

There are spectacular floats the size of our old house in Surrey decorated in the magical forms of underworld fantasies and fairy tale scenes. Party music pulsates in the air drowning out everything but laughter and squeals of wonder. Everyone is happy. Dad and Elizabeth point out jugglers and acrobats breathing fire to the girls, who are buzzing with excitement, their eyes shining with joy. Philippa smiles at me smugly, proud to own this whole scene and I grin back in relief. We are having a nice day.

Along the edges of the bustling, rapturous crowds, clowns and princesses tip their upturned hats and flower baskets towards children who reach in eagerly for handfuls of sweets. Philippa holds the girls back.

Ballerinas and teddy bears pass us offering toffees with huge generous smiles and as the girls stretch out to take some, Philippa trills *no sweets before lunch.*

A gigantic spotty dog unfurls a hot fluffy paw full of gummy bears and lollipops. *Don't you dare,* my wife hisses and glares into the wide enquiring eyes staring back at her.

Every other child is taking them and mine don't understand why they're being punished like this. Their little chins wobble and before I allow the first tear to splash in the middle of this perfect morning, I hand them one hardboiled sweet each. The repercussions are fierce. Philippa snatches them back out of their tiny plump fingers and as they burst into heart-breaking wails, she lets loose with a tongue lashing that creates a small clearing around us, which is lucky because the next thing she does is drag us all out of there.

We drive home in silence, save for the girls stilted sniffling and Dad and Elizabeth's sympathetic murmurs in the back. Then I'm marched to my bedroom and shouted at for two hours solid, which is shameful but it's two hours less than everyone else must endure.

I put forward a few weak arguments in my defence in the same flat, lifeless tone I always use when I speak to the love of my life now but in the end it's easier to let her run her course. I use the rest of the time to picture her bruised, broken body lying at the bottom of a canyon then realise this is too pleasant, so add a couple of fallen boulders onto her crushed legs and a pack of coyotes circling her, trapped but alive. Then I take out the coyotes and leave her to dehydrate, her helpless screams out of hearing range, her twisted torso out of sight. And then I add the coyotes again.

When she's spent, she glides down the stairs as though entering a dance in a ballroom at which she's the guest of honour. Dad and Elizabeth have managed to put together sandwiches and she exclaims effusively, marvelling at their ingenuity. They're not quite sure how to react to this benevolent display of obsequiousness and merely smile almost convincingly in return.

The parade is never referred to again and after lunch, Philippa excuses herself with gushing regret and allusions to the incredibly important and complex essay she must finish. Nobody troubles her for more information and the tension in the atmosphere lifts the moment she skips down to the basement.

After half a dozen references to the fact she's tired, Elizabeth's finally persuaded to go upstairs for a nap and my dad and I get to spend some time together on our own with the girls. The swimming pool's idyllic, the mood's light, the kids splash around and we cheer enthusiastically as they jump in from the side a million times and swim underwater like fish.

My dad asks me if everything's okay in the code we use whenever we talk about Philippa, but it's clear he knows the answer. Everything is not okay. Almost everything is awful in fact. I can barely relax in my own home. I daren't breathe too loudly or too often lest it upset my wife. I'm under surveillance the whole time. Accused of having affairs despite never going out. Accused of spending too much in the liquor store despite barely drinking. Accused of not doing anything around the house despite doing everything while my wife merely looks on scornfully in disgust. The goalposts are moved constantly but the more I rise to the challenge, the more she hates me. I am the primary caregiver to two children as well as working full-time and I'm so tired I want to cry all the time.

But my daughters are magnificent and their love for me is almost as great as my love for them. They make me laugh, they make me happy, they keep me sane. They can be sassy and stubborn like any other child but I won't tolerate rudeness, so I teach them to be respectful and polite. If they're naughty, I discipline them, but I do it calmly and consistently. They try their luck on occasion and God knows getting them dressed and out of the house is a special type of torture they should introduce at Guantanamo Bay, but they know there are boundaries and they're all the better for it.

This dissolves the moment their mother walks in the room and intermittently praises them for creating a marvellously artistic landscape out of Cheerios on the sitting room floor - *What's all this, you clever monkeys?* - and screaming wildly, her teeth bared, eyes bulging at the same scene a day later. *What the hell are you doing? Clean this mess up now!*

Katie is the most noticeably traumatised by her mother's whims of fancy and behaves in my absence and for a few hours afterwards, like a shell-shocked veteran suffering the effects of PTSD, but there's no Post about it. The attacks are ongoing and unpredictable. Unpreventable. They are only reduced by my presence and so I put up with being treated like an unruly delinquent who's chopped the heads off the daffodils and defiled the lawn. I put up with being woken after only a few hours sleep because the dishwasher needs emptying. I put up with being put down for being a good father because Katie and Lauren are the light in my life. The only light and if I leave them, we will all be left in darkness.

To my father, I simply shrug and say only eight years to go before they can legally choose to live with me and he pats me on the shoulder with such a forlorn expression I have to sink below the surface of the water to compose myself.

At six o'clock we sit down to eat. Elizabeth is red raw again having come down to help me make dinner at the same inopportune moment as Philippa appeared to find out why it was taking so long. She was promptly sent out to the poolside, lest she make my life in any way easier.

It is testament to how little Philippa cooks that she has no idea that waxing my chest hair would be preferable to having my stepmother by my side in the kitchen so I revel in secretly getting one over her and I even allow myself a small chuckle at Elizabeth's expense (although I don't tell her this as she seems slightly less tickled about it than me).

I'm still in a relatively good mood by the time I head off to work at half past six. Dad's been hinting about having an early night so they only have a few hours to get through before they can reasonably slope off to bed and as long as I don't sleep for more than thirteen minutes in the morning, I can get everyone out of harm's way before Philippa is even up.

The girls nuzzle into my neck and tell me they love me and they'll miss me and I squeeze them with all the tenderness I have and remind them to be good. As for the rest of the evening's events, I have to cobble them together from a range of different sources over the following few days.

Everyone agrees that Elizabeth does the washing up (although how well and to what extent varies considerably) while the girls show my dad their scrapbooks full of pictures they've drawn. Philippa's overflowing with compliments and pride and my dad, though marginally less impressed, smiles encouragingly and makes all the right noises. Elizabeth, on the other hand, starts telling everyone how good her daughter's children are at art and how they've won competitions for it at school.

And this is where the two accounts begin to differ. Elizabeth says that Philippa makes a rude remark about nobody caring, but rather than retaliate she walks calmly across to the table to admire Katie and Lauren's work.

In Philippa's version Elizabeth strides over bellowing, *aren't those pictures wonderful? Aren't they amazing? You must be geniuses,* really sarcastically, a manic, crazed look in her eyes.

In this version, Philippa is confused and turns to my dad saying, *George. What's wrong with Elizabeth? Why's she doing this to us?*

In Elizabeth's version, Philippa says *George, call your dog off* and as Elizabeth turns away she mutters something along the lines of *fucking bitch* under her breath. This is bad enough, but as far as Philippa is concerned, Elizabeth screams *you fucking bitch. I'm going to rip your face off* and then throws the glass she's drying at my wife's head.

Elizabeth says she fumbled and dropped the glass, which lands by her feet and rolls harmlessly under a chair but Philippa gathers the girls into her arms and cowers with them on the floor crying, *get away from Nanna. She's going to hurt you.*

By this point, Elizabeth has picked up the cracked glass from the floor and is heading for the bin. Philippa maintains she's about to throw it at them and starts screaming at my dad to get Elizabeth out of the house. The girls are crying. They're petrified. My dad doesn't know what to do. Elizabeth storms out the front door and as she paces the driveway George apologises profusely, telling Philippa his wife gets violent when she's been drinking. Philippa tells him Elizabeth is never setting foot in her home again and will most definitely never, ever, ever get near the children. George keeps saying he's sorry and explaining he and Elizabeth are having marriage problems and he's going to divorce her.

My dad agrees that he does say he's sorry, because he is, although he has no idea what the hell is going on. He doesn't recall disclosing intimate details about his relationship to his mad daughter-in-law. He just follows Elizabeth outside where they shake for some time.

This is the point where I get the phone call, thirty minutes into a twelve-hour shift. If Mike Chan had a little diarrhoea, I have the sort of seismic bowel shift that creates continents.

My wife has kicked my stepmother out on the street and is threatening to call the authorities to have her removed from the country and banned from ever entering again. My girls are terrified and distraught. I leave immediately and by the time I get there, things have not settled down.

My dad's permitted entry to quickly gather their belongings and although I'm allowed to help him book a room at the Lakeview Hotel, I am not under any circumstances to drive them there. Instead I have to call my own father a cab because his wife is not welcome in my house. Ever again. And I don't know if I'm angrier at Philippa for setting the trap or at Elizabeth for running straight into it. Either way, I'm certain that my life has been irreparably screwed.

But I'm wrong once again. It's much worse than that.

Plan B

If there was ever a List before, it may as well be ripped to shreds. There's a new List now and there's only one name on it that matters. One name but it's intrinsically bound to another. George hasn't actually made it on there himself but he will be on Elizabeth's (if she has such a thing) if he goes so far as to make the eye-watering effort it'll take to rebuild the bridges his wife first doused in petrol and then incinerated before diving headlong from the charred remains into the fires of hell.

And so that is that. They stick around for a few days reliving the moment they shattered my life to smithereens on an endless time loop, refining details and reinforcing their denials until they're absolutely certain it was all Philippa's fault.

And I'm sure it was. I can empathise with anyone wanting to throw a glass at her head, but I can't see Elizabeth firing one at the children, no matter how provoked and I know my wife. For all I don't understand her, I know she did this. But all that's irrelevant and I can't quite swallow the resentment I feel at being put in a position I've fought so hard to avoid. There was one condition. One. Shut up and put up.

I get over to see them at the hotel a few times, without the girls obviously, who are certainly less traumatised than Philippa would like, though she encourages them to relive the ordeal by going over it a hundred times until it's lodged in their memories. Or at least her version is.

She's already emailed the rest of my family to let them know what a sicko Elizabeth is and to warn them not to let her near children or tableware. The sympathetic responses she receives (at my bequest) fuel her further and as far as she's concerned, everyone in the world is rightly on her side and my stepmother is whacked out of her tiny senile mind.

She's still threatening to contact border control and the exam board where Elizabeth invigilates once a year to let them know what sort of child-hating maniac they're allowing to walk unchained among their students.

In the meantime my dad's been on the phone to my mum back in England and they've formed something of an uneasy coalition. The three of them have agreed to email all their conversations to each other as though communicating for the first time so that when (not if) it all goes to court, there'll be as much evidence to back up Elizabeth's claims as there is for Philippa's.

And it will go to court at some point because as everyone knows Plan A is to stick this out for as long as I can and then walk away with full custody of the children. Or joint custody at the very least and for this my family's presence in the girls' lives should be a bonus not a reason for a judge to think twice.

I am keenly aware that these latest developments are being discussed and dissected with anyone who'll listen and it's mortifying. This is no soap opera. This is my life and I need to preserve it, bat shit crazy nut jobs and all.

Dad and Elizabeth haven't slept since the incident and live in constant fear of Philippa coming to the hotel to scream at them some more. Or rather scream in response to some imagined attack that will land them in jail (where they seem determined to end up one way or another) and by and by they pay a thousand pounds to move their flights forward rather than take the risk.

Sad as I am to see my dad go, I'm also relieved. Things at home are far worse than they've ever been and it's only now that I realise I've never given Philippa credit for holding back the full extent of her true feelings about my family. Until now. A few days on from the scandal and the sympathetic emails she receives are lacking sufficient outrage and no one seems quite as appalled as they should be.

I apologise on their behalf and say I'm sure everyone is as horrified as they say they are and she turns on me with fire in her eyes.

'If they truly cared,' she spits through a set of clenched teeth she could pull trucks with. 'They would never speak to Elizabeth again.'

'We don't know that they will.' I stare down at my hands as I always do when I'm forced to talk to her these days.

'Of course they will, the fucking bunch of lily-livered-wank-busters. That's what they do. They stick together like some giant fatberg in a sewer. And that's where they belong, in the sewer, the two-faced dirty traitors. They're shit-for-brains, arse-licking losers the lot of them and you can forget it if you think any of them are setting foot in this house ever again. I'm not having their toxic negativity around my girls anymore. I wouldn't piss on a single one of them if they were on fire.' (Which is a relief of sorts. It's hard to imagine a less effective way of helping anyone engulfed by flames.)

I could just let it go, but I know she will not. Instead I assemble my face to its factory setting, lower my voice and attempt to sound calm or at least stop it squeaking.

'I know you're upset, Philippa and you have every reason to be, but what Elizabeth did was really out of character and no one else would ever dream of doing anything like that.'

'I guess we'll never know. I'm certainly not going to sit around waiting for one of them to start throwing kitchenware at me again.' She has her hands on her hips and I back away slowly, disguising the urge to run away with a lame stab at tidying.

'I'd be really surprised if this was more than a one off,' I say casually. 'And besides, we agreed it's really important for the girls to see as much family as possible.'

'They have my mum. I'll get her over more often. Anyway, I'm their Mother! They don't need anyone else.'

She's radiating fury and indignation. I can feel her from halfway across the room. I steady myself against the side of the sofa and wipe it half-heartedly to hide the fact that I'll fall if I let go.

'I know but it's good for them to see their grandparents and cousins and stuff as often they can. They love being with the family and they miss them.'

'They'll get over it. I'd rather shoot myself in the head than have to put up with a single one of them again.'

'Okay, but you know my mum's coming out next month.'

'No she's not. Not fucking here anyway. She can sleep under a bridge with the rest of the street dogs, the stupid ugly bitch. I'm not having her under my roof expecting me to run around after her, cooking and cleaning while she puts her feet up and does the crossword.

'She doesn't even like Katie and Lauren anyway. She's only interested in your twat-faced sister's kids. What's she even coming for? She just wants to be waited on hand and foot. Well, not on my watch. Tell her to get herself a free holiday at someone else's expense. She's done here.'

I swallow. Press my hands against the cushions, dig my fingers into the foam. 'I understand you're upset and rightly so but she's my mum. She's got nothing to do with what happened and anyway, she's already bought her ticket.'

'That's not my fault.'

'Philippa, try to be reasonable. The girls'll be devastated if they can't see their gran. They're looking forward to it.'

'Bollocks,' she snarls. 'They couldn't give a rat's arse.'

'I can't tell my mum she's not welcome in my own house'

Philippa's indignation propels her across the room like a blast of diarrhoea. She has me cornered. Even my cushion can't protect me.

'Make your choice, you pathetic worthless piece of flying shit. It's your mum or me.'

And there it is. The moment I've looked forward to and dreaded for six years, but it's all happening too soon. The girls are too young. I don't have any plans in place or any money to wing it. I have nowhere to go, nobody to lean on but in the moment I hesitate, Philippa's eyes narrow.

'Well go then! Fucking go! Get out my house, you fucking prick. You dick-licking arsehole. Go and have yourself a sausage fest with all your buddies if that's what you want, but I'm warning you, I will fight you. I'll fight you for every penny you've got. You'll never see Katie or Lauren again. I'll make you wish you'd never met me, you rim-loving cocksucker.'

It's nothing new. I've heard this all before but I don't have the strength to do it anymore. Not if she's really going to stand in the way of the handful of loved ones I have left. She's gone too far but as I turn silently to leave, she suddenly grabs me by the arm, her eyes wide with terror.

'Stop. Where are you going?' she wails.

'I'm leaving you,' I say, so calmly even I am taken aback. 'But let me be very, very clear about this. I am not leaving the girls. I will continue see them everyday and don't even think about stopping me. I'll take care of them like I always do and then I'll go because I can't be around you anymore.'

She's on her knees now, clinging to me as I head for the stairs, choking on hard ugly tears, a trail of snot smeared across her loathsome face. She's frantic and frenzied, an injured animal clawing at a locked cage, grotesque in her desperation and it's surreal to be finally leaving her.

I pack a small bag with nothing but my toothbrush and a change of clothes for the morning and as I do this, I watch myself as though suspended from above. As though I'm completely outside of my body and just observing, unemotional and unaffected.

Philippa flings the bag across the room screaming *I hate you* and then she crumples to the floor as I go to retrieve it. I haven't said a word since we got to the bedroom but now I turn to her and say I'll be here tomorrow after work to give the girls tea and put them to bed.

She cries *don't leave me. I love you* and I say I haven't loved you for years. I'm not sure how I ever did and her outstretched arms sink to the floor.

I turn around and head back to the landing, past the girls' bedroom where they're sleeping, oblivious to the life-altering events unfolding outside their door and I vow to be there for them no matter what happens from this point onwards until the day I die. I'll do everything in my power to make this a positive change and as I close the door behind me, I finally exhale.

More fool me for thinking I could.

Dog Days

So Version 3 of myself is dead and buried (well before his time) under newly laid floorboards in a basement I spent months renovating and will barely use again. Instead I spend two nights at Motel 27, which is about as pleasant as a shipping container with the added luxury of one grimy window that disgusts even the flies.

The walls are thin enough to keep me abreast of every mundane conversation and magnified climax either side of my room and I still can't afford it. We've spent all our savings on an unnecessary trip to Disney World, on building fences that don't need building and on builders who don't build. I'm earning approximately the same wage as I was on at eighteen when I was renting a one-bedroom shoebox, only now I must pay off a crippling mortgage on an unaffordable family home I don't live in and support three other people, one of whom is racking up credit card receipts at Tommy Hilfiger and The Gap like there's going to be a strike in Bangladesh soon.

Every day I go back to the house, where Philippa follows me around like a puppy and it would be easy to put this behind us and stay. But behind my back, she's emailing all my friends and family again expressing her concern that I'm having a nervous breakdown and I'm clearly depressed, which after six years of living with her is not surprising but I'm reminded that she's still as unhinged as a Jack in the Box and more than anything she has no idea how this could have happened. What she could have done to make me walk away from this paper perfect life but then again, I can hardly explain how I got here either. Why I chained myself voluntarily to a storming lunatic and once trapped, choose to tiptoe around her instead of gnawing my limbs off to get away.

But now I don't have a choice. She built a house out of cards and blew it to pieces. There's nothing to pick up and no way to rescue it. I can only salvage what's precious inside. And in a way, nothing's changed as far as Philippa's concerned. She is still in control. She has the nice big house, the nice big car, control of our finances – at least for the time being – and as long as I continue to look after the children (which I do with a ferocity like never before) she can enjoy life. The only real difference is when she tells me to leave because she hates me, I do.

As for me, things are slightly less enjoyable. A vintage Ford Mustang is not a car built for comfort and I am currently living in mine. The temperatures are still soaring in the midst of a baking summer and even with the windows down it's so humid, my shirt sticks to my back and sweat drips down the leather bucket seats that don't lend themselves to sleep.

Most nights I drive around for a while and because I have nowhere else to go, I eventually park up in an alleyway between Walton Regional Police Station and a pub I can't afford to buy a drink in. It's generally quiet after closing time and I can hunch up and rest, but during the day the heat is brutal, so after a nightshift, I head out to a little patch of greenery behind the car park and stretch out in the long grass.

It's surreal to stare up at the sky and long for sleep in a field only a mile up the road from a house I actually own and where my kids are. To feel so lost and far from home. So separated from my girls. But I have no other option. I have no money and no one to turn to because the only other adult I really know here is the one I am trying to escape from. On the plus side, I'm never late for work.

Philippa's emails to my mum, dad and sister become increasingly worrying and I force myself to read them, even though every one of them makes me physically ill. On the surface, she's so eloquent and well meaning, even I begin to wonder if I have actually lost my mind and she's been right all along. She details succinctly the depths of despair I have sunk to and yet all the while she attributes my depression to work, to the things I've seen and been through as an officer of the law, which admittedly is no picnic but there's nothing

I've witnessed that compares to the look in her eyes when she screams at me night and day and then into night again.

She reaches out to my family, begging them in turn to reach out to me. She is desperate to save me, save our marriage and save our family and she implores everybody to please get in touch. To contact me as though they haven't. As though while all this is happening, the people I'm doing it for, can't even be bothered to drop me a line.

She has no idea that behind the scenes, calculated operations are already in action. She's brought my parents together in angst and dismay for the first time in decades. They are constantly in touch with each other and with me, only not on the email account she frequently hacks and never on the phone when they know she's there. But as her accusations of neglect on their part become more indignant and robust, it becomes impossible to deny we talk frequently and rather than please her, this only serves to antagonise her more, as I knew it would. Nonetheless, a few days later, she's on at them again, outlining her concern for the attention I bestow upon my service weapon, need she say more?

Not at all, but she does. In the meantime, my main concern is not falling apart in front of the kids and finding the strength to leave them alone with her every time I say goodbye.

She suggests we see a counsellor to talk through our troubles and though I have no desire to overcome them, I agree. I've wanted her to seek help for her mental issues for years and this presents an opportunity, which in the long run may help her understand that she needs urgent medical intervention, a cocktail of debilitating drugs, then sectioning and eventually, a lobotomy. Still, baby steps, I've had my hopes dashed in the past, but Philippa is adamant that Canadian counsellors are far superior to British ones because they are fully trained as psychiatrists and are infinitely better in every way.

All except for our one who completely dismisses Philippa's version of the showdown with Elizabeth and repeatedly tells her to stop interrupting until she storms out the room halfway through our session and refuses to come back.

I'm both disappointed that she's not stuck around long enough to be detained under the Mental Health Act and relieved to have met an impartial, unbiased professional who sees through her. Who reminds me that I'm not barking mad even though that very notion has been drummed into me so many times I can't help but wonder sometimes if it's true. It would certainly explain how I got here but I instead, this Master of Psychiatry (a woman no less) confirms that I am right to feel undermined, belittled and bewildered.

Philippa doesn't stick around long enough to get a full and complete diagnosis but *Narcissistic Personality Disorder* is bandied about more than once. There are technical, medical definitions for her condition, but in layman's terms, she is a cunt.

None of this helps my immediate predicament however, but it does narrow down my Google searches and hone the advice I need to navigate the tempestuous waters I have entered (or more accurately, been thrown into prematurely against my will, better judgement and desire).

It's a few weeks before anyone notices what's going on at the station and a few days after that before they comment. I downplay what's happening but there's no getting away from the fact that I'm between homes and those homes are my car and a field.

Fortunately my humiliating situation is dwarfed by the unsatisfactory performance of the Toronto Blue Jays this season, which soon takes over the conversation but during the course of the day, my sergeant sidles over to give my back a good beating which in man-speak means he's worried about me.

He's the one of the few decent guys in the department. In another life we might even have been friends, but in this one I'm too busy having affairs and getting drunk to fit much else in. Busy, busy but it doesn't stop him telling me I look like a sack of shit and insisting I stay with him and his wife for a few weeks before I'm back on my feet. A few weeks! The optimism of the man.

The British arises in me and I vehemently deny there's any such need, but the Canadian in him is stronger and I find myself actually sleeping for the first time in as long as I can remember, on his sofa with an awful Jack Russelly sort of thing on my ankles which barks every time I dare move, but I'm not complaining. Quite the opposite. I'm humbled by his generosity and ashamed of all the mean things I've said about Canadians.

That being said, when I return the second evening, a crate of beers in my grateful, sheepish hands, Luis and his wife, Giselle are in the middle of – what I at first take to be – a heated row about me. But I'm forgetting that Canada is full of people who can only communicate as though they're standing at the end of a pier in a storm and this is simply a discussion about the fact Scout, the Jack Russelly sort of thing, has jumped onto the table and eaten a very large lump of butter.

I am not involved in this conversation, despite being in the room and even though the main cause for concern is the fact he's vomited on the sofa. Or as I call it – my bed.

I stick my head gingerly into the sitting room and there's the cushion, complete with stinking stain humming away exactly where my torso spent the previous night. An opportunity has arisen, albeit grotesque and nauseating, to repay some of the kindness that has been bestowed on me and so I immediately offer to clean it up. But I am a guest and this offer is refused with the same gusto as an attempt to donate a kidney to save the family cat.

Giselle wrenches the cushion out my hand with mock outrage and props it up by the side of the wall and there it stays for the rest of the evening. Nobody does anything else about it and all I can do is keep darting my eyes in its direction in the vain hope the golden puddle slowly curdling in the heat has disintegrated.

I can't offer to wash it off again, but since no one else does, at the end of the night I have to go to bed with that entire section missing. And it is not mentioned at all.

I pull the two remaining cushions next to each other, which doesn't cover the sofa, of course, but it's more comfy sleeping with my feet trailing on the springs than it is with the middle bit missing. It's better than a boiling hot Mustang but the dog joins me again and there's no getting away from the fairly strong smell of butter-vomit in the room all night.

I stay there for a week (on day three I take matters into my own hands and clean the cushion which either no one notices or assumes I'm happy to sleep on, puke and all) and in the meantime, Linda arrives to reinforce the battle lines that Philippa's drawing as she simultaneously begs for my return.

She isn't aging well, but who can blame her? She looks like she's made of wax and has melted a bit. There's a hardening in her demeanour as though she's realised her daughter's meal ticket, and therefore her own, is about to run dry. On the surface, she is warm and understanding, sympathetic and fully acknowledges Philippa's faults. But to her daughter, she is equally empathetic and feeds her manic diatribes with applause and adulation.

She's making plans to move here, reluctantly, because Philippa cannot cope with doing everything for the girls on her own in addition to continuing to run the household, cook and clean for everyone, deal with the children's ongoing confusion and pain as well as placate an estranged, volatile, suicidal husband battling depression. Not to mention, sort out the finances, which on the last bill, included $500 for air conditioning to refrigerate the house, while I slept in a field to keep cool.

Linda has her own agenda with regards to the money and she is keen to clarify all the details before she up sticks and joins us in this circus charade. She's referring to the £70,000 she once cunningly transferred into an ING account in Philippa's name in order to claim poverty and free housing on the jolly old welfare state. She's enjoyed the generous hospitality of the British taxpayer for several years, but now she's being forced to pull the brakes on the gravy train, she will require all of her money back. Which is a shame, because Philippa has spent it.

That she didn't see this happening from a million miles away (or even three thousand and forty-seven miles) goes to show the extent of her own idiocy and highlights the role she's always played in nurturing and facilitating her cuckoo offspring's own delusions. However, as amusing as I find this, I soon realise that despite never having access to this account or even logging on to the website, I'm being held accountable for frittering its contents away on M&S online purchases and an assortment of musical instruments I only now realise I haven't seen for some time.

I don't deny that I existed when Philippa spent the money. I was certainly breathing and somewhere in the vicinity, but the debt is hers and hers alone. She worked her way through our savings so thoroughly it hadn't occurred to me that she'd spent even more.

I explain all this clearly and concisely and regardless, I have no money so I'm happy to share the sum total of zero with anyone who wants it, but that £70,000 is everything Linda has put aside for old age and assuming Philippa doesn't drive her to an early grave, this won't be the last I will hear of it. Not by a long shot.

It's a reminder to change the terms of my will immediately leaving everything to Katie and Lauren in trust so their mother can't spend it all on their behalf while they're minors. I have no cash savings but there's equity in the house and I have a pretty hefty pension I'm intending to retire on early.

In addition, I make my daughters the beneficiaries of my private life insurance as well as of any future killed-in-the-line-of-duty type compensation (assuming Philippa and her mother don't get to me first). And I make sure both the money-grasping witches know this, as uncomfortable a clanger as it is to drop and at last, my wife seems to realise that from now I will refer to her as my ex. And I'll be damned if, from this moment on, I'm not back on The List.

My mum arrives in the middle of all this and let's just say, she is not greeted with open arms. She is welcome at Luis and Giselle's place however, which they continue to reiterate really loudly in the days leading up to her arrival even after I've explained repeatedly that she'll be happier in a motel than curled up with me on the sofa. It's incredibly kind of them to offer though (fifteen times) and I feel terrible that it's all I can do not to overturn the kitchen table in rage if they insist one more time.

In the end, we both stay at the motel. The single supplement is a killer anyway and so I might as well. Of course, I'd have preferred my own room, but since my mum is paying I don't like to mention it and all of a sudden I'm eight years old again, in one of two single beds, sharing a bathroom with a woman I would rather be on less intimate terms with. But there are no bony animals yapping intermittently on my feet and I'm not woken by her stale breath blasting onto my face as she scowls at me because I've slept (which is normal apparently...?).

We talk endlessly about the girls, about Philippa, about her mother, about everything I've been through, past, present and future, covering old ground and new and there's still more to say. Philippa is the gift to conversation that will never stop giving and for the first time in years I don't have to conceal the worst of it or hide anything to protect anybody else. I open up more and more every day and the more I reveal, the more questions follow.

My mum is no stranger to this story and neither of us knows how it will end. Or if it ever will. We cry and we vent and we break wind self-consciously when we go to the toilet while the other pretends to be absorbed in the bible, but all in all it's cathartic.

The next day, we visit the house and everyone in it. I sense the kids have been discouraged from being too pleased to see their *other* grandmother and they're awkward around her under their mother's watchful eye.

Philippa is fully immersed in the role of Wronged Wife and she's composed herself graciously as though refusing to stoop to our level. Linda has slightly less self-control and pulls my mother aside every time I'm distracted to enlist her as a bench sub for their team and bring me to my senses.

I notice in the kitchen the chalkboard displaying my name and list of duties has been changed to *Tin Man*. From now on this is what Philippa calls me and the suggestion I have no heart is not lost on me and neither is the irony, but I have no strength left to address either. My mum is under siege and after two days, I have to go back to work leaving her to fend for herself.

I'm nervous when I drop her off at the house, but she's focused. Unfortunately so is Linda and without an audience, Philippa's own calm composure is slipping. For ten straight hours, they regale her with tales of my deterioration into madness and self-destruction, into depression and aggressive instability. They rebuke her for the lack of support she's provided for either me, Philippa or the girls and when she reminds them we speak constantly, that she asks after the girls all the time and that when she does ring the house phone, Philippa passes it immediately to me, they refuse to believe it. Even her very presence isn't enough to convince them she cares – not in the way they want anyway.

She is failing to chastise me for relinquishing my responsibilities. Worse than that she's more shocked at hearing Philippa's done good on her threat to report Elizabeth to Bournemouth Borough Council and the Canadian Border Police than she is at the violent outburst itself which is further proof, if it were needed, that she's a hindrance not a help.

Linda hovers over her and the girls wherever they go, interrupting and trying to join in or take them away, but my mum holds her ground steadily, refusing to bend to their will with a benign smile on her face which by the evening gives her lock jaw. When I come to collect her, the kids hug her a little too tightly and beg her a little too loudly to stay.

The next day when we go to the house, they're not there. Nobody is. The cupboards and drawers have been ransacked, piles of clothes lie discarded on the floor, the passports have gone and the car's not in the garage. I leave twelve urgent messages on Philippa's mobile and one pointless one with a colleague at Walton. After forty-five minutes she texts to inform me they've taken a trip and will be back sometime next week. After my mum leaves. And there's nothing I can do but report it again officially and scream silently inside as I'm told that without a court order stating she can't take them, she can, she just can't leave the country.

Once again she's taken control and reminded me she has the power and the will to destroy me. And she intends to, whether she disappears with my children off the face of the earth or she comes back and takes me down in pieces. She's gunning for me now like never before and this is merely a teaser. A preview of what's to come. The war has begun and the only hope I can cling to is she comes back to fight it, because if she doesn't, I will never see my daughters again.

Bend Over. This Won't Hurt A Bit

It's four days until I'm able to sleep for more than a few moments before my head jerks and my eyes fly wide open. Philippa screens my calls to the girls allowing me access to them only every fifth or sixth attempt and then she lurks in the background, fielding my questions as I try to stay calm. As I try not to reach inside the phone and wring her proud turkey neck. As I try to keep the escalating panic out of my voice so as not to alert her to my overwrought state and encourage her to prolong it.

She pulls up to the house a few hours after I drop my mum off at the airport, full of smiles and brandishing a small fluffy Golden Retriever. The girls' squeals of delight and sweet garbled chatter drown out the irate preamble of the speech I've been practicing for days and by the time I can get a word in, I've registered the perverse satisfaction playing on Philippa's curled lips.

Linda smirks in the background and a hunk of fury the size of a sausage gets caught in my throat but I refuse to play into their hands so we behave as though abducting my children was a misunderstanding, a minor miscommunication, probably on my part. But we all know that if I don't tow the line, it will happen again.

I pause briefly and fantasise about taking off with the kids myself. Packing a bag for us all, getting in the Mustang and driving until the dust is too thick to see Philippa writhing around on her knees in the dirt behind us. Weeping into the earth as fourteen years' worth of maintenance and spousal support disappears into the distance.

But my job is the only thing separating any of us from destitution and they tend to get funny when I don't turn up. I have to work to earn money to survive. There's no way around it. I'm the only one who actually can without resigning three weeks in or getting sacked and there's the definite promise of a promotion on the horizon, which might be less easy to swing in the midst of a nationwide manhunt.

So I let Philippa drone on about how much the girls love the puppy and what fun they had travelling around and when I mention that if she takes them away she needs to run it past me, she looks me straight in the eyes and says *I did let you know*. I say you know what I mean and she replies *about that. We should probably get something in writing* and so she does.

The following week, she produces a separation agreement and I know without reading it that she will feed me to the wolves but even I haven't appreciated how many wolves there will be and how hungry they are.

My priority is having access to Katie and Lauren and the only real advantage I have is I know Philippa would rather boil her eyeballs in bleach than be responsible for them all the time. Even with her mum helping out, she can't cope with the two of them. Worse, the more she has them, the more she has to put up with her mother as well.

But she would limit me to supervised visits once a fortnight out of spite or if I step out of line, so instead we play a game of cat and mouse with her pretending joint custody is a gift she is graciously extending and me pretending, every time she reconsiders her options, not to throw up a bit inside my mouth.

And all I have to do is give her 70% of whatever we get for the house when we eventually sell it and 90% of my wages for the foreseeable future. A bargain! It's a good job I only spent forty quid getting her grandmother's ring resized all those years ago or this might push me over the edge. Oh, and they want Linda's seventy grand back too.

I would bite her hand off to get that 50/50 childcare split in writing but even in my delirious, panicking state I realise I can't possibly live on 10% of a teenager's salary and low cost of Canadian living my arse, even with a promotion, I'll be raising my kids in the back of the Mustang if I don't hold at least some ground.

We try to negotiate face-to-face but it's impossible. I can't even make eye contact with her and Linda's never far away egging her on. Not that she needs it. I've become so intimidated by her over the years I'm only able to stare at my feet like a terrified child in her presence. She's combustible at the moment and I'm tempted to walk past her with a naked flame to see if she'll explode, but she'd take me down with her. So to the lawyers we go at $300 a pop, which represents roughly a day's wages. Or two if you consider I have to pay for hers too. And not just once. Many, many times as we flit back and forth, but what is money but an illusion? Whoever thinks that should try sleeping in grass.

It's now been six months since this impromptu chain of events was set in motion and we're no closer to signing off on a deal. The threat of withdrawing my custody rights isn't real, but then neither is anything else that goes on in her head so I can't blithely take it for granted.

Apart from the Mustang, the field, a couple of car parks and two motels, I've also lived in three different basements. One with an airbed and no window, one with an airbed and a window and one with a sofa bed and a window but no heating, which I timed very badly over winter. Brittle toes aside, I've been overwhelmed by the number of people who've offered to help me and while even the most intelligent of Canadians still wears a baseball cap inside and has an irrational fear of imminent bear attacks (in the city) there's no shortage of kindness here.

Were it not for the soulless breeze block buildings, wooden houses wrapped in fake bricks and tiles, people called Brad, huge beards on young people, waking up to find the car buried under ten-foot of snow, roads called Apple Tree Hill when there are no apple trees or hills for miles around, people called Dwayne, ice hockey – in fact any of their televised sports which are actually mainly bloody adverts – people called Colton, stupidly large cars with six-litre engines which can nevertheless be outperformed by a Ford Fiesta, people honking their bloody horns at nothing, conversations concerning the merits of one restaurant's steak versus the merits of another restaurant's steak, people who describe themselves as Italian yet have never been to Italy, people on medical marijuana, having to walk a dog on a lead even in the middle of nowhere, having to carry a gun - make that bear-fearing, baseball-capped morons carrying guns – people called Chad and the fact the person I hate most in the world is right here, I would probably learn to like it.

But it's still the wrong country. I can't describe what it's like to know you're on the opposite side of the world to almost everything you care about. To have my two most important assets besides me, but no one to share them with and nowhere to go.

Until now I've had to visit Katie and Lauren at the house in Burlington and leave them there every night. My blow up mattress is as comfy as a sack of oats and regardless of how much I want to have them to myself, it's in their best interests to stay where they are until we've finalised the terms of our divorce and I'm sorted.

Katie's started at the elementary school at the end of the road and it's supposed to be one of the best in the area. Even the worst would have been pretty good given how high the standards of Canada's state education system is (I will give them that) and as long as I don't try to squeeze sleeping into my schedule I can usually take Katie there and pick her up every day. She's made a few friends and seems settled and happy. Lauren is only a year behind her, but in the meantime it's nice to have a bit of time on our own.

Katie and I have always had a strong bond and these few hours alone together give me a chance to focus on Lauren instead. To push her on the swings and teach her how to ride a bike, to kiss her better when she falls off, to play with all her horrible My Little Pony characters (okay, I admit it. They're quite cute). To hang onto every word as she tells me their names and all about their adventures. To dress her up in her warm winter coat and take the new fluffy dog for a walk (which is also my job now and I'll never let on how much I love doing it). She's still into death – Lauren that is, not the dog. It's all she can talk about.

'Will you take me to the hospital if I die, Daddy?' I can't help but roll my eyes.

'Yes, darling, but you're not going to die.'

She chews on her lip for a moment then says, 'If I get squashed by a car, will I die?'

'Well, you might but that's why you have to be careful crossing the road.'

'But if I do get squashed…' she cries triumphantly. 'Will you take me to the hospital?'

'Yeeessss, but as long as you don't run into the road, you'll be fine so let's not worry about it.'

'What if you forget to take me to hospital?'

Is it too early to drink? 'I would never forget to take you to hospital, sweetheart. That's the first thing I would do, but it's not going to happen.'

'I don't want to die like Candy's hamster, Daddy.'

'You're not going to die, Lala. Try to stop thinking about it.'

'Will I never die?'

I take both her warm clammy hands in mine, bend my knees with a crack and hold her gaze.

'Look, you're not going to die for a really long time. Most people don't die until they're really, really old.'

'I don't want to be old.' She seems quite sure about this.

'Well…you can't have it both ways. You have to get old if you don't want to die.'

'I don't want to be old like you, Daddy.'

'What's wrong with being old like me?'

'It's boring coz you can't go on trampolines or you'll break it.'

I place a kiss on her forehead. 'Fair enough.'

At times like this, I am prepared to sign over every cent I ever make along with the house to get the custody agreement in writing before the loopy narcissist decides the girls can't live without her. She is their *Mother* after all. This is where spending a month's wages on solicitors comes in handy, especially one who, after being introduced to several of Philippa's many personalities, has now developed her own personal vendetta against her.

Stella refuses to let me bend over and be shagged up the arse by my soon-to-be ex's giant penis-shaped demands but even she can't stop her dipping her red throbbing head in and ultimately, we settle on a compromise. And when I say compromise, I mean a financially-crushing, soul-destroying pit of misery from which I will never recover but with Linda back in the UK instead of jollying her along in the background, Philippa drops the £70,000 debt claim and from the original nine tenths of my salary, I wrangle her down to a smooth 80%. Plus, and this is the biggie, she agrees to sign away any rights to my pension.

For once it works in my favour that she's always too busy grasping at the cold hard cash to ever plan ahead. Or maybe she thinks I'll be dead soon anyway. She would know.

The solicitors have to register the separation agreement at the court but we'll officially be divorced within a month. I can hardly believe that it's over. The six years of hell she's put me through, the money she's wasted that we'll never see again. The decades she's shaved off my life, but I'm done with it now. I won't be followed around for hours at a time being screamed at anymore. I won't fear going home for what awaits me as I walk through the door. I won't quietly absorb the endless criticisms and insults that wear away at my confidence and judgement until I've lost track of what's normal. Of what's acceptable. Of who I am.

I have survived, bruised and broken, but alive. And she's won ultimately, because she's got much more than she deserved but she left me still breathing and that was a mistake. It's ridiculous that she expects me to support the girls on 20% of my salary, despite having them half of the time, but I'm pumped up with reason that we can revisit this absurd financial arrangement at a later date. The important thing is that for now, I've achieved my objective. Joint custody of my own children. And all I have to do is find somewhere to live and bring them up on thin air.

I'm technically homeless but other than that things seem to be going quite well. The girls and I are in a pretty good routine and I can come and go as much as I like at the house as long as I clean up after myself and everyone else afterwards. With Linda back in England tying up loose ends, Philippa lets me stay over on the nights I'm supposed to have the girls. I suspect she would actually let me stay over all the time now the staff is away, but she's enjoying my new role as a Hobo too much. I'm definitely being yelled at less often these days and while she's still as dodgy as a week-old burrito, she seems to be slightly less gloweringly nutty now she's got what she wants.

But wait! That was yesterday. Since then she's decided she's bored of Burlington and her massive four-bedroom home with a fully renovated media room slash playroom, huge front yard, enormous back yard and unnecessarily fenced off swimming pool. It's imperative that she move to Toronto and rent a gardenless apartment in the middle of town. Now.

'I'm sick of it here. I feel like I'm suffocating.'

And it's non-negotiable. It has to be because it's already happened.

I'm torn between horror at her uprooting the kids without consulting me, especially Katie who can look forward to a forty-five minute commute each way to school now and unabated glee (which I keep to myself) because Philippa is inadvertently freeing up my 30% of the house a decade earlier than I expected and it's possible that I will now be able to afford my own cardboard box to live in under a railway bridge.

She's already rented a property and it's marginally disorientating walking into a room I've never been to in my life and finding it full of all my stuff. The sideboard and matching dining set my gran gave me when she moved in with my dad sit pride of place in the kitchen-diner along with the old lady tea set the mad cow bought in Epsom, which she's welcome to. The table and chairs less so, but she'll sell them shortly so at least they won't offend me anymore. There are paintings I had before I met her adorning the walls and half the mugs in the cupboard say *Best Dad Ever*. I'm paying for this apartment but I can't actually stay overnight anymore because there isn't enough room to swing a cat in it. (Though why would you want to?)

Philippa's concerned about poor Katie having to travel so much every day and so she swiftly pulls her out of the lovely (free) school in Burlington and enrols her in an exclusive (private) school she's just read an *Article* about *Online*. And then she demands I pay for half of it. I remind her that I'm sleeping on a sofa bed in someone else's basement because I have no money. At all. But I have money for solicitors she reminds me and tra-la-lahh! The separation agreement has not been registered yet. We can change it absolutely any time, annihilating anything in it that takes our fancy. Wahey!

We are back to square one, only now square one is in the most expensive part of the district and I have no choice but to agree to pay for a school that costs more than I can afford to spend on rent. And even better, Philippa's signed Lauren up for kindergarten too so I get to spend even less time with her and pay for the privilege. Or we can talk about supervised visits again and though I know she'd never get that past a judge, it could be months before it even went to court and years before it was resolved.

And of course I have to deal with the sale of the bloody house by myself because a week later, Philippa gets into it with the realtor who rings me afterwards, still shaking, to say she's never been spoken to like that in her life. She has no idea how I put up with her for so long but she will never talk to that lunatic again. Hurrah for me.

I've obviously had my fair share of experience with estate agents so I'm not best pleased at the prospect of having to go through it again so soon but unlike in the UK where nobody involved in the sale of properties seems to have the slightest interest in actually selling them, here in Canada, it's almost as though you'll pay them thousands of dollars if they do.

Patty's job is made easier by the fact I've spent nearly two years renovating it to a beautiful finish (although a blind, one-armed chimp could have done a better job, I'm told) and since Philippa's stripped it bare, it no longer looks like a rummage sale at the back of a community centre. We accept an offer on it quickly. Philippa has her eyes on the prize and is too short sighted to see she has screwed herself over and handed me the opportunity to rebuild my life (less school fees and the side-splitting cost of the uniform).

With what remains of my piffling 30% I'm able to rent my own place for the first time. It's tiny, but I have virtually no furniture, which makes it seem a lot bigger. And it's not in a basement in somebody else's house so I can finally bring the kids here when they're in my custody.

The first time Philippa sees it, she actually laughs. She's so tickled pink at the sight of what she's reduced me to, she doesn't even mind when I ask her if we can swap our days around so I can pop back to England. My gran's poorly and she needs an operation. It isn't serious, but I haven't seen anyone apart from Mum, Dad and Elizabeth since we came out two years ago. I miss them so much it hurts and now some time has passed, I feel sick to my stomach that I didn't really thank my gran properly for lending me the deposit for Burlington.

But I'll make it up to her. I have my money from the house and for the first time in years, I don't have to ask for permission to do what I want. And what I want is to tell her that I'm grateful and I love her. But more than anything, I want a plate of her hot, steaming roasties fresh out the oven and dripping in salt-laden oil.

I do my best to replicate them for dinner but they're never as good (unless you define good as not life-threatening). Lauren holds a knife out in front of her and says, 'If I accidently cut myself with this, will I die?'

And I say, 'To be honest, honey, you would have to accidently cut yourself with that particular knife for about a month before you even got a blister, but yes, in theory, you should always be careful with knives.'

'What about if I accidentally fell on top of it?'

'It's pretty hard to fall on knives at the table.'

'But accidentally?'

'Well, yes, if you did somehow manage to fall on it accidentally, you might really hurt yourself so eat nicely and finish your food and that won't happen.'

And then Katie says, 'When will I die, daddy?'

And I say, 'You are never going to die, either of you. Nobody is. No one is ever going to die.'

And then my dad rings to tell me that I'm too late to tell my gran I'm sorry because everybody dies in the end.

Over The Rainbow

I've forgotten how much it rains in the UK. How grey it all is, but I like grey. I think it suits me. I get back a few days before the funeral and go straight to my dad's. I didn't grow up in that house but it still feels like home. My gran's newly converted bedroom feels empty even though it's crammed full of her old junk. The drawers of string and toy soldiers have gone and in their place is a wheel chair that should count itself lucky the girls aren't here to give it a test drive.

My dad and I sit on the edge of Gran's bed in silence for a while but it's one of those high ones that bends up in the middle so it's awkward and we end up perching on the side. And then I give him a long, silent hug and when I pull back, his eyes are red and I've left a patch of damp tears on his shoulder.

'She's with your grandad now,' he says. 'Wherever that is.'

And I know she's not tired or in pain any more, but I still wish I could have said goodbye.

I hang out with my dad and Elizabeth all afternoon, but the conversation never moves on from *The Incident*, as it is known. I can only go over it so many times and besides, they keep insinuating it was probably for the best. That somehow bringing my master plan forward by at least five years with no money or plans in place and only two minutes warning was a good move. It got me out of the house anyway. And into a sweltering pub car park with the windows of my new home wound down so as not to die of heatstroke. But still, it had to happen one day. Really, they did me a favour.

I'm not ready to thank them quite yet and even when my dad leaves the room and I simulate a narcoleptic coma on the sofa, Elizabeth can't be stopped. Most concerning is the prospect that Bournemouth Borough Council won't invite her back to invigilate this year's GCSEs now she has this dark blot against her name. It is a worry, I agree and thank goodness that's one thing I don't have to add to my own list of headaches. For all my troubles, there is always someone – oh no, wait... Ignore me.

I'm not sure how many more times we can talk about this and I'm getting so wound up, I'm starting to defend the fruit loop. Thank the stars, most of my school friends still live in Bournemouth so a few phone calls later, I'm able to make my escape before I start my own List.

We meet up in a pub that feels strange and familiar at the same time and no one has changed apart from me. Philippa's been in touch with them all, firstly with misgivings about my various addictions to bourbon and penises (if only I had the time) and then after the split, in despair about the state of my mind.

She has *implored* them all to *reach out to me. To try to think of her not as a wife but as a concerned friend with only my best interests and welfare at heart. To understand that I've slipped into a dark place. Even darker than in all the years she's known me and this emotional retreat has only got worse since the breakdown of our marriage* (which is a symptom of my unrelated misery) *and where the fuck is everybody else when I need support? Why is it all down to her to sort this shit out? What I need are people telling me to get my arse out of the sand and suck it up like a Real Man with responsibilities so why the flaming fuck can't any of my so-called friends and loving family give me an effing call once in a while and tell me to shut the fuck up and grow a pair? Because she can't communicate enough how worried she is.*

It's hard to imagine a time when I'll ever laugh about this, but it's certainly easier to try with a pint of Harvey's in front of me in a pub surrounded by friends I've known my whole life. It takes a shot of tequila or two, but all of a sudden the strangest sensation begins to creep over me. I recognise it and if memory serves, it's called *'happiness'*. I'm having fun instead of continually looking over my shoulder and making a mental log of all the exits. My cheeks hurt and my belly laughing muscles haven't had this sort of work out in so long I know for sure there'll be consequences.

It's only Tuesday and everyone has families, work and various other things they haven't managed to screw up in their busy lives, but still, there is a curry house two streets away that I've been fantasising about for years now and I won't be dissuaded from dragging all their sorry, sagging moobs there. It's not like it's completely impossible to find an Indian restaurant in Toronto, but they're nothing compared to the ones here. I don't know if it's the burger masala or the bottles of ketchup they serve on the side, but it's never quite the same (Only kidding). I'm sure they probably say the same about ours in Mumbai, but if they do they've never been to the Moonlight Palace in Old Christchurch Road.

The vindaloo doesn't disappoint, or at least not on the way down. Partaking in the whole meal again when it comes up in the morning is somehow less enjoyable, but I soon wash it down with a full English breakfast at my mum's around the corner. My sister's staying there with her brood until the day after the funeral. Her little ones, Maya and Lucas, have both grown so much that if it weren't for all the bloody photos Julia sends me all the time, I wouldn't recognise them. I wish my two could be here with me, but at this rate they'll all be teenagers before they ever meet again. My own sister's kids – virtual strangers, even to me.

They're shy at first, but I've bought them horrible Canadian chocolate and loads of cheap souvenirs so before long they're bouncing off the walls, which does me no good at all in my delicate state. I have to sneak off upstairs to my old bedroom under the guise of Skyping the girls, but we all know it's to vomit. I Skype them anyway, though to be honest, I'm surprised when they answer, but it's early over there and Dragon Breath is probably still asleep.

The connection's bad like it always is and they burst into tears when they see me. I want to draw them both into my arms but I can't so instead I run my finger across the screen and try to keep my voice from cracking when I ask them what the matter is.

'Gran's dead like Candy's hamster.' Lauren croaks, her little chin wobbling. Giant tears roll down her cheeks and drop out of sight.

'Oh, Lala. Gran's fine. I've just seen her.'

'Mummy said she died.'

'That was my gran, sweetheart. Da-Da's mummy. The one with white hair in the photo on the fridge.'

'Are you sad, Daddy?' Katie asks, spreading a transparent trail of snot across her lips and licking it. I have an urge to make her stop, but it seems to be cheering her up.

'Yes, I am, sweetheart. I loved her very much.'

'What was she like, Daddy?'

'She was funny. She used to take her teeth out and clatter them about to make you laugh when you were little.'

'Take her teeth out?' Lauren's back on high alert.

'She had false teeth. Because her old ones fell out.'

'Will my teeth fall out?'

'They might if you don't look after them but not until you're very, very old.'

'I don't want to get old.'

'I know, Lala. Try not to think about it.'

I realise too late that not telling them about my gran was a mistake, but it wasn't something I thought they needed to know. Not with everything else that was going on and their already sizable obsession with death. I wanted to protect them, but I was forgetting not everyone feels the same.

Philippa's told them I came to England on my own because I didn't want to take them with me. I tell them that's not true and I'll definitely bring them next time. That I'll be home soon, like I promised and I'll bring lots of their favourite treats back.

I take the phone downstairs so they can say hello to everyone but they get upset when they see my mum and remember she's dead. Just as I'm calming them down and they're starting to laugh again, Philippa appears behind them, hair dishevelled and face creased like a badly peeled grapefruit.

'I knew it!' she snarls, snatching the iPad away from the girls. 'You couldn't resist rubbing their poor little faces in it, could you? It's been a nightmare here, dealing with all of this, not that you care. And just as I've finally sorted it all out, you have to phone up and set them off again. What's wrong with you? It's bad enough you go on holiday without us, but I'd really appreciate it if you could refrain from constantly torturing the kids so I don't have to listen to them wailing about it for the rest of the day.'

'Can I talk to Daddy again?' Katie asks faintly off camera.

'Daddy's too busy having fun without us all.'

'No, I'm not. I'd like to speak to them.'

'And I'd like you to lift,' she lowers her voice and hisses into the speaker, her face blurry and magnified only millimetres from the screen. 'A ruddy finger around here to help out once in a while but it's not going to happen, is it? Certainly not this week.'

'Philippa. Can I talk to the girls please?'

'We're going out. You'll have to talk to them later.'

'Just let me say goodbye properly.'

'You're upsetting them, Dan.'

'Mummmmmmy.'

'Stop shouting. Go and put your shoes on.' They aren't even dressed. Katie's trying to grab the iPad back. Lauren's crying. 'Stop it! Naughty girl! You could have broken it, you little idiot. I said go and get your shoes on and don't you dare answer me back.' Then turning to me, 'You see what you've done now? They're both in tears. You've totally ruined the whole day once again and I have to deal with it all. You are a selfish bastard, Daniel. I don't know how you can live with yourself.'

She hangs up and the last thing I hear before the dialling tone is the sound of my children sobbing and calling out for me.

The silence that fell in the room when she took over the call isn't broken for a moment, but then it's hard to say much with your mouth hanging open. Andy's the first to speak but all he manages is 'wow'. It's not the first time they've seen the lunatic in action of course, but she's like a human water board. Or maybe human's the wrong word. Either way, I'm tied to her and I feel like I might die.

In fact the truth is, I wish I could. I wish I could end all this. Make it go away forever. Not think about it anymore. Not live in dread and fear. Not catch my breath every time the phone rings. Not stuff my hands in my pockets to hide the fact they're trembling when I'm around her. I could make it all stop this very moment or later on tonight. Or tomorrow. It's all I think about almost all of the time, but then who would look after my girls? Who would stop it all happening to them instead? I am trapped.

Julia says, 'It's no better now then?' And I shake my head.

Of course it's no better now. I still have to deal with her every day and she's irate because she had to find out about my gran dying from me. Imagine that. At the very least, she'd expected a phone call from George to let her know and make sure she wasn't too badly shaken. They were still family after all. A piece of paper couldn't change that and it was inconsiderate of my father not to invite her to the funeral. And to add insult to injury, she has to look after the kids for five whole days on her own while I'm here having the time of my life.

Any happiness that may have inadvertently crept into my soul dissipates like a stream of piss hitting hot sand. It's days before Philippa answers my calls again and only then because the girls are at a play date and she wants to shout at me. I use the time to see my friends, visit old haunts, catch up with Andy and Julia and buy several kilos of dried meats and heavily flavoured peanuts with the sole aim of declaring them all at the airport.

It's overcast on the day of the funeral but the rain manages to hold off and every so often the sun breaks through the clouds. We file into the crematorium and embrace each other sombrely, nodding at vaguely familiar faces but avoiding small talk for now. The only thing worse than putting my gran to rest right then, is having to have the same conversation twenty times about my pitiful life. I stick with Julia and Andy while my dad makes the rounds, greeting cousins and distant friends of the family in a hushed tone that's easy to ignore when he tries to catch my attention.

My mum's looking after Maya and Lucas back at the house so the three of us file into the pews behind Dad and Elizabeth. A woman welcomes us and begins to talk about death and I find myself staring distractedly at the back of Elizabeth's sparse grey scalp. Her hair's so brittle with spray and over-styling that any exposure to sunlight could start a wild fire. I'm almost drawn to reach out and check it's real, but no one would choose it and anyway, the woman's introducing 'Ivy's son, George, who'd like to say a few words.'

My dad's been up all night going over the eulogy but as he stands in the pulpit, his eyes fill with tears. He holds a sheet of paper in front of him, but it's shaking too badly to read. He gets as far as her name and then chokes back a whimper with a wobbly smile. We're all silent for a minute as he lifts his head and tries again, but he gets no further. He looks as helpless as a vulnerable child and I'm reminded that it doesn't matter how old he is. He's still lost his mum.

I stand and smooth my suit down. Slide myself out into the aisle and our eyes lock as I take the few steps up towards him. His mouth quivers and I smile reassuringly. Taking the sheet off him and with my hand on his back, I lead him away gently and wait a few seconds for him to sit down. Julia leans forwards and presses her hand against his shoulder and with the other, she dabs at the tears on her cheeks.

I stare down at his speech, allow the soft sympathetic murmurs to fade and begin to read. Only I can't because it looks like a spider's crawled through a pot of ink and made its way across the page. And halfway there it changed its mind and went back and forth and round in circles. And then it had a fit.

I'm standing in front of dozens of heartbroken mourners, here to pay their respects to a woman they loved. I only recognise my immediate family but she had a lifetime's worth of friends and seven siblings who all seemed to have bred. I don't know them other than from stories my gran would tell me, but every one of them is looking at me expectantly and the silence has gone on for too long. I fold the page up. Stare out into the room.

'Thank you everyone for coming. My name is Dan and I had the pleasure, and honour, of being Ivy's grandson.' A few people smile at me. People I recall vaguely from my grandad's funeral two years before. People I won't see again until my dad dies.

'My grandmother, Ivy, was the archetypal grandmother and by that, I don't mean any disrespect to your grandmothers, but I have to say, they couldn't possibly have been as perfect as my gran. If I could've put her in a bottle and sold her, I would have, but I got here a few days too late….' I look around the room. A sea of hankies is suspended in the air and all eyes are on me. There's a moment of slow comprehension, then bemusement. I cough to clear my throat and break the stillness.

'I hadn't seen her for a little while, other than on *The Skype*, as she called it, and I don't know if you've ever tried to Skype an old person? It's like trying to have a conversation on an intercom in a deserted office block. All I'd get is this big image of her chin because she'd insist on picking up the tablet and shouting into the speaker.' There's no response from the audience. Not a flicker. I plough on.

'One of the things I'll remember most about her was every year she'd get a little smaller. I know my dad was hoping if she hung on long enough, he could save himself a fortune and bury her in an old tin of Quality Street.' Only Andy laughs. Julia nudges him sharply, her eyes drilling into me, her mouth set in a line.

'Sorry. Dead people humour. I'm doing my best not to corpse up here.' Still nothing. There's no pleasing some people. 'I probably need a stiff drink.'

Julia's lips have disappeared and Andy is looking down at his song sheet trying not to giggle, but not in a good way. I glance at my dad, sitting bolt upright now, salvaging his dignity and I pull myself together, take a deep breath and remember why I'm there.

'Sorry. I'm a little nervous. Wasn't expecting to do this today. Would love more than anything in the world not to be here, because being here means my gran has gone and the world is a sadder place to be now.

There isn't a time in my life, obviously, that I haven't known her. That I haven't been able to rely on her. She's saved me more times than I remember, both when I was little and in more recent times. And I'll never be able to thank her enough for that.

'You all knew her, of course. You have your own memories of her and your reasons to be here today, but what

I'll never forget are all the little things that made her my gran. That made her so special.'

I pictured her in my mind. Back in her house, when I was small and she was still bigger than me. When my parents got divorced and turned our world upside down, but she turned it back again. When I grew, gawky and awkward at first then gradually taller until I towered above her, but she was always there for me. No matter what, she was my rock. I can't believe I'd let us grow so far apart.

'Don't know if you ever noticed, but she used to make tea in a pot and serve it in these horrible glass mugs that cooled down about half an hour after the tea did so you could never drink it. Couldn't even pick the thing up, until it was scummy on the top and stone cold but it was still the best cup of tea in the world.

'And they always had Wagon Wheels, her and my grandad, which are possibly the most ludicrous biscuit on earth. Have you ever had one? They were the size of a small child's head and it goes without saying that no parent would ever buy them, even in the eighties. It's a real grandparent treat, like paint guns that leave massive stains on the wall – that's going out to my own dad,' I look at him and grin. He shakes his head sheepishly and holds back a smile. 'I can't ever see a Wagon Wheel without thinking of her.

'And she'd always have stories that went on forever, but you never wanted them to end, they were so funny and confusing. And she'd lean in towards you and laugh so wickedly all the way through that you couldn't help but join in even though you never knew who she was talking about and you'd already heard it fifty times before.

'I'd never be able to take my eyes off her mouth when she spoke because no matter what, no matter what time it was or how poorly she was feeling, that woman wasn't dressed if she didn't have some orange lipstick on her teeth. Was she?' There was a little slow rumble of laughter around the room. 'It was always there. This little patch of orange and your eyes would be drawn to it the whole time she was speaking, but you could never say anything, because she wouldn't have been her without it.'

People were nodding and smiling. These strangers who knew her. Who thought she was theirs somehow too.

'We went through some tough times growing up. Everybody does, but Gran and Grandad were always there for us. They made us laugh when we were sad, they made us calm when we were anxious, they made us use that freezing downstairs toilet because the one upstairs was just for guests.'

Lots of people laughed at that. I wondered how many of them were close enough to my grandparents to have been forced into the ice-loo too.

'My gran and grandad had the sort of marriage I aspired to – together for sixty odd years, never a night apart. They'd met in the war and loved each other ever since. They fitted together and that takes a lot of effort, I realise that now, but they made it look easy. They were a package and one didn't really work without the other, like her old knitting needles or chopsticks. They come in twos.

'The pair of them would finish each other's sentences, only they wouldn't be sentences from the same conversation. They'd both be talking to you about two completely different things, one in each ear and seemingly with no idea the other one was speaking. They were so used to each other, they were like white noise in the background but in other ways, they were so totally in sync it was like they were two parts of the same person.

'And I never heard her complain about Grandad fixing everything with sticky tape and bits of leftover carpet. When he died she gave me a pair of his boots he'd hardly worn because they were too big and inside were two shag-pile insoles. I've still got them in a box. The rest of my memories of the two of them, I'll keep up here forever.' I tapped the side of my head. Drew a breath and swallowed the lump in my throat.

'I don't know what's supposed to happen next. If there's a heaven or reincarnation or nothing but whatever they're doing, they're in the same place and I know wild horses couldn't stop them finding each other again. And for that, I'm truly grateful they're together, even if it means we're not.

'So with that, I'd like to turn it over to Judy Garland singing *Somewhere Over the Rainbow*, because it was Gran's favourite song and that's exactly where I'd like to think she and Grandad both are right now.'

I glance up at the watery expressions gazing back at me with a tenderness I haven't seen in years. Julia smiles at me and squeezes the hand my dad is resting on his shoulder and he nods at me with something like pride.

When the service is over and we've filed past all the flowers and pretended to read the cards, we head back to my aunt's house for the wake. There are old sepia photos of my grandparents on display in the sitting room and it's impossible to avoid talking to anyone as I try to reconcile the old faded images with the people they became.

It's disconcerting how many people seem to know all about me and I make a mental note to thank my dad for making it easier to relive the darkest moments of my life repeatedly all afternoon. Because who wouldn't want that? At a funeral.

I head to the kitchen and wedge myself out of sight between my aunt and sister for protection. Andy passes me a beer and takes the opportunity to re-enact extracts from my performance and it's only now that anyone can laugh.

'So how is the stand up going anyway?' my aunt asks. 'Are you doing any over there?'

'In between twelve-hour shifts and trying to stop the pyscho bitch from hell from destroying me and my children, you mean? Or out on the streets with a little hat in front of me, by my cardboard bed?' She reddens but I didn't mean to make her feel bad. I put my arm around her shoulder and squeeze it. 'I'm kidding. I haven't had a chance to get around to it. Besides, I'd need subtitles flashing up behind me or the bastards wouldn't be able to understand anything I said.'

They've got that look on their faces. That expectant awe I know will be there until it's broken by the creases of their smiles. The sound of unbridled donkey-like braying as though they haven't a care in the world and for a moment it feels like I don't either. They're still looking at me, waiting. 'Honestly. Most Canadians can't distinguish between an accent and a camel hoofing up a hairball. It's like over here, even if someone asked you something in German, you could probably work out what they were trying to say, but there, unless you sound like you're having a stroke, they haven't got a clue.'

Their eyes are shining, lips parted. I can practically hear the laughter bubbling in their throats. It's beginning to feel good. It's beginning to feel normal.

'What do you mean? Can't they understand your chavvy intonation, the poor twats?' Andy asks.

'Understand me? For a start, they all think that I'm Australian, even though there are no Australians in the entire country, it would seem. And then in addition to this crippling defect, they're all morons. Every single one of them.'

Julia giggles. 'You're so rude. They can't be that bad.'

'No? Explain this then. The last time I went to a pub – a *pub,* have you got that? I'm in a pub – and I ask for a beer so the barmaid looks at me with this totally flummoxed expression that would have made a walnut look attractive. So I repeat myself. *Can I have a beer, please?* And she leans towards me and goes *a b....?*

'I say *a beer.* We were in a pub, remember. It's not like I could have been asking for anything else. It's unlikely I wanted a bear or a boar. A bar would have made more sense since we were standing at one but even then... I'm there, like, enunciating with all the strength I can muster in my little overworked mouth muscles and pointing towards the two hundred different bottles off the stuff on the shelves behind her, but she's unable to drag her eyes off me to turn around because I'm this crackpot who can't even speak properly, right?

'So finally I take a deep breath and say it again – grudgingly I might add – in this ridiculous Canadian drawl and she goes *ohh, a beer!* I'm like, *what in the hell else could I possibly have been asking for, you imbecile?*'

'Oh my God, Dan!! Did you say that?' Julia's laughing so much there are tears rolling down her cheeks.

'No, but it wouldn't have mattered if I had. She wouldn't have understood me, the pinheaded dunce. They are all stupid, I am telling you. Actually I lie. They're not. They just go out of their way to give the impression they are. The ones I have to deal with at any rate.'

'You're so mean.'

I am mean. It's not even true, but it feels good to be mean sometimes. Feels good to feel like myself again, that's for sure.

'I thought you said they were really kind and friendly. You told me they'd all been looking out for you.'

'They have. They're still all as thick as poor Julia's ankles though.' I got a punch in the arm for that one, but she's still giggling. 'Even Andy could probably beat them at Trivial Pursuits, if one of the kids helped out.'

He throws his head back and bellows 'And he's back, ladies and gentlemen!'

I laugh that time, but Andy's right. I feel more like myself than I have in years. Just being around these people, absorbing their warmth and not treading on eggshells, living in dread and being criticised all of the time, it almost feels normal, but in the back of my mind, I know that it's not. Not my normal anyway and tomorrow I must get on a plane and fly back across that shark-infested ocean and face the consequences of the life I have made and cannot undo.

My balls drop to my knees at the thought of leaving my home and the closest people to me but my daughters are on the other side of that ocean for reasons I no longer understand and so I must get on that flight, not knowing when I will ever be able to come back.

It feels like the limit of what any man should have to endure but I'll do it for Katie and Lauren and I'd do it a hundred times, even if it breaks me and I know one day it will. Only now, going back is going to hurt more than ever before because I've remembered what it's like to be me, the way it was when I was me. Version 1, back when he didn't even know he had tiny hands.

Easy Come, Easy Go

It is official. The divorce has finally come through. To this day I have no idea when I got married, but I can recite the date it all ended in my sleep. I am single again but no longer young and certainly not free. It's a milestone, but there's still a long way to go before I will really be allowed to move on.

I go to a bar that night to celebrate and as I sit there on my own nursing a beer as slowly as possible so as to avoid having to ask for another, I get chatting (reluctantly) to the dishevelled, scary, tattooed guy next to me. I'm lonely and the options are slim, so when he tells me he's just been released from prison, it doesn't bother me. I spend most of my day with people who are en route to or from jail in some capacity or other and more often than not I've found the only difference between them and me was circumstances or a bad choice somewhere along the line.

The upsetting bit comes later when he asks what I'm doing all the way over from Australia and after the briefest synopsis, he replies, 'Holy Christ, that's depressing!' It really provides some perspective when an ex-con feels sorry for you.

And so he should. The destroyer and I aren't married any more, but she will continue to squeeze my tender nipples until she's milked me dry. I'm handing over $2250 a month to an arsehole I now legally own on a financial level. She doesn't work and she doesn't need to. I am her own personal welfare state and there's always more stuff to pay for. More extra curricular activities she's signed the girls up for so she doesn't actually have to parent them at any time. More dance classes that require special shoes and new costumes every time there's a show, which she'll insist on sitting next to me throughout. More gymnastics training, which necessitates completely different but seemingly identical leotards as the ballet. More tap dancing shoes and outfits, which appear to be – well, see all of the above.

I am grateful she doesn't sign them up for horse riding lessons until, of course, she does. And I must pay my half of every one of these new hobbies without complaint or be subject to a barrage of abuse about my failings as a father and a man. I disagree but I've learnt to pick my battles. I've had to. I'd spend my whole life fighting them if not and there's nothing that would please her more.

My sister says I'd feel better about things if I accepted that Philippa is genuinely mentally ill and managed her with the same detached judgement as I would any old fruitcake reeking of piss and paranoia. But that would take empathy and compassion and I'm years beyond either. This chain around my neck has wrung me out of any understanding and she continues to bleed me for anything she can get. Any overtime I do is gleefully divided between us, in her favour. Every pay rise for me is money for her.

Between Philippa and the taxman, I get to start a ten-hour shift at eight o'clock in the morning and by eleven o'clock I'm done. I've earned my dollars for the day. The next seven hours belong to the state and the creature I hate most in the world and hilariously she wants to use my *borrowing power* so she can get a mortgage (in my name) when the sale of the house in Burlington goes through. But that would mean I wouldn't ever be able to get one myself yet I'd be tied to her financially for all time, so I refuse.

I'm actually getting better at saying no to the big things now I have an irrefutable right so see my daughters. Standing up to her doesn't help my domestic situation at all though, because while I have the credit history and income (at least on paper) to get a loan, I won't have a big enough deposit to buy my own place for the next fifty years, while Philippa could afford a small apartment with her share of the old house, but would rather rent something wildly disproportionate to her (my) income which is nonetheless more befitting of her style.

But then my gran comes to the rescue one final time. My dad has calculated how long he has left to live (optimistically in my opinion) and deducted that exact sum from his inheritance. The rest he's divided between Julia and me. My sister's going to put hers towards a loft extension like a normal person who has not pissed their life up the wall so many times they have no walls left to piss up.

And I, in a total reverse of fortunes, can suddenly afford to buy some more walls of my own. Dad only lends me the money indefinitely since Philippa's madness doesn't extend to fighting for 80% of my debts and once the other sale goes through, I'm able to put it all into a one and a half-bedroom apartment on Kings Street West.

The half is not a bedroom at all, but more of an alcove off the sitting room with huge floor to ceiling windows and a view of the bustling street below but I can fit a bunk bed in it and have plans to somehow divide it off although that will leave the rest of the room in darkness. It's not ideal but it's so far removed from sleeping on sofas and airbeds, it feels like a palace. There's a communal laundry room on every floor, a gym and a swimming pool in the basement, which becomes exclusively ours the moment Katie and Lauren let out a blood-curdling shriek as they practise their dive bombs.

The rest of the residents are mostly fresh-faced singletons with trendy careers and social lives that don't involve playgrounds or ball pits and I doubt any of them have realised the corner they set the Xbox up in is actually a second bedroom or even a bit of one, but after everything we've been through it's more than we need. It's a sanctuary. It is peace and it is ours.

I'm a long way from the end of this journey, but as I listen to my daughters breathing gently a few feet away there's a small and broken part of me which slowly starts to believe I can do this. There are a few metres cubed on the earth I can sit in without anybody screaming at me, even during the hours I might reasonably be expected to sleep. I'm allowed to exist here without being followed around and shouted at. Keep it spotless knowing that no one will make a great fat mess everywhere and then expect me to clean it.

It is an oasis, a place of safety for the three of us. It's our home and no one else has the key. For the first time in their little lives, the girls can relax and be themselves.

It's so nice in fact that when the maddest woman never to have been sanctioned comes to pick them up for the first time she goes completely berserk and drags them out without their shoes on, yelling all the way down the corridor that she is destitute while I'm living in the lap of luxury. It's a very small lap, but apparently she preferred it when I was reduced to residing in a rented shithole even if her own children had to live in it too. Their distraught wails are muffled by the elevator doors closing as it takes them away and I return to my oasis and cry, only realising then that I'm far from being out of reach from the one person I want to hide away from.

Philippa is lazy, demented and completely out of her box but she's never been stupid and she knows full well my dad will be long dead before he asks for his loan back. By her logic we were still officially married when my gran died and so therefore she's entitled to a share of her money. The phone calls to my father begin shortly afterwards and the time difference is no obstacle to her, but then she's not the one trying to sleep.

What begins as a slightly uncomfortable chat about the nature of our financial arrangement soon becomes a demand for compensation, firstly because George is responsible for raising the sort of selfish, neglectful bastard who would abandon his family and leave them with nothing and secondly for introducing me to the *Art of Adultery* at an early and influential age and then thirdly (it did go on a bit) for bringing the *home-wrecking bitch* he left us for across to Canada so she could ruin our marriage as well.

She's relentless but she's also on speakerphone and hell hath no fury like a woman scorned at two o'clock in the morning. If Elizabeth was incapable of squeezing her butt cheeks together and holding it in when my whole life was at stake, I can only imagine what came out when she felt she had nothing to lose. I have to imagine because I only hear the censored version from my dad and Philippa's own wildly exaggerated adaption, which naturally does not include the prologue or the purpose of her call.

A few more lively debates are exchanged until Dad and Elizabeth finally stop answering the phone so never one to play favourites, Philippa turns her attention to my mum who she blames for letting this happen. For allowing her own grandchildren to live like paupers while their father squanders away all their (her) money on a bachelor pad in downtown Toronto. She's not impressed when my mum (who's been rehearsing this speech for a while) points out that it was her idea to move to Toronto and those grandchildren live in that bachelor pad half of the time. Not only that, but since Philippa did so staggering well out of the divorce settlement she could probably afford to buy the penthouse upstairs (I'm also not impressed when she says this). Thankfully, old moneybags has already spent a huge chunk of it on a Lexus (which is excellent planning if she intends to eventually live in it).

The only one who isn't treated to an early morning wake up call is Julia but she gets quite an email instead, mainly regarding the lack of sympathy (and legal tender) she has bestowed on Philippa and the girls since the separation and now divorce. I only know about this because Julia replies in the heat of the moment and then calls me immediately afterwards to apologise.

'I'm so sorry. I don't know what came over me. I just couldn't hold back anymore.'

My heart sinks but I tell her she'd feel better about things if she accepted that Philippa is genuinely mentally ill and managed her with the same detached judgement as she would any old fruitcake reeking of piss and paranoia.

She laughs sheepishly and I manage to convince her that I'm less irritated than I am. But I am irritated. I get that my family all have their own beef with the nutcase, entirely at her own invitation of course, but just because I no longer live with her, doesn't mean she isn't everywhere I turn.

If she were to fall – accidentally say – from a burning building and onto some railings where she was impaled and roasted alive, I would be gutted because I'd never be able to enjoy a doner kebab again without thinking of her. As far as the rest goes, I would turn the rotisserie myself. But until that day, keeping her relatively stable is still my main focus and it's bad enough trying to tame Elizabeth, let alone the one person I thought I could trust to understand the consequences of engaging in battle with a psycho who also happens to be my ex.

Philippa's emails and the phone calls stop abruptly, but I know this won't be the end of it. It's merely the calm before the storm but for now she reverts to just making my life a misery, which is easier to handle but will never be okay.

Part of any parent's job is keeping their children safe and in my case this means teaching them how to cross a minefield of incomprehensible emotions and survive. There are rules we must adhere to in order to reduce the risk of unwittingly setting off a chain of events that starts with, for example, a throwaway comment about the weather and ends with someone threatening to drown the dog in a bucket full of rain.

I don't want to talk badly to them about their mother. She is their mother after all and while she's utterly deranged, I don't want them to know that, not exactly. But I do need them to understand how to handle her. What to say, what not to say, how to react and how not to. How to identify a safe place and hide in it when the person who's supposed to protect them, is unexpectedly derailed.

But there are things a five and a six-year-old say without fear of the consequences such as revealing they've watched My Little Pony on the iPad, eaten Chococrispies for breakfast or had a sweet in the park. Any one of these might be perceived as indications of child abuse and an infraction on my part results immediately in sharply toned emails and irate voicemails left unanswered on my phone.

It's hard to get the balance of trying to give the girls a nice time, a normal time I should say, like any other kids and keeping them out of harm's way. And so depressingly I tend to err on the side of caution. Too afraid of their indiscretion to shower them with the treats and rewards they truly deserve. But kids are simple. All they want is attention and I'm accomplished at providing it in droves.

Philippa's left the dog with us again because the girls miss him terribly when they're with me. He's also a massive inconvenience, needs walking twice daily, has reflux and is hard to take skiing, but that's irrelevant and nothing to do with it.

He is quite cute admittedly and I enjoy it when he stays so I make a point of seeming put out whenever she ditches him on me and so she ditches him as often as she can. He's up to my knees now and still growing. One huge drooling ball of fluff that leaves traces of himself wherever he goes, like crumbs in a children's story, only gross.

Fortunately, there's a playground and a garden in the grounds of the apartment complex. It may be small but it's free and I can get them here without scooters, roller blades, bicycles or losing the will to live. Between this and the money I save on public swimming pools, I figure by the time they're teenagers the condo will have paid for itself.

Sometimes we meet a flame-headed, tattooed English guy there with his equally red-haired (but as yet un-inked) daughter, Sadie. He's in more or less the same situation as me. Divorced, trapped and totally buggered, though his ex doesn't sound quite as scary as mine, but I'm biased. She's certainly awful enough and though I wouldn't wish what I've been through on anyone, it's been good having Dom the Butcher to talk to, especially once we'd established that he was an actual butcher, not an assassin (it was a disconcerting introduction).

There's no sign of them, but no matter. The girls have each other and there's a climbing frame, a swing and a slide they can play on while I walk the dog around on a lead behind a mist of his smelly flyaway hair.

Lala hangs off the ladder. 'Will I break my leg if I fall off the monkey bars, Daddy?'

'Well, you might so hold on to it properly.'

'Will I break my other leg?'

'Probably not, but don't fall off it.'

'If I break my leg and my other leg, will I still be able to poop?'

'Yes, Lala. You will still be able to poop.'

It's starting to turn chilly as the sun begins to fade. I give the first of what will be at least seven status alerts regarding the need to head upstairs in a minute. I'm on the third when out of nowhere a rat in a leopard skin coat and booties scuttles around the corner. I say a rat. It's one of those dogs ladies keep in their handbags, presumably to stop them from scaring passers by. Its dubious canine heritage is established over the course of an intense bum sniffing session which I do not partake in since I'm too busy rolling my eyes sympathetically at its owner and good for her, if she's embarrassed to be seen with it (she should be), she hides it fairly well.

'Oh my God!' she exclaims Canadianly from behind an oversized woolly scarf and ridiculous pom pom hat. 'He's so gorgeous. What's his name?'

I glance down at the source of scrappy clawing at my feet and bury the urge to kick the thing over a bush.

'Stan,' I reply.

'No it's not, Daddy.' Katie leaps off the slide to get a closer look at the freak fest. Lauren follows her over and starts swinging around my thigh. The rodent hybrid sniffs her and I try to recall when she last had her tetanus shot. 'It's Starlight Twinkle Toes.'

'Stop it, girls,' I admonish, rubbing the scruff of Stan's neck. 'You're embarrassing him.'

'It's what?' Pom Pom cries. 'Star...? Oh my gosh. I love it! Did you name him yourselves or did your daddy come up with that?'

'I choose Starlight and Lala wanted Twinkle Toes.'

'That's awesome. You guys should give my little doggy a new name. He's called André, but I don't think he likes it.'

'André?' I say, one eyebrow arching involuntarily and my voice higher than is natural.

'Yeah, I know. I thought it was funny at the time.'

'He looks like a Rainbow Fairy Dust to me,' I continue.

'You reckon! What do you think, girls? Shall I call him Rainbow Fairy Dust?' and they laugh and say that's not a real name.

'Silly Daddy,' she cries and the way that she says it makes me look at her again.

'Daddy, let's go,' Lauren wails. 'You said one minute and that was fifty-ninety minutes ago.'

'Well, you've got five more before the sun goes down completely.'

Pom Pom ruffles Starlight Twinkle Toes' ears and a lock of blonde hair swings gently across her eyes. She straightens up and as she brushes it away, she smiles and I can't even tell if I am smiling back. I seem to have lost control of my face.

'*Now*, Daddy.'

'Three more times down the slide.'

'I'm cooooooooooooold!'

'I'll let you go,' the blonde grins. 'But I guess I'll see you around. If you live here…?'

'I do. We do. Me and the girls. They're here half the time. I share custody, with their mother. We're…'

'Wow. That's amazing. We should arrange a play-date then, for Rainbow Fairy Dust and Starlight Twinkle Toes.'

'He'd like that.'

And with that she's gone and the girls and I go back to the apartment to play *Princessopoly*, which is even more boring than it sounds, but for the first time in ages I can't seem to stop smiling.

Not Quite Wales But Somewhere Like That

It's been six months since Tammy and I got together and I still can't say her name without sounding sarcastic, but things are good. It was a novelty at first being thanked for making dinner by someone who then told me how delicious it was, but I'm slowly getting used to it.

She lives three floors above me and rents one of the bigger apartments with a friend, who seems very nice, but she doesn't go out much. All that really means is that Tammy stays over at my place most nights when the girls are at Philippa's, but so far when they're here we've kept it casual, more out of fear of upsetting Crazy Eyes than alarming the kids who think she's wonderful, but then she is.

Stan and André greet each other every other week as though they've never stuck their noses into such lovely anuses before and although Tammy and I stopped pretending to be surprised whenever our dog walks coincided months ago, she's only recently begun to join us afterwards for an excruciating game or two of something idiotic while I get on with making tea.

'What are we playing, girls?'

'Chutes and ladders!"

'Again? Come on then, but I'm gonna beat you this time!'

She's an absolute natural with Katie and Lauren. Makes cookies and does crafts, has already learnt all the Little Ponies' names and plays with them for hours. She's like an aunty who doesn't have kids of her own and can still bring herself to spend time with other people's when she could otherwise be drinking alone. She even talks to them as though everything that comes out of their mouths isn't charming nonsensical gibberish.

'Do you know I do a poo when I laugh?'

'Wow, that's…I don't really know what to say to that.'

'Do you do a poo when you laugh?'

'No, but I sometimes do a wee when I sneeze.'

'I like sneezing.'

'I like sneezing too.'

'I know.'

'Next time we can do a sneeze together.'

'That sounds awesome. I'd love that!'

'In the toilet.'

'Yeah, sure.'

It's also quite nice having sex with someone who doesn't make me want to peel the skin off my groin afterwards to feel clean. She's five years younger than me and earns a third more which is somewhat refreshing after the last few years of austerity. What's more, I'm pretty sure I like her job even more than she does. She's in charge of marketing for a beer company, has ambition, travels the globe and brings home lots of samples. Not only that but she's contractually bound to use the company credit card to buy three thousand dollars worth of booze every year to keep their sales figures ticking over. Any booze as long as it's their own. Wine, spirits, beer obviously. It's almost too perfect. And when I ask her, my heart in my throat, how she feels about children, she says she likes them but she's far too busy with her career to want any of her own. Ever. Boom!

The situation is ideal for both of us. She has a readymade family, but gets to do the fun bits and leaves me to deal with the everyday tedium of trying to put their shoes on for half an hour when we're leaving the house. Of insisting they take their coats because it's freezing only to carry them awkwardly over my shoulder for the rest of the day. Of telling them they can't go to the toilet during dinner and talking about nothing else until they do. Of not losing it completely when they eventually return and complain their food's cold. Of not letting them watch fat men fall over on YouTube and if they do, making sure that they don't tell their mother. Of asking them to do everything at least fifteen bloody times.

Meanwhile Tammy (even writing it…) actually listens and responds when they talk, praises them in proportion to what they've done, not as though they've cured cancer one minute and released a deadly nerve gas the next, encourages them and shows them by example to aim high, work hard and never stop trying. To be proud of being strong, but to never use that strength to hurt or belittle other people. To be independent women with voices that should and will be heard. She's a breath of fresh air after years of smog and diesel fumes choking my lungs and withering my gonads.

Philippa heard all about her from Katie and Lauren on day one, of course and even before the dog walks turned into play-dates she'd realised there was more going on than me simply being on friendly terms with the neighbours.

She's adamant it's too confusing for the girls if she stays over and for once I don't completely disagree. I wouldn't have even introduced them by this stage if they hadn't met already but since they had and Tammy's such a positive influence, I broke my own rules and invited her into our lives.

When we're together, it feels like we're a real family, the way it was always meant to be. She even looks like the girls with her blonde hair and blue eyes so when people assume she's their mother, it's easier to go along with it than bother to explain. Plus, it makes the little fantasies I still have about the soul sucker not being around all the more authentic.

Philippa insisted on being introduced to her and though I managed to put it off for a few months, it had to happen at some point and fortunately when it did, old Lizard Face was on the charm offensive trying to make a good impression.

'It won't last,' I warn Tammy, but I can see that no matter what I've told her, she's surprised that my ex is nothing like she imagined. But then that was the point. She's lowered her guard and all Philippa has to do is sit back like a spider and let her walk into her web.

But then maybe not. The real reason I've gotten away with any of this is she's also seeing someone. Barry's a banker, a millionaire no less, who she's fond of telling me all about, especially if it involves a private yacht or the Montreal Gran Prix. He has his own grown up children and a wife who is as yet unaware of the situation. It's tempting to drop her quick line but Philippa's enjoying her new role of Mistress of the Manor so much, it's nothing but advantageous for me.

It's slightly ironic that I'm genuinely delighted she's landed herself such a prize but she's overjoyed at being screwed for money (there's a word for that, but I forget) so long may it last.

As long as she's deliriously happy and otherwise preoccupied she's not thinking up ways to shaft me. She's finally passed her degree and is planning on doing a PGCE. My heart goes out to the poor saps that end up with her for a teacher, but if her time scale is anything like that of the last course she'll be eligible for retirement before she's even qualified.

For my part, I've passed my Detective's exam (again) and been promoted. The hours are better and I don't have to do nightshifts anymore, which means I no longer feel like the walking dead when I pick the girls up for the handover on zero to two hours sleep.

We have them for one week each now rather than four days, which is less unsettling for them and means I have to see the hustler slightly less. The team that I work with are great too. That is to say they don't walk like a bunch of pigeons and can talk about more than ice hockey and football (which is not freaking football at all. Use a different word. The ball gets kicked about once every bloody game). They are almost (but not quite) completely inoffensive or maybe I'm getting used to them now.

The promotion came with a pay rise, which is of more benefit to my ex than me, so I barely notice it. More importantly, as far as my sanity goes, it's got me out of traffic duty and onto more interesting cases so I don't feel like driving headlong into fifty-ton trucks as they hurtle towards me endlessly on the highway. The next step is taking my Sergeant's exam and at that point I'll be almost back to where I was when I left the Met nearly three years ago.

Things are finally falling into place. I have a house (one and a half-bed apartment), I have my daughters by my side (50% of the time), a girlfriend (complete with rodent infestation - or dog as she calls it) and a job that doesn't drive me mad with colleagues I don't want to kill (all the time) so apart from the fact I still have a Philippa (and a Linda, who's back from the UK and yapping at her heels), life is good and I finally feel like I'm moving forward instead of treading water.

Banana Brains has even agreed to let me take the girls to England in the summer without putting up a fight. She can't object because she's already taken them away on various Barry-funded trips to Barbados and several different ski resorts, as you do. I have them for three weeks in August (she has them in July) but even so there was a time when she would have challenged me. But those days are behind us.

Whether or not she likes Bazza for his striking wit and personality or for his money (hmm?) she's on best behaviour, probably until she gets herself knocked up and invites him at point blank range to shackle himself down to her. I've met him and he seems like a pretty decent bloke. Apart from cheating on his wife, but who am I to judge with my deviant history? I almost feel I should warn him, but there's no one on earth I like that much. So off to the slaughter he must go, poor little lamb while I sit and plan a lovely holiday with my made-to-order family.

There are a number of issues that I need to discuss with Philippa in terms of logistics and maintaining contact with the girls while they're with her and vice versa so we meet up in a coffee shop. I feel so carefree and cheerful I don't even mind when she orders her $4 cappuccino and walks away to find a table leaving me at the counter to pay for it and bring it across like the staff.

I'm about to suggest we Skype the girls every day when we don't have them unless they're travelling or she's been crushed in an escalator or contracted rabies (though how would we know?). What I'm totally unprepared for is Philippa announcing she thinks that when I take them to England, we should stay there forever and she'll join us. With her mum.

It's everything I've dreamed of for years, but I don't understand why it's happening right now. I say I thought she was happy. She says she is but if she does her PGCE in Canada it'll cost her (me) $30K and they're inundated with teachers here so there's no guarantee she'll even get a job at the end of it. Meanwhile in the UK, they're so desperate they'll actually give her a bursary to study, bite her arms off to employ her and make her head of department within the week. Probably and assuming they a have a governmental quota of physically challenged employees to meet.

I say I've got an apartment here. She says *you can sell it*. I say I've just got a new job. She says *you can still transfer back*. I say what about Barry?

'What about him?' she says. 'I'm just thinking about the girls and their future. They have family in England, but over here it's only us and my mum. They need a bigger support network and it's really important to surround them with people who love and want to protect them. It takes a village after all. We still know lots of people over there and the girls will make new friends really quickly. I'll be working soon. I can't be around all the time to look after them and who knows how long your parents have left? They're pretty old after all.'

I don't ask what about Tammy? I already know. But even so, we have talked hypothetically about moving to the UK and she said she'd love to. Her company has offices all over the world and there's one not far from Epsom. She's close to her family but they could easily visit (there's always a downside).

A little bubble of excitement is growing inside me. I need to check I can get my old job back in London and I'm not sure I'll be able to afford much to live in, but with Tammy on board we could probably buy something quite nice to get us started. I can't believe it's really happening. For once I'm not even dreaming about lacing Philippa's coffee with drain cleaning fluid.

I almost bounce back from our meeting, hardly able to keep my thoughts straight in my head. I call the HR department at the Met before I speak to anyone else. There's no point getting everyone excited if I can't get my job back after all. There's no way that I can start at the bottom for the third time so it has to be Detective Sargent or nothing.

I hold my breath and a little piece of my heart back as I explain that I left three years before but I'd like to go back and it's all I can do not to shoot one out there and then as I'm told that it's no problem at all. Not at all. It wouldn't matter if I'd been out of work all this time or spent it delivering online grocery shopping. As long as I reapply within five years of leaving there's no issue at all with me picking up from where I left off. Unless of course, I've left the country for more than one year. One year.

It doesn't matter that I've been in Canada, not training for jihad in an undisclosed location in the Middle East and it's totally irrelevant that I've been working as a policeman for the entire time I've apparently not been a policeman. The fact my station has a picture of Queen Elizabeth II in every other office is of no consequence either. I may as well have been renting my sweet buttocks out at an hourly rate.

There's only one way I can return to the Met and it's as likely as sharing a burger with the Dalai Lama or successfully giving yourself head. In order to get back in I would have to receive special permission from, at the very least, the Deputy Commissioner, which is the second highest-ranking position in the entire force. So no biggie.

I think, at first, the whole deal is off, but then I remember that my old Superintendent, Jim Nichols is best friends with said bigwig. *Like brothers*, I believe was the phrase. And although I haven't personally met him, Jimmy Boy speaks to him on my behalf and while there are a few hoops to jump through, it may take some time and isn't guaranteed even then, he doesn't think it'll be a problem.

It's not as straightforward as it could be, but then when is anything I ever do? I have to make this happen, even if it means relying on the skills I honed in public toilets during my alleged, if unmemorable, gay phase.

Next I speak to my sister to talk it through and check it would be okay to stay with her when we go over. It'll take a few weeks to find something to rent and we certainly can't buy until Tammy and I have both got a few payslips under our belts. Julia's even more elated than me if that's possible and I'm pretty sure I can still hear her shrieking after we hang up the phone. Long story short, we can stay with her for as long as we like. We were going to anyway for most of August and if we start looking as soon as we arrive we can probably find something short-term to rent that will do us until we can get another mortgage.

'It's so exciting! I can't believe it! Whatever it takes, Dan. Just get yourself back here!' I put a tick in that box.

I start to feel guilty about Dom the Butcher. Ninety per cent of our conversation consists of reminiscing about home and fantasising about going back, but I know what he'd tell me.

'Do it, mate! What are you waiting for? And take me with you, ya bastard. Where am I gonna find another sad wanker to bore the tits off me now?'

There is someone else I should probably mention all this to, but I know Tammy's going to love the idea too. She's already told me she does. But it turns out when she said *it would be amazing to live in England*, she meant *it would be amazing to live in England*, if all of her family, friends, job and dog were not here.

I say that André can come too, in her hand luggage probably, unless pest control get to him first. I also point out her company has an office in Weybridge, a mere twenty-five minute drive from Epsom, which is even better than her current commute. Besides which, she's always travelling so instead of flying to the UK and Europe all the time, she'd be going back the other way to Canada so she'll probably see more of her friends and family than she does now. And, of course, they'd be welcome stay with us in Surrey (as long as they keep a wide berth).

It's a big ask obviously but it's what my family will have to do if I continue to stay here and she did say she wanted to live in the UK but it turns out she was speaking Canadian where everything is awesome and amazing until you realise it isn't.

I'm gutted but I have to keep moving forward with this and I'm convinced if push comes to shove, Tammy will see that emigrating is a real opportunity for her, both career-wise and for our relationship. She loves the girls too much already to let us leave and it's a gamble, but I need to be back with my family and the friends I've known for years. I had thought that going back for holidays would keep me sane but now I realise it will never be enough. I need to live there. I need a really good belly laugh at least six times a day and to moan about the weather because there's a little bit of drizzle and not a mountain of snow I've got to dig my way out of. I need to buy food in packets that feed a family of four not four hundred plus guests and puts your back out trying to get it into the car. I need to have conversations that don't make me want to smash the face in of whomever I'm talking to. And I really need to be with the people I love.

Everything is slightly out of reach and I know it will be an uphill struggle but if it gets me home it will be worth risking it all and so I agree to meet Philippa again to talk it over and maybe finalise details.

She's over the moon when I tell her I'm almost convinced going back is the best course of action. There are a number of outstanding issues I'll need to resolve if it's all to work out but in principle and all being well we should be able to move back to Epsom over the summer and get the girls into school there by September. And then she tells me she's just read an *Article Online* about Shropshire.

'Apparently it's one of the safest places to live in the world.' She purrs and the hairs on the back of my neck stiffen like there's a storm coming.

'That may be…' My fingers tighten around the mug and I focus on the heat searing through it. 'But would you even be able to find it on a map?'

'I'm not taking them back to live in a warzone, Daniel.' The nostrils are out. I clear my throat and swill the coffee.

'The leafy suburbs of Surrey are hardly that.'

The air is electric. 'You might not care about putting the girls lives in danger, Dan, but I do. I'm their mother and while we're at it, maybe you could remind your little Tampax friend of that.' Ha, Tampax. Good one.

'It's just that if I am going to give up everything all over again, I need to be close enough to London to commute.'

'They have policemen all over the UK, Dan. Are you an idiot?'

Probably, but I still know there's no point moving back to the middle of nowhere. Instead I say, 'What happened to needing people around when you go back to work?'

'The girls will have my mother. And their father if you can be arsed to lift a finger to look after them. Which will be the day,' and then she snorts and I realise this is madness. That either Barry has some links to bloody Shropshire or else it's just another symptom of her utter lunacy.

If I move back under her terms, I'll be no better off than I am over here, miles from anyone I know and with far less reason for them to ever come and visit. I mean Shropshire, for God's sake!? I'm sure it's very nice but we don't know anybody there. But she will not be moved. It's Shropshire or nothing. So I say nothing then. Nothing changes. I'm not risking my job, the roof over my head and my relationship to go somewhere I don't know and start all over again.

If we even get there. Knowing Philippa she'll let me hand my notice in, sell my apartment, break up with Tammy, buy my ticket and then inform me that she's just read another

Article Online about how cheap the property market is in Syria these days and how if we hurry I could pick her up a bargain. This is another one of her temporary delusions and even if it's not, it makes no sense for me to agree.

So that's what I tell her. If we can't move back to Epsom or somewhere close to London and my friends and family, we're not moving back at all.

'Well in that case you can forget about taking the girls to England this summer or ever again. I withdraw my consent and I will fuck you up, Daniel. I will screw your whole life up until you beg me to forget you ever said no, you fucking arsewipe. I've put up with enough of your shit for too long. You don't get to tell me where I have to live. This is my life. You're just dead weight clinging onto it.

'Well, fuck that. This time you're going to let go before I sink you. And I will fucking sink you, Daniel. You want a war? Well, congratulations. You've got it. God damn Tin Man.'

I don't want a fight on my hands, but I have one. There's no going back now and no escape. Everything else I've been through before this will compare to a disappointing minibreak to Blackpool by the time she's done with me. I never asked for this war, but she will take me dead or alive and if it's alive, I guarantee I'll wish I'd been disembowelled when I had the chance.

As my sister says, if only Philippa used her powers of evil for good, she'd have been a national treasure by now, but I have a feeling this is not going to be one of those occasions. Her powers of evil are going to be otherwise engaged in battle and all I can do is batten down the hatches and pray. And get myself a bloody good solicitor or this isn't going to end well. If indeed it ever ends at all.

White vs. White

By the time we go to court I'm shitting myself. Between the maintenance, spousal support and school fees I'm left with almost nothing to live on but air, which I hardly dare breathe in case I've missed some hidden charges in the small print. The cost of plane tickets is going up daily and I've already spent a fortune on solicitors getting the paperwork in order. The separation agreement stipulates that I have joint custody of the children but there's nothing about leaving the country in it. Even if there were, Philippa has the girls' passports and without them we can't book the tickets, let alone fly.

My lawyer, Stella, is brilliant but she's pregnant and I only hope she can hold the baby in until the trial. She has years of experience but she's never dealt with anyone as toxic and deranged as my ex-wife. She's confident this is an open and closed case but I know only too well Philippa makes a great first impression when she wants to and can bend any truth into a lie. Or just lie. Fabricate, deceive, misrepresent and distort anything so confidently that in the end she believes it herself. And how do you deal with that?

How do you reason with someone who's completely unreasonable?

Paradoxically, for all Philippa hates Tammy and she really does hate her, let me clarify that. This is no state of hostility, animosity or loathing, this is the sort of reaction you might expect if she'd raped, flayed and murdered the children, not taught them to play Ludo and done their hair in French plaits. But all her hatred has achieved is to push us closer together, both emotionally as Tammy supports me and stands by my side, as well as financially because something had to give other than my knees. She's moved in and pays half the mortgage or rather the court fees, which is swings and roundabouts, because it is all the same thing. A dark hole that only seems to get deeper every time I try to dig my way out.

I'm haemorrhaging money I don't have, but if I don't stand up to Philippa on this one issue, there'll always be something else and I won't be blackmailed into doing what she wants every time she changes her mind. I have to take a stand even though the consequences are far-reaching and vile.

Every day when I drop off or pick the girls up from school I'm the lone male in the playground and I have to stand and wait with dozens of women glowering at me. Every last one of them has been told that I'm a wife beater, an adulterer or worse and I have no way of defending myself without terrifying every one of them simply by approaching or opening my mouth.

I'm not a *Mother* after all, merely a weird dad who actually wants to be a part of his daughters' daily lives and not just take them for ice cream every other Sunday. I must deserve this suspicion and so I endure the disdainful expressions, the dirty looks and hateful whispers that follow me around like I'm a predatory pervert that must be monitored.

I despise every last one of the malicious gossipmongers and look forward to the day they unwittingly put a foot wrong with the maniac and feel the full weight of her wrath. And I'll know exactly when this happens because in a complete about-turn, there'll be big smiles and how-are-you-Dans the way there always are when they realise they've been duped and strung along. When they finally get to meet the real Philippa and she sucker punches the supercilious smirks clean off their startled faces.

Linda's also desperate to get back to England and start living off the state again so like a dog with a bone, she has her teeth bared and is gnawing away on the gristle. I avoid them as much as I can, but they insist on coming to watch the girls at their after-school activities on my time and sit behind me conspiring and glaring at me. Then there are the multiple phone calls, texts and emails that turn my phone into a Taser, setting me off balance even though I'm constantly taut with tension waiting for the beep.

There are complaints about me administering medicine when Katie has a cold, complaints about me not administering it for a graze, complaints about Lauren's teeth which the dentist said needed two fillings and is down to me only feeding them sweets. Complaints about the fact dentists and doctors are free in the UK, but over here they cost a fortune. Complaints that I refuse to lie on my insurance declaration at work, which means Philippa can't claim for medical and dental cover as well as the girls. Complaints they are watching too much telly and eating too much crap, going to bed too late and not doing enough homework. They're on the iPad all the time and playing up after the handover and none of it's true except for their behaviour when I take them back to her house every week only to wrench them out of my arms and leave them wailing on the doorstep as she holds them back from running after me. And then I drive home feeling sick with guilt and reliving the moments I shared with them as I try not to cry.

'Am I your special girl, Daddy?' Lauren's nose has a special way of crinkling when she's testing me.

'Yes, darling. You know you are.'

'But you said Kiki's your special girl.'

'You're both my special girls. Kiki's my Special Kiki and you're my Special Lala.'

'But if I'm special, will a bad man steal me?' She turns to me, all eyes and elbows.

'What? No, Lala. Where have you got that from?'

'If he steals me, is he gonna to steal me or is he going to steal money?'

'He's going to steal money, hon, he's not going to steal you.' I kiss the top of her head and she looks up at me with a sincerity that threatens to break my heart.

'But I've got monies.'

'He's not going to steal your money. Don't worry about things like that.'

'But I thought bad guys steal money.'

'They know better than to come here looking for money, sweetheart.' I hug her tighter and stroke her soft hair, inhale the scent of it. Rest my eyes for a moment.

'Does Mummy have money?'

'Yes, darling, Mummy's got lots of money but no one's going to steal it. They'd be silly billies to even try.'

'Also I don't want you to die or turn into a granny.'

'I promise I won't turn into a granny.'

'I love you, Daddy.'

She stares up at me and this time my heart really does break. My chest hitches and I take a shallow breath to steady it, clench my teeth until I'm able to speak. 'I love you too, Lala.'

The court date finally arrives and if it needs clarifying, I haven't slept at all in the weeks building up to it. This is not the first time we've been here, but it's the day we'll present our case before the judge and he'll decide if I'm able to take my own children to my own country to see my own family or if he'll open a Pandora's Box of horrors which will plague me for years.

I'm quietly confident, not only in as much as I'm obviously in the right, but because when we filed the initial court order and booked the hearing we heard the same judge rule on the case preceding our own. It was a similar dispute to mine in many respects only this guy had a job that paid eighty grand a year and he quit it. His reasoning was that when he worked, his ex-wife took all his money and he was so busy he could hardly see his kids. Her response was to stop him seeing them at all but as he ruled, Judge Weiner's words ricocheted around my head.

'I have sat here for thirteen years in front of men informing me they don't have the time or money to spend on their kids. On the rare occasion I have a man telling me he wants to see his children, I am always going to listen.'

And I heard what he said and thought did you catch all of that, you insane arsehole? But if she had, it hadn't sunk in because she steamed ahead until now, the day of reckoning and the day all this ends.

Philippa has employed the world's most expensive solicitor. An ugly, steel haired battle-axe, covered in moles, who takes the time to turn around in her chair and glare needlessly at me from two feet away with no idea that she's the one representing the psychopath. They try to get Tammy thrown out of the court, but there's no law saying she can't sit behind us so Philippa resorts to simply scowling back at her for much of the proceedings.

Linda's not here, which I find staggering since they wipe each other's arses but it's telling that neither is Barry even though he's clearly footing the bill. I can only imagine she doesn't want anyone seeing how well she can lie and the lengths she'll go to annihilate me. And anyone else who doesn't comply. Stella pats my hand and I glance down at her bump.

'All okay?' I ask tentatively and she winks.

'We're going to get through this. Don't worry.'

But I can't not. The contents of my bowels have turned to liquid and I can only squeeze so much. I look back at Tammy and she smiles, bravely ignoring the filthy energy my ex-wife is projectile vomiting at her two rows ahead. My stomach grumbles and my rectum muscles tense.

I'm relieved when Judge Weiner shuffles in, almost eighty if he is a day but not dead of a heart attack yet, though there's still time before the end of this hearing so I will him to survive a few more hours. Or even longer if he'd like. He's a small man with a friendly wrinkled face, little round glasses and a pair of Nikes under his gown. I try to read him, but he's completely impartial and never wavers from his torturous neutral expression and unloaded tone.

I'm the one who brought the case against Philippa for not allowing me to take the girls on holiday and it's she who must try to defend her stance. Her main bones of contention are that firstly she does 't understand why the children need to see family they hardly know in England, when that very same family have already visited them numerous times here in Canada. Equally she feels it's important to immigrate back to the UK so the children can maintain strong relationships with the family she doesn't want them to see.

On top of this she's their *Mother* and they cannot be expected to survive all alone with only a man to look after them. It goes without saying that she's worried the girls will not cope with being apart from her for such a long period of time and yet according to the separation agreement she wrote herself, they'll be apart from her regardless for three weeks whether it's here or in England. But of course, if they're here she can continue to turn up uninvited and see them during the time they're meant to be with me.

She's concerned the girls will be travelling around so much they won't have a chance to stay in contact with her regularly over Skype (which they need in order to maintain the high levels of anxiety they exhibit whenever she calls) and worse, if they're to be dragged from pillar to post (who even has a pillar or a post?) they won't recover from the jetlag and may suffer irreparable neurological damage or feel a little bit woozy.

Fortunately I'm able to alleviate her fears her as we will be spending the first ten days in London with Julia so they'll have plenty of time to get over the trip. The same trip she has no qualms about doing if we immigrate.

But there's a problem with my sister's house too, she cries shrilly over the top of her lawyer. She's visited it numerous times and can personally vouch for the fact it's too small to accommodate four extra guests, so it must be a relief for her to hear that since then, not only has Julia added a huge extension onto the back of the kitchen but there are two extra bedrooms in the loft. If that's too many numbers for you, altogether it's a total of five and they only use three. Plus there's a separate lounge with a sofa bed if needs be, but that's getting silly. Suffice to say, we will not be in the shed.

But this brings her to another problem and one that has her on her feet. The house might be passably okay (if we're simply to accept the loft complies with planning and building regulations) but Julia is unbalanced and quite possibly dangerous as proven by a barrage of abusive emails with language so extreme they appear to have combusted into the ether for she's able to produce only one.

And I know which one it is. It's The One and I've seen it already. It was included in the bundle of evidence she had to file before the start of the hearing and I read it, hands trembling with tears in my eyes.

And then she wrenches a copy of it from her lawyer's fat man hands, bats her away and addresses the judge.

'I think this demonstrates succinctly, Your Honor, the sort of aggression and abuse I have long put up with from both my ex and his family. The very family I'm expected to allow around my daughters without any supervision and no means of escape. May I?' she pleads and Judge Weiner lifts his eyes disinterestedly from the paperwork in front of him and nods his little unbiased head.

'Dear Philippa,' she reads, her voice dripping with sarcasm. '*I'm sorry* that you feel we have not expressed enough concern for you following the *breakdown* of your *marriage* but I assure you that my *entire family* and all of our friends are filled with *regret*.

'We have watched for years now, as our once carefree, happy Dan has been *chipped away* by the constant *criticism, nagging, ingratitude and rage* directed at him and *his* beautiful children. We've remained quiet, while you *ground him down* with vociferous *anger, disregard* and a total *lack of love* or understanding. We've listened to you *lie, pontificate, self-glorify* and *run rings around yourself* as you struggle to keep track of the stories you've told and we've swallowed the desire to call you up it.' Her lawyer places a restraining hand on Philippa's arm and she turns on her like cat to a dog. The grey haired harpy withdraws and lowers her head, her eyebrows arched and her lips pursed like an old goat's vagina. Stella sits a little straighter and I almost feel the baby doing somersaults besides me.

'We've watched you order Dan around with *contempt* and longed to *wipe the sneer from your face*. We've listened to you run him down like a *wretched fishwife* and then bitten back our own *anger* as you systematically *abused* us all. We've watched and held each other back because Dan has begged us time and time again to let you get away with it for fear of the *horrendous repercussions* against him and *his* daughters.'

'Philippa,' her lawyer interrupts, starting to stand and she spins around and hisses *get your giant hands off of me.* Philippa looks right through her with daggers in her eyes and then smiles back at the judge.

'Where was I? Oh, yes. We're all afraid of what you'll do next and how far you'll actually go before you *destroy* Dan completely. We've wept for him and the pain he endures trying to bring up *his* daughters in an environment where people *throw their own mothers out on the street* and *scream in violent rages.* Where the most they can hope for on a good day is *neglect.*

'*Well, we've had enough. All of us.* So I ask you politely to never, ever contact any member of my family again. You'll *refrain* from the *continual attacks* on all of them and if you still have something to say, take it up with me because I've held back for six years and I'm *sick of you poisoning everyone* and everything around you. You had it all and you *spat it back with anger and distain.*

'I'd give my all to have one day back with my brother the way he was before you *broke* him. I'd give anything to see him laugh one more time and to get to know his children the way that normal people do, but I know that *you'll* never let that happen.

'So *I'm sorry* Philippa, if that's what you want to hear. *I'm sorry* you've done this to my brother and to my entire family. *I'm sorry* you think you can say whatever you like about us and it won't bring us closer together. *I'm sorry* you don't know how strong we are and how, no matter what you say, you can *never, ever touch* what we have. *I'm sorry* those two lovely girls are trapped there with you and your *narcissistic paranoia*. I'm sorry you will take this out on them and Dan and that you will never understand the *dark and persecuted* world in which you live is woven from *fabrication* and the *rage inside your own head*.

'Please don't ever think that you have slipped from our minds. We think about you constantly and our hearts go out to Katie and Lauren. Take care of yourself, *Philippa* and by that I mean *get some bloody help*. Julia'

She lifts her head triumphantly and even Judge Weiner's dispassionate expression falters as we all stare at each other as though we may have missed something. All but Philippa who seems to have read something else entirely and her lawyer who is scrambling at the files.

'A fairly contentious example of the sort of animosity my client faces, I'm sure you'll agree, Judge,' she says rising to her stumpy, swollen feet. Philippa finally sits and as her sanctimonious arse slaps down on the seat, she turns to me with a victorious sneer. I ignore her but inside I'm dancing. Stella says, 'We have nothing to add to that, Your Honor' and he replies, 'No,' and writes something down.

Next they introduce the unending issues with Elizabeth and the peril the children face at my dad's house or indeed anywhere along on the south coast where she lives and by that time the judge has heard enough. He goes off to deliberate and we file out into the corridor where we form a protective circle around each other and the baby.

Philippa and her own lawyer appear to be at loggerheads outside the men's toilets, so I can't even go to check if I really have shat my pants. It would be absurd for things not to go our way, but I wouldn't be here if absurd things didn't happen all the time. It's agony waiting for our names to be announced but eventually after twenty excruciating minutes, the clerk calls us back. White verses White.

We stumble in behind the desks and Philippa narrows her corrosive eyes and stares at me until Judge Weiner calls her attention and invites us to sit.

'I've considered the matters raised in this court concerning Mr White's right to take his daughters on holiday this coming August. First off,' he says, not looking up from the bundle of paper in front of him. 'It's joint custody so there's no issue with the time frame here. This is all set out in the separation agreement and it's very clear that both parents have equal entitlement to provide care over the summer period. That being three weeks per parent with telephone or videophone access to the other parent at least once a day where physically possible and on such occasions as the children request further interaction with the other parent.

Secondly, looking at it from the children's perspective, I see no reason to deprive them of a really nice trip.'

He looks up at me and smiles. Barely, but he smiles.

'Mrs White, you're ordered by the court to provide details of the children's passports to Mr White immediately and to hand over the passports themselves no less than two weeks before the date of departure. As your lawyer will inform you, any failure to comply with this order is considered Contempt of Court, which is punishable by a fine or imprisonment. Mr White. You are ordered to inform Mrs White of your departure date when it is known to you and to ensure that a reasonable amount of contact is maintained with her while in the UK. I wish you a pleasant holiday.'

If I wasn't already sitting down, my legs would have given way. There's certainly a loosening somewhere south of my smaller intestines. Philippa starts to object, but her lawyer turns on her with a growl and leads her outside before she gets herself hauled away. We thank the judge and make room at the table for the next case and as we head to the door Stella high-fives me and Tammy leaps into my arms.

We've done it. We looked into the eye of the storm and survived. And there is nothing Philippa can do. I can't believe it. We've won. Me and Tammy. Me and the kids. This is it. We made a stand and we've been vindicated. In writing. There's nothing that horrible joy-sucking hag can do to hurt us now. She's dive bombed so spectacularly, there's no way she can come back fighting after this. She'd be insane to even think about it. Right?

Booby Chains And Small Knickers

We are three days into our two and a half-week trip and I get an email from Philippa telling me she can't afford to send the girls to private school any longer so she's transferred them across to a public one, which in Canada means free. Free!

I'm caught somewhere between resentment at her making another life-changing decision without me and relief that it is…well…free.

It is however, a good hour away from downtown Toronto, where she can't afford to live anymore apparently, so she's moved out little more than a year after dragging us all there. When I take the girls back to her place, it'll be to yet another apartment they've never seen before, smaller than the last one but still within five minutes of a Whole Foods. A girl's got to spend $50 on a tub of quinoa after all.

Only trouble is she can't really afford to live there either so she's already planning to move again within the next term or so now the kids have been accepted which will do wonders for their sense of security and wellbeing. And none of this merited discussing months ago when she set all this in motion, but why would it?

No matter, she's done it again. Pushed things forward with me and Tammy. We start cautiously looking at town houses in the northern district, just online for the moment (we are in England after all), but we're having a conversation we wouldn't have had if my ex-wife hadn't forced us to consider our options.

The majority of the houses up for sale are made out of wood like the old one, but I refuse to pay that sort of money again for something which is, in all reality, a posh shed that probably won't outlast even me. The odd brick version comes up every once in a while but they're few and far between, which is fine because there's no real rush. It'll just mean commuting for four hours a day to and from the apartment, their school and then work. It's a bugger but I've been buggered before. Repeatedly, as you know.

My sister's delighted that we might buy a bigger place, especially since we'll have enough space to put up her clan who are finally old enough to travel without dosing up with antihistamines to make them sleep through the flight.

But this is all a pipe dream for now. Tammy and I have been together for less than a year and it would be prudent to take our time before committing to a massive financial investment together. Still, it's nice to think ahead and fantasise once in a while about seeing how the other half live.

And by the other half, I mean ordinary, unsuspecting folk like I used to be.

The kids are happy here in England and I still feel a tinge of regret that we can't stay, particularly given how awful it was getting over here in the first place. The thought of reliving the nightmare fills me with dread and I've got to take my hat off to Philippa for convincing the girls that flying is so unnaturally terrifying, they'd be lucky to make it alive. You've got to admire the ingenuity. At least I could if it hadn't led to poor Katie being so petrified she didn't stop crying and vomiting for the entirety of the flight.

And I don't know if the nutbag was driven by her insatiable urge to ruin our trip or by her love of drama. By her desire to have a child with Something. Some phobia. Some allergy. Some definition made up of acronyms. Some diagnosis she'll eventually grind out of a doctor who'll give her anything she wants if she'll only go away. Some childhood disorder she'll cope with heroically. Some ailment she can cure or that'll make her stand out vicariously through the children and their ordeal.

And little by little, her destructive obsessions are doing the work nature can't. The girls are displaying signs of afflictions that have been hard earned through tireless persuasion. Through relentless suggestion and conditioning. At least they were until finally, away from the indoctrination, they've begun to free themselves of the labels weighing down on them and return, restored and relieved, back to me. Back home.

The sand on Bournemouth beach makes its way into our picnic and the nostalgic crunch of my disappointing sausage roll takes me back to an age of innocence. The sun is shining but not so much that we'll die if we stay in it for a few hours and we do, soaking up the sound of the waves that crash gently on the shore drenching Katie's shorts and washing away one of Lauren's new rubber shoes. I can't be cross. I'd only just told them both to be careful, which has never helped anyone but did mean that I knew exactly what was going to happen, but I let them do it anyway. And it was worth it to hear their little squeals as the swell of freezing water inched up their inner thighs.

'Daddy, is it gonna to flood?' Lauren hobbles back towards me, stiff with salt and goose pimples.

'No, Lala. The tide won't come in that far.'

'But if it does, will it flood?' She steadies herself, blue lips arranged in a thoughtful pout.

'Yes, probably, but it won't. It only floods once in a while when there's a really massive storm.'

'If there's a massive storm now, is it gonna flood?'

'No. There's not a cloud in the sky.'

'But if a storm comes and it floods will all my toys go down the drain?' Her hands are on her hips.

'No. Even if it does flood, your toys won't go down the drain.'

'But you said it wasn't going to flood.' For some reason, she thinks she's got me.

'It isn't. It's not going to flood.'

'Then why will my toys not go down the drain if it floods?' Arrrrghhhh.

Everyone has met Tammy now and they all agree she is lovely. Dad tells me he had very low hopes of me ever meeting anyone in my position i.e. divorced with two kids, no money and a crazy ex-wife. He can't believe I've somehow attracted a seemingly functional, intelligent woman with a high-flying job. He's almost too surprised she could ever be interested in me, which is always nice to hear from your own father.

'Of course,' he warns me in the same voice he uses to grumble about the high cost of petrol these days. 'She'll be wanting her own kids soon enough. How are you going to afford them?' and I tell him easily, the way he's worrying himself into an early grave. But she doesn't want kids anyway. That's the beauty of it all.

She's not the only one flying high in her career or at least not taking a nosedive. I've passed my final interview and will be starting in the Human Trafficking Unit as soon as we get back to Ontario. I'm finally more or less doing what I was meant to be. Albeit with far less hair and nerves so stretched any fiddler with an ounce of talent could scratch out a tune.

We've been here for thirteen days and so far every one of them has been scheduled around the five o'clock Skype call that dictates the abrupt termination of every daytrip and no matter how lovely a time we're having, by three o'clock a dark cloud overshadows my mood. But this is how it is and how it's always going to be. Philippa will call the shots and I will duck to avoid having my head caved in.

She's insisted on being shown around, first Julia's house (which is smaller than she remembered), then my dad's (which is dangerously cluttered with junk) and tomorrow she'll examine my mum's even though she's been there more times than I care to remember since picturing her there makes me want to throw up.

My family feel slightly violated, like the victims of burglaries who find their underwear strewn on the floor, but they smile stoically at the girls as they traipse through their homes with the iPad and ignore the catty comments that accompany each tour.

Only minutes after ending her fifteenth call, I get another email telling me that I may have some trouble getting back into Canada as she's reported me to Border Control for marriage fraud.

Marriage fraud?! It was a farce, I'll agree. A giant turd in the history of mankind, but the idea that getting a visa to a country I never wanted to go to in the first place would be incentive enough to suffer untold misery and a life of total destitution was even more mental than her. And that was going some. I'd have been better off braving the Atlantic in a dingy alongside forty other poor desperate souls with only the use of our fingernails for paddles if I'd wanted it that badly. My life for a visa and the opportunity to start back at rock bottom, continually trying and failing to claw my way up. For God's sake.

I know what's coming now, but it is still makes my voice squeak like a twelve year-old boy's when I see it in writing a few days later. The girls' *Mother* has filed for sole custody with visitation rights for me on alternate weekends and one evening a week. She's really doing it. I'm going to piss another ten thousand bucks away just trying to keep what is rightfully mine. The very custody agreement she suggested herself back when it wasn't worth her while to have the girls all the time.

But this isn't about me seeing them or her seeing them more. This is revenge for me not agreeing to up sticks and move somewhere near Wales for absolutely no reason. Revenge and a reminder that I can make it all go away with the simple destruction of my life in Canada.

She wouldn't even be able to cope with the girls full time, let alone jet off to St Lucia (twice already this year) but then that's what her mother's for. Linda already picks the girls up from school three or four days a week but then it's nice to be retired and have the time, I suppose. It certainly takes the load off Philippa and up until now I've even been glad the old bag has been around to absorb the worst of her daughter's unchecked insanity (the bulk of which I blame her for anyway). But it does me no good now I've got to say. At the same time, the nutter has no grounds to even bring her case in front of the judge.

Of course she knows that, which is why a few days later she informs me she's also filed a report with the Met and Walton Regional Police complaining of historic domestic abuse. By me, not the other way around which would explain why I literally tremble in her presence but wouldn't help her in her court case in any way.

Instead, serendipitously she's remembered that I throttled her when she was seven months pregnant with Katie and punched a hole into the wall of every house we ever shared. I don't recall trying to strangle her, which is a shame because I would love to have that image in my mind to replay whenever I feel a bit down. And to be fair, it would make more sense than the reality which was years of me cowering like a king prawn before a sushi chef as she ripped me to shreds even though I was twice her size.

I did admittedly attack the plasterboard in the basement in Burlington, which I instantly regretted. It really hurt and it was a ball ache having to fix it, but if I'd known it would multiply over time like a couple of Mormons at a bible retreat, I'd have broken them all.

It is puzzling that she's never mentioned any of this before. Personally I'd be a little more concerned about leaving my children with a violent, abusive women-hater I couldn't trust not to smash up their home. But this is not the first time she's made up mad shit about me. The fact she's put it on record however, suggests there's a lot more to come.

My parents say no one will ever believe it, but they've got no basis for that. She can't prove that I did, but I can't prove that I didn't. This is going to be hell whatever the outcome and I don't know how much fight I have left in me. And then Lauren comes into the kitchen and lifts her face up to mine.

'Daddy.'

'Yes.'

'Is there a heart in my eye? '

'A what?'

'A heart in my eye? '

'…No.'

'But I love you so why is there not a heart in my eye when I love you? '

How are you not supposed to give your everything for more of that? Even so, Philippa may not have stopped me taking the girls away on holiday, but she made sure she monopolised the whole thing. I can think of nothing else for the rest of my time here. I can't even enjoy being with everyone I missed so much and all we can talk about is endless scenarios all accumulating in my ex-wife's unexplained and mysterious disappearance.

The kids are watching the tablet when Katie strides over angrily and says 'Daddy, can you get rid of this please?'

I roll my eyes and take the iPad off her for the millionth time, only on this fortuitous occasion there's an image of a semi-naked woman straddling a hairy man on a bed. It's not fortuitous for me, I should probably mention. It's one of those porn sites that's embedded into every bloody webpage (in this case My Little Pony) and I've forgotten to put the child settings back on the tablet after I was messing around trying to connect it to my mum's shitty router.

This is bad. I close the pop up and freeze not knowing whether to draw attention to the image and make it bigger than it is or ignore it and hope they haven't even noticed it.

I ignore it, dickhead that I am. I ignore it because it's not like they'd even know what it is. It's just two unattractive people gurning and all they care about is getting back to their programme. I ignore it because they're bound to forget all about it unless I bring it up again. But they don't. Katie asks her mother why a lady in a booby chain and a small pair of knickers would want to squash a man on a bed.

And from that moment on she has me for showing the girls pornography. *Violent pornography*, which would be about right, because I used to watch hours of it back-to-back in Epsom too apparently. No wonder I didn't get much bloody sleep.

I can't tell the girls to deny they've seen it in case they tell anyone I've told them to deny it. All I can do is explain, but the damage is done and I inadvertently did it to myself. But then again, don't I always?

Bring It On If You Have To

The game is back on and Tammy and I do everything we possibly can to improve our position. We start with putting the apartment on the market and searching actively for a house in the same area as the girls' new school so there can be no suggestion that the commute (which has been forced on me) is reason in itself for them to have to live with her.

We find a three-bed detached brick town house ten minutes walk away from where they'll be and make an offer on it there and then. I'm going to put the $90,000 I'll receive from the apartment into it and Tammy will use the $30,000 she has saved towards the necessary renovations and will then pay the mortgage moving forward while I cover the bills.

Over time this will all work out even somehow, but it doesn't matter because we're in this for the duration. It'll be a stretch, but it's worth it in the long run. Katie and Lauren will have a bedroom each and I can do up the basement for guests. As long as I don't keep punching holes into the walls.

It all takes time though, even with the strict realtor rules that nearly cost me my family and my sanity the first time around, but the wheels are in motion so that's the main thing.

Tammy's almost as dedicated to this fight as I am and she's started to filter the emails Philippa sends me up to ten times a day so I don't have to read through them all. They're the volatile inconsistent work of a madwoman, but they're carefully crafted to support the hard-done-by persona she's cultivating ready for an appearance in court and they all demand money, which is wearing me down.

Though demand isn't the right word. They plead with me to pay what's due to her as she struggles to raise her beloved children at poverty level, while I enjoy the high life and refuse to give her what she's owed.

'See reason, Daniel. If not for me then for the sake of our daughters.'

Her on-off relationship with Bazza is definitely off. The girls say he's not around anymore though whether she's managed to destroy him like a snail under the heel of her foot or is still planning on winning him back, I can't say. He's quite a catch to let slip through her fingers so I'd be surprised if she takes it lying down. (Though lying down seemed to work out well for her the first time.)

Either way, he's not bank rolling her anymore so the old bulldog barrister's out. But wait! By lucky chance, Philippa's spent most of the proceeds from the Burlington sale and has no other money (apart from most of what I earn) so she qualifies for Legal Aid, while I, who literally barely even eat when I don't have the kids, have to pay for my own. There is a God after all. And he's a twat.

My lawyer, Stella's on maternity leave now, which is gutting (for me, not for her hopefully). It's hard to imagine I'll ever find anyone as good to represent me, but she recommended a colleague when she left *just in case* and our initial conversations leave me feeling quite positive.

Steve seems to know all about my situation in advance and I realise my life has been the source of entertainment at the office. So be it. I'd probably find it all rather amusing myself if I didn't have a starring role in it. And especially if I wasn't playing a giant penis being squeezed in a vice day in and day out.

The girls have started at their new school and they seem more anxious about going than before. Lauren's settled in more easily but Katie's struggling to make friends and keep up with the work. Her literacy level's below expected standards although everyone says she's bright, but she's timid in class and freezes up when the teacher pays her too much attention.

We start doing more reading at home and really concentrate on lifting her grades, not because we want to put any pressure on her but rather to make school a little easier. She seems unnecessarily preoccupied by unlikely scenarios and frequently breaks off from our studies to ask questions I can only guess the origins of.

'What would happen if I go to jail, Daddy?'

I tap the question she's supposed to be reading. 'You won't go to jail, sweetie.' I tap again.

'But what if I do naughty stuff?'

'Don't do naughty stuff and you won't go to jail.'

'But if I do go to jail, can you open the door?' I put my pen down.

'Yes, Kiki. I can open the door.'

'But what if you go to jail?'

'Well, if I go to jail, we'll be together so we'll be fine, won't we?'

'But what about Mummy?'

'Let's keep our fingers crossed that Mummy goes to jail too, sweetheart.'

'Oh! I know. When you do naughty stuff, don't tell the police.'

'That's my girl,' I say and she looks relieved. I tap the question again and try not to dwell on it.

She worries a lot about disappointing people too and so seems to push them away when in fact she craves acceptance and affection. She doesn't quite seem to know how to relate to her peers and her only real friends are Lauren and Dom's daughter, Sadie, who we'll have to see less of once we move out of the apartment.

It's troubling and I feel like I should organise some play-dates with her new class mates but what parents in their right mind would allow their child anywhere near an abusive, porn-loving paedo, not to say let them go to his house?

Philippa's been busy again and is making the most of a whole new audience. I feel like I've been allocated a part in an impromptu immersion theatre production but I'm not keen on my character and judging by the disgusted looks I receive in the playground, neither is anyone else.

To make matters worse – if it's possible to feel worse than being branded a vicious nonce at your children's primary school – in addition to the extra-curricular activities (and there's at least one a day) Philippa's started to appear regularly at random drop offs and pickups, where she conspires with a group of turtle-necked cronies and accuses me of stalking her.

There's one day every week when I can't collect the girls after school and so Tammy gets them for me. That is she did until Philippa got wind of it and refused to let them go with her. And by refused, I mean screamed her head off as though they were being dragged into the back of a van by R Kelly.

I had to leave my shift early in order to sort it out but I may as well have gone and had a little wank for the good it did me. Within days Philippa had appeared with an emergency court order prohibiting Tammy or anyone else from ever picking them up for me again. She doesn't understand why I would ask a third party to get them when she or her mum would happily step in themselves. I don't understand why someone hasn't smashed her face in or run her over in their car by now but I don't shout about it. I just tell her it's unfair that she's allowed to rely on her mother, while she expects me to do everything myself, including work so I can pay for her cocktails and olive tapenade.

Her comeback is to turn up to everything all of the time. Every club, every pickup, every time I turn around, she's there. And she's not blowing me kisses.

She's lurking outside Kiki's classroom one afternoon when I pop in to see if Katie's getting on any better now. Her teacher's unusually standoffish, but I'm so used to this sort of reaction it barely even registers anymore. Only when she kicks professionalism to the curb and tells me outright that it's shocking I don't pay Philippa any maintenance (she clearly hasn't heard about me breaking down walls with my bare hands if she's shocked about that) do I actually notice.

I'm taken aback at the balls of her laying that on me even if it were true, but as luck would have it, I've just come from the bank and am able to brandish a receipt for the $2478 I had transferred into her account.

Her face drops like shit from a donkey's arse and suddenly she has nothing to say. Not for a couple of seconds until she gathers herself and begins apologising frantically. We could ask her if you like, I say nodding my head towards the lunatic who is rehearsing for her latest role of Supermom in the playground and she backs away, shaking the palm of her hand saying, 'I probably shouldn't get involved in your business.'

Now she says that, but as she scrapes her chin up from the floor, I note that I've made an ally.

'I'm so sorry again,' she repeats and I point out she may hear a few more things about me she should really ignore and as she reddens again, I realise she already has.

I leave her squirming on the spot like a beach worm trying to dig itself into the sand but I leave with a smile, which I flash at Philippa, even though I'm seething inside.

Stan is with her and he lurches towards me as I call the girls over and tell them to make their goodbyes. I've barely seen him since she realised he spent most of the week with us nose deep up André's crapper.

A small group of idiot sidekicks are watching expectantly and Philippa doesn't disappoint. She's admirably stoic as she breaks away from her poor helpless daughters, balefully and with her lips trembling to ensure they are nothing if not wary of their immediate fate. Stan's yanking at the lead, desperate to join us and she drags him away whimpering and forces him into the back of her car.

The last thing I see before she suddenly curses aloud is him throwing up all over the boot. Even the bloody dog's terrified of her, but bless his soul, he's the cherry on the cake of my day. It's still a pretty shit cake though.

In retaliation for me laughing (which was more of an explosive snort, in my defence) she demands we get the OCL to take over our case. The OCL, or the *Office of the Children's Lawyer* as it inexplicably likes to call itself given how clunky that sounds, is an independent law office which represents children in custody and access disputes such as ours. It's like social services only with the resources to actually investigate what's happening behind closed doors and do something about it.

I can't believe it. This is the best news I've had since I heard Philippa had fallen off of a cliff and landed on top of her mother, but that turned out to be only a dream. This on the other hand is actually happening and at her request. Both parents have to consent to them getting involved and I never dared to imagine she would agree to such an imbecilic move but then that's the extent of her mental illness. She genuinely believes no one will ever see through her and maybe she even thinks what she's saying is true. But it's not and all I have to do is let her be herself and be myself too.

They interview us, the kids, their doctor, their dentist, headmistress, teachers, my boss and Philippa's mum. I have to choose someone who can speak on my behalf too and Tammy suggests her brother, Wayne. I have to find a nice way of saying I'm not even comfortable leaving the girls alone with him much less allowing him anywhere near an investigation into their wellbeing.

He's younger than Tammy and twice as wide. If I pressed my forefinger into his belly it would keep going right up to my elbow and if I used a fork, he would pop like a water balloon. Suffice to say, I've done neither but mainly because he makes my skin crawl and it turns out there is no nice way to phrase that so I just say I've already asked my dad.

Thankfully, the OCL are happy to do the interview over the phone and he tells them what he knows, which is essentially that we're all scared of my ex-wife because she's nuts. The type of nuts that can instantly leave anyone she comes into contact with clutching at their throats and in fear for their lives.

He tells them when the children were little she used to shout at them so loudly people passing the house would actually stop in the street. He's seen how the girls get upset when they go back to their mother's but I always reassure them it'll all be okay, that they'll see Starlight Twinkle Toes and I'll call them every day because I love them. Because I really do love them.

He recounts the late night phone calls and accusatory emails, the way she lost it completely and threw them out of the house. The attempts to get Elizabeth banned from Canada or at least onto the Most Wanted list. The complaint to Bournemouth Borough Council they're convinced cost her the job there. Her irate accusation that they'd turned her in to the Open University for living abroad in an attempt to get her thrown off her course when it turned out she'd asked the providers herself if she could take her exams in Toronto (which she promptly forgot and blamed my parents for when she was questioned about it). If there's one thing my dad excels at, it's fretting about Philippa and for his sake I am glad he didn't pay for that call.

Tammy tells them she's committed to helping me raise the children but would never try to replace their mum, who is one of a kind. It's inevitable that Philippa should be suspicious of her but she only has the girls' best interests at heart. She's keen to provide them with some much-needed calm and stability, patience, understanding and a positive role model.

The only times she's ever picked them up from school they've run into her arms and then spent the hours until I get home doing homework, making cookies and playing endless games of My Little Pony Top Trumps, so if anyone is suffering it is her. Ha ha ha.

She's concerned Philippa's relentless ambush of every occasion and activity is having a negative effect on us all, exposing the girls to parental conflict, ruining our lives and if this were sixteenth century England, she'd have been drowned as a witch by now and good riddance (she may not have said that. I'd had a few beers by the time we debriefed).

Philippa's clearly had a bit of time on her hands and has used it to report me to Walton Regional Police for bringing my service weapon home several years prior when we still lived together instead of checking it into the station when I worked an overtime shift (all perfectly legal).

Her efforts to actually cost me my job despite living off my wages sadly fall on deaf ears, mainly because I don't have a choice. I'd rather take my chances with a sausage than carry a firearm at all, let alone wield it at the kids but since no one's stupid enough to pay me overtime to take my gun back if I'm the other side of Toronto at the end of my shift, it has to come home with me, disassembled into ten different pieces in a locked box I put high out of reach. And they even pay me for it. There's more chance of Houdini rising from the grave and reassembling it under water before the kids ever could. A hammer would be more dangerous. Even the blunt end of a spoon. Not that I've given it that much thought I'm keen to clarify when they ask me about it.

I'm still irritated that I handed Philippa Porngate on a plate and I apologise and put my hands up to it straight away. On one unfortunate isolated occasion they did indeed see an inappropriate advert pop up by accident. What they didn't do was re-enact it in front of a group of aging clergy I'd found on the dark web, though anyone would be forgiven for thinking otherwise given Philippa's reaction. Feigned reaction, I should say. I know she was delighted about the whole incident and if she had any manners at all she'd have sent me a thank you card.

A few weeks after the interview (this whole process takes three months if you can imagine the ball-crunching stress of trying to live through it every day) the OCL investigators come to the apartment to watch us in action and we all go into character like slightly stiff, yet amiable versions of ourselves.

We're supposed to behave as though the women taking notes on the sofa are cushions we haven't really noticed and are yet to plump up. The girls are bouncing off the walls by the time they arrive, forty-five minutes late – 'Oh, the traffic!' - and all I can think is, my God, please don't blame me because they're starting to go wild.

Lauren does some colouring while I read Katie a story from her school bag and Tammy makes a horribly weak cup of tea for us all (I keep intending to have a word, but she means so well) and when Katie starts jumping off the top of the bunk beds we quickly gather our swimming kits and head to the pool as we do every evening to tire them out. With the women following, we keep our voices light and breezy even though Kiki's already stripped off and dumped her clothes by the lift and Lauren's doing roly-polies all the way down the hall.

'Such energy,' we exclaim indulgently.

The girls flip and jump from the sides of the pool, as immune to this whole surreal episode as they are to the demise of the polar icecaps. They're a little too loud and a little too boisterous but thankfully when I tell them to quieten down, they obey without a murmur and leap into my arms. They're happy and comfortable and fortunately when we get back to the apartment, which seems suddenly tiny with so many people inside, they've chilled out (a little).

Tammy dries Lauren's hair in the bedroom while I start making spaghetti meatballs for dinner and when she's finished, Katie goes through and Lauren joins me at the counter in the kitchen.

She's starving and asks me for something to eat and I tell her she can only have a cracker because I'm literally making tea. Her smile turns upside down immediately and suddenly she's frowning and refusing to speak. I try to jolly her along, but inside I'm dying and willing her not to melt down completely. Not now.

She has no idea how much is at stake and as she starts to ask again, her voice grating dangerously, I have to hold myself gentle but firm. It's agony trying to keep it together but I pick her up and hold her on my hip as I finish the meal, all the while chatting merrily as though we haven't a care in the world.

And it's taking bloody ages. I've forgotten to turn on the hob for the pasta and the sauce is already spitting out of the pan. I have to push it out the way of Lauren's dangling legs and pretend that the arm holding her with isn't starting to shake. She's grumpy but rests her head on my shoulder and I'm overly chirpy and all I want to do is beg her not to do this right now.

I pass her a cracker and as she spills crumbs on my T-shirt, I ask her incessant questions about the herbs and the oil until she slowly starts to uncoil and her little mouth stops pouting. In the background I can feel my houseguests making notes about it all.

An hour passes and they finally leave. The girls have been amazing but even I can see objectively their behaviour is sometimes more savage than sedate. It's only when they're under a microscope that I find myself judging them the way other people must. The way I judge other people's children myself and blame the parents when they're not well behaved enough.

My thoughts are spinning as I replay the previous few hours over and over in my mind, my heart sinking every few seconds as I wonder how certain parts came across. I'm so drained by all of this and my only hope is that when Philippa is observed, they're all having a really bad day. Or regular in her case.

I wilt onto the sofa like a tube man deflating in a car dealership. It's over. There's nothing I can do to change it now and there's nothing more to add. We've done our best and all we can do now is sit back and see if people I've barely met will either grant me permission to raise my own children or make me an every-other-weekend dad.

This whole process has felt like a demolition and as the wrecking ball finally slams into my stomach, I run to the bathroom and hurl every one of those meatballs back up. And then I sit and wait for their appraisal and I hope more than there are stars in the sky, that we have all done enough.

Don't Let The Fat Lady Sing

I can feel Philippa's eyes boring into the side of my head, but for once I don't mind. She's shooting toxic fumes across the courtroom with only the power of her mind, interrupting every time I speak, waving her paperwork around and shouting over the top of us as she tries to convey to the judge how terrified she is of me. My lawyer almost stops the hearing a couple of times, but I'm happy to let her continue so instead I go quiet, my head bowed while she disgraces herself.

This isn't the lawyer Stella recommended. This is someone else entirely who is less familiar with my case, but also less familiar with my ex-wife, who in an act of pure ingenuity managed to track the first idiot down on a dating app.

Her shock when she realised she'd been messaging my lawyer with details of the case (as you do in the flirty opening stages of a relationship) was indescribable, though she had a good shot at it when she reported him to the *Law Society* accusing us both of conspiring to entrap her.

As if getting her screwed while screwing myself was all part of the master plan. The first I heard of it was nine days before we were due to go to court when I got a sheepish email from Steve telling me he had to excuse himself or he could jeopardise the trial.

'What are the chances in the whole of Toronto?' Pretty damn high if you take chance right out of the equation.

Anyway, it was done and I was passed over to Greg 'Halitosis' Kowalski – a dysfunctional, sandal-wearing weirdo who worked out of one of those social hubs, but let me be clear, any money he was saving was not passed down to me.

He had a week to get up to date with my entire case and the only advantage I had over the Wicked Witch of the West was that I knew her attorney wouldn't even pick up her file until two minutes before he walked into court. These Legal Aid people are just there to get paid. I, on the other hand, had my whole life at stake, I knew the details inside out and I could nail the opposing counsel on every single point.

The fact we shouldn't even be here in court is by the by. The recommendations from the OCL inspection were published months ago after twelve hellish weeks of intensive scrutiny and investigation. Philippa wandered into it all thinking she would win but the results were conclusive. The *Office of the Children's Lawyer*, a totally independent organisation she had handpicked herself determined we both cared for the children beyond a shadow of a doubt.

However, they found they were being unnecessarily exposed to conflict due to their mother's insistence on attending all their extra-curricular activities. They stated that we should both choose one a week (not five hundred) and go to both if we wanted, but only during our own parenting time. Same with drop offs and pickups at school, about which I'm entitled to a joint share in the decision-making. Oh, and Tammy has the right to pick up the girls on Tuesdays and so do my mum or dad if they happen to be here.

We should only email once a day (not thirty) and restrict ourselves to talking about the children. No calls and no texting, especially not unhelpful threats and references to my girlfriend's overactive thyroid gland, imagined or otherwise.

The kids' health and dental hygiene was within the realms of expectation for their age and so rather than blaming each other for every filling and graze, Philippa is to sort out their medical appointments while I take care of the dental and optometry checks. Except in an emergency, which is an emergency and not an excuse to throw accusations of child abuse around.

They summarised that while Philippa undoubtedly loved the children, sometimes her concern for them was overwhelming and completely disproportionate to the situation giving the girls the impression they were unsafe. Not only did this have a detrimental effect on their mental and emotional stability, they were also exhibiting signs of anxiety which reflected her own.

When interviewed she displayed a distorted preoccupation with concerns which would then be forgotten and replaced by other equally worrying issues, creating an unnecessary sense of turmoil. Her thoughts appeared to be disorganised and she frequently put forward totally contrary parenting strategies within a matter of minutes. She continued to insist both parents should attend appointments and birthdays together even after it was established that this created problems and should be avoided.

At the conclusion of the twenty-two recommendations against her, Philippa was advised to seek separate independent support services (counselling) to help her cope with being a fucking loon (they may not have phrased it exactly like that, but it was clear reading through the softly-softly social workery speak that it was implied).

I turned the page to read the comments about me and there were none. Not a one. Their description of me sounded more like the man in the Athena ad in the 80s cradling a baby on his bare manly chest. They even put in that I'd kissed Katie's forehead in the swimming pool and held Lauren in my arms when she was cross like I was Father of the Year.

They also stated that my dad had said that she'd shouted so loudly at the kids the neighbours had come out of their houses, which was not accurate as he'd actually said people stopped in the street (but that accent...) and resulted in a renewed flurry of late night calls and emails describing him, amongst other things as a *LIAR!*

You would think that would be it, but in Philippa's lawyer's opinion it was all highly prejudicial. She was the one who called them in. If it was going to be prejudicial against anyone it should have been me, but then she wasn't counting on them realising she was totally bonkers.

Anyway, it goes without saying she didn't concur with their verdict and so she took her same concerns to the *Children's Aid Society*. They didn't take long to draw the same conclusions. They found no safeguarding issues and closed the case, but that still wasn't enough.

'They're all corrupt, every one of them!'

Next we tried mediation, which went down like a snog at a funeral and ended with Philippa storming out because she doesn't actually want to compromise on anything. She wants it all and any suggestion of less is tantamount to offering to violate the dog for a fee.

So despite humiliating herself spectacularly several times with a variety of completely unrelated law associations and child protection services, she continues to believe she's right and the rest of the world is out to get her.

She won't stop until she's got what she wants. Nor will she listen to advice, take on board any recommendations or stop attempting to annihilate anyone who crosses her path and so now we are back here in front of Judge Weiner at my insistence, to have the findings of the OCL inspection added to the original separation agreement so that she's legally obliged to stick to the terms.

And she's fuming. She thinks all she has to do is to possess boobs and shriek *I am their Mother.* But therein lies the problem and now I have a stack of impartial reports about her unstable character and mental issues to use as evidence against her. Even without a single one of them she's doing herself no favours. As I'm sat here telling the court she's aggressive, she's screaming across the room at me in furious denial. I almost feel a moral obligation to stop time and say to her do you know how bad this looks for you? I'm telling the judge that you're a head case and you've literally been behaving like one for half an hour. But I don't. I just let her illustrate my point so thoroughly it's almost a cliché.

'Your Honor. The man's got a gun and a licence to kill. It's terrifying. He's insane. Violent and insane. It's just a matter of time. I can hardly sleep at night.'

She denies she's stalking me and supervising the girls drop offs and pickups. She volunteers at the school and any crossover is entirely coincidental. She agrees she did tell Katie's teacher I don't pay her maintenance but it was a joke (what a cracker!). No need to overreact. She insists, despite the findings of two separate agencies that it makes the girls happy to see their parents together so she continues to turn up and glower at me wherever I'm scheduled to be.

She's still struggling to get by with no money at all (other than most of mine) and no chance of ever getting any since she's chosen to pursue a career path she herself describes as pointless because there aren't any jobs going in the teaching sector. I, meanwhile, am living in a mansion with all the latest mod cons, half a state-of-the-art kitchen, new furniture, a trampoline and a hot tub in the garden.

The hot tub only arrived a few days ago. I haven't even told the girls about it because I wanted to surprise them the following weekend. There's no way she could've known about it unless she'd seen it with her own eyes. She's inadvertently confirmed what I suspected all along. That alarmingly she's been to my house when I'm not there and had a good snoop around, including in the back yard and through the windows.

I point this out to my lawyer and he points it out to the judge and by way of defence she starts yelling over him that she's simply concerned for the children and since I won't let her into my home, she has to do what she can to ensure they are safe.

And they're not! It is a death trap! A building site! We're in the middle of an expensive renovation even though I claim to be broke and rather than let the kids stay with her where they'd be out of harm's way and undisrupted, we're encouraging them to play with nail guns and chainsaws amongst deadly sheets of plywood with hazardous corners.

She's right about the house being a mess. We moved in about five months ago and got the builders in as soon as we could. If I had any money to spare we'd have rented somewhere else until it was more habitable, but I've put every cent I have into the equity and Tammy's paying for the renos (which is impossible to say without sounding Australian and I've stopped trying to explain).

It's still a wreck but I can see where it is going now. It's been absolutely freezing and pretty much open to the elements for much of the time we've lived there but we have sliding glass-doors on the back now and I can hardly drag myself away from the view.

There's a racoon that lives in a tree in our garden and he likes to steal rubbish from the bins and trail it all around the drive which is always nice to deal with at six o'clock in the morning, so I've started leaving food out for him and now he joins us for breakfast on the decking while André goes berserk smashing his ugly little face against the windows trying to chase him away. Little by little I'm teaching these damn Canadians a thing or two about manners, starting with eating off a plate.

There are black squirrels too and tons of birds that fight over the feeder we put out for them on the apple tree. It's only half finished but it already feels like a home. The girls love it but they think we're mad and don't understand why we keep moving the walls. The dog is also mad and doesn't understand why we keep moving the walls. We must be mad because we keep moving the walls and Tammy still can't make a decent cup of tea so nothing's changed (apart from the walls).

My dad's moved on to worrying about how we're going to pay for it all but at least it's a distraction from worrying about Philippa slipping into the country and murdering him in bed because of what he *didn't* say in the OCL report and for *not* reporting her residential status to the OU. I must say I do wonder how we can afford it myself but as long as we don't eat or leave the house for the next two years, we should be okay.

The trouble is, there's a crap version of everything, but it's very difficult when you're deciding what floor/doors/toilet/tap/hinges you'd like to see in your house for the next forty-five years to say, 'Oh look, there's a Basics range that we'll regret for all time. Let's get that.'

Of course, the alternative is adding up, but it'll be worth it and amazingly I got a tax rebate for $6236 without even asking so that covers about 0.000007% of the debt. Or I can sit tight and wait for the phone call from Elizabeth letting me know that Dad's brought on his own heart attack and I can go ahead and order the granite worktop after all.

It's the middle of November and the builders still reckon it'll be finished within a couple of weeks. I can't see how since they've taken to disappearing for days at a time, but they better had sort it out. Julia and co are coming out for the holidays. We have no decorations, toilet paper or light bulbs as they're all in the basement and we can't get to any of them behind the new floor/doors/toilet/taps/hinges. I refuse to buy more so we're in for a shitty Christmas (on more than one level) if they don't get a move on.

Dom the Butcher will be joining us for the twenty-fifth too. His ex has stopped him seeing his little girl, Sadie so he has his own court case to deal with and in the meantime he's starting to go out of his mind. He only has her at weekends as it is and like me, he has no other reason to even be in this country.

We make a right pair of miserable saddos but it's a massive consolation having someone around who shares the same edgy dark sense of humour and unfulfilled yearning for Marmite. Someone who understands what I'm going through and doesn't say 'Why don't you just tell her to fuck off?' when Philippa pulls the latest boiled bunny out of her hat. There's no way I was going to let him mope around by himself on Christmas Day. Plus he's bringing the turkey. Get in.

Tammy wants to invite her weird family as well and I'm struggling to come up with an inventive excuse not to have them. They're all slightly odd with an undertone of freak. Her father, Dwayne, is a larger, wobblier version of Wayne (classic) who needs to rest for five hours if he does more than a challenging poo in the mornings. I say rest. I mean plough through a ton and a half of fried chicken. A man's got to work out after all.

Her mum, Chelsea, started off as a skinny person (there are soft focus portraits of her cupping her only chin circa

1983) but since then she seems to have rolled through a vat of sticky lard. She wears her hair in the style of a helmet because it's too heavy when it's too long. The woman's the size of a pregnant hippo, but it's her hair that weighs her down. It's not a cool helmet either. It's like the ones they give flat-headed babies but it's about three sizes too small. She doesn't say much, which is slightly disconcerting, but I'll take disconcerting over my last mother-in-law's inane pointless yakking any day.

Then there's Wayne of course, the creepy, masturbating brother with a fat belly and legs like moss-covered pylons which just leaves one older half-sister, who's inherited the family genes and likes to accentuate them with a strong and off-putting aversion to soap. I thought Tammy was messy (And she is. Let me be clear. She's a pig around the house) but I've seen garbage trucks with cleaner interiors than Darlene's apartment or as Lauren summed it up in a voice that echoed in the silence that followed, 'This is icky, Daddy. Can we go home?'

The woman's a virtual recluse and she lives in a tower of congealing fast food containers because who's got the time to clear that up when you're at home all day?

And don't get me started on the aunt. The first thing she ever said to me was 'I have a prolapsed vagina'. What do you say to that? She looks about ninety but she's only sixty-five so God knows how the rest of her insides are doing. I don't care, but now I can think about nothing else when I see her.

So the idea of inviting them over to meet my sister and her perfect little clan isn't one that I'm keen to promote, but Tammy doesn't seem to have quite the same disgust for her family so it's getting hard to think of ways to get out of it. There will be thirteen of us if they do come (assuming the recluse stays holed up in her apartment) and since none of the bastards cooks (not including Dom, Julia and Andy who are the only ones I consider guests not parasites) it'll be me who gets to make the whole dinner for everyone, even though they'd be happier with pizza.

Tammy has put on a bit of weight herself, which she blames me for because I'm always cooking proper meals for the girls. I say it's not the homemade Shepard's pie and broccoli that's the problem. It's the box of Buffalo Wings that barely made it through the front door, but she just laughs and accuses the builders of hiding their rubbish at the bottom of the recycling bin.

Her idea of dieting is getting through an entire tub of hummus and a box of breadsticks in between meals. She tries to tell me it's healthy and I say it's not if you eat the whole lot and wash it down with a bottle of OJ.

'But that's fruit!'

Nevertheless, all of this is irrelevant because right now I have Philippa shooting laser beams at me with her eyes and telling Judge Weiner that I involve the girls in our disputes and have told them she's got all my money and should go to jail. That's not strictly true. I mean, it's true she's got all my money and should go to jail, but I'm not stupid enough to say that to a five and six-year-old with no filters on their innocent little minds. But then I remember I probably am that stupid but there's no opportunity to either admit or deny it since Philippa's too busy testifying against herself.

She's shrieking about the abuse she suffered for years, which she's only now found the strength to mention but the judge has heard enough and informs her she'll have to be removed if she can't contain herself.

Her lawyer is finally up to speed and stares at her like he's discovered an unexploded grenade in his garden and can hear it ticking. He rounds up his arguments as quickly as possible so he can flee the danger zone and all Halitosis has to do is breathe his pastrami sandwich through his sweaty pores and the judge sends us outside to await his deliberations.

Philippa's slime bag of a lawyer, like everyone else she's ever met, has gone from sending me evils and waving his cock in my face, to hiding in the toilets until we're called back in. It's only five minutes this time and as Tammy and I sit outside, our thighs pressed together and our hands clamped in hope. I can't believe it won't go our way again, but there's always that chance he'll believe her. That she's thrown enough mud around to make some of it stick.

When the clerk calls us in my stomach drops straight out of my arse with a little squeak, which I disguise with the scrape of my chair. I roll my eyes in disdain at the back of Greg's polyester jacket as Tammy screws up her nose. I'm pretty sure she believes me but by the time we sit down I'm insufficiently braced for the verdict.

Judge Weiner clears his throat and begins to sum up his findings in his customary diplomatic tone, which has so far always veered on the side of reasonable. Even so, my heart is hammering so loudly in my chest I'm in danger of being thrown out myself.

'With regards to the allegations of domestic violence brought against Mr White,' He looks right at me and it's not until he opens his mouth to continue that I realise I'm holding my breath. 'In my experience when there is no evidence, it's because it didn't happen.

'In my opinion there's no question of any risk to the children while in Mr White's care.' Philippa springs to her feet and starts to object. 'Ms White. You will be silent or you'll excuse yourself from this court.'

Her face twists as she lowers herself down again and her lawyer leans gradually towards us as though if he moves slowly enough she won't notice him creeping away. Judge Weiner holds her stare with a dispassionate expression that begins to embarrass even me on her behalf.

'As for the OCL and CAS recommendations, I concur with all points raised and order Ms White's counsel to resubmit the original separation agreement with the updated specifications included, particularly those pertaining to Mr White's partner, Ms Bainbridge, in order to ensure she has access to the children during school pickups and drop offs.

'It's understood by the court that Mr White is both entitled and bound by necessity to work and should be able to do so without judgement or impediment. In short, what Mr White does on his own time, is Mr White's business.'

The rest of his conclusions all fall in our favour and the final thing he says to us is 'Good luck you two,' and he looks straight at me and Tammy with a little smile, which was sweet.

Of course, he thinks he's seen the last of us but then, who doesn't? It's so non-negotiable. There's nothing that could go wrong. Philippa's been ordered by a judge in a court of law to comply with the findings of her own investigation and a sledgehammer of relief that it's over smashes through me. The adrenalin that's got me through the last few months evaporates instantly. I could sink to the floor.

If it weren't for Greg patting me on the back with a greasy paw and Tammy bouncing over, I'd collapse there and then. A few metres away, spittle is flying from Philippa's contorted mouth and her lawyer is beating a hasty retreat as though she might detonate at any moment. Tammy hugs me and links her arm through mine, her face radiant with a joy I can't allow myself to feel until I am holding the updated separation agreement in my hands.

'That was amazing, Dan!' she cries once we are safely out of earshot. 'Oh my God! That was so awesome! I can't believe she did it again.'

'It's not over yet,' I say.

'What do you mean? You heard what the judge said.' She's skipping down the steps of the courthouse but all I can do is lag along behind her. 'You did it, honey. You won! She can't do anything to hurt us after this. It's all gonna to be in writing and if she tries anything, she'll be breaking the agreement.'

'I don't know…'

'Honey! Would you stop it? It's over. Everything's gonna be okay now.'

I stop in the street and turn to her and for the first time, I allow myself to smile. Barely, but I can almost feel it. I have won and little by little, things are getting easier. I'm still broke, but I have some financial support now. I'm still terrified all the time, but I have someone to lean on. I'm still unbelievably tired, but I finally have a bed I can sleep in without fear of what will happen in the night. It's all slowly coming together. I have the love of my daughters, my family and this wonderful woman who has entered my life at exactly the right time. I'm still spinning too many plates and battling both mental and physical exhaustion but I have everything I need and for that I'm grateful.

Tammy hugs me and as she pulls away, she giggles and says, 'You know what, sweetie? I've been giving it a lot of thought…'

'What is it?' I say, sweeping her fringe out of her eyes. 'Spit it out'.

And she takes my hands in hers and says, 'I think we should start trying for a baby.'

Balls And Bags

The first thing we do when Julia arrives is go to Walmart (Asda) and Winners (TKMax) because they've forgotten both the kids' suitcases with all their clothes in, including the skiing gear Andy's been accumulating off eBay for the last six months because he's a tight bastard.

'Tell me again. How is it possible to forget two of your five bags?' I say pulling into a space in the car park that's the size of a national park.

'It was Lucas's fault, apparently,' Julia says, leaning across the back seat to unbuckle his seatbelt. 'Because he didn't bring them down when Daddy packed the car in the middle of the night.'

'You didn't notice either!' Andy's voice is as arched as his eyebrows.

'I didn't blame my seven-year-old son for forgetting them though. Besides, you told me you'd packed everything. Honestly. We got to the airport at five o'clock in the morning and I swear to God, I've been packing those bags for weeks. They had literally everything in them for this whole trip. You know what it's like and Andy got everything out the boot and Lucas went "Where's my bag?" and we looked at him like, uh,' She drops her jaw in bewilderment. There's no need really. She hasn't slept for twenty-six hours and she already looks like her chin's sliding off but all the same everyone laughs. 'Andy was like "What have you done with it, Lucas?" And I pictured it suddenly up in his bedroom all packed and lovely, waiting to go. And Maya's next door in her room...'

We head towards the faceless warehouses, Maya on Julia's hip and Lucas on my shoulders. He weighs a ton compared to my two. I'm starting to regret picking him up. The girls are due across tomorrow, but Christmas Day falls midweek so I've only got them until two o'clock and then they'll go back to their mother's until New Year (Barry's back in their lives and taking them skiing.) but then I've got them for ten days. (I'll be taking them to the playground.) Julia's going to head off to the slopes (different slopes) the same week they're away so the kids can have as much time as possible together when they're all here. They're hiring a car and Tammy's sorted them out a special deal at an awesome ski resort through her work. I'll bet it is awesome, but the only special deal I can afford at the moment is one that pays me to turn up.

'Oh and mate,' Andy groans. 'I've spent months trying to save a couple of quid here and there on all their bloody gear too and you know the little bastards are going to grow out of it all by the time we come back –'

'Andy! They are here!'

'What? They know they're going to grow, don't they? Luckily, you didn't forget the big bag, hey, Lucas? I really would be upset then. Can you imagine having to replace all of that?'

'All their Christmas presents…,' Julia mouths as we step into the unflattering strip-beam lighting of North America's favourite superstore. 'Oh my God! This is huge!'

We spend a good couple of hours there. They're so excited that it's all so cheap they end up buying twice as much as they need. Julia tries to show me a packet of peanuts as if I've never come across any in the four years I've been living here and I have to explain once again that they don't compare to the six family bags of KP dry roasted I made her lug over along with Peperamis (green and red), Bombay Mix (not the nasty cheap stuff she usually gets), a few bricks of Cathedral City Extra Mature (Tammy's favourite), Crunchy Nut Cornflakes (for the girls) and two lumps of beef dripping (for my roasties).

I told her not to listen to bloody Dad (who's still going on about nearly getting arrested when he first came out three years ago). I said sign your landing card where it says you have nothing to declare and come right through like normal people. They could care less. And she said, 'It's they COULDN'T care less! Not they COULD! If you can't handle it out there, come home!'

And I wish I could, but I have to stop thinking like that. My life's here now so it's *could care less* along with every other nonsensical bastardised version of the English language I have to say to make myself understood. At least until the girls are old enough to decide for themselves and maybe choose to go back to the UK.

Of course by then, Dwayne-Wayne Junior the fourth will probably be in the picture to complicate matters, but it's weird. I can't help feeling I'll never love this new kid the way I love the girls and it's not like when I was throttling Philippa as she carried our second child and thinking I couldn't possibly have room in my heart for anyone else. It's more that I just have to look at the rest of Tammy's family to wonder what sort of three-armed, boss-eyed buffoon we're going to end up with and I can't help but feel a little resentful that she's doing this to me.

One of the first things I ever told her was I didn't want any more children, but I get that she does (even if she said she didn't, many, many times) and now I even get it's a *deal breaker* as she so delicately put it after waiting until I fundamentally needed her and we shared a house and everything we own before she thought to bring it up. I'm just not sure anyone looking at me from the outside would necessarily think it was a good idea to be knocking out a few more sprogs when I'm still having panic attacks all day long, I'm not sleeping or eating and I'm in and out of court every few months trying to hold onto the kids I've already got.

But she's given this some thought. Not for Tammy, leaving it to chance and letting nature take its course. She's clearly been investigating this for some time. When she suggested trying for a baby outside the courthouse, I was a tad lost for words so she had plenty of opportunity to fill me in on my role as a Fertility Facilitator. As luck would have it she was ovulating right then and since we'd be celebrating our win anyway, it made sense to get my balls rolling.

I put up a little show of resistance but it was futile. I knew the jig was up. I'd fallen once again for the promises of a childless woman of childbearing age, but at least this one doesn't repulse me and she isn't completely insane.

She's thorough though, I'll give her that. The first month, we tried five times in four days, which might be bog standard fornication fare for all I know, but I'm so ground down with exhaustion and stress that I'm currently injecting myself in the leg twice a week to boost my testosterone levels so I can get through the day (at $25 a pop).

My doctor told me he'd never come across such a low reading when he saw my results and recommended I take a bit of time off, but that's not an option as I'm in the middle of the fight of my life and I know if I allow myself to fall or to even slow down I'll never be able to find the momentum to start going again. So I get up and go to work everyday even though I'm pretty sure I must be dying of the one thing I haven't already been tested for.

Fortunately, Tammy doesn't want wining or dining, let alone foreplay anymore. She wants to *crack on* and then lie there afterwards with her buttocks raised on a pillow to maximise the chances of my poor dilapidated sperm sliding powerlessly down towards her deformed DNA.

It didn't work that time round and she was cheerfully stoic about it (I was ecstatic) because it is statistically unlikely to happen on the first attempt so we've crossed that off the list. I don't tell her it did twice the previous three times I tried (not that I was trying the first time) because I think I may have programmed my sperm to self-destruct within three seconds of leaving my ball sack.

It's a peculiar sensation, willing the person you are actively trying to impregnate, not to pregnate and I'm sure there are more scientific methods which do not involve placing my penis inside her, but I'm buggered if I can think of a way to retain my relationship without looking as though I'm at least trying to provide her with her very own humpback or Mr Potato Head.

Julia says it's great we're trying, but then she loves babies and thinks everyone should be afflicted by them. Plus she thinks I'm exaggerating about the state of the gene pool. *But Tammy's so nice* she exclaims. *And normal* and she is but if you want to feel physically superior go to a Bainbridge family do.

The last one we went to was in a room full of mutants with limps and wheelchairs everywhere. There was not a single able-bodied person in it but none of the buggers was born handicapped. They'd actively made themselves that way. I spent the whole day trying to keep the children away from the wild-haired uncle walking around in a pair of torn boxer shorts you could see his arse through, but I felt like a god by comparison.

Plus Tammy smokes which is not going to help matters if by some laughable twist of fate I do somehow knock her up. She pretends that she doesn't having gone out of her way when we got together to tell me, unprompted, that she definitely doesn't but she stinks when she gets home and there's ash all over the car. I'd rather she admitted it but then I'm reminded by every three out of four emails hounding me throughout the day, that it could be worse.

Philippa's decided to ignore the advice of the OCL and indeed the decision of the court and so continues to plague me with every thought that goes through her infantile mind, especially the dark ones which accuse me of owing her money.

Inexplicably here in Canada, the way the law works is the losing side has to write up the judge's order and comply with it. Let me re-phrase that in case it's so mind bogglingly incomprehensible you can't work it out. The side that loses the case, the side that doesn't actually agree with the verdict, has to write it all up and so all her pie-eating lawyer has to do is tell me *my client doesn't consent to this* even though the court's ordered it.

So I realise now that there's no end. There's no winning, only losing. My life gets worse every day and there's nothing that can stop this hideous person who's intent on destroying it because every time I think I've got somewhere she goes for the next thing and she's not working so she has all this time on her hands while I'm on medication because without it I'll implode.

I'm banging my head against a brick wall, which has been reinforced with steel barricades. Every time we beat her, she ignores it. The only way to get her to adhere to the previous judgment is to spend thousands of dollars taking her to court again, only to have her disregard it all anyway.

She's after the money now. The seventy grand Linda hid in her account that I frittered away in boutiques is back on the table. My half of the previous private school fees she explicitly agreed I'd paid her in full for, but which I stupidly didn't get in writing. My half of all the extra-curricular activities she's not even supposed to be signing the girls up for, which I rightly refuse to pay. My tax rebate that she's somehow found out about. Her share of my gran's inheritance. It is constant and it's never going to stop. We're always due back in court at some point. I finally understand that now.

The only hope I have is when she tries to claim all of these so-called debts off me, I can challenge the amount of maintenance and spousal support I pay. The girls are old enough now for Philippa to easily work although according to her it's impossible with the few hours she has free between pickups and drop offs. It's a wonder I manage it when I have them every other week and the law says the

State can't make her work but they can deduct the minimum wage for the hours she could be doing from the amount I pay her every month. Which would frankly be life changing, if nothing else than for my dignity (if I can scrape it off the floor).

But in retaliation she's going for sole custody and primary residence with access for me on alternate weekends and one midweek evening again. So in retaliation for that, I'm requesting sole or joint custody and primary residence or equal time which I already have but my worst case scenario is that Judge Weiner is ill the day we go back to court and I get someone who hates blokes or who falls for Philippa's charm or the lies, whichever is dominant that day. And then I lose everything I've ever gained. Not that I've really gained anything.

My one consolation prize is the OCL report. The physical evidence that an independent, unbiased professional body identified my ex-wife as a nutter. And she knows it too. A few days after the last court case I had the girls' headmistress on the phone to me trembling because Philippa had been screaming at her to *never open the report*.

That she will eventually show her true colours and fall out with whomever she comes into contact with is guaranteed, but the timescale fluctuates unpredictably leaving me vulnerable. But this time I had pre-warned the school that there might be trouble and sure enough when Tammy turned up to pick up the kids, Philippa was already waiting for her. Or waiting for me really as in her opinion Tammy shouldn't have been there at all despite the judge's ruling. So it was Katie and Lauren's teachers who had the unenviable job of insisting the girls go with their father's slut-faced whore (not their words, I believe) rather than with their own *Mother*.

Their persuasive powers failed in the face of Philippa's outrage and it was at that point that the headmistress was summoned to deal with a situation, which was clearly beyond the teachers' pay grade. And this is also when Tammy got the OCL report out and Philippa let rip in front of the children, the school staff and half the parents in the playground.

'I'm going sue you! This is slander! Girls, come here. Come here! Don't you dare let that woman take my children from me. That report is fake. It's all lies. Give it to me or I'll see you in court.'

But the head stood firm, God bless her, so I suppose I have to look forward to a barrage of emails demanding we move the girls again. So let her try because one of those twenty-two recommendations against her requires she involve me in all the decisions about schools now and she can't transfer them without the headteacher's compliance. And she's not getting that now without me. Or the opportunity to volunteer there anymore.

I fill Julia and Andy in on all of this in the car on the way back. Their kids are sleeping like zombies with their glazed eyes half-open and their mouths gaping wide. Julia's head keeps lolling and then jerking to attention but Andy's fine despite denying he slept at all on the flight over (Julia appears to disagree).

Tammy's home by the time we get there and she's parked on the garden hose again even though I've told her a dozen times that's not what the people who designed it had in mind. I let everyone into the house while I move her car and then mine into the driveway and when I finally get inside I see Tammy has made dinner. This is only the second time I've ever seen her cook if you count the chargrilled blocks of carbon she said were fishcakes and fries the last time.

We decided pretty early on that we both have our individual strengths. Hers is bringing home endless supplies of alcohol and mine is cooking, cleaning, tidying up, doing the laundry, DIY and opening jars of peanut butter. But she always says thank you so I don't mind at all.

Today, however, she's out to impress and I'm touched that she's conscious of coming across well in front of my family. She needn't worry. She had them when she said *I have endless supplies of alcohol* but it's really sweet of her to cook when I know it's not her forte.

It's not very nice for everyone else though, it has to be said. She's made pasta, which she's managed to break down into pure starch and burn to the bottom of my favourite non-stick saucepan, which she's also gone to the trouble of destroying with a fork.

She scrapes the pulp into dishes, passes me a jar of Dolmio to open and pours it on top, all the while chatting away merrily. She doesn't even heat it up first. It's just cold tomato sauce and mashed carbohydrates that even the kids won't eat (but then they have grown up with Julia's *fucking pasta sauce* so the stakes were always going to be high). They're falling asleep at the table (or playing dead) so my sister apologises and takes them down to the basement to bed, where she's probably filling herself up with my dry roasted peanuts and Peperami.

It was hit and miss whether the basement would be ready on time. The build turned into a nightmare in the end, predictably really, given the violent stream of diarrhoea blasting through the rest of my life. Wallace, the contractor we'd hired on the recommendation of a woman at Tammy's office stopped turning up one day, but he was swiftly replaced by a bombardment of other people hammering on the door demanding cash for things we'd already paid him for. He'd skipped away with the money and disappeared off the face of the earth. One guy was about to register a debt against the house, which is a fun thing you can do over here to screw up other people's lives if they owe you money, but we didn't. We'd already paid but we damn well paid again when he shared his plans with us. And would you believe that when Tammy told her colleague what was happening, she said, 'Oh my gosh! He did that to us too.'

That's what I mean! Holy Mother. What's wrong with these people? They're delusional. They can never say something's shit. It has to be awesome, even if some bastard crook has completely shafted them. How was that? *Great! Amazing!* Would you do it again? *No.* Just say it's frigging awful (except when it comes to Tammy's cooking but equally don't overdo it or she'll make it again).

So with four weeks to go before everyone was due to arrive, muggins here got his guns out (not literally, before this ends up in court) and enjoyed a few excruciating work outs with my old friends The Hammer and Mr Hacksaw, all the while reliving the last time I'd found myself in that exact same position on a ticking clock and no sleep. Needless to say, it was not pleasant but at least this time Tammy kept the kids out of my way so I could get on with it without smashing them in the head or sawing my finger off trying to watch them do cartwheels on the joists.

And I've got to say, I'm pretty pleased with my handiwork. I got a proper plasterer in to finish it off because that's a skill you need a steady hand for and I've had a tremor in mine since I walked down the aisle but I redid the bathroom, plumbed in the washing machine and dryer, put up two new walls to create a den that people can finally stay in and I did all this without killing the rabid beast that is Tammy's dog/rat/burden.

It looks bloody amazing and by amazing, I mean amazing, which would obviously confuse anyone here. I've probably added about fifty grand to the value of the house, which doesn't make up for the ten grand we paid to *Where's Wally* but does at least instil a little sense of pride. Everyone's very complimentary about it but then they would be. Because it's amazing. And to clarify, by amazing, I mean amazing. Of course, it would have been more amazing if the contractor had just done what we'd paid him to do and saved me the grief and half a dozen fingernails, but that's the least of my worries at this stage in my life.

'I'd have made you do the loft extension last time you were over if I'd known you were this handy.' Julia's smiling but I know inside she's kicking herself for not making more use of me when I was seeing out the last of my days at her house back in Blighty.

'It's all practice,' I say. 'You just need to buy and then lose several houses within the space of a few years. That's all it is.'

'Every cloud, hey?' But every cloud seems to end in a massive downpour.

My inseminating skills have been in demand all week and I thought I'd finally been released for the rest of the month, but Tammy's decided not to leave anything to chance and is taking advantage of Julia and Andy heading off for an early night. It's statistically unlikely that we'll master the incomprehensible art of procreation until we've had at least a few more attempts, but someone must be swinging those numbers and Tammy has apparently been discussing our (her) plans with anyone who'll listen and they all have advice.

The pharmacist in Shoppers Drugmart has suggested taking Pregnacare even before she is pregnant, because it'll be a few weeks until a test can confirm that she is and besides, it's his job to sell exorbitantly priced supplements to desperate people whose only dietary requirements are a range of breaded animals and fries.

She's bought some multivitamins for me too and suggests I need to avoid smoking and drugs (done), stay out of the hot tub (I'm still paying it off. I'll stop getting in that thing once and only once my giggle bags look like raisins), cut down on alcohol (but it's free…), exercise more (in between work, looking after the kids, cooking for everyone, cleaning everything, preparing endless documents for court, dealing with limitless hostile demands for money from everyone from carpenters to psychopaths, defending myself against the deluge of accusations fired at me by people I've never met but who appear to know my ex, answering one in every fifteen vilified emails that shave a day off my life when I read them and ferrying my family around because the only way I can see anyone I love is to make them fly over here and live off me for weeks) and reduce my stress levels (seriously?).

A good friend, Sara-Jayne, who I've never even heard of has explained that if I enter Tammy from behind in a spooning position, my penis will penetrate her vagina more deeply increasing the likely trajectory of sperm towards her uterus when I ejaculate. Bob Delany from accounts also added that she needs to keep her hips raised for at least twenty minutes afterwards, not the five she gave it last time. It all sounds very romantic and spontaneous and I am delighted my knobbing techniques have received so much attention from so very many close friends and associates.

She heads upstairs to have a poo so she doesn't need to worry about it afterwards when my bad boys are speeding towards their destiny and as I hear the bathroom door close, I pour myself a large glass of single malt and down it in one. Then I pour myself another and sip it more slowly with my balls cupped in my warm, sweaty hand as I contemplate whether or not she'd notice if I had a quick fag.

Deck The Halls

Tammy's racing around the playground with the kids, all four of them. She's set up an obstacle course and they've been running around it for at least twenty minutes. Julia, Andy and I are huddled together banging our toes on the snow dusted ground to keep warm, huge winter coats bunched up over our ears, hands encased in thick gloves we're squeezing under our armpits as we admire her energy and enthusiasm, but make no attempt to join in.

'You can see she doesn't have any children of her own,' Andy smirks.

'Wait till next time we come. I guarantee she'll be standing over here with us,' Julia adds and the whole joke hinges on Tammy having a baby by then and being as jaded as the rest of us. I can't bring myself to join in.

'She's so good with them all,' my sister continues.

'*She's awesome, man. Can we take her back with us?*' Andy's attempt at an accent is more Jamaican than Canadian. He's always been terrible at impressions and that alone makes me laugh.

Tammy is good with the children. She always has been. She's chasing them now and they're screaming and giggling and enjoying themselves effortlessly. And so is she it would seem, but like Andy says, this is still a novelty for her. She spent the morning making gingerbread houses with them all and decorating the tree in candy canes for the third time and later I expect she'll teach them to crochet or make a reindeer out of papier mache. There was a time when I might have done that too but suddenly it feels like there aren't enough hours in the day, despite simultaneously seeming like there are far too many.

'Daddy!' Katie grabs at my leg as she darts past.

'Don't look at me,' I have absolutely no intention of moving. 'Ask your Aunty Julia here if you need saving.'

'I would, Kiki. But it's my knees. Andy. You go and join in.'

'Bugger off. I'm on holiday.'

'Daddyyyyy!!' Katie stumbles rapturously out of Tammy's reach as Lauren throws herself into the monster's path like a sacrificial lamb with a weakness for tickles. Then all four of the kids hurl themselves around Tammy's thighs, convulsing in fits of laughter as her fingers poke joyfully into their sides.

It's quarter past four and everyone's having a great time but I'm starting to feel anxious. The Thousand-Yard-Stare will be calling the girls at five as usual and they need to be warm and calm by then, pink noses suitably thawed and any trace of excitement vanquished from their little voices so their mother doesn't overreact to any accidental display of happiness. Any deviation from vacant indifference will be met by a spiralling interrogation, which will end in tears and the announcement that she's taking them to the moon just to put us in our place. And she'll be charging me half for the tickets.

She's already called nine times today and sent six emails stating the girls were devastated when they hung up last night and they'd insisted, through hysterical wails that must have been drowned out by the radio, that they'd call her again this morning. Neither of them have mentioned it and they're having a wonderful time not being grilled about everything my sister has said or done, so I've left it.

The agreement is one call a day at five o'clock unless they specifically ask to phone her. She can't stand that they are here with Julia's children and she has no say anymore. They're Tammy's family now and while Philippa doesn't want them, she doesn't want anyone else to have them either. Or worse, for them to actually like my girlfriend more than they like her, which is hilarious. I could literally invite a lice-addled junkie to join us over here and we'd all have more affection for her than we do the crazed lunatic who continues to ruin my life.

But Philippa's aggrieved Julia declined an invitation to meet up for coffee as though that's standard etiquette for two people who've each accused the other of threatening aggressive behaviour and slanderous attacks. She's dealing with my sister's rejection of this offer the way she always does - by strenuously interfering with the time we have together and spoiling it as much as she can.

'You alright?' Julia asks and I make a noise, which is supposed to convey that I am, but it's more of a grunt and does little to reassure her.

'We've got time,' she says. 'Don't let her get to you.'

And it's so easy for everyone else to dismiss her. To roll their eyes and say 'What a bitch. Let's go and grab a hot chocolate'. But I can't. She's a cancer that continues to eat away at my soul and is always at the back of my mind. For every moment of unhampered joy, there are fifty minutes of relentless hellish torment to pay. For every second I let my guard down, there's an hour of pain and retribution for the toll it will take bracing myself again.

She's in a bad place at the moment. The kids say she was arguing a lot with Barry when they went skiing, but that's not exactly atypical so I don't know if I should read anything into it. The silly cow has her emails linked up to the girls' iPad so we have total access to everything she writes or receives. She's been contacting schools in the UK asking about teaching positions and I know she has an interview lined up in February near the old house in Surrey but she hasn't mentioned any of this to me. And she'd have to.

My dad's certain she's planning to run off with the girls again but she can't. That actually would be child abduction now we have the separation agreement, plus she wouldn't get any more money from me if she did so I can't really guess what she's up to. She put a post up on Facebook asking for recommendations for cheap deals on flights as though she thinks she can go back there every other week or, I don't know, go in term time. But even she can't be so mad as to think she could maintain two houses or that I'd let the girls fly back to England on their own six times a year to see her if she relocated back there.

She's been trawling Rightmove though, looking up places to rent in the same area and Julia asks me, 'If she's that desperate to go back, why don't you do it? Why don't you come home?'

And I tell her with tears in my eyes that I don't trust her to go through with it and even if I did, Tammy doesn't want to emigrate.

And Julia says 'But if she knows you're this unhappy…?' and I say she does know, but her whole life is here and I don't want to make her feel like I do.

I don't want to emotionally blackmail her into leaving her job – a job she could easily do in Weybridge, or the house we could easily sell and replace, or her insipid idiot friends she hardly sees anyway and her pervy, gross family that I could easily never set eyes on again.

They all joined us for Christmas. There was no getting out of it and I don't know if it was all psychological or if I was genuinely ill, but I was so completely broken that once we'd got through the frenzied pretence of Santa dumping tons of cheap Chinese crap in our house, I had to excuse myself and go back to bed. I had bags under my eyes I could have steam roasted the turkey in and I was shaking from my head to my toes, but this is my default position these days so what's the difference?

Dom the Butcher had driven over on Christmas Eve complete with a bird the size of an ostrich, allegedly to make the most of the free-flowing booze and hot tub, but I could tell it was so that he wouldn't have to wake up alone.

That probably hadn't helped matters as far as my head went and with three hours to go before the Addams Family arrived, Julia and Andy had to take over the cooking. I say take over. I hadn't prepared a thing and Tammy was best kept out of it. Her job was to entertain the children, although I'm not sure who was entertaining whom.

They did it all, while I lay under the duvet shivering with exhaustion and trying to gather the strength to simply get up. And as I lay there, it hit me again and again as it has a hundred million times. This was all I had to look forward to for the rest of my life. It was a farce and my only contribution to the world was not dying for a brief period of time.

I don't know how many hours had passed before I heard a tentative knock on the door. Dom creaked it open and peered into the room.

'Alright, mate?' he whispered and there was no need to tell him I wasn't. 'Hair of the dog?'

I shook my head. 'Driving the kids across to the nutcase's later.'

'One won't hurt.'

'Better not hand her the ammunition on a plate, just in case.'

'Fair enough.' He hovered in the doorway. 'Anything I can do?'

'Just feeling a bit out of sorts, mate. Probably coming down with something.'

'Yeah, right. Something. I think I might be coming down with that too. Candice won't even let me talk to Sadie. She's saying my own kid doesn't want to speak to me, but I know that's bollocks. Unless she's been filling her head with all sorts of shit about me.'

'Sorry, mate. I should have asked how the call went.'

'It didn't, to put it in a nutshell. The stupid cow wouldn't even tell Sadie it was me on the phone.' He was still talking but I couldn't take in what he was saying. My mind kept drifting back to Philippa and the last time I saw her.

'I will fucking have you.' Her face was screwed in that perennial scowl, her eyes blazing as spit flew from her misshapen mouth. 'If I do nothing else for the rest of my life I will make it my mission to ensure that you suffer, you arsehole. Every time you go to sleep, every time you wake up, every time you draw a breath, know that I'll be thinking of ways to get even with you, you self-serving dickwad. You think you've got the better of me, lording it over us in your ivory tower with that slut-whore at your side while your daughters and I have to live in a shithole surviving on food stamps.'

'You got most of the money, Philippa. You still do,' I say and regret it immediately.

'Does it look like I got all the money? Is that what you tell yourself so you can sleep at night, poor baby. Who do you think is going to believe that? Look around. You haven't got your skanky family here right now to back you up, you righteous wanker.

'And they'll be leaving you again soon enough, but you keep telling yourself they care. That they're not just here for a free holiday. And don't worry. Believe me when I say that you won't be alone when they fuck off back to England because you'll still have me. Everywhere you look, every time you turn around. I'll be there. And don't you ever forget it. You belong to me, you pathetic piece of shit.'

'It's a bitch of a day this one, hey?' Dom was staring at me as though he'd been waiting for an answer for a while. 'Well, I'll leave you be. Come down and join us when you're feeling up to it.'

I don't know if I'll ever feel up to anything again. I could lie here forever and it still wouldn't be long enough. Nothing is working out here. The house is finished more or less but it took it out of me. Tammy's great but this baby business is really getting me down and there's nothing I can do about it if I want to hold onto her. The girls are brilliant but I never really feel like we can all relax when they're here in case anything gets back to Philippa and sets her off again. Like she needs an excuse.

Even work is terrible. There was a short stretch of months when it was bearable. When it was actually interesting enough to be a tiny bit stimulating and a break from the usual monotony of being metaphorically kicked in the knackers every time I woke up. But that all changed when they brought in a lying arsehole to run the department. He's fabricated his entire career, but the big bosses lap up his bullshit and fail to realise if you take away the veil of sanctimonious pretence, all you're left with is a nasty little turd.

And so young vulnerable girls hardly older than my own kids are being pimped out and abused every day that this arsewipe is laughing his little legs off while they're having theirs spread by some stranger their so-called boyfriend's introduced them to. And not one of these teenagers doesn't have daddy issues, whether they've been abused or deserted or unloved. They haven't chosen to be there. They've been chosen because nobody cares where they are, especially my new boss

So I carry on doing my job and these kids carry on doing theirs. I've almost convinced one to testify against her pimp but she keeps getting close and then changing her mind. He loves her, you see. And for the money she makes him, I expect he probably does. He has another five girlfriends he loves just as much though and the last time he beat her I came as close as I've ever got to bringing her onside.

But then she had second thoughts, the way they always do and so I wait every day for the inevitable call over the radio saying they've found someone matching her description, if they're able to identify her at all. It's frustrating and upsetting and ongoing, like everything else. Nothing ever seems to get better and everywhere I turn someone's standing in my way, making sure I achieve nothing, help no one and never move on.

I lay there for hours unable to sleep but unable to drag myself out of bed while downstairs my mate, sister and brother-in-law were preparing a ridiculously huge meal for the weirdest bunch of people they would ever meet.

They arrived in dribs and drabs over the course of the morning and as I heard the volume rising in Julia and Andy's voices – as though if they spoke loudly enough these dumbbells would eventually understand them – I realised I had to go down and put them out of their misery. Despite appearing briefly to say hello in my jogging pants and a T-shirt that was covered in holes, I was pleased to note I was still better dressed than any one of them, but we were family now after all so why not put comfort ahead of cleanliness? I should be flattered they don't feel they have to make any effort around me, I suppose.

Dwayne had brought the fifteen-stone fat suit he always wears and was so exhausted after lugging it all the way from the car to the house, he immediately sank into the sofa where he stayed for the next seven hours, nursing his Type 2 Diabetes with handfuls of my dry roasted peanuts (who put them out?) and wiping his fingers on a cushion I would have to throw away.

My lovely mother-out-law was sprawled out next to him in a dress that rode up higher than was decent or even tolerable but I was too preoccupied by the combined weight on the sofa to let a mere display of excess flesh bother me. I had enough horror left to be suitably apprehensive though when the girls were invited across the sea of laps to open their presents – one, because I wasn't sure if I'd ever get them out again and two, because I was certain the sofa wouldn't take it, so I suggested subtly that they sit on the floor.

Dwayne and Chelsea had brought presents for Julia's kids too though which was a nice touch. I did appreciate that. I still would have preferred it if they'd posted it all and stayed home instead.

By the time I was showered and presentable (dressed for kings by some standards) Wobbly Wayne had arrived and Tammy was stretched out over him on the other sofa throwing her head back and laughing as her legs melded into the depths of his jelly thighs. She wasn't laughing at that. She hadn't noticed, I don't think. She's just unaccountably fond of him, despite the drivel that crawls out his mouth and the way he makes my stomach turn, not in the least when she does that – places her feet inches from his penis as though that's not creepy at all.

I could tell Julia and Andy had clocked it but they didn't say a word. They wouldn't. They're far too polite. Instead they smiled sweetly and made small talk with these half-baked simpletons who seem even worse in comparison to people of above-average intelligence and below-average waist size. It's embarrassing, but at least I am pretty sure that not one of them will accuse me of stealing their money or beating their daughter, which counts for a hell of a lot more than their appearance or IQ these days. Not that some soap would go amiss.

But the fun wasn't over. Tammy's cousin, Michela was yet to arrive, although nobody was expecting her since she dropped by without her mother (the recluse) or even an invitation, but she did bring another boyfriend we'd never met to replace the last five who didn't stick around either. I'd tell you his name, but it's immaterial. No one bothered with an introduction. We all knew we'd never see him again. It's enough to know that his teeth looked like sweet corn and his left eye was bigger than the right.

I've had to make Tammy ban her cousin from bringing her boyfriends to the house when the girls are here but obviously this is a special occasion and we had no say in the matter. I don't know any of these geezers from a bum on the street and I'm not even certain that she does.

I came home after work a few weeks back to find Tammy and Michela in the hot tub with the last one and she'd lent him a pair of my trunks. I was so livid, I had to throw them out (my trunks not the drunk fools in my garden, though I should've). Tammy thought I was overreacting and I said 'How would you like it if a total stranger stuck his knob in your gusset?' but I should have known she wouldn't care. She's not affected by stuff like that and who knows? Maybe it's better her way. Maybe I've got enough to worry about than adding hygiene into the equation. It certainly doesn't seem to bother anyone else.

So with the cousin and the interloper that made fifteen and we were eating at one so that I could share Christmas dinner with my daughters before I had to drop them off at the loon's apartment at two. Too many to all fit around the table which at least meant I didn't have to sit and watch any of them spill food all over their faces and besides they were more comfy sitting as they were. The whole room is open plan anyway so I sat at the table with all the kids, Dom, my sister and Andy while Tammy's lot squeezed a few years out of the lifespan of the sofas, but it was nice enough.

I felt mildly guilty about leaving everyone else to organise lunch but no one seemed to mind and as the free wine flowed, the general goodwill went up proportionally to the alcohol going down. Though to be fair, I think I was the only one who was ever actually grumpy.

'Have some carrots,' I lumped an obligatory spoonful onto Katie's plate and she gagged.

'I don't like carrots.' Like I'd taken a mid-meal dump on her plate.

'You eat carrots all the time.'

'Not cooked ones.' Obviously.

'What's it matter if they're cooked? They're still carrots.'

'They don't taste the same. They're yucky.'

'Yeah! They're yucky,' all the kids agreed.

'Don't you two start.' There were times my sister was not to be messed with. 'Eat them up please.'

'But we don't like them.'

'Nobody cares if you like them. They're good for you. They'll keep you healthy.'

'But Grandpa Dwayne and Grandma Cheesy eat carrots and they're–'

I shut Lauren up with a forkful of peas while Andy tried to pretend that the noise that exploded through his nose was just him choking on a green bean.

Then Michela announced, 'We told Duke's best friend, Reece, to drop by later. Hope that's okay.'

'Yes, of course!' In situations requiring a stern *no*, I could always rely on Tammy to be Canadian. 'That'll be awesome. The more the merrier!'

The doorbell went and I let out an audible sigh that was totally wasted in a room full of deaf ears. Michela bounced off the arm of the sofa, dripping gravy on the carpet as she scrambled to the door.

'I'll get it!' she shrieked as though there was a remote chance of anyone else bothering to get up.

I gritted my teeth and stabbed more carrots onto Lauren's fork with the ubiquitous threat involving her not getting dessert.

'Mummy,' she said by way of response and it took a moment to register what she meant.

The hairs on the back of my neck stood up immediately and the blood drained from my suspended arm. I dragged my unwilling eyes from the wall of open mouths facing me and I turned around slowly.

'Happy Christmas, everyone! I thought I'd save you the trip, Dan.' Philippa's eye were glassy, her smile fixed.

My hand wilted and a carrot dropped onto the plate. I said, 'You're forty-five minutes early.'

'I know. The roads are deserted. Aren't you going to introduce me?'

I said nothing. This was five hundred times worse than a knob in my man gusset. This was a knob in my living room and nobody spoke, not even the children.

I could see Philippa's nostrils beginning to flare dangerously and then suddenly Julia leapt up with a huge smile and strode across towards her, her arms outstretched wide.

'Philippa! How nice to see you. I'm so glad you came by. I was worried we wouldn't get the chance to see you before we left. You look wonderful. Andy, look! It's Philippa.' As though he might not have noticed, but he took his cue like a man (who has been condemned to die horribly) and stood up with a brave trembling grin.

They kept her busy at the door with compliments and inane conversation that centred on her achievements (the most eeked out degree of all time and her as yet incomplete PGCE) and observations about the tourist attractions they'd visited, the glories of which they managed to accredit to her.

It took a few minutes to gather up the girls' bags and though they didn't want to leave (they had another forty minutes before I had to hand them over.) I couldn't have that charm sucker in my house a moment longer. Her poison had already ruined the meal and any memory I'd have of that day. It was almost inconceivable that only a few moments before I'd thought it couldn't get worse than entertaining a bunch of bloated ignoramuses. Now perspective had raised its cocky head once again to remind me how good I had it now. I told the girls to say their goodbyes and they did, reluctantly and then I bent down to hug them.

'Can Lucas and Maya come too, Daddy?' Katie asked and Julia smiled sweetly down at her.

'Not this time, Kiki. You're going on holiday with your mum and we're going somewhere too, but we'll all see each other when we come back. Have a wonderful trip, Philippa. You must be fantastic at skiing now.' Then bending down to kiss the girls. 'Have a fabulous time, you two. We want to hear all about it when you get back.'

And with that they headed out the door, Philippa adjusting her coat around her inflated ego and stroking her restored pride. We watched the plumes of our warm breath spread towards my daughters as we waved them goodbye and I stood there in the cold for a few moments longer composing myself after they drove out of sight. Trying not to pass out with the strain of not breaking down. Of not collapsing in a ball and staying there forever.

'Well, she seems nice,' chirped Michela and I slammed the front door, grabbed a bottle of whiskey from the side and brushed past her on my way back to bed.

The Lion, The Witch And The Wardrobe

Tammy's parked on the hose again. I'm not surprised. Every time I get back from a ten-hour shift at one in the morning or thereabouts, I have to get out of my own car and move hers. I warn her repeatedly that it'll blow and the next day she'll have parked on it again. It's quite a mission too in a decent-sized drive so I've got to give that to her. This time however, she's ruptured it and flooded the basement.

'I never thought it would actually blow!' she says incredulously.

Naturally, she's only travelled as far as the TV since she got home so by the time I discover it, the damage has already been done. But still, it's nothing that won't take a few months to dry out with the heating on full blast and I can easily replace the warped floorboards by ripping the whole lot out and starting again.

The collection of annuals I've had since childhood have had it though, along with any dreams I had of selling them for a vast fortune one day. But it's fine. The timing couldn't be better. It's garbage collection day tomorrow, which she's also forgotten despite the fact there are three hundred bins lining the street.

And at least I've moved her car already because normally she parks it right in front of the wheelie bins so I end up having to carry four hundred pounds of rubbish over my head to get it to the pavement (or *sidewalk* for anyone who would otherwise fail to understand what those strips of concrete lining every street are for).

It's not even her car. It's my car, which is on its last legs but as long as I look after it properly I should be able to keep it running for another year or so. Her car arrived home one day with the wing mirror hanging off and the wires dangling out with seemingly no explanation for how this had happened. So it's in the shop. It's ready. She just hasn't got round to picking it up yet and I can't get it because if I do, I'll have to pay and I have no credit whatsoever and still hundreds of bills to settle.

So I'm in my work car, which I'm only supposed to use when I'm on duty and if I suggest picking hers up together she's always too tired to go and get it right then. If she's tired now, I don't know how she'll cope with being woken up five times a night by a baby but as yet, it's not an issue.

We're six attempts in and *statistically* we're heading towards the home stretch, but staying optimistic is taking its toll on Tammy who's becoming increasingly desperate to turn my already hellish existence into Dante's Inferno.

She's taken to shovelling Brazil nuts down her throat twenty-four seven because they're an excellent source of selenium which ironically prevents DNA damage in the egg (like a few nuts are going to undo several generations of inbreeding). I told her maintaining a healthy diet and exercising also increases fertility but, for reasons I'm choosing not to contradict, she prefers to take her chances by downing her body weight in monounsaturated fats instead.

She's also trying to cut back on her hours to reduce the stress she's under while simultaneously going out a lot more after work, which seems counterproductive to me but she says having fun will improve her mood and her chances of conceiving. I don't know why she thinks she can't have fun with me…

We've just made it back from a long weekend away in the country where a colleague has a cabin by a lake in the middle of some woods. It was fairly idyllic or at least I can imagine it would've been if Wayne hadn't joined us. AKA the boy who turned up on holiday without a toothbrush or a phone charger. He even went to a shop while we were there and came out with a new charger. **Didn't bother himself with the toothbrush though.** It was only four days after all, but it wasn't all bad. By the end of it, he could clear a path of midges every time he breathed and those things could bite.

Not that Tammy was much better. I asked her on day two are you going to be having a shower while we're here? And she said, 'I'm at the cottage!' like that explained why even the flies were better groomed than the pair of them.

It was four hundred degrees and all I wanted was to lie under a running faucet all the time and it's a good job I did. It was about the only time I was safe from her advances. There's nothing sexier than smelling your girlfriend when she's in the next room, particularly when she's picking the fluff out of her own brother's cavernous navel.

The girls seemed to have a good time though, the way kids always do when you stick them in the middle of nature and turn off their screens. They spent most of the time jumping off the dock into the ball-shrinking water and dragging me out on a dilapidated rowing boat to an uninhabited island [mound of earth with a couple of trees growing out of the lake] where they searched for buried treasure and came back with a couple of beer caps that meant as much to them as a chest full of gold. I didn't want it to end (but for the eye-watering stench in the air), but like all good things, it did.

'Can we come back soon, Daddy?' Katie was resting her head against the car window, squeezed (or squeezing herself) away from Wayne. Her breath steamed up the glass.

'Maybe. We'll have to see if we're invited. Did you have a nice time?'

'It was the best, Daddy!' I glanced back through the rear view mirror and the light in her eyes tugged at my heart.

'Even better than Gran's?'

'No, not as good as Gran's because she's got spiders.'

'And that's why you like it?'

'They eat the flies.'

'They do eat flies. Maybe that's why she keeps them.'

Katie nodded thoughtfully as Lauren snapped forward, her elbow listing like a sinking ship into Wayne's stomach.

'And she's got a tiny telly.'

'What's wrong with our telly?'

'Our telly's okay but hers is so cute.' They were both nodding now.

'Really? There's no pleasing some people.'

'Don't be sad, Daddy. We love our telly too.'

Which was the sloth's cue to turn on the DVD player in the back and regale us all with running commentary about the lack of realism portrayed in *Tinkerbell and the Great Fairy Adventure*.

He went home for a few days but he's back here again, farting mid-conversation on my sofa, only now as I'm explaining to Tammy that we can't use the basement for a while as I've had to dump almost everything in it into the middle of the floor, he's reached out for my tape measure and is stretching it along the length of his imaginary penis. Fourteen inches no less. Even André looks disgusted and he spends 95% of his time whacking himself off and rogering small children.

I can't be in the same room as either of them anymore. I'm actually grateful the basement is so devastated I have to go back down to sort the whole damn thing out at ten o'clock at night and all the while I'm plagued by the image of Tammy holding a mini-blob like him in her doting arms.

It'll be awful and there is nothing I can do to stop this bucket of slime landing on my shoulders should my unsuspecting testicles hit a home run. If they're even up for the task in hand (so to speak). I'm still stabbing myself in the thigh twice a week with a needle I could use to knit scarves with. Not that it's doing me much good – I honestly feel closer to eighty than forty. I'm still exhausted and unable to keep a straight train of thoughts in my head. Or maybe I'm blocking all of this out.

The girls are excited because they know we're trying. That is to say, they kept asking for another little brother or sister and *you never know* became *maybe someday* which turned into *any time soon, girls* which I wish Tammy had never said because of course it got back to the ex and now she's on about us sharing details of our sex life with the kids as well as making sure they know the minute we have another baby, we won't want them around.

Which couldn't be further from the truth. They're the only things keeping me sane in all of this and much as I love Tammy, if I'm honest, what I love most about her is how much she loves the girls and how much they love her back. For all her quirks, she's the antidote to Philippa's madness and without her, I couldn't cope. Not with the hours I have to put in at work or the crap I have to deal with on a recurring basis just to keep our lives from being ripped apart. So if all I have to put up with in return is a swimming pool in my basement and an extended family I could hide refugees in, it's a small price to pay. As Andy said, 'They seem like good people. They're a bit whiffy, is all.'

Philippa's still chasing interviews in England and I know for a fact the last time she supposedly went to the Bahamas with Barry, she went to Surrey instead. Her mum's living back there, having apparently exhausted Mitch's generosity or maybe she ran out of excuses not to sleep with him. She doesn't have any savings hidden anywhere anymore so she legally qualifies for free housing for once, which leaves Philippa stuck over here looking after the girls by herself and we're all bearing the brunt of her suffering. The hail of constant threatening harassment is like gunfire now and there's nowhere to hide. It only stops when we go back to court and then it starts again immediately. But she's lashing out because she's unhappy so at least I have that. It's nowhere near enough to make it bearable, but helps.

I've had to stop Tammy going through her emails and her web history on the girls' iPad though. She was getting obsessed to the point that I was becoming more irritated with her than I was the paranoid crackpot herself. We all know she's unbalanced but I've reached the point where I'd rather sear my own eyebrows off with a blowtorch than know any more about what goes on inside her deranged mind. But Tammy is a voyeur, a reality TV junkie and there's nothing more entertaining than the demise of the villainous star. Only Philippa's not going anywhere. She's always in the shadows and where there's light, she sucks it inside like a black hole. But we know that and it's our job to absorb as much darkness as we can which is why Tammy and I had our first real argument a few weeks ago.

It wasn't entirely her fault I suppose, but she showed Katie and Lauren a text message the demented maniac had sent which was full of the usual insults and they ran to me in tears. Everything the old witch had written was uncalled for but nonetheless, she's still their mother and if I can manage not to tell them what I think of her, I don't think it's too much to ask that my own girlfriend try to protect them as well.

'They deserve to know the truth!'

'No, they don't. They've been through enough.'

'Well, so have I. How is it that bitch can say whatever she likes about me and I have to act like she's awesome?'

'Because she's their mum. They don't need to know she's insane. Keep them out of it.'

They're exposed to enough of her crazy without knowing how deeply it runs through her veins and how much she hates us. She's even on about putting Stan down now that she has to walk him herself instead of dumping him on me. I can't see her going through with it, if for no other reason than he's the one thing she has that I don't, but even so the girls get hysterical if I don't let them Skype her three times a day to check she hasn't actually done him in yet.

And to top it off, work's taken a turn for the worse, which is remarkable since it was already a bog brush of excrement to begin with. I'm at the point of bringing in the teenage trafficking victim to testify against her boyfriend but my boss isn't convinced there's enough for a warrant for no other reason than he's never anywhere to be seen.

This aside he wants to micromanage the entire case and take the glory for bringing this flesh-peddler down, but it's taken me months to get this girl to trust me enough to even open up about what's happened to her. I don't give a shit if he wants all the credit. I just want Kaylee out of harm's way, but all Detective Sergeant McTwatish wants to do is claim for overtime he hasn't worked and tell me to *get it sorted* while making it almost impossible for me to sort anything, including leave work on time so I can pick up the girls.

'Where are ya?' he roars down the phone hours after I've clocked off.

'Where are ya?' when I'm out doing my job and he's sat behind a desk licking jam off his fingers.

'Where are ya?' when I'm trying to persuade a seventeen-year-old prostitute to bring down the forty-year-old man who made her what she is. The same man who'll dump her battered corpse in a forest without breaking a sweat or even bothering to dig a grave because who gives a toss about another dead whore anyway?

I need to go out and have a good vent to get this all off my shoulders. Or maybe not talk about any of it. Just get bladdered and probably drunk-cry knowing me, but I've hardly seen Dom the Butcher since Christmas and when we have got together he's been distracted and edgy. He's got his own psycho ex to deal with; he doesn't need me banging on about my problems too. Continually reliving the crap that keeps getting thrown at us. It never seems to help anyway. Every living breathing moment is like something out of hell and it keeps getting worse.

Every evening I come home to find the house is a stinking mess even though it wasn't when I left and all Tammy's managed to feed herself is a bowlful of wings she's bought from the pub but I remind myself it's a small sacrifice to pay in return for the chance to live an almost ordinary life.

Only one night, about two weeks after we get back from the cabin, I can't find Tammy anywhere. I call out her name, but she's nowhere to be found. There are fast food wrappers spread across the kitchen and some ketchup has dripped onto the worktop but has yet to congeal.

I try her phone and in the silence I can hear it vibrating through the floorboards upstairs. I call out for her again, but there's no answer. Just her phone ringing where I find it at the bottom of our bed. And as I hang up, I hear a muffled scuffle in the wardrobe and I know before I've opened the door that there will be no coming back from whatever's inside.

But it's just her, huddled up in the darkness weeping and there's a pregnancy test in her hand. What's going on? I ask pulling her out and she answers 'Nothing, honey. I'm being silly. It's all going to be awesome.'

And my heart sinks because I know that it's absolutely not.

More Than Any Man Should Have To Bear

Dom's on a high again. He is going to see Sadie for the first time in months and he's bouncing around his sitting room like a small child with his first bag of Haribo. It's a supervised visit for forty-five minutes at a family contact centre but it's better than nothing.

'If I can just tell her, mate. If I can make her understand none of what her mum's been saying is true. She's gonna know, right? It's all bollocks. I've got a record of all the emails and texts I've sent her. All the times I've tried to call. The old bitch can't get away with telling her I haven't bothered to get in touch.'

'No, of course not,' I'm all teeth and shiny-eyed for him. 'It's brilliant, dude. I'm really happy for you. You'll get it sorted. Like you say, you need to see her face-to-face and tell her what's been happening. Maybe not in detail, but just make sure she knows you're fighting to keep her in your life and that none of this is her fault.'

'Court ordered supervised visits though, mate. What's that about? She's my own kid and I can't see her without some stranger in the room making sure I don't…what? What the fuck do they think I'm going to do?' He's on his feet again. He can't keep still.

'It's not worth thinking about. Try to focus on what you're going to say to Sadie when you see her. It's going to be great, mate.'

'It's been too long, Danny Boy. I can't wait.'

I can't imagine what it must feel like to be in that position. The fear of it has always kept me towing the line with Philippa when in my fantasies I tell her to jump off the nearest high bridge whenever she pulls a fast one, but the longest I've ever had to go without seeing the girls is three weeks. And even then, I get to Skype them everyday.

'I should leave you to it, mate. Let you prepare what you're going to say.'

'I know what I'm gonna say. I'm going to tell her I love her and I want to keep seeing her every week. I'm not this alcoholic womaniser her mother's making me out to be. I'm the same man I always was when we all lived together and she was Daddy's little girl. It's not like I've ever done anything to make her think otherwise. It's all Candice spreading lies and innuendo about me coz she's a dumb bitch and she's trying to get back at me for the affair. It doesn't change how I feel about Sadie. I'm her dad and I always will be.'

'I know, buddy. I get it. You might not want to throw the phrase *dumb bitch* around too much though,' I grin. 'Stick to telling her how much you miss her and remind her of all the good times you had together. Once she sees you, she'll remember you're nothing like Candice says and then at that point, you've got a much stronger case when it goes back to court. Don't worry, you old wanker. She'll be back here every weekend soon enough.'

I stand up to leave and give him a congratulatory punch on the arm, followed by a man hug and a whack on the back. I'd give him a kiss too if I didn't think he'd knock me out.

'Here. I almost forgot.' He pulls away and grabs a couple of white greaseproof packages from the fridge. 'There you go. Best burgers in Toronto. Don't say I never give you anything.'

'A bag would have been nice but much appreciated, as always.'

He sticks one into each of my jacket breast pockets and pretends to give them a squeeze. 'That's a nice little rack that. If all else fails, you can get yourself a job down at Hooters. Earn a bit of extra cash.'

'Long as you leave a big enough tip, I'll save you a booth.'

'That's the best offer I've had in ages.' He waggles his eyebrows suggestively.

'Which is why,' I say reaching for the front door latch. 'You need to call that friend of Tammy's, you dirty lug.'

'I will. I will.' He shakes his head dismissively, pushing me into the corridor.

'You keep saying that. Just do it. Might do you good to get out once in a while instead of choking the chicken in here every night on your own. It's either that or I'm going to get you a goat so I don't have to worry about your gonads exploding. I'll pick you a feisty one. You deserve a bit of loving after all that you've been through.'

'Let me get this visit with Sadie out the way and I might take you up on it. The friend not the goat! Now get out, you soppy bastard before you make me cry.'

And I give him another hug which squashes the burger meat but I still look like I'm walking around with a pair of double Ds I should be proud of so I strip out of my jacket again and fling it on the back seat when I get to the car.

I don't see as much of Dom as I did when I lived in the complex but it still warms my heart on the odd occasion I get to spend time with someone who understands this whole situation. Who knows what a cantankerous bastard I am because I'm British and that's perfectly okay because he is as well.

I can have a really good laugh with the man even though no one else has a clue what's so funny. I can call him a twat as a form of endearment and if a bird were to crap on his head, I could rib him about it for months instead of asking if he needs therapy to cope with the trauma. And if he feels shit, he tells me or at least he doesn't make out everything's great. That having your world ripped apart and taken from you isn't character building. And defending yourself every day against the spiteful accusations of an enemy who has nothing to lose isn't fundamentally ten times harder because she is a woman and no one ever believes that a man could be the victim. Could be frightened or abused.

But we are. All the time. There's no saying when the next malicious attack will occur, where it'll come from and whom it'll affect.

The latest is Philippa warning the girls against letting me into their room at any time. Not only at night, which would still be unforgiveable but I'd expect that of her. I barely ever need to go in there once they're asleep, so it wouldn't be an issue. She'd still be a vindictive sicko, of course but I could tuck the girls into bed and read them stories without explaining that it's alright. I could still sit on the floor and let them paint my face in glittery make-up and put thirty tiny ponytails in my hair. I could never think twice about hurrying them along when they take two hours to get dressed in the morning or take a bath. Now we have another layer of awkwardness to deal with, as if trying to raise them before wasn't stressful enough.

'Daddyyyy? Can you put more hot water in?'

'Not really, love. Can't you do it?'

'The hot tap's too hot. Can you come here?'

'I – er – no. Listen, it's probably time to get out now anyway.'

'But I don't want to.'

'Come on. Get yourself out and put on your pyjamas.'

'Can you help me? Nope. You're a big girl now.'

'Daddyyyyy.'

'Come on, quick as you can.'

The depraved liar has done that to me and to them. She's tainted the purity of our relationship and left the girls questioning their affection for me. She's sullied that innocence and I don't think we'll ever really get it back, no matter how many times I tell them and myself it's all okay.

It's late by the time I get home but Tammy's away on business so the house is immaculate and I reward myself with a few minutes stretched out on the sofa enjoying the silence. And then I remember the girls are not sleeping upstairs and my stomach drops like it always does when I know they're in the so-called care of someone intent on clouding everything they know about me with lies.

It's only Tuesday and the week will stretch ahead indeterminably until I have them back under my roof, except this week is worse than usual because the old hag's birthday is on Saturday and so she's getting them for an extra day.

My sister tells me over and over again to make the most of it. *What she would give to only have to look after her kids fifty per cent of the time!* To be able to leave the house spontaneously, if only to pick up some more milk at the corner shop without it feeling like a military operation (that is destined to fail). To say nothing of going out in the middle of the week without paying fifteen-year-old girls forty quid to sit in your house eating Jaffa cakes and the Wotsits you'd been planning to put in the kids' packed lunches the next day.

'And then as if that weren't enough, you have to drive them back home at the end of the night so you can't even drink!'

And I sympathise but there's nothing satisfying about having more time to yourself when that time's being used to build a great wall of deceit all around you and you even can't be sure your children will be back when it's your turn to have them.

And so maybe that's why I barely put up a show of resistance when Tammy informs me, the night she's back, as my semen slides wearily down her elevated vaginal canal that we're going to see her brother and parents on Saturday or else we'll only end up moping around the house.

All my misgivings about the whole day dragging with only each other for entertainment are suddenly laughable, but I don't raise even a chuckle. Instead I turn the groan that slips inadvertently from my sagging jaw into a yawn and murmur something unintelligible but relatively enthusiastic (relative to getting lumped with a handful of garlicky dough balls masquerading as my in-laws when I should be with my kids).

As much as I can't bear spending time with her family, I'll never make Tammy feel that she can't. I remember all too clearly how it felt being deliberately isolated from everyone I knew and loved and going along with it because it was so much easier than having a row that would never be resolved. Even so, this is going to be awful and if I had a choice, I'd rather spend the day milking the engorged dripping teats of a frenzied porcupine than go over to their place, let alone have them all over here.

But I've misunderstood and we're supposed to be meeting them at the CN tower which is great because it's all the way over the other side of Toronto and I've only been there about two hundred times with all the people I actually do want to spend time with. But I roll my eyes and say well, let's both drive down then so I can pop into Dom's on the way back and find out how it all went with Sadie. And she hasn't got a clue what I'm talking about because she never actually listens to anything that doesn't directly affect her.

I follow her down there in my work car because she hasn't picked up hers from the garage yet so she's still in the Mustang. There's a strange sort of odour wafting around it that I can't put my finger on and I have to wind down the window to let in some air. It's been getting progressively worse over the last few days and I could almost swear Wayne's been using the car behind my back, but he couldn't have been unless he'd taken it out in the middle of the night. Which I would not put past him, but he'd have had to have broken into the house to get the keys. Although, I bet he's got a set for the front door *for emergencies.* The only emergency there'd ever be is if I ever found him in my home uninvited and creeping around in the dark. And he'd need more than the police to come and save him, the slimy, otter-toothed weasel.

I'm still seething at the hypothetical notion of it when Tammy and I eventually pull into the car park and set off together on foot in the direction of the heaving tourist attraction we've unnecessarily planned to spend an otherwise glorious afternoon inside.

'Did you see the queues to get in?' I grumble to disguise the real object of my discontent and she slides her hand through the crook of my arm.

'Don't worry about it!' she exclaims. 'We're not going up.'

I stare at her sideways. 'What do you mean we're not going up?'

'We're not going up. We're meeting everyone here at the bottom.'

'And then we're going up?'

'No. We're going to grab a coffee in the cafeteria.'

'At the bottom of one of the tallest buildings in the world?' She's looking at me like I'm the idiot.

'What? You didn't want to go up it again, did you?'

'No. I just think it's a bit weird to come all the way here if we're not actually going to ride to the top.'

'We've all been up it.'

'I know!'

'Well, what do you want to go up it again for?'

'I don't. I just don't know why we're here.'

'To meet my parents and Wayne for a coffee. Jeez, Dan. I don't know why you're getting so uptight.'

And neither do I really. I don't want to go up the CN Tower. I don't want to queue for hours for the ticket and I certainly don't want to pay $20 to get in when I have to take all my friends and family up it whenever they visit. I just can't get my head around the fact we could've gone anywhere in that case. A nice coffee house in the north of the city where we live instead of a soulless café that's resembles a hospital waiting room with a kid's softplay bang in the middle when none of us has brought any kids.

And she's right. Her grotesque family are there when we arrive. Already seated and nursing some mediocre beverages they could've ordered from any old horrible hot drinks dispenser. And they're all so grotesque I think I might die if I spot anyone I know. It's impossible not to see Tammy in a totally different light when she's in this sort of company. Even the way she behaves around them gives me the heebie jeebies. It's not right, surely they can see that. They make my own family look like the Beckhams.

Dwayne starts telling us that he might have to have his left leg amputated as though it's a matter of course. I say, 'Your left leg amputated?'

He nods and gives it a tap. 'It's part of the condition,' he says sorrowfully. 'The docs have said it'll have to come off if they can't control the diabetes.'

And with that he rips open four sachets of sugar and pours them piously into his cup. Tammy leans across the table and squeezes his hand.

'Oh, Daddy. You poor thing. Can I get you anything?' And they all agree on cake.

I can't sit there any longer. I've put in twenty-five minutes. I think that's enough. No one on earth should be subjected to this idiocy. Not even Philippa deserves to have to put up with this mindless drivel and flagrant stupidity. I stand up too abruptly and my chair makes a screech, which is fortunately drowned out by the unpleasant high-pitched screams resonating around the playhouse behind us.

'I'm so sorry,' I announce. 'I said I'd drop in on a friend. He's been having a hard time of it lately and I promised I'd call by to check on him.'

'What? Who?' Tammy cries in a way that makes my jaw clench.

'Dom. I told you. He's expecting me. That's why we brought both the cars.'

'Oh, yeah, right.'

'Sorry to love you and leave you,' I say but I'm not. I almost skip out the building and as I get to the car, I spot my jacket on the back seat and have a sudden flashback that makes me laugh so much I sound like I'm barking.

The burgers Dom gave me have been festering in my pockets for nearly a week. Thank god it hadn't been that hot or I can only imagine what the maggots would've done to the car. It's not even mine. The jacket's unsalvageable though and I have to drop it into the nearest bin, my eyes weeping as I carry it at arm's length dripping blood past a gaggle of horrified Koreans.

I'm still laughing when I pull up to the complex. I haven't even had a chance to tell Dom I'm on my way but I can see his lights are on so I leap up to the third floor two steps at a time and immediately regret it. I've clearly allowed myself get marginally out of shape and have to climb up the last set of stairs clinging to the bannister. No matter, it's less painful than sitting in a windowless basement watching red necks literally eat themselves to death.

I ring the doorbell and a man I instantly recognise as Dom's older brother because of the flaming hair and wrinkles, opens the door and it's really nice to see him. To put a face to the name that's always coming up in conversation. Then I see some other gingers behind him who must also be family and a woman I assume is his mum comes to the door and I say, 'Sorry. I didn't mean to interrupt. I popped in to see Dom. Is he here?'

And then they tell me that he's died and they're sitting shiva and I don't even know what that is until I look it up when I get home and realise he was Jewish and I don't think he ever mentioned it.

Maybe I didn't know much about him after all. I didn't know Sadie had failed to turn up to the contact centre. I didn't know Candice had refused to take his calls and when she'd finally answered, she'd told him to stay out of their lives for good. Told him Sadie never wanted to see him again. I didn't know he hadn't gone to sleep that night, but instead he'd downed a bottle of bourbon and God knows what else and then at some point he'd gone down to the gardens and that's where he was found. Hanging from one of the trees there at six o'clock the next morning.

And I'm so angry with him. I'm so angry that he did that right there where the kids played. I'm so angry that he didn't even care who might find him. That it could have been a child who had come across his body. I'm so angry he could have done what he did to Sadie. That he was so far gone on grief and hopelessness that he hadn't called me to let me know what had happened. To tell me what was going through his head as though there was no other way. As though he were alone. I'm so angry that he hadn't come to me. That he thought there was nothing left for him here. That he couldn't keep fighting anymore.

And then, as the pain of what he'd done overwhelms me, I start to cry and I don't know how I'm ever going stop.

Done

It's been three months since Dom did what he did and I'm still not used to him not being here – at the end of the phone or sat on a bar stool next to me. Every time my phone pings I expect to see his name there and some dirty GIF he's forwarded from his mobile. But it never is anymore. It's always Philippa or Tammy. It's always something that makes my heart sink. Never anything to make me laugh anymore.

Things are tense between Tammy and me and as much as she likes to make out it's because of what happened, there's more to it than that. It's the endless stream of little things that are no longer endearing or even excusable really.

For a start, she's blown up my Mustang which I'm not going to pretend was worth much, but it was one of the few things I'd managed to cling to when I lost almost everything I owned and it meant something to me even if not all my memories of it were good.

It was my own fault I suppose. I'd let her hang on to it for a little while after she finally got her own one back from the garage because the air con wasn't working in hers and since she drives quite a bit, it made sense for her to use it. Even so, every time I got in it afterwards the oil sign would be on and I'd say 'How long has that been flashing? You have to keep the oil topped up or the engine's going to seize up.'

And she'd deny that she'd ever seen it until one day it died. By which I mean it literally exploded on the highway. She'd killed it. Driven the bloody thing into the ground and then she took ages choosing another one to the point where I was actually having to hire a car to get around.

And when she did get a new one, she kept it and I got her crappy old one with the mismatching wing mirror, which was as hot as a Swedish sauna on a midsummer's day. Like I say, the Mustang wasn't worth much but I could've got a few grand for it, but I didn't even get an apology. If anything, I got the blame for making her late for her meeting.

We're still trying to sabotage the population with our very own bundle of defunct chromosomes but much to my relief and her unrivalled frustration (if you class frustration as more or less moving into the wardrobe) we've been unsuccessful so far. Unfortunate side effects on her part include losing all interest in my children and repeatedly snapping at them for seeking her attention, which they're doing less and less as the weeks pass by.

A few days ago I came home to find them in tears because she'd washed off a picture they'd drawn for me in chalk on the doorstep. It said *we love you, Daddy* but before they had a chance to show me, Tammy had stormed outside and thrown a bucket of water over it, all the while berating them for making a mess. This from a woman who decorates the house in empty fast food packaging every night and thinks her clothes live on the sofa and every other stair. I wasn't impressed obviously, but she's under a lot of strain, even though I'm under far more and yet still manage not to take it out on Katie and Lauren.

We've been back to court yet again and nothing's changed. Philippa's relentless. The hostility and the daily demands for recompense, the accusations and the lies, they go on. Nothing the OCL report recommended has made a difference. Regardless of how many times I win, I never gain anything. She just comes back at me with even more nonsense. Every time I'm victorious, it doesn't mean I've succeeded in getting what I want. It means she hasn't yet. She won't be happy until she's taken the kids away from me and so every time she's told she can't, she ignores it and carries on trying.

She wants the maintenance increase she thinks I'll get stung for and it makes no difference to her how many times she has to demand it from the judge. She's not paying through the nose for a lawyer because she really is living on the poverty line now albeit it still with the lion's share of my monthly wage. She has nothing. *Nothing, you effing bastard,* I believe was the phrase. She's spent all of my money and she's renting a shithole, which is somehow even worse than the last hovel they were in.

Tammy and I dropped the girls off a few weeks ago and there was rubbish and graffiti all over the place. I didn't even want to let the kids out of the car it was so run down and there was Tammy laughing at the depths Philippa had sunk to while I was on the brink of tears because my daughters are living in that dump with her half the time.

Her reaction drove a wedge between us that I can't address. It was proof that as much as she may enjoy playing a part in their lives, no real parent would ever take pleasure in the knowledge their children are living in such a place.

And that's the difference, when it's your own kids. As mind bending as it is, I would rather she was shacked up with Barry in some five-bed mansion on the outskirts of town but I've heard through my contacts at Walton that he's taken a restraining order out on her now and so has his wife so I guess she's blown her chances there and I'm not even pleased about it.

Tammy's still sneaking off with the girls' iPad and trawling through the latest updates in Philippa's imaginary world where she can commute to England every weekday, only Katie's started to notice her walking off with it now and no matter how many times I tell her to leave it alone, Tammy can't help herself from cyberstalking my ex.

What's more I've realised she's also snooping through my phone. Only my messages and email accounts as far as I can tell. All of them, because she knows the secret ones as well.

There's a distance between us and I don't know how to fix it. She has a lot of business trips and that never bothered me before, but now she's started posting photos of herself on Facebook when she's away and she's always with this one guy in particular. I even showed them casually to a colleague who, without any prompting, got halfway through and suddenly said, 'Who the fuck is this guy in every picture?'

I don't think there's anything going on, but he's always leaning on her and I can't help but feel that it's a message aimed squarely at me. You don't accidently post a dozen photos of yourself draped over someone else unless you want to make a point, but if she's trying to warn me what could happen if I'm not careful, it's not working. She's just making the gap between us harder to fill.

We're going to the UK in a few months and I'm hoping the break might do us good. Philippa's going to take the kids in July and I'll meet her there in August and bring them back two weeks later. I'm still harbouring a faint hope that when Tammy gets there, she might change her mind and decide we should stay. I keep telling her my family adore her, she'd get a brilliant job and we could have a good life. Even Philippa might ease off a bit if she gets what she wants. But she's still not interested.

And I can't do it without her. Not that I'd want to. We've made a life together. I made her a commitment when we bought the house. She may have sprung propagating the species (and what a species) on me, but I agreed to it –

mainly because I didn't have a choice – but also because I want her to be happy. I need her to be happy and continue to provide the stability that the girls desperately need in their lives. And my hours are all over the place. My boss is an unsupportive wanker and my ex-wife is always looking for an excuse to drag me back into court again.

'No offence,' Julia says when I call her. 'But you're not the only person in the world to have children as well as a job you know. What do you think the rest of us do?' and I say 'Philippa won't stand for me using any form of childcare though. If she thinks I can't fit the girls around my schedule she'll use it against me.'

'And that Judge will tell her, like he has a hundred times, that you have to work especially if she wants you to keep paying her a shedload of money each month. Besides, she hates Tammy. I'm sure she'd rather you were paying a childminder or for wrap-around care at school than using your girlfriend.'

'I'm not using her,' I say my voice suddenly clipped.

'Yes, you are. You are. And she's using you to get what she wants and that's fine as long as you both want the same thing. But do you?'

I don't know what I want anymore. Things haven't felt right for a while but my mum tells me Tammy's a Godsend and when I mention tentatively moving back to the UK, she tells me house prices have gone through the roof and I'd be lucky to afford a one-bedroomed flat in Newcastle which is a hell of a commute down to Weybridge. Besides, she didn't think Tammy was up for it and I tell her she's not.

'Well then, stop thinking about it,' she says. 'You've made yourself a nice life there. Just get on with it.

And so I do. I keep getting on with it. Every day and every night. I keep moving forward. Keep trying not to think about my friend hanging from a cherry blossom that I'll never see flower again. Keep tiptoeing through this strange life. Keep dealing with Philippa. Keep penetrating Tammy. Keep telling myself that it'll all be alright.

And every day brings another unwelcome surprise but I get on with it. If it's not a court order or a snide accusation or an unforeseen bill, it's an impromptu visit to one of Tammy's weird relatives. It's her half-sister again this time. The tramp with the back fat she can live off if she ever gets trapped behind a tower of her own trash, but she's had a little clear out. It's actually possible to see a couple of chairs now but I would still rather lay my children in a sewage outlet than let them sit down on either one of them. We all stand awkwardly in the middle of the dining room refusing tea and trying to balance staying in the same spot for so long we stick to the carpet versus exposing ourselves to latent diseases by pacing around.

She's moved a stack of boxes from one side of the room to the other and for the first time I notice that what I thought was a cupboard, is in fact a toilet. It's an actual cubicle like the ones you get in public bathrooms where the wall sits a foot off the ground and three foot off the ceiling. Can you imagine being sat there eating dinner and someone comes in and has a giant dump? It's beyond all belief. Who does that?

I hold the girls tightly either side of me and for once they are still and totally silent. We shouldn't be more than five minutes. I'm pretty sure we wouldn't survive much longer than that anyway but suddenly my phone rings.

It is Paxton from work. One of the few good men in the entirety of Walton Regional Police. The closest thing I have to a real friend here now that Dom's not around. It is refreshing to find a Canadian who calls a spade a spade, not a super-duper dirt-shifting sensation. It almost makes up for him being a raging alcoholic with a penchant for throwing cups full of wee at me in the middle of a stakeout. He could almost be British, if it weren't for his stupid name.

There's been a report of a man threatening a badly injured woman with a gun in Glendon Forest and I know instinctively that it's my witness. By the time I get there, she's being carried into an ambulance with a face that looks like she's walked into a moving propeller but she's alive.

The boyfriend made a dash for it earlier into the trees and a team of aviator-wearing officers are scanning the area, their chests puffed out and their weapons raised high. They'll catch up with him somewhere. We know all his usual haunts and he has too much business here in town to do a runner. But I have her. I have Kaylee and I know for sure she'll turn this time. He's gone too far and they have to let me take her somewhere safe now, but it's too little too late.

I stay by Kaylee's side at the hospital until she's taken into surgery to have her jaw pined and then I tell her I will be back in the morning. And I will be. I'm not going to let her give in to her insecurities and go crawling back to that creep this time. I am getting her out of here, as far away from him as I can, but in the meantime, she needs to sleep.

I knew Tammy had taken an Uber from her aunt's place and it's late when I get back so I'm surprised when I realise that the light's still on in the girls' bedroom. I know something bad has happened the moment I walk in the house.

Tammy's stretched out on the sofa in the dark and when I turn the lamp on, she won't look at me. Only her hideous dog leaps up, its horrible claws catching on the blanket on the top of the sofa as it bounces around snarling like he's never seen me before. Tammy pulls him back onto her chest, stroking his scrawny little back and murmuring sickeningly.

'What's going on?' I say.

'Katie's in a strop. I told her off for kicking André.'

'Kicking André?'

'That's what I said.' Katie's never hurt an animal in her life. Not even this feral substitute baby. 'They're still up. They won't let me put them to bed. I told them you'd be ages like you always are, but they wouldn't listen.'

I pull my jacket off and hang it on the coat rack, peel my trainers off and place them inside the shoebox. I throw

Tammy's in for good measure while I'm down there, then without looking back at her, I make my way upstairs where the girls are sitting on their bedroom floor playing My Little Pony.

'Hey, you two.' King Sombra seems to be riding Fluttershy. At least I hope that's what he's doing. 'It's late. What are you still doing up?'

'We were waiting for you, Daddy.'

'That's nice.' They take my hands and I pull them up into a hug. 'I'm here now though so let's get you into bed. Have you brushed your teeth?'

'Yes.'

'Lala?'

'I did, Daddy.'

'Okay. Well, hop in then.'

They both jump onto the bottom bunk. They always like to sleep together. The top bunk is nothing but a storage shelf for ten thousand cuddly toys they never play with but will sense immediately if I cull. I tuck the sheet over their shoulders and into the side.

'Do you want to tell me what happened this evening?'

Katie doesn't answer. Her eyes are glazed. I haven't seen that look for a long time. Not here in my house.

'Tammy pushed Kiki over,' Lauren sits bolt upright, indignation flaring in her little nostrils.

'What do you mean?'

'She pushed her over. André was biting her and then Tammy pushed her over.'

From what I can piece together, the little bastard had been jumping up at Katie, snapping at her and scratching her legs. Katie was screaming and had tried to push the damn thing away and that's when Tammy burst into their bedroom, grabbed André and knocked Katie to the floor.

I was sure she hadn't done it deliberately. You could blow either one of the girls down with a badly aimed sneeze, but that wasn't the point. Instead of asking if she was okay or, I don't know, saying sorry as you do when you send a small child flying halfway across a room, Tammy had flounced out with the dog, leaving Kiki with a huge throbbing bruise and the unchallenged impression that the person looking after her had done it on purpose.

I try to convince them that it was an accident, that Tammy didn't mean to bowl into Katie. She was just trying to get to the dog before he hurt either of them and she bumped poor Kiki over with her (big, ha-ha) bottom. But there's nothing I can say to explain why my girlfriend didn't pick her up afterwards and make it all okay.

I tell them Tammy would never hurt anyone. That she loves them like they're her own and I cuddle them the way she should have at the time and as I tuck them back in, I pray I've done enough and they won't tell their mother. But the last thing they say to me as I turn out the light is 'We don't like Tammy any more. She's not nice.'

They are Philippa's words, but it doesn't matter. I know the battle is lost. And I get it. It's hard enough to keep fighting for your own kids. It's even harder to keep fighting if they're not. At some point, you're going to run out of steam. I'm beginning to remember the feeling but it's not down to the girls.

I take them back to Philippa's for the handover in the morning and the next few days pass in virtual silence. Tammy and I don't refer to the incident again. Not after the initial row we had as soon as I walked back downstairs.

She's simmering with passive-aggressive resentment because I've taken Katie's side over hers, but I know exactly what happened. That dog went for my daughter because she'd laughed or picked up the doll he wanted to piss on or whatever and when Tammy stormed in, she accidently bumped Katie aside. Which is understandable. I've done it hundreds of times. It's impossible to turn around without swinging into one of them. If there's a pair of feet anywhere in the vicinity they'll do their upmost to get right under them. I can picture the scene exactly but what was unforgiveable was walking out of that room without checking my seven-year-old was okay. Without kissing her better and making sure she knew it was all a big misunderstanding.

My girls put up with enough drama at their mother's house, without feeling threatened in this one. And so we haven't spoken much since then. It isn't really an option. Tammy is usually upstairs hiding in the wardrobe *in a pit of despair,* despite everything being *absolutely awesome* any time I try to talk about it.

There's a knock on the door and I get up grudgingly and swing it open.

'Good afternoon, Mr... White? We're from the Children's Aid Society. We're investigating a complaint about possible child endangerment and abuse at this address. Is it convenient to come in and discuss it with you right now or would you prefer to make an appointment to come down to our offices? We're going to need to speak to your partner as well. Is she here?'

And with that, we are done.

Poker Face

I say 'Alright' when Julia picks up the phone but that's the last thing I can get out for a minute and we listen to each other breathing until she says, 'You've done it then?'

It takes a few moments longer but then I sigh and say 'She did it really. I told her I didn't want another baby and she said, *"Well, that's it then".'*

'How are you feeling?' Julia asks and I don't know. I don't know if I've made another colossal mistake or if I've finally done the right thing. But I do know that I couldn't have brought another person into all of this, even if against all odds it didn't look like a great hairy bollock with a set of teeth I could use to open baked bean tins. An all singing, dancing, farting, burping numpty with the mental capabilities of a cheese ball like every other member of the Bainbridge family clan.

Even without the daily stream of shit I deal with, the endless cycle of free flowing crap that flies at me from every direction, take all that away and I'm still left with a stranger I didn't fall in love with. If I ever really loved Tammy at all. I'm not even sure what that means any more. The girls worshiped her and she seemed to adore them too and that was all that mattered to me. She was everything they ever needed, the sort of mother figure they deserved, but when that changed, when she withdrew her love from them and her affection turned to resentment, all that was left was a vacuous, overweight cheerleader chanting for her own team. And we weren't on it. We were just a means to an end.

'So what are you going to do now?' Julia says.

'I don't know. We'll have to sell the house. She's gone to stay with her pervert brother, but I can move in with Paxton for a few months while we sort all this out and then... I don't have a clue.'

'So come back.'

'I can't.'

'Why not?'

There's a silence. I draw a breath and my head sinks back on the sofa.

'Philippa won't do it. She'll agree and then she'll pull out and I'll lose what little is left.'

'Why would she?' Julia doesn't get it. 'She's desperate to come back, you know that. She's been wanting to for years. It's you that keeps saying *no* and I could understand when you were trying to make a new life with Tammy, but there's nothing stopping you now.'

I close my eyes and rub my temple, tired of explaining. 'I can't lose the kids. I've worked too hard getting joint custody. I can't go through it again.'

'But why would you?'

'Because the separation agreement's only valid in Canada. It wouldn't mean anything over there.' Why does nobody understand this?

'Well, tell her you'll only come back if you can stick with the arrangement you've got. And get it in writing. Anyway, it's not like she really wants the girls all the time. She'd go mad.'

'She is mad.'

'Madder then.' Julia sighs. 'She's only threatening to take them to make your life a misery. Give her what she wants and she'll leave you alone.'

'She doesn't know what she wants. She'll change her mind again.'

'What's it matter if she does, as long as you're all over here? She can't take the girls out of the country if you don't let her. You need to get here and then take whatever happens as it comes. And seriously, what on earth can she do to you, that she hasn't done already?'

The sound that explodes through my nose is like gunfire. 'Are you kidding? She hasn't had me locked up yet.'

'Well, alright, but it's not like she won't try that over there. At least here you'll have us to support you.'

'Visit me in prison, you mean.'

'Well, it'd be a damn sight easier to get to Wormwood Scrubs than all the way over there. Especially if they'll only let us in for an hour every week. It's bad enough listening to

Dad moan about the price of the airfare every time he goes over to see you. It'll kill him if he can't even sleep on your sofa when he gets there.'

'He can get himself caught smuggling salami at the Canadian border. They'll probably put us in the same cell. Be much cheaper than a motel.'

Julia laughs. 'Stop it. You're going off track. I'm trying to convince you to come home.'

'You don't have to convince me. I want to come home. It's all I've wanted since I got here, but it's not that easy.'

'Yes, it is! It is that easy. You're the one making it hard. Don't think about it. Just do it.'

I take a few moments to answer. 'It'll cost me. She'll want paying off.'

Julia doesn't miss a beat. 'So pay her off if you have to, but I don't think she will. She's always on about working in the UK, isn't she? And she'll qualify for benefits and tax credits and God knows what else. You could even try and renegotiate the ridiculous amount of maintenance you're paying at the moment.'

'She won't go for that.'

'I promise you. There's a reason she wants to move back. She's not stupid. She's already got all this figured out. She must know that she'll get free housing or enough welfare hand-outs to make it worth her while or why else would she even be looking?'

'Because she's nuts!'

'She might be certifrigginfiable, but she can sniff a pound coin out from down the side of a sofa.'

I can hear the kettle boiling in the background and the speaker sounds muffled for a couple of seconds. I know without her saying anything that Julia's squeezed the phone between her chin and her shoulder and she's making a cup of tea. Picturing her pottering about in the kitchen gives me a nostalgic pang.

'Listen, I've been looking online and with your half of the house in Toronto, you could afford something small here.'

'I know. I checked.'

'Something bigger if you move further out.'

'No, it's got to be near whatever school they end up in. And if we are going back it has to be to Epsom. I can still commute to London and it's close enough to Mum and Dad that they can help out if I need them. Plus the girls have still got friends there, Linda too. The loon'll be planning to palm the kids off on her as much as possible or it won't be worth her while.'

'Alright, well you can still get a two or three-bedroom terrace once you get yourself a mortgage. You'll have quite a bit of equity after all.'

'I don't have a job though.'

'So get one. Ask your mate to pull a few strings with old Whatsischops. Get the ball rolling now. You're coming over in a few months anyway. You've got time to get this sorted and stay on when you get here. Think about it. It's perfect. Crazy Horse is coming over in July with the girls and you can aim to tie up all your loose ends by August in time for them to start school in the autumn. It couldn't be more convenient.'

I hear her take a loud swig of tea.

'I don't know. That's not enough time to organise it.'

'How much notice do you have to give at Walton?'

'Four weeks.'

'How long will the house take to sell, do you think?'

'A few months probably. I wouldn't need to stick around once we had an offer on it though.'

'Okay.'

'That doesn't help me negotiate terms with Philippa though. She'll take everything I've got and screw me sideways with a shovel if she knows this is what I want. '

She's slammed the mug down on the worktop. I hope she finished it first.

'Well, don't tell her! Don't let on that you're as desperate to go back as she is. You've got to play this like it's the last thing you want. You've got your life there. A career. Your lovely house. Loads of friends. Don't let on that you've split up with Tammy. Make out you're only doing it for the girls, but it's a real ball-ache for you and you'd be happier staying there forever if you could.'

We fall silent again.

'Look, Dan. She's an awful, unstable, unbelievable bitch and she's ruined your life, but you need to stop acting like she's a normal person who thinks and feels in the same way we do. She's a mess, a total meltdown waiting to happen and that's why you need to make her think that she's in control. That she's forcing all of this and shafting you in the process. Think about who you're dealing with and use her weaknesses to get what you want.'

'You don't know her.'

'But you do. You know her. You need to manage her –'

'Like I would any old smelly fruitcake stinking of piss and paranoia?'

'Exactly!'

I drag the sides of my mouth down but my hand is trembling so much I have to press it against my chest.

'You are so unhappy over there and you've been through so much what with Dom… and everything else, but now the main reason that you went wants to come back and the main reason that you stayed has gone. Gone nuts actually, which is a bit of a recurring theme we're going to have to talk about before you start dating anybody else.'

I'd laugh but it's still a touchy subject.

'You're the only one standing between spending another fifty years living on the opposite side of the ocean to almost everything you love… and coming home.'

'I don't know if I've got the strength to go through this.'

My voice cracks and Julia says 'I know you don't. But I do.'

My sister checks availability at the schools in and around Epsom and one of them has spaces in year two but not year three, one has year three but not year two and one of them has quite a few places in both, which is not a good sign.

I know Philippa prefers the first one so Julia suggests putting Lauren's name down and once she gets a place, Katie will be top of the list because they prioritise siblings. It's risky, but we can always change our minds in September and enrol them in the same (rubbish) school at the last minute if no slots open up in year three before then. It's not completely straightforward but it's a long way from impossible.

She also speaks to three different solicitors (three free trial-consultations because she is my mother's daughter after all) and they all say the same thing. That there's no reason for the joint custody split to be overturned back in England as long as there are no grounds for changing it. And there are none, of course. Instead, I have the OCL report, which is worth more to me than any money. Fortunately, as there is no chance of me having any for a very long time.

In fact, if anything I have all the evidence I need to go for sole custody, but I wouldn't. Crazy as my ex-wife is, now the girls are easier to handle, she's less volatile with them and while I can't trust her not to peddle suggestive gossip behind my back, I'm not crapping my pants all the time about them being with her. They need a mother and while I wouldn't have implicitly chosen one like her (Yes, alright. I know I did, but in fairness, that was actually Mavis's fault, if you remember – may her adorable sweet soul rest in peace) Philippa does love our daughters so I wouldn't want to take them away from her anymore but at least I'm protected if she tries to take them from me.

As far as the monthly payments go, Julia reckons the lawyers say that not only is there is no such thing as spousal support in the UK but if I have the girls half the time, there wouldn't be any maintenance either. Not only that but if she's working and I'm not, she might actually have to pay me for the time I have custody, which is not a door I'm silly enough to open, but it does give me some sort of leverage if I only had the balls to use it.

My dad's woeful imaginary voice is niggling away in my head but if she did abduct the children when we got back, she'd have to spend the rest of her life in hiding and couldn't sign on or work or get a nice free house or anything. Not to mention she'd be holed up with the children by herself.

Even in my most paranoid, negative state, I can see it doesn't make sense for her to do that and anyway, she could run off here if that was her end game. But it's not. It's not. But I don't know what her end game is. I'm not sure what she's going to get out of this that she can't already get over here. This is what she does. She latches onto things and when she's done, she lights a match and laughs as it burns to the ground.

This is all a pipedream. A fantasy. It's never going to work. It's insane to even try. She'll get my hopes up and destroy me before I even know what's happening. If I think my life's bad now, if I think it's a nightmare, wait until I put it all in her hands and watch her crush it like an empty crisp packet and blow it into the wind.

And the more my sister drones on about how easy it'll be, the more I believe her and I shouldn't because she has no idea. She's got a nice house with a kitchen extension and a loft conversion she doesn't even need because she's got nothing else to spend her money on because the only contact she's ever had with psychopaths is through me. She hasn't woken up every single night for the last nine years of her life in a cold sweat. She hasn't contemplated jumping from every building she sees.

'And what about you?' she cries when I throw it in her face. 'Does your heart stop every time the phone rings because you think it's going to be someone telling you your little brother – who you're suppose to protect – has blown his head off with his own gun? Has killed his kids because that's the only way he can see out of this whole awful mess? This isn't all about you, you know. I mean I know it's shit, but Jesus Christ. It's not like the view gets better from here.'

' I can't do it,' I say.

'You don't ever have to do anything that you don't want'.

But then she writes an email and phones me to make me read it.

'Here are a few of my ideas,' she says. 'Add anything you want and then send it.' There's no way I can send it but I read it anyway.

Dear Philippa, it goes and even the sight of her name sends goose pimples right through me. *I got your previous emails about ballet club starting next Tuesday but before we sign up for it, I wonder if we could have an open and honest discussion about something that seems to be on the girls' minds.*

Over the last few months, I've noticed they've become obsessed with going to England. At first I thought they were just looking forward to their holiday in the summer but recently I've begun to think it's more than that. I, for one, am very happy here and I think they are too, but as we both have Katie and Lauren's best interests at heart, it would be irresponsible of me to ignore the possibility of moving back to the UK if this is something they genuinely want.

Obviously, this would be a massive upheaval for me and quite frankly, it's one I would hope to avoid. I have a number of commitments here as you know, including a house, a job and a relationship, none of which has been easy to come by.

However, I realise that if this is to be an ongoing issue, the girls are probably better off dealing with the disruption of a move now while they're still young enough to re-settle in England, rather than later when it will be harder for all of us.

I'm concerned, however, that the last time we talked about this, you had Shropshire in mind and if that's still your preference, then I don't think it will be in the girls' best interest to uproot them from the life we have here. The only benefit of going back as far as I'm concerned would be moving closer to our families and it goes without saying that I would only agree to this on the condition the custody agreement we have here remains the same. That is to say, we each have them every other week with an even and alternate split over school holidays and special occasions.

In addition, I'd need to be close enough to London to work and since the schools are all very good in Epsom and we all still have friends in or near the area, in my opinion it makes sense for us to return there. As far as I understand, your mum's moved back to the area herself so please let me know that you are in agreement with this, hypothetically, should we decide to explore this option any further.

To be clear, the only reason I'm even mentioning this is because I know the girls' wellbeing is a priority for both of us and this may be the last opportunity we have to really make a decision about it one way or another.

However, this isn't something I'm comfortable about discussing with you unless we both feel we can approach it with mutual respect and understanding for each other. Despite what's happened in the past, we're clearly both committed to putting our children first regardless of the personal sacrifices we may have to make in order to ensure they are happy, but as I've mentioned this would not be without its complications for me so if I've misunderstood Katie and Lauren's intentions and you are not considering going back, please let me know asap so I can stop worrying about it.

Obviously we'd need to involve the girls in whatever decision we make but in the meantime and without any guarantees that this is something we could actually make happen, I'd appreciate your thoughts.

If I don't hear back from you, I'll assume you are happy here and won't bother you with it again. Best wishes, Dan

'What do you think?' Julia says.

What I think is that I'm going to defecate myself right there and then if Julia doesn't stop talking.

'It's good, right? There's nothing else you need to say, is there?'

'I'm going to vomit.'

'You can do this.'

'No, I can't.'

'Yes, you can. Copy and paste it into an email right now. Don't think about it. Do it.'

I can't speak. My heart is working overtime. I have to hold it to stop it bursting out of my chest.

'Do not make me come over there and press send, because I will.'

My hands are shaking and there's a lump in my throat that hurts every time I swallow.

'Do you want to come home?'

I start crying.

'Do you want to come home, Dan?'

'Yes, I do.'

'Okay then. That's what we're going to do. We're going to get you home.'

And with that, I take a deep breath, open a new email, stick it in and press send. And then I sit back and wait.

Everything Is Awesome

'She still hasn't answered.' I keep pressing refresh but nothing's happening.

'It's only been half and hour.'

'It's been forty minutes.'

'She might not have even seen it yet.' Julia's making a cup of tea again. Good to know I'm the only one with guts like a chewed-up balloon.

'She would have. She always answers immediately. It shows up on her phone straight away.' I check the router again.

'Well, maybe she hasn't looked at it yet. She's probably in the middle of something. Even if she has seen it, she's going to need a bit of time to think it over. Don't read anything into it.'

The Wi-Fi light looks fine. I probably need to turn the Internet off and on again, but then I realise it must be working because I'm using it to make this call and then it hits me.

'She knows.'

'Knows what?'

'That she's got me.'

'Dan, you need to relax.'

My palms are sweating. 'I guess I can offer her thirty thousand from the sale of the house.'

'Thirty what! What for?'

I jerk the phone back from my ear and wince. Jesus Christ, it's like talking to Mum.

'As a one-off payment to make all this happen.'

'But she wants to go back. Why would you pay her?'

'Because money's the only thing she understands. It's the only thing she wants.'

'Of course it is, but you're already going to be paying her for maintenance when you don't need to. If anything, you should tell her you'll only be able to afford to move back if you pay less.'

'I can't do that.'

'Dan, you keep forgetting that she's wanted this for years. She doesn't know you know she's had interviews in Surrey and whatnot. We know she's desperate but as far as she's concerned, you're not. In fact you've made it clear you'd rather not go and that's the only way to play this. You've got to hold your nerve.'

'I can probably stretch to forty but I wouldn't be able to buy another house for a few years. I can rent though, until I've got myself sorted.'

I hold the phone away from my ear reflexively.

'Dan! Do not offer her any money. Wait it out and see what she says.'

'I know exactly what she's going to say.'

But I don't. I have absolutely no idea because two hours later when she gets home from a play-date that's cost me three billion calories burnt pacing the floor, she finally writes back and says *OK, understood.* As in OK, understood. No more playing silly buggers. No more destructive behaviour. No more toying with my life like a cat with a mouse. OK, understood.

And from that moment on she becomes this whole other person. She is sweetness and light. She's a cloud full of fairy dust. And she's even more terrifying because I know what she can do once she's reeled me in close enough to her. She'll bite my head off and spit it out in the stagnating pond of my life.

She has questions. This has all come as a bit of a shock and she apologises if her emails come in bits and pieces but have I split up with Tammy?

'Don't tell her. Don't tell her that. She has to think you'd rather not leave.'

So I say we're still together but Tammy's very supportive and understands that if the kids are better off in the UK, I'll have to go back and realistically we won't be able to maintain a long-distance relationship from there. But if I stay, nothing will change. She'll still be my girlfriend and play a huge role in our children's lives.

She says she sees only one major problem and that's the cost of shipping all our stuff back to England (Here we go). The dog alone would cost five thousand dollars and she has no money whatsoever.

'That's fair enough,' says Julia. 'You know that much is true. You've got to pay for yours anyway. What if you bung it all in together?'

'I can't send the dog in a shipping container. It takes six weeks.'

'Not the dog! Wait a minute. Are you smiling?'

'No.'

'I can hear you smiling.'

I'm not smiling. This is nowhere near done yet. This is the tip of the iceberg. First it's paying for the removals and Stan – which costs ten times more than my bloody ticket by the way – and then it'll be a deposit for a house.

'She'll get housing benefit. She won't need a deposit.'

'But she'll need a car. And a brand new wardrobe. And a pony.'

'Let's take this one step at a time.'

'She's going to use it to wrangle more cash out of me. What if I tell her I'll give her that thirty as a one-off payment and she can do what she likes with it so long as she doesn't ask for more. '

'No! Stop it! What is this thirty bloody thousand, you keep talking about? You don't owe her anything. She's practically biting your hand off to leave. Just relax.'

Relax? Holy Christ.

'Write back and say that seems a bit much but you'll look into it. Do not roll over and start wagging your tail. Let her think this would be a huge stretch for you. If you agree straight away, you're begging her to come back for more.'

Philippa agrees the joint custody arrangement we have here should continue but she'd like to review the amendment banning her from attending the same activities and social engagements as me. I don't tell her to shove it which is what I really want to say. Instead I reiterate (or rather Julia reiterates and I cut and paste) that as long as we can wipe the slate clean and develop a healthy relationship based on trust and respect then there'd be no reason not to re-evaluate certain conditions in the future.

'But I don't want her turning up to everything all the time,' I cry.

'Fine,' Julia says. 'Add something about really enjoying the time you share with the girls and say if she can give you the space you deserve together most of the time, you won't kick up a fuss about every little thing. But make sure there's a caveat there. Make sure she knows none of this is going to happen at all if she starts messing you around.'

But she does seem to know. It's bizarre and she has shocked me before but this is genuinely Topsy-Turveyland. It's like a shape shifter's moulded her body but they couldn't fathom out how to make the crazy work. She looks the same, but I can almost hear her giggling as she writes.

'This is weird. She's going to blow,' I say.

'She's excited. That's normal.'

'There is no such thing as normal when it comes to Philippa. Even you told me that.'

'And I told you to handle her mental illness. It's working, isn't?'

Handle Philippa? Sweet Jesus. You don't try and handle a great white shark. Why does no one else get this but me? But even I don't get it. The woman who has laid waste to everything I've ever loved or held dear says she hopes we can repair the damage we've done to our relationship and return to a time in our lives before it got so bad between us. I don't even think I own T-shirts that date back that far, but it's a good sign, I guess. That is, it's better than a death threat as long as she means it.

'I think she does mean it,' says Julia. 'She wants you to do what she wants. And that's move.'

'No. It's all too easy. She's up to something. She's going to hit me for a pay-out. I should get in there first or she'll come out with something exorbitant. If I go in now with twenty, it gives me room to negotiate.'

'You will not! You are already going to pay for the move and the dog. She hasn't asked for anything else.'

'But she will.'

I can hear Julia grinding her teeth the way she does when she's trying not to tell off the children. She takes a measured breath that reminds me of water draining down a dirty sink.

'Look, the very fact you're planning to keep paying maintenance when you don't have to is outrageous enough. If you're going to insist on giving her a lump sum then she needs to agree that all the rest of it stops. You can't do both and anyway, she'll get benefits if you don't pay her and she probably won't if you do, so maybe say something now while she's on a roll, but still... Don't make it sound like this is all a done deal. You're laying your cards on the table but you'd still rather stay in Canada if you can, right? What did she say about the schools?'

She wants them both to go private if they can (naturally), so she'll try to get a job in a fee-paying primary because the children of teachers go free. Which is all well and good, but we all know she'll be fired from wherever she ends up within a month so where will that leave the girls?

'You're going to have to play that one by ear,' Julia says. 'But write down immediately that you can't afford to pay for a private education under any circumstances.'

'Well, I can't.'

'So get it in writing right now. And say you won't stand in her way if she wants to send them to a public school but that you don't want them moved around once they've started. Make it clear the free schools in the area are excellent and you see no need to pay, but you'll support her decision if she wants to. Emotionally! Not financially!'

'I'm just going to say I can't afford it, but I won't stand in her way if she can sort it out somehow.'

'Alright, Shakespeare. Just get something down.'

So then Philippa asks me about my work plans and I tell her that I'm not sure that getting back in the Met is a viable option and since I can't even start looking for anything else until I'm back there in August, it would probably be best to request a career break from Walton so if it doesn't all work out in the UK, I'll still have a job to come back to. There's no point burning bridges after all.

'Smoothly done,' Julia says. 'You're getting good at this.'

So then she asks me where I'm planning to live and if I want to get a place all together. Julia says 'WHAT THE FUCK???' and I reply that I appreciate the offer but it would probably be best to rent two separate houses near the school or it might be confusing for the girls.

I'm not quite sure how this is going to go down but the next thing she wants to clarify is that once we return to the UK, all spousal and child support payments will stop. She is not clarifying that they won't stop, she is asking me to agree not to pay her anymore. I read it again.

'That's what it says, isn't it?'

Julia's thinking. This could take a while.

'Erm…I think so.'

'She is definitely after confirmation that we won't be claiming anything from each other once we get back.'

'That's what she's saying...'

'It doesn't make sense. What's she playing at?'

'It must have something to do with the millionaire boyfriend, right? It must be back on and she thinks you'll try and sting them for some money.'

'He's got a restraining order against her. She's not allowed within fifty feet of him.'

'Since when has that ever stopped her from getting what she wants? His wife's probably kicked him out and Philippa's thrown herself at him, legs open wide.'

'I don't know…'

'Well, it's either that or she's worried she'll get a job and you won't and then she'll end up paying you maintenance. She's obviously spoken to some solicitors too. They must have told her how it works.'

'Maybe.'

'Look, whatever it is, she thinks she's better off without your money. You need to jump on that right now.'

'Oh my God.'

'Oh and Dan – don't forget to insist she take that thirty grand while you're at it.'

'Mother Mary in heaven.' And we laugh. We really really, really laugh.

So apart from having to ship all her stuff over and the dog's private jet or whatever it is I'm paying five thousand bucks for, I am quids in. Instead of handing over most of my salary each month to a psychopath, from now on whatever I earn will be split between me and the taxman, who is also a bastard but at least he understands he's better off not wrecking havoc with his cash cow.

And the best bit is that somehow Philippa thinks she's getting one over on me and I don't even care if she is. I don't want her boyfriend's money. I just want to keep my own as controversial and outlandish as that may seem.

Tammy's decided she'd rather buy me out of the house than sell it, which is a good move on her part, I think. She might never get a chance to get her hands on a property like this again and I'm happy to let her have it for a good price for old times' sake.

She's been really sweet actually. We've been texting each other every day to make sure we're both getting by and I've remembered what it used to be like. When we would hang out in the hot tub all evening, drinking endless supplies of alcohol and gazing up at the stars in the sky. And it was lovely and it wasn't her fault that the whole time she was sat in my arms, I'd be wondering what those stars looked like from the other side of the earth.

And that's a shame because we had something. It wasn't the most passionate affair in history. She didn't blow me away, but she's a good person. She's special and despite what we went through this last year, I still care deeply about her.

Not as much as she deserves and certainly not enough to give her the baby she's always secretly wanted, but even so I hope all her dreams come true. That she meets the right person who doesn't have the baggage I haul around. Who can appreciate her kindness and treat her like the star of the show.

And maybe, you never know, once all this has settled down. Once I've got my own place and I'm not in and out of court all the time, when I'm not giving away almost every cent I earn and living on the breadline, when I wouldn't rather have a hedgehog wedged up my sphincter than drag myself out of bed each morning, I might even start to feel differently about that baby.

And if she started to feel differently about coming over after all, well, who knows? My parents would be delighted, that's for sure. I hardly dare tell them we've split up yet let alone that I'm coming back to England, cash rich but unemployed and homeless (again). There's no point until all the loose ends here are tied up or I'll be going home to nurse my dad back from a stroke (assuming I can get my mum off the phone long enough to catch my flight).

But I'm feeling pretty positive about everything and it's always possible that things could work themselves out in the future. It's all coming together, so why not this?

I call Tammy for a chat and to see if she's okay. To find out if there's anything she needs or wants to talk about. To let her know she still means a lot to me and after everything we've been through, I'll always want her in my life. And then I tell her what's happening. How I've convinced Philippa that she's convincing me to go back home. And just before I tell her how much I'd like her to visit she says, 'Oh, fuck you. I always knew that was all you cared about, you asshole. I should have known better than to hang all my hopes on a miserable coward like you. At least I know now. That's awesome. Thanks, Daniel.'

In retrospect, I probably shouldn't have mentioned leaving the country until she'd bought me out of my share of the house. But that's the thing about retrospect. It's like money and I only ever seem to realise too late that I'll never have enough.

And, of course it's bloody awesome. Isn't everything always? At least it is, until I bugger it all up.

Closure

The move is happening. What started as an almost insurmountable pipedream has snowballed and is now pretty much a blizzard. There are some unavoidable upfront costs that I hadn't really factored in when all of this was a flight of fancy and I have no capital other than the money in the house, but all that means is that Tammy needs to buy me out before I fly home.

Of course, it also means that when she tells me she's decided to only give me $100,000 instead of $150,000, there's sod all I can do about it. I mean I try, don't get me wrong. This is fifty thousand dollars we're talking about, but ultimately I can either accept this pathetic, debilitating insult or insist we put the house on the market and split what will be a considerably higher profit.

By this point however, as she knows, I've almost worked out my notice, I have no possessions because they're already winding their way back across the ocean and I'm supposed to be leaving in less than a week but without the money from the house I can't afford to go anywhere.

I beg again. My urethra has recoiled so tightly I can't pee, but no. She's very clear. Since she paid for all the lawyers and court fees as well as a higher share of the mortgage each month, I owe her.

I try to point out that she paid for the court fees because I'd put $90,000 upfront into a house she could never have afforded otherwise. I've spent a small fortune since then doing it up, not to mention the time and the energy it's taken and all she's offering me is ten grand more than I'd have got if I'd sat in my old apartment jerking myself off seven times every day for a year. And quite honestly it would have been more satisfying.

Ten grand! I'd spent three times more than that on bills and getting the place sorted while she was dipping chicken drumsticks into barbeque sauce. If it'd been left to her, the house would have been full of landfill by now and I've no doubt that it will be before long. She has neither the skills nor ambition to keep it clean, let alone do it up and I swear, I'll stick the bristle end of a courgette up my anus if she can even find the bins or figure out how to use the washing machine.

But the memory I'll cherish the most is walking out of the solicitor's office after she'd completely screwed over, not only me but my daughters and she sang, 'Let me know if you need anything!'

Let me know if you need anything? At least on these sorts of occasions Philippa always had the decency to bear her buttocks and light a fart in celebration. Of the two, that was far less offensive and there was nothing I could say except how about my fifty grand back? To which she had no answer because she has the mental reflexes of an ingrown toenail.

Annoyingly, I'd already moved out of the house in a conciliatory gesture that pre-dated her swindling me or I'd have buried some kippers under the floorboards. If they even have kippers here.

I've been staying with Paxton on his sofa which is strangely reminiscent of times gone by, except nobody's barfed on it. Stan is keeping me company, the dumb smelly hairball and he weighs as much as ten little Jack Russelly things that have eaten ten other Jack Russelly things and a whole lump of butter, but I don't really mind. For the amount he is costing to sedate and fly over in a huge plastic box that cost me $330 even though I'll use it only once (unless I'm reduced to living in it now I definitely can't afford to get a house) the least he owes me is a few days of affection, though I'd rather he kept the silent windy pops to himself.

We decided it was easier if I held on to him so that Philippa was free to go for interviews, look for houses, visit schools with the girls and prepare for a hundred other things I'm no longer pretending won't happen if she doesn't play ball, because she is. She is loving her latest role as a Co-Parenting Virtuoso and tells all and sundry how progressive we are. How extraordinarily well we work together, putting the girls needs ahead of our own and raising them in a cooperative, supportive environment. To be fair, she's creaming her Spanks because she thinks she's forced me to choose between Tammy and her and she won.

So be it. I guess we both got what we wanted, albeit I also wanted a block of human waste to fall out of a plane as she was passing and I'd have quite liked $150,000 to start afresh when I get home, not $100,000, less $5000 for the dog and $15,000 to pack up and transport all our stuff back on the trip of a lifetime. Well, its second trip. I don't even own anything worth over a tenner. I should have left it all there but it was going to cost $12000 to take Philippa's so $3000 to add mine seemed like fantastic value and I'll take my emotional highs where I can get them these days.

I'm fully aware that this collaborative state of unity and respect is all temporary and the higher the peaks of perfection I scale, the harder I'll fall when I sneeze out of line or accidently part Katie's hair in the middle when it should be on the side.

But despite still sleeping with only one eye closed at night, I must admit things are going even better than I could have imagined. Now that my ex-wife doesn't spend her days dreaming up ways to destroy me, she has loads more time on her hands and has already got herself a job in a prestigious private school and when I query what will happen to the girls if she 'decides to move on' she tells me that she's already made Barry (who it turns out is moving over too due to the fact he has business in Shropshire of all places) sign a contract committing to pay for their education, no matter what happens between them until the day that they graduate or he dies, whichever comes first. God help us all should she ever run for prime minister.

I've finally told Mum and Dad what's happening. My dad can't believe that I've split up with the only woman disillusioned enough to put up with me and everything I bring to the table and I'm too embarrassed to tell him I let myself be sandbagged again. That the woman he keeps wistfully hoping might come and join me at some point (because how else am I ever going to cope with two girls on my own?) turned out to be the right bollock to Philippa's left.

My mum was equally nonplussed until Julia pointed out that I may die trying to ever get on the property ladder again but at least they won't have to repatriate my body. It's expensive enough getting a chest of drawers back from Canada and besides I've been broken and risen many, many times before. I will survive this and whatever happens, no matter how frightening jumping into the abyss again might be, they'll be there to drag me back out.

As the date of departure draws closer and the fragmented world around me falls into place, they've even allowed themselves to believe it can actually happen. I almost believe it myself.

It was strange and exhilarating packing up the house. The girls don't quite understand that they're not coming back and let's admit it, as much as I used them to expedite going home, they were completely oblivious to the whole contrived scheme but you know what kids are like. Katie was more worried I'd forget her insect collection than she was about leaving pretty much everything that she remembers behind.

'Where's my pot, Daddy?' she wailed three rooms away from where I was packing (over-considerately since this was before I realised I'd be needing every knife and saucepan I could salvage).

'What pot?'

'The one that I put my dead bugs in.'

'Oh.' I roll my eyes and stifle a groan. 'It's on the breakfast bar.'

'That's Lala's pot.'

The groan escaped. 'I don't know then.'

'Can you look for it?'

'No, I'm in the middle of something.'

'Daddy.'

'No.'

'Daddy. Can you look for it?'

'I don't know where it is, Katie.' Was it okay to take some toilet roll or was that rude? 'You look for it and if you can't find it, I'll come and help.' I took one. She'd be needing the other seven if her brother came to stay.

'I can't find it. Can you look?'

'Oh, for goodness sake. Are you sure that's not it on the breakfast bar?'

'No! That's Lala's. I've got a bumblebee and a fly and she's only got a fly.' Pausing only to take out my frustration on a pile of Hilton-embossed towels and flannels, I strode into the kitchen and lo and behold – 'What's that if it's not a bumblebee?'

'You found it, Daddy! Thank you. I knew you would.'

'Yes, funny that.'

'You're the best daddy ever ever.'

Not sure the bumblebee and the fly would agree.

Philippa's on such a high, I even took her up on her suggestion I take them all to the airport when they left ten days ago. Me and my crazy ex-wife in a car when only two months ago, the closest we got was pretty frigging close because she was stalking me, but at least now I wasn't in fear for my life. It was as though the last ten years of embittered hatred had passed like a difficult stool.

Surreal doesn't even begin to describe it and now that I've cleared out the house and moved the last of my bags into Paxton's, all I have to do is work out the last few days of my notice at Walton, stick two fingers up at Sergeant Dickless (who unbeknownst to him is about to be caught out and thrown back into uniform where he'll be able to sit on his arse making up his fictitious career forevermore but will do a lot less damage).

This all sounds fairly tranquil I'd imagine so let me clarify it is a living hell. Again. It's been relentless and draining and awful just like it was when I did it the other way around.

I have ten thousand things to organise in two vastly different countries, one of which I'm not in. I have ten million questions to answer and two trillion decisions to make. I'm sleeping on a sofa for what must be the fiftieth time. I'm alone (apart from the dog who seems more intent on releasing methane gas into the atmosphere than providing any comfort to me) and despite the simmering euphoria that occasionally surfaces at the thought of going home, it soon pops like a huge dirty bubble splattering doubt all over my plans. I'm on the verge of completely freaking out all the time. I wake every night at 3am and sit bolt upright shaking and pouring in sweat as if I'm under a shower.

So many things have been destroyed in the wake of this disaster. There are so many things I'll regret and so I'm grateful when Tammy drops me a little email to say *Hiya Dan, How are you and the girls? I hope you're all set for England. There must have been a lot to sort out but at least you're finally going home so I know you must be happy.*

Just wanted to say you've got some mail here so if you let me know where you'll be staying in the UK, I'll send it over. Also, the dishwasher doesn't seem to be cleaning anything properly and I can't find the manual so if you can shed any light on why it won't work, could you please let me know? Hope the move back goes smoothly and that you and the girls are doing well. Best wishes, Tammy

I am grateful because for the last ten years of my life I've been too scared of the consequences of expressing my feelings to ever open my mouth, but unhappily for my ex-girlfriend, I'm an IED of emotions at the moment and I'm about ready to detonate. And she hopes that we're well.

I probably shouldn't, but I write back anyway and you know how you always feel bad immediately after replying on impulse and sending it before you've had a chance to cool down? Well, I don't. And I won't. Ever.

Instead I say *Thanks for your email, but to clarify, you seem to have convinced yourself that we split up because I wanted to go back to England, but let me be very clear. I could have gone home two years ago, but I didn't because I wanted our relationship to work both for my sake and the girls'. The sacrifices I made over those years and the desperation I felt about being so far away from my friends and family, were due entirely to the fact that I chose you over them all and even when you decided you wanted a baby – despite my situation and misgivings – I relented, again, for you.*

However, when, over the course of the last six months, you became increasingly erratic, volatile and frankly, downright unpleasant toward my children, I must admit alarm bells started ringing.

When you began to treat the girls with undisguised contempt and resentment resulting in social workers popping by to discuss your behaviour towards them, my feelings towards you, did indeed start to change.

When you put the separation agreement that I'd spent four years fighting for in jeopardy and made it very clear that it wouldn't bother you if you never saw my daughters again, I have to say, I questioned how good it was for them to be so attached to you, especially if we did have another child and the novelty of spending any more time with mine would quite clearly evaporate completely. If it hadn't already.

You made the fact you'd had enough of Katie and Lauren so unforgivably obvious that the idea of having another baby with you and making the situation a hundred times worse, suddenly seemed even less appealing than when I'd simply been embroiled in a bitter and exhausting custody battle with my ex, four thousand miles away from home, all the while struggling both physically and emotionally to get through the day.

So, yes, when you said it was a baby or nothing, I said I didn't want a baby. More fool me for not realising when you said nothing, you meant it.

I am not going to suggest our time together was wasted or that I didn't lean heavily on you for support during one of the most difficult periods of my life. You paid for the court cases as all my money was tied up in the house and of course, I couldn't have been more grateful. I must say, I didn't realise it would all be thrown back in my face if I *didn't do what you wanted, but fair enough, we can write off the $20,000 in costs now at least, with $30,000 interest.*

So, in answer to your question, how am I? If we take into account, the $100,000 you grudgingly paid me for a house that'll be worth a million before too long, less all the money I put into it and that you cost me by flippantly grinding my car into the ground I'd say, I'm ok, but each of my children is at least $15,000 worse off for knowing you. We will struggle financially and have to rent somewhere for years, unless I cash in my pension and look forward to working for the next five decades.

And why? Because you took advantage of the situation I was in, exploited it and cheated them. You spent three years ranting on about Philippa and then you did the exact same thing to us.

If one good thing has come out of this, it's that I found out who you really are and I guess I should thank you in part for helping me become strong enough to recognise a toxic situation and have the guts to walk away.

With regards to the dishwasher, you have to put a tablet in the drawer before you turn the machine on. With regards to my post, you may bin it.

And that is what they call closure.

Thank you for having me

It's kind of dark outside waiting to go on. A dim glow made darker still by the brightness of the auditorium. There's nothing forgiving about this lighting and there's nowhere to hide, but that's okay. It's time to stand up tall and this is diddlysquat. This is bouncing on a trampoline with a safety harness compared to my usual plunge into the depths of a fiery inferno. Or my day, as I like to call it. This is pudding after vomiting my own intestines through my nose and I don't say that lightly. It's been five years since I last stood on a stage, since I last stared into a sea of expectant faces, confident that I had only to open my mouth to make them all laugh. Not so tonight. I'm not even sure they'll understand me, but what the hell. It's my last night. I can say anything I like.

Paxton's there in front row with a few of the other guys I should have got to know more while I had the chance. Good people who'd have been better friends in better circumstances. It's too late now. Sweet Jesus, it's too late to do anything. My name's being called. I draw a breath and stride on. Grab the mic. Nod to Paxton, flash a self-assured smile around the room. Get a few smiles back. A ripple of welcome applause.

'Ladies and gentlemen. Thank you so much.' I pause. Look around me. It's a full house tonight. I feel a wave of nervous energy hit me and then I use it. Fill the silence with it. The room is mine.

'My name's Dan White, but most people here in Canada know me as Justin Glish. Didn't intend to change my name but whenever I get talking, someone will ask me if I'm Australian and I'll say no, I'm British. And that's usually the point where they start speaking very slowly like I'm deaf or something.' I can feel the crowd leaning forward in their chairs, ears pricked, anticipation heightened.

'Some of them'll start signing at me like I won't be able to understand them unless they mime our whole conversation.'

I start gurning and twirling my hands around. I form a penis with the curl of my fingers, move it slowly up and down with a baffled expression. Set off a few chuckles.

'So I'll say *I'm not deaf* but by then I'll be enunciating every letter myself.' I distend my lips around the words like a horse shitting hay. 'In fairness that could be a bit confusing, so I'll repeat, I'm not deaf. I'm *just English.*'

I leave it hanging in the air. Let the penny drop. Or the cent. A collective good-natured groan rolls out around the room. Paxton's snorting beer through his nose (not a good look). Everyone else wants to laugh, they've got that look on their faces but I'm not sure they understood a word of what I said.

'This guy's got it in the front row. I've worked with him for a year and he's only now realised my name's not Justin. Justin Glish. From Australia. The guy with the speech impediment.' A few more people join in. I'm making myself laugh, that's the main thing.

'And you know what they say, when they realise that I'm either deaf or stupid or not from round here? It doesn't matter which. It's always the same response. *Oh my God. That's awesome.*'

A table full of ladies to my right cracks up at that. Not sure if everyone else is laughing at them or with me, but I stick with it.

'That's what all you Canucks say. Any occasion. My mum's died. *That's so great!*'

I've got my jazz hands out. A crazed look on my face. The rumble of laughter spreads like a Mexican wave.

'I mean, I love your enthusiasm but it's confusing to the rest of the world, you get that, right? There's got to be a distinction between amazing and totally shit or it's all the same. You're just sabotaging yourselves.

'Take my mate, Paxton here, for example. The other week he tells me he just got a new car from the same garage he got the last one from a year ago. I say, the one that kept breaking down? He says, *yeah. It couldn't be fixed in the end. Had to buy a new one instead.* I say from the same guy? He says, *yeah.*'

I raise my palms upwards, give my head a little incredulous shake. Paxton's mates are elbowing him in the ribs. He's got his face in his hands.

'I say, why would you go back to the same guy who sold you such an awful car in the first place? *Well*, he says, *last time he gave me an amazing deal!* An amazing deal!'

I look around the audience totally aghast. The tittering is starting to turn into a full on guffaw. The ladies nearest me are leaning against each other for support, tears rolling down their chubby red cheeks. They're easy to please, this lot. Maybe it's the accent. Or maybe they still think I'm handicapped in some way. I'm getting the sympathy laughs. I carry on. Try to speak more clearly.

'That's not an amazing deal! He sold you a car that lasted less than a year! He deserves to be kicked in the bollocks by The Rock, not enjoy return business! How's that working out for you by the way, Paxton? Those flashing lights on the dashboard keeping you entertained? Amazing.'

He sticks his finger up at me but he's grinning. I wink. Saunter back across the stage.

'*I got an amazing dose of herpes the other week.*' I say with a Canadian drawl and an eyebrow waggle. An inviting glance at a woman at the back. '*That guy gave me the most amazing broken nose. It's so awesome!*' I stroll back again.

'*Went to the most amazing restaurant the other day.* Would you go back? *Probably not.*'

I shake my head in bemusement again, eyes widening. Make a sort of okay, whatever sort of gesture with my wrists.

'And there's no need to go back anywhere really, is there? You can literally go to any restaurant here, confident you'll be getting the exact same meal as every other restaurant you've ever been to. I don't even look at the menu any more.

'I'll just take a wild stab at it when the waiter comes over. Give me the jumbo wings with medium sauce and the bacon burger with your no doubt 'famous' fries please. No, I've never been here before. Yes, it was a good guess. Wings and burgers.'

I slap my belly appreciatively. Swagger back a little bit.

'You guys could do your bit for the environment if you stopped bothering to print menus. Issue one to everyone who lands here at point of entry and they can use it for the duration of their stay. You could probably halve the nation's carbon footprint overnight. Save entire forests. It'd be awesome.'

God knows how much anyone here is actually getting of this. Thank Christ for beer. They're either laughing or hiccupping really quickly. I stick the mic back in the stand.

'So I've been here for five years. This is my last night. Going back to the UK tomorrow and you know what it's like when people haven't seen you for a while, you want to look good, right? And I've got to admit I've put on a bit of timber while I've been here. *Wings and burgers.*' I pat my stomach again. 'So I've been trying to tone up a bit. Cut down on the alcohol, do some exercise, you know the drill. You've probably read about it.' I smile mischievously. Avoid looking at the fatties in the front row. No need to offend the fans.

'Anyway, I thought I'd break myself in with one of those exercise bike classes. Revolutions or something original like that. And this is the first time I've done any sort of exercise class in about twenty years, but I figure, it's like riding a bike, right? It's literally like riding a bike. Fuck me. It is nothing like riding a bike.' I stagger forward, gripping my heart, my mouth contorted.

'First off, we do a two-minute warm up which nearly kills me and this instructor – who's quite hot I have to admit or I would have walked out there and then – tells us to stand up. Stand up, but keep cycling. Like that's a thing. Who the hell stands up to cycle? Why would they put a frigging seat on if they didn't want you to use it? You've paid for it after all…? Idiots.

'And this lasts for eighteen minutes. *Eighteen minutes.* My legs are shaking like little leaves. In a massive shit storm.' I stand quivering, ankles spread, knees trembling. 'And then finally she lets us sit down, the instructor. Thank fucking God. My face is the colour of a baboon's arse and I've got this vein coming out my neck the size of a skipping rope. My eyes are bulging but I'm hanging in there. Just about.' I draw a breath. Wipe my brow theatrically. Let out a little sigh of relief.

'Then suddenly the rest of the class starts reaching around to pick up these weights from behind their bikes. Just little ones. And I'm like alright, you pussies. I'll show you how this is done and I grab a couple of the medium-sized ones. I'm not showing off or anything. Don't want to make them feel bad, but I go to the gym, I work out. I can do this.' I flex my biceps appreciatively, a cocky half-smile on my face.

'But wait! We're not lifting them. Oh no. We gotta hold them right out and leave them there.' I stretch my arms out either side of me, a look of panic beginning to form on my face.

'And I'm thinking to myself what have you done, you dickhead? Eighteen minutes. Eighteen sodding minutes.' I'm cycling on the spot now, arms outstretched, my lower jaw sticking out. The roar of laughter is building, led mainly by Paxton who's thumping the table rapturously at the thought of me in pain.

'I've given up after three. I'm holding the weights down by my sides, just letting them hang there as all these other tits in their fancy leotards break into a frigging river dance.' I leap up and down gleefully with my arms out, a manic grin stretched from ear to ear.

'Eighteen frigging minutes. *Eighteen*. That's long enough to cook, eat and digest an entire burger. And shit it out afterwards. Or it would be if I didn't have kids.

'Kids. They always want to talk to you in the toilet, don't they? The minute you step in and get comfy. It's *Daddy...*' I pause. Cock an ear. Wait.

'Daddy...' Pause.

'Daddy...' Pause.

'What! *What are you doing?* I'm in the toilet. What do you think I'm doing? *Can I come in?* No!' My mouth drops into a sneer. 'Come into the bloody toilet? Oh yes, lovely. Welcome. Make yourselves at home. I'll just be five to ten minutes depending on how much fibre I've managed to shoehorn into my diet. Look girls, this is what happens when you eat all your vegetables! Not going to happen, but they've still got to ask, right? Every time.' Everyone in this room has definitely got kids. They're all laughing anyway. All bobbing their heads and nudging each other. Dabbing their eyes with the back of their fingers.

'Anyway, I'm still on this bloody bike. I'm about to have a cardiac arrest, but God forbid I let anyone else know that, right? I would literally rather die than let these lily-livered pansies show me up. And the whole time I'm trying to remember how long the class is. We've gone past the half hour mark, but it could be forty minutes, no? It could be, but it's not.

'*Put your weights down*, says this damn instructor and I almost smash a hole in the floor, I drop them so fast. And I'm like, Holy Christ. I've done it. I've survived. And then she goes, *now stand! Oh my god.*' My face is a mask of pure horror. '*Eighteen more fucking minutes.* It's like a medieval torture. Donald Trump needs to hear about this. Screw waterboarding. Just put a semi-attractive woman in a room full of terrorists with some exercise bikes and sit back and let them torture themselves to death. They'd be begging to confess after six and a half minutes.'

I'm cycling frantically again. '*Picture your goals* she says. This is her motivational speech. Picture your goals and I'm like my goal is to get the hell out of here. What's *wrong* with you, you sadistic arsehole? Jesus Christ. *Eighteen more minutes.* And you know how long that feels when you're waiting for a bus? Triple it! And all I can see is this line of perfect tight arses in front of me. All men so I can't even focus on them without having to explore three shades of hidden depths. And I'd even go there. Happily if it meant getting out of that bloody class. Sweet Lord.' I stop cycling. Stagger around the stage. One hand held out for balance, the other holding my chest.

'I almost ruptured my spleen. But I did lose weight. Not then obviously. I put a pound on. Between entering and leaving that class, I actually put on a bit. That's always motivating. But then after the class, that's when I lost weight. I couldn't walk or lift my arms up or the next three days.'

I mime trying and failing to raise a glass to my wobbly lips.

'I almost died of dehydration, but I am down seven pounds. No pain, no gain as they say. Wankers. I haven't been back. Decided to start a new thing. It's called Eating Less and Moving More. It's a fad. It'll never catch on. Beats showing my face back in that place though.'

I pick the microphone out of the stand. Walk around a bit to catch my breath. Parade a little.

'I know, some of you are probably wondering why I need to lose any weight at all.' I give it a cheeky smirk. A self-satisfied strut. 'But things are different back in the UK. It's like Lilliput compared to here. I've never felt so bloody small. Back home, I've been known to actually bend down to talk to people. Here, I've got a weekly physio session to fix the crank in my neck. But everything's big in Canada. Shops are big, cars are big. All your animals are big. You're all so used to it no one ever even seems to notice.

'In fact, no one seems to know much about any of the wildlife here, unless its head is hanging above their fireplace. When I first came across I was stunned that every time I looked up in the sky there were these prehistoric-sized birds up there gliding around with the wingspans of a bloody Cessna! I asked four people what they were and no one knew! How can that be? You have birds of prey big enough to carry away your new-born baby and you've never noticed. Just look up next time you go out. Unless you're from here in which case, duck. *Turkey Vultures*, they're called. I'm not joking, that's their actual name. Why's that woman laughing?' I point to one of the ladies in the front who immediately breaks into a giggling fit that sets all her mates off. 'You're welcome, by the way.'

I tap my temple and click my tongue with a knowing wink. Turn back to the mic stand. Fiddle a bit.

'So, this is it. My last night in this beautiful, big, *awesome* country of yours. It's been a hell of a ride here. Had its ups and downs. Well, its downs. Unless divorce, homelessness and custody battles are particularly high on your bucket list.' Someone laughs. It takes all sorts.

'Real reason I'm leaving though… I've got to get the hell out of here before winter comes round again. I say winter. The only winters I ever knew before I came here were about as cold as it gets standing in front of the refrigerator with the door open for a few minutes because you forgot what you wanted. That's about as intense as it gets. I might have got chilly toes once. They didn't snap off when I took my boots off or anything though.' I glance around the room. Let the tension build a little.

'And then I came here. Jesus Christ! Where are the notices? Where are the signs? There should be government forces driving through the streets with megaphones distributing puffer jackets and ski boots. What you have here is not winter. It's not even a season. It's a National Crisis. You should call it Death. Why sugar coat it? Give the folks some warning. That way maybe a few less people might drop dead shovelling two tons of snow from their driveways. Can you imagine the humiliation?' I lower my voice, bow my head respectfully. 'How did he die? He fell. Over. Is there a more pointless end? Or anything more predictable than possibly surviving the early morning shovel-a-thon only to be squished while then driving in a blizzard by a huge truck also driving in a bloody blizzard.

'If you called it *Death*, people might stop leaving the house at least. Think about it. More people are killed by winter over here than by zombies. You know why? Because if there were three-feet of zombies covering every freaking surface no one would go out! Think of the lives that would be saved if you all called it what it is.'

Paxton is practically convulsing. I'm glad I asked him to come. I'm going to miss him. He makes me snigger to myself as I go on.

'I can't do it anymore. I need to go home before this "*winter*" gets here.' I create apostrophes with my fingers and raise my voice sarcastically. 'I cannot subject myself ever again to the ordeal of walking out of my house at 5am and trying to work out which of the big white snow piles in the street has got my car under it.'

Every single person in this room knows what I mean, but I doubt they've ever laughed about it before.

'But I shouldn't grumble. I've got a brush to sort that out after all.' I pull an imaginary nine-inch snow scraper out of my back pocket and shake it, a huge demonic grin on my face as I pretend to sweep a bank of snow off my bonnet. 'What I need is a four-man crew with shovels and a digger but that's cool I've got this. And pneumonia.

'But fair play to you guys though because you're all out there doing it without complaint. I've got to respect that. We can't even get out of bed in the morning without a cup of tea in the UK. The entire economy would collapse overnight if we ran out of teabags because we'd literally refuse to leave the house but here you are, cheerfully going to work every day in near death conditions for months of the year. So good for you. I will be sure to think of you fondly when I'm lighting my barbeque on the beach back in Australia. Or wherever the hell I come from.

'So, time's up, ladies and gentlemen. And Paxton. Apologies if you didn't catch the whole act. It wasn't very good anyway. Or as you would say. It was *amazing* so never mind.'

I swing the microphone back in the stand. Take a bow and as I stand, I really mean the smile on my face for the first time in years. I can feel it. A ripple of indulgent applause and a whoop drown out the cackle of laughter that threatens to burst out my throat.

I don't belong in this place and I can't put into words what it's like being so far from home. It's not as bad as finding myself halfway through a tour in Afghanistan with a hole where my foot used to be, but it's still a world of pain except now that I'm leaving, I can finally be here. Just exist in this moment, knowing that's all it is. Just a moment. And when I wake up tomorrow I'll be a stranger for the last time.

This fight will continue until the day that I die but I've won this round. It's far from over, this life I've ballsed up so many times and yet despite everything, through all the torment and heartache. The chaos and the waste. The different versions of me. Throughout it all there has always been one thing that's given me the strength to rise up and face every new day. My girls and in a few hours I'll be on my way home to them. I lift my hand above my head in a salute.

'Thank you for having me, Toronto. And good night.'

And The Bell Tolls

The tarmac's the same dull black as at every other airport and the seats are as narrow and uncomfortable as always but today it feels different, as though they're charged with electricity. Everything is sharply focused like I'm seeing it all for the first time. The minutes pass by agonisingly slowly and yet I feel almost completely at peace.

I say at peace. I keep getting the odd tingle of anticipation like a fifteen-year-old virgin giddy at his first flash of boobs and I'm not sure when it hits me whether it's audible or not. I have the ubiquitous fat bastard to my right who I already despise and whose man-spread will consume 85% of my attention for the duration of the flight. The other 15% will be firmly concentrated on the fact he's already taken his shoes and socks off.

The stewardess is surely the love child of a drag queen and a satsuma and is in no way responsible for my occasional snorts of excitement. I close my eyes as she launches into the on board safety demonstration and the plane begins its slow taxi to the runway. I've already decided that in the event of a crash I'll use my neighbour here as a floatation device and so instead of pretending to listen to instructions which will be about as useful as an audio recording of the latest John Grisham should I actually find myself hurtling towards death, I reflect on the events that have led me to this moment.

From a chance meeting at a gig in my favourite comedy club to a rushed marriage and a bride hiding something I let myself be too hurried to see.

To a miscarriage and the chance to walk away. A chance I didn't take.

To the birth of two girls who would leave me no choice but to stand tall in the face of a storm I can't describe or fully explain. That I won't try to justify or ever understand.

To the realisation that my best could never be good enough and to the feeling of entrapment that can only be truly understood by those genuinely unfortunate enough to have nowhere to turn or to hide.

To the last resort of a desperate man escaping to a foreign land with a lunatic in the hope she might stop hurting the things he's trying to protect, only to realise for reasons he'll never comprehend that she's turned even crazier at the border.

I'm stronger now than I ever thought I could be but I'm also more broken than I imagined was possible. I've spent nearly a decade now living in fear of a person who's half the size of me, but nonetheless has ten times my anger and my ability to hate.

The abuse she doled out was never physical but I don't know if that made it better or worse. If she'd have hit me I might have seen it for what it was earlier. I could have acted upon it. But instead she chipped away at me little by little every day until there was nothing left of anything I recognised. Nothing to draw strength from. Nothing of me to save.

But from great weakness comes great strength and proof that life can endure in the absence of all hope. I can only sit here now, still not free from those chains, because when I close my eyes, I see my family and friends all standing by my shoulders. As one. And she doesn't have that. She doesn't have them. Not even anything close.

If I had words to explain the last ten years it might help me understand them better, but I don't. I'm not who I was anymore and it'll take me some time to get back there, if ever I can. Life has changed me but I will no longer be attacked and insulted and I will not be controlled by the past. As I sit here with blood still running through my veins and with breath in my body and the strength to continue slowly growing inside of me, what I want most in the world is to tell everyone who stood by me that I'm grateful for their loyalty and generosity.

I want to thank all the people who let me sleep in their spare rooms and on their sofas. I want to thank my friend's brother who paid for my meal when I had absolutely no money and I want to thank my colleague's father-in-law who let me use his cottage for free so I could have a summer holiday with my girls. I want to thank my family who gave me deposits so I would not be homeless and who came to see me as often as they could to lend me support and remind me that I am loved. I want to thank Dom the Butcher for making me laugh through the bad times and to tell him I'm sorry I couldn't do the same for him. I want to thank everyone, both sides of the Atlantic, who got me through this.

I also thank Canada for keeping me and my girls safe and just about together for five years. In another lifetime we could have been friends (apart from the ridiculous spousal support thing). Most of all I'd like to thank the Honourable Judge Weiner for treating me without malice or prejudice. For allowing me to parent in the eye of the storm.

I feel as if I'm on the cusp of a freedom I haven't felt in years. Though I don't know exactly what the future holds, I make myself and everyone else a promise that I'll embrace it with open arms.

I return to my country happily divorced and the father of the two finest living things I've ever seen and this will never change. In that regard I can say the last ten years have been worth it. The challenge now is to go on from here and make it all mean something. And I will. Football may still not be coming home but I sure as hell am and I will not be going anywhere soon.

The plane swings around towards the runway and the orang-utan takes her seat. I grind my teeth as the fat man's bulging arm brushes mine and then I smile as it finally sinks in that I'm on my way home. I take a last look out of the window and as we begin our ascent, I start to laugh. Just quietly, but I laugh.

Because I can. Because I did it. I survived and I'll never be fooled again. And no matter what happens from now on, I know, I'm not alone.

For the last few years, every time I've closed my eyes at night, I've pictured myself on a boat. I'm on my own in the darkest waters in the highest, stormiest seas. It's pitch black and there's not a star in the sky. A bell chimes as it lurches treacherously and despite the thunderous noise of the ocean, it's the only sound I hear.

I stand on the deck motionless, head down and soaked by the sea as wave after wave comes crashing down on me. My chin rests on my chest so as to breathe under the weight of the water. My eyes are closed to keep the salt from stinging them. Then from beside me in the darkness tiny hands reach up to take mine and for the life of me I don't know who is holding up whom. And the waves keep crashing over us as in my mind I repeat to myself *stay the course Dan, stay the course.*

And in the darkness, a light at the top of the mast of that boat begins to shine.

Printed in Great Britain
by Amazon